The Devil's Descendants

By

Amylynn Bright

Whenever you make love to someone, there should be three people involved – you, the other person, and the devil.
-Robert Mapplethorpe

Previously in

The Devils Descendants

Everyone thinks they know the story...

In the beginning, Lucifer fell in love with Adam and Eve's daughter, Rachel but when God learned about their love affair, he forbade it. The lovers foolishly did not heed the Father's decree. Lucifer's angelic brothers tried to convince Lucifer to give her up, but he would not. The lovers made a plan to escape to be together. God saw their plan and, in his righteous fury, he evicted Lucifer from Heaven and the Garden and cast him to the Underworld. Rachel pleaded with God to allow her to go with Lucifer, promising that she'd give anything to be with him. When God asked if she'd give up her soul for him, she agreed saying she would make any sacrifice for Lucifer. Lucifer was furious with God and, before taking Rachel down to Hell, he disguised himself as a snake and tempted Eve with the apple. If Rachel couldn't have Eden, then no one could.

The lovers still managed to be happy together in Hell, and when God learned that Rachel had sons he sent the Archangel Michael to retrieve the boys and deliver his curse. Lucifer would rule Hell until a child reached adulthood when he would descend and take over rule of the underworld, each generation giving one male heir to rule Hell *infanitum*. Lucifer ascended from Hell to spend the rest of his days in a cage of his own making in Heaven, alone and separated from the woman he loved. And Rachel, the soulless mortal woman, was to remain in hell for all eternity, tormented without the angel she loves or the sons they made together.

The Curse... God's curse upon the Mephisto bloodline demands that the first-born sons of Lucifer and Rachel's descendants shall each bear one of the Seven Deadly Sins, passed on to them by their fathers. During their fortieth year, a ceremony is held, choosing one of them to reign as the new Devil for a generation, and the burden of bearing the Sins is passed on to the younger Mephistos to start anew.

In Heaven and Hell... A young angel, Juliet, and a demon, Neil, join forces to reunite the original lovers. They're working together to free Rachel from her hellish confines, but first they have to find her. Neil is on his own quest through the perilous Levels of Hell while Juliet searches Heaven for a runaway Cerberus.

Chapter One

T he aroma of coffee and cinnamon wafted its way into Asher's dream. It was that weird one with the centaurs and Vincent van Gogh. Except right when the Viking vampires were due to come in, a gorgeous, leggy brunette strode through with a mug of coffee.

"Asher." Her voice drifted in his ears, low and husky. "Time to get up, Ashe."

He sighed and let go of the dream. Stretching his legs and flexing his feet, he encountered a warm body. He found the same when he extended his left arm. The slide of cool sheets against his skin brought him further into consciousness and, when the soft mewl of one of his bed companions breached the surface, he opened his eyes.

At the end of his bed stood his gargoyle. At just over 6 feet, 6'5" when she was wearing stilettos, his gargoyle, Esther, was formidable. This morning she was wearing skin-tight, red leather pants and a black tank top with a rhinestone devil emblazoned across her chest.

Ashe snorted when he saw her. Unlike most of the gargoyles, Esther was irreverent when it came to the one she called, The Dark Overlord.

"Good morning, Esther." His voice sounded husky and unused from sleep. Once he sat up, she handed over the mug. He hummed as he sipped.

The woman on his left rolled towards the magical smell. "Oh, is that coffee?"

Ashe couldn't remember her name. Sandy? Stephanie? No, it was something unusual. Eh, it'll come to him or it wouldn't. Her hair was a tangled riot of blonde.

"It's not just coffee," Ashe explained to the uninitiated. "It's Yemen Mocha Mattari." He took another sip and let the glorious brew fill his senses. Yemen coffee was easily the best-smelling coffee on the planet, and the taste was out of this world. The chocolate and fruit tones melted on his tongue and consummated with a sensuous almost wine-like finish. He moaned lustily.

The body on Ashe's right stirred. His other bed partner was flat on his stomach with his face turned into the pillow. "Mornin'." His voice was also slurred and throaty from sleep. He kissed Ash's hip as he pushed himself up.

Asher observed the young man through the steam rising above his cup. This one's name he remembered. Liam. With the dark eyes and dusky skin.

Liam hummed as he took the cup from Asher and sipped. "That's incredible."

Ash retrieved his cup and kissed the man's lush mouth—mmm, mocha. He slid his hand under the covers and gripped a warm, muscular thigh while feminine fingers circled the small of his back.

"Uh, uh, uh." Esther's voice was insistent at the end of the bed. "It's morning. Time for all good boys and girls to find their respective underwear and depart."

The girl next to Asher—Susan? Simone?—giggled. "What if we weren't wearing underwear when we got here?"

Esther put her hands on her hips. "That's for you and your laundress to worry about."

"Huh?"

The gargoyle tossed a sequined miniskirt and a pair of boxer briefs on the bed and gave a toss of her head to indicate everyone needed to get up.

Asher took another long sip of coffee and smiled. The girl was pouting. He wound a finger through a lock of her hair and gave a little tug. "Tell me what your name is again."

"Symphony," she cooed, morphing from a childish pout into a sex kitten. "Remember. You said you were going to play me like an instrument."

Asher chuckled but was pretty sure he heard Esther gag. "Ah, that's right. And I did, didn't I."

Esther left the room with dirty glasses in her hands and an empty bottle tucked under each arm. "Chop chop," she called behind her.

"Who is that woman?" Symphony asked. "She's mean."

"Totally," Liam agreed. Asher enjoyed the view as Liam crawled towards the side of the bed and rose.

Asher feigned reluctance but flipped back the comforter to make it easier for them to untangle from each other. "That's my gargoyle," he explained. Esther definitely could be mean when the situation warranted it. So far this morning, she was only using her stern voice.

"This is the biggest bed I have ever seen." Liam spread his arms wide in comparison. "What is it? Like two king beds?"

Symphony struggled to make it to her side. Her ass was equally plump. "Yeah. Like, where do you find sheets and stuff for a bed this big?"

Asher drained his coffee before answering. "I have no idea. That's the gargoyle's job."

Liam emerged from the bathroom with his jeans on. He paused in the doorway and asked Symphony, "Did you see the shower? It's just like the bed—freaking huge. There are five shower heads in there."

The naked girl trotted in behind Liam to look for herself. She returned with a towel wrapped around herself like a blanket. "Bed, shower, these towels. Everything in here is huge."

"Thank you very much," Asher said with mock lechery. He tied the sash on his favorite bathrobe. It was navy silk, and he loved the way it slipped across his skin.

"Why does anyone need a shower with five shower heads?" she asked.

"Because you don't want anyone getting cold when you have a crowd in there."

Liam raised his eyebrows at the implication, but Symphony gasped and jumped up and down. "Let's take a shower! All three of us. Pretty please?"

Asher grasped the sides of the towel and brought her in flush to his body. He gave her a deep kiss, but he didn't turn on the Lust. He did have things to do today and, as easy as it would be to make happen, he couldn't spend all day in bed. Or in the shower.

"Not this time," he told her. He let the towel drop to the floor and scooped up a black lace bra and handed it to her with the miniskirt.

"Another time then?" she asked hopefully.

When he glanced up, Liam was waiting for the answer, too. Ashe smiled and quirked his eyebrow suggestively without answering the question. The truth was, probably not. When Esther put them each in an Uber and sent them home, she would do so with a dab of oblivion, just enough that they would have sexy memories, but not enough clarity to remember the details like his name or where his house was located.

That was Esther's worst nightmare. She lived in horror that one morning all of his lustful conquests would turn up at his front door expecting an orgy or something.

"You don't have to go home, but you can't stay here," Esther called from somewhere in the front of the house.

Liam already had his boots laced up and his shirt on, but the girl moved slowly and with reluctance. Asher left her hunting for her shoes under the bed and went to embrace the man.

Liam was tall and wiry. Ashe didn't have to duck his head to kiss him, which put him about just over six feet. Wrapping his fingers around the back of his neck, he pressed his lips against Liam's full mouth. Morning scruff chaffed at Ash's chin. Delicious.

A muffled voice came from under the bed. "I can't find my shirt. Now, I know I had a shirt when I came here. I may not have had underwear, but I never leave the house without a shirt."

Ash gave Liam's bottom lip a little suck before pulling away. "I'll give you a t-shirt to wear home."

Esther had a line item in her household budget for t-shirts for his lovers to wear home. She kept a stockpile of them. There were also flip flops in assorted sizes for the ones who couldn't find their shoes. She swore Ashe's conquests did it on purpose, left an item at the house so they would have to come back. Of course, when they got home they were confused about where they'd lost their clothes. One of Esther's superpowers was the ability to find each and every one of these people and get their shirts/shoes/panties/what-have-you back to them.

"Your rides are here." Esther strode in from the hall. "Why aren't you wearing a shirt?" she demanded of Symphony.

"I was just going to get her one?" Asher asked.

Esther rolled her eyes and disappeared into the walk-in closet.

Symphony flinched. "Is she mad?"

Ash snorted. "Mad? No. She's just a gargoyle. They're all like that."

Liam shook his head. "Dude, I would not call her a gargoyle so loud. She might hear you."

"I always hear him," Esther announced as she emerged with a brand-new shirt on a hanger.

"Eep!" Symphony jumped.

"Everyone dressed now? Excellent." Esther marched them from the room.

Ashe slipped away from the parade towards the exit. He'd said his good-byes, and now he was going to let Esther do her thing. If he followed along with them to the door, the goodbyes would linger and the whole scene could get messy. He ducked into the kitchen and poured himself some more coffee.

He checked the oven to find a coffee cake baking so he perched on a bar stool to wait for his gargoyle to return. He loved his kitchen. It was one of his favorite rooms in the house. Done in cobalt blue and exposed brick, it was very European in style. Esther always made sure there were fresh flowers, and this morning a pitcher of sunflowers contrasted beautifully, yellow against the blue. Fresh herbs hung in the window adding to the fragrance and ambiance of the room. He had no idea who cooked with them. He could cook and he did so capably when the mood struck him, it just didn't strike very often. Esther flat out refused to cook, and everything was catered in. Coffee was the only thing she'd make from scratch. Even the cake warming in the oven was from the boulangerie around the corner.

It only took her a few minutes to finish up before he heard her heels tapping on the hardwood floors.

"That girl had the potential to be a stage-five clinger," she told him as she crossed the room. "I hit her twice with the wammy just to make sure. Did you know her name was Symphony? Who does that to a kid?" She drained the coffee pot into her own mug. "Are you going to want more?" she asked, gesturing with the carafe.

"Um hmm." He nodded. "To go with the coffee cake. It's right there in the name."

She didn't say anything but got the beans down and filled the grinder.

"What's on the—"

Esther hit the button and the coffee grinder went to work at about ninety decibels. Ash waited until it quieted down.

"Do I have any—"

Whiiir, it started up again. A short burst of about twenty seconds.

"Do—"

Whir! Esther pulsed the machine with a smirk on her face.

"Are you done?" he asked when there had been an extended pause between pulses.

Whir! Finally, Esther chortled. "I think so."

Asher rolled his eyes. "What are we doing today? I'm restless."

She pulled the cake from the oven and took to cutting slices from the pan while it was warm. "My agenda is super exciting. I'm changing the sheets on your bed and finding Symphony's shirt."

He gave her a look. "You say that like you're actually changing the sheets instead of supervising the maid and sending the laundry out."

Her shoulder rose and fell in a practice gesture. "There is a lot of organizing that goes into all that. Besides, I still have to find that shirt."

Nibbling on the cake while he watched the carafe fill with aromatic mocha, he asked, "Do you remember that great wine I found for Wrath's groundbreaking thing last week? It was made from apples."

"Obviously, I remember." Esther set a plate in front of him. "I'm the one who tracked it down, as a surprise for the apple lady. Jeb loves her," she said referring to her gargoyle compatriot.

"Yeah, she's a doll," Ashe confirmed. He couldn't believe that Luke—Wrath, of all people—had become so domesticated. It was confounding, both repulsive and sweet at the same time. "So I've been thinking." Esther leaned her hip against the counter, listening. "We've just about got the diamond contracts sewn up."

Esther perked up. "No more trips to Russia?" She clapped her hands. "I've never been so cold in all my life. Arkhangelsk is the most godforsaken place. Why would anyone want to live at the North Pole? There just isn't enough vodka."

"Come on, you loved it. You made me buy you that matching gray sable coat and hat."

She let out a blissful sigh. "I looked freaking amazing in that. Remember that old movie, Dr Zhivago? That was me every time I wore it."

"Anyway, I think we've about wrapped that up and I was thinking of another project."

The creation of Eros Unlimited had come about because he couldn't find quality silk for his bathrobe. At the time, he'd been bored and twenty-three and he'd became obsessed with the idea that Lust needed a bathrobe better than Hugh Hefner's. In truth, Hef wished he had the powers of Lust. Asher had begun the search in couture houses in Europe, and it took him two years wenching his way across that continent and moving on to Asia before he'd found success in a perfectly average trader's market in India.

Pheresata Silk had a painting of a stylized white *bombyx mori* moth painted on the side of the building, its gorgeous white wings spread out like the heavenly host. *Pheresata* meant angel.

Perhaps it had been serendipity or just blind dumb luck that brought him to West Bengal and led him to the angel silk dealer. Whatever it was, it seemed to Asher the name was calling to him. He negotiated a deal to import the silk right there in the sultry, buzzing market and his first independent fortune was made.

Two years later he found himself involved in a wager with his cousins, Seth and Jacob, over caviar. If asked now, Ashe couldn't tell you the terms of the bet, or even what brought it around in the first place but, guaranteed, alcohol was involved. As always with the cousins, stakes were high and the three of them wound up in a Russian thug's living room, eating outrageously priced black-market caviar on top of baked potatoes, "as the real Russians do it".

Seth had been fascinated with the texture and taste, letting Gluttony out to play. Jacob, on the other hand, didn't really enjoy it but the price tag-per-pound made Greed sit up and take notice. Asher asked a million questions, intrigued by the whole process—especially the underground/mobster part of it all. He hadn't decided he wanted to be involved until their Russian host referred to the eggs as *kheruvim*.

"What does that mean?" he'd asked thinking it sounded an awful lot like cherub.

"You know, fat baby with wings," the big Russian had said while flapping his fingers on his shoulders.

"Why are they cherubs?" Ashe asked. The eggs were round and black; he didn't see it.

"Mother fish looks like angel to me, under the water, silver and magical."

Asher just blinked at him. It was an off-hand comment, but again it was as if the universe was calling to him. He was in. Dealing with the Russian mob was more difficult than the fabric merchants in India, but he had the Devil on his side. And now he could indulge in all the delectable caviar he could ever want.

In his silk bathrobe.

Really, if he had to deal with the Devil in his life at all, he might as well get something out of it. Unlike his cousin Luke, Ashe was a bit more levelheaded about his family connections and wasn't squeamish about using whatever tools were available to him. It didn't take long until the Russian mob was happily using his connections to make even more underhanded money and Ashe had been able to tuck one more "angel" in his portfolio.

Eight months ago, he'd received a call from his Russian "family" who needed some help with another situation. There had been some bad blood within the organization, which caused a hole in the distribution of diamonds from one of the largest mines in the world.

Who knew so many diamonds came from Russia? Asher certainly hadn't. He wasn't sure he really wanted to bother with the politics and bullshit that came hand in hand with dealing with the touchy mobsters any more than he already did. That was, until he found out the mine was in Arkhangelsk.

Diamonds from a place called Archangel.

It was like he didn't even have a choice in the matter.

And now he could sit in his silk bathrobe, eating caviar, covered in diamonds if he wanted to.

Pretty fucking fantastic.

Esther pulled him out of his thoughts with a rap on the granite countertop. "So, what is the new idea?"

"Empyrean Vineyards"

It took Esther a second, and then she grinned. "Empyrean as in Heaven."

"Um humm." Asher toasted with his coffee mug. "I find myself thirsty for the Holy Spirit. What do you think?"

"Not necessarily for breakfast, but what do I know."

.

Chapter Two

E vangeline Dashiell was walking the rows of Gewurztraminer. The sun had begun its ascent less than a quarter of an hour before, so the sky was streaked with shades of hopeful pink and gold, but it was dark in the shade of the vines, so she only saw the shadows of her booted feet.

Empyrean Vineyards was withering.

Spring had been warmer than usual moving right into a summer that promised to be blistering. May was already a good five degrees above normal and, while that might not seem like a lot to the average person, her experimental Gewurztraminer vines were languishing in the heat. Merely thinking about August made Eva's heart palpitate.

She'd already done the monetary calculations for constructing a sunshade, and her sister Maggie had wheezed dramatically over the cost, but it had to be done or these grapes were going to be raisins before the solstice.

She pushed the leaves back and cupped a cluster of fruit. Sweaty globes of cloudy mauve grapes lay in her hand. She closed her eyes and summoned her grandfather like she always did when the vineyard made her anxious. She imagined him beside her, his old work chinos shiny at the knees from kneeling in the dirt, his face shaded by the ubiquitous straw hat he wore in the fields. In her mind's eye, Pops leaned forward and cocked his ear next to the fruit and listened. He did this often and it amused her to no end when she was little, but as an adult she had begun to suspect he actually could hear something. He would furrow his brow and nod his head, making little noises of acknowledgement. Finally, he would rise to his full height which towered above hers, even when she was grown, and announce whatever mystery the grapes had told him.

"Shade," her long-dead grandfather said in her mind.

"Yup, shade," she agreed.

She picked up her pace until she got to the end of the row and the dirt track that circumnavigated the fields. She climbed into the old pickup truck with the Empyrean logo fading on the door and slowly, so as not to spray dust and gravel, made her way back to the house to break the bad news to her sister.

Magdalena was just where Eva knew she'd find her. It was a twin thing. Ever since the womb they'd always known right where to find the other. Convenient in malls and amusement parks, annoying when playing hide and seek or sneaking out with a boyfriend.

Maggie set her coffee cup on her desk. "It's already hot, isn't it?"

"It's sultry," Eve corrected and launched into the sales pitch for the awning. "And the sun is barely up. We really have no choice. I know it's expensive, but losing all those grapes would be even more fiscally irresponsible." She used her sister's own words against her, trying to keep her emotion out of it. "Just think how much revenue those grapes have the potential to infuse into the company."

Her sister closed her eyes and sighed. "We can funnel some money from the rehab of the banquet hall. It just means it'll take longer before we can start making money with weddings. As I've said before, there's a hell of a lot more money in weddings than in experimental wine."

Eva took off her ball cap and wiped her brow with her forearm. "I know, believe me, I know. It's just that the thought of letting that whole field wither and die makes me want to throw up."

Maggie sighed again. Her sister had a whole vocabulary of sighs. She spoke English, Pig Latin, a little Spanish, and Sighs. "I know."

"I'm gonna start on it this morning," Eva told her. She pulled open the top drawer of their shared desk and plucked their company credit card from the flotsam of pens and paperclips. "I'm gonna nab Ernie and get to the lumber yard as soon as it opens. Are you going to be okay here alone?"

The look Maggie gave her was a mash up of a sneer and a query. "What's gonna happen while you're gone? Are a thousand mad Shriners going to descend and demand a banquet hall?"

Eva rolled her eyes. "I meant... I don't know what I meant, but now that you mention it, a thousand Shriners would be super exciting. You should hope for that."

"Nah." Maggie made an exaggerated face of disgust. "Shriners are old and wrinkly and probably crabby. Not a one of them is handsome and dashing and sexy."

Eva held up a finger. "But, point in their favor, they do drive those tiny cars at the circus. You can't tell me you wouldn't love to get your hands on a tiny car." She pretended to drive, hands on a make-believe steering wheel, and made engine noises. "I can see you, rippin' ass through the fields."

Maggie laughed. "You're the only one who wants to drive the tiny car."

"So, if the Shriners come in, you flirt with them up and to the point where I get a tiny car."

Maggie snorted into her coffee mug. "What the hell is in it for me? I seduce old men for toy cars for your benefit? I don't think so, chickadee."

"Don't be shortsighted," Eva told her with a grin as she walked back out the door. "You can convince one of them to pay off our company credit card."

She found Ernie, their jack-of-all-trades foreman, in the barn. Ernie had been around the vineyard as long as Eva and Maggie had been. He was practically family. His father was the foreman until five years ago when he had a massive heart attack at fifty-three and died right there among the rows of cabernet. The sisters had only been managing the family business for a couple of months when that tragedy struck, right on the heels of burying their grandfather. The three of them cleaved together, Eva, Maggie, and Ernie, to keep the business afloat earlier than they'd ever thought they would have to. Once the shock was no longer clouding everything in a mournful haze and the three of them got past the dread of waiting for the mythical third tragedy to befall them, they slowly began to implement some changes.

Ernie had set up lasers as high-tech scarecrows and had plans for more technological advances.

Eva bought some root stock from the Alsace region of France and lovingly nurtured the Gewurztraminer grapes that her grandfather had never gotten around to attempting.

Maggie wanted to build an event center next to the idyllic pond south of the house. Where Eva's Gewurzt would hopefully bring in a marginal flush of cash, Maggie's plan would infuse their business with enough capital to rehab the old monastery that was their family home.

The first Dashiell to immigrate to America had wandered to California in 1870, taking Horace Greeley's directive to "Go West" literally. Maurice traveled light: he came with his trusty steed, a very nice beaver hat he purchased for the occasion, and a pack filled with cuttings from his family vineyard in Bordeaux, France. Upon eventually discovering himself in the lush valleys of the Pacific Northwest, he knew he'd found home.

Finding the monastery was a stroke of luck. The Spanish mission was in a terrible state of repair. The only building still standing was the old monastery. The church had been burned nearly to the ground. Only the south wall remained. Blackened by soot and dirt and months of grime, the remnant of a stained-glass window tilted dramatically towards the ashy floor. Maurice rescued it and cleaned it gently until the artistry gleamed through. Unlike the usual Madonna and Child or some other typical biblical theme, this glassmaker had immortalized a vineyard.

Maurice knew beyond a shadow of a doubt that this was the location of his destiny.

He moved into the monastery and began the arduous task of planting a vineyard. He married Milagra Angelica Navarro, a lovely young woman of Spanish and Chinook descent with a name befitting the serendipity that ruled Maurice's life.

Six generations later, Evangeline & Magdalena, named in the biblical convention Maurice & Milagra started, inherited the property, skipping their mother, Delilah, who couldn't possibly have cared less. Eva and Maggie had never actually met their father. He'd come for the harvest, sewed his own virgin field, and disappeared back into the world when the job was done. Delilah blamed it all on the name she'd been saddled with. She'd vacated the farm as soon as she'd been able, left her babies with her parents, and ran as fast as her legs could carry her. She'd never looked back.

"Hey, Ernie," Eva called out. "What are you doing?"

He tossed her a confused look. "What you asked me to do. Winery stuff before your sister ropes me into building that damn screen."

Eva laughed. Even knowing the sisters his entire life, Ernie still confused them for each other. In all fairness, Eva and Maggie looked remarkably similar even for identical twins. When in town, they often didn't even bother to correct people. Sure, it made for confusing conversations, but that was kind of the fun.

"This is the sister." She laughed when he rolled his eyes in consternation. "I'm totally roping you into this. Come on."

It took most of the morning and they'd had to go to more than one place to find all they needed, but Eva had made a comprehensive list of supplies and they stuck to it. After the bed of the truck was loaded up with lumber and high-density polyethylene, they wandered down to the diner for something fortifying. That meant coffee for Ernie and a fruit smoothie for Eva.

They chatted up their neighbors and friends. Eva commiserated with several other farmers in the area. Her lineage and unearthly understanding of the earth and grapes meant her thoughts and opinions were often sought out.

"Did you see that car?" Toby asked no one in particular, interrupting a conversation between Eva and his father. Toby was fifteen and as car crazy as any teenage boy ever got. He was a good kid, and Eva liked him. His family owned the apple orchards to the west of their property. Sometimes he came and helped Ernie with projects or with harvesting for some extra cash.

"No." Eva looked over her shoulder, but the only cars out there were the usual.

Toby ran to look out the window in the glass door. "Man, when's the last time you saw an Aston Martin?"

Surely, that was a rhetorical question. They saw plenty of fancy cars in wine country. There were enough wealthy people who loved to tour the wineries and vineyards that they saw just about everything. Aston Martin's, however, were just unusual enough that Eva had no idea when she'd last seen one.

"It was red, and I swear I could hear it purr from in here." Toby craned his neck.

Eva paid the check and signaled Ernie it was time to go. "Have your dad drop you off when you're done working for him. Ernie and I can use all the help we can get with this project."

"Yeah," he said distractedly. "I'll see you in a while."

Eva eyed her old pickup as they approached it. It was classic in the sense that it was old. 1973 Ford F350. It was red in the sense that when it was new it had been candy-apple red. Now it was also red in the sense that it was oxidized rust. It still ran alright, so long as you were gentle with her. The tires were old and the bench seat was slick vinyl and duct tape. She imagined the new spark plugs they put in last month were worth more than the whole truck, but it was trusty. And it had been their grandfather's. And there was no way in hell they could afford to replace her until some of these projects panned out.

She hadn't told the ghost of her grandfather that she was worried, but she suspected he knew anyway.

He must have been reading her mind, because Ernie turned to her as they neared the turnoff to their property. "It's all going to work out, you know. We'll get the shades up, and the weather is going to break eventually. We'll get the rains and then we can worry about flooding and rot and mold."

Eva made an effort to release the tension she was holding in her shoulders. "I know. You're right. Maggie keeps telling me to relax, too, but I can't seem to let it all go. As soon as I stop worrying about the vines withering, I worry we'll harvest too early. Or too late. I worry about the cold storage. Then the plumbing in the house. That old building is gorgeous, but it's falling apart at the seams. What if this truck finally dies? When I finally go to sleep, I have nightmares about fires and locusts and, I don't know, space aliens landing in the fields."

Ernie chuckled. "Wow. You're a mess. Let's just tackle this one thing and then we'll move to the next one."

"I know, I know." She shook her head like some of the anxiety might come loose and fall out. "I just can't take one more thing on my plate right now."

There was still dust hanging in the air when she turned onto their long dirt driveway, which indicated that another vehicle had been there not too long before. It wasn't possible that Toby had beaten them here, and they didn't do tastings on Mondays.

They came around the final curve of the drive and under the bigleaf maple tree and Eva's question was answered.

"Hey, isn't that Toby's Aston Martin?" Ernie asked.

Annoyance flashed through her. She wasn't sure if it was because of the looming delay on building the shade or if it was because of the man unfolding himself from the driver's seat of the car. He had entitlement written all over him.

He for sure wasn't a Shriner.

"Shit," she said, thinking that just about covered it

Chapter Three

Asher was charmed by everything he saw. Empyrean Vineyards was bewitching. As he steered his car down the lengthy driveway, he had the sense he was going back in time.

Or to a fairy realm.

Once the car emerged from the tree-lined drive and into a meadow that served as the front lawn of the old monastery, his cousin Benji let out a low whistle. With the classical building in the front and the rolling hills of the vineyard behind, the scene was heartbreakingly idyllic.

"Well, isn't that a photo op?" Benji sat straight and showed interest. Asher and the other five Sins had taken to dragging Benjamin around with them in an effort to keep Sloth from becoming one with his sofa. None of them ever asked Benji if he wanted to go; they just shoved him in a car and away they went.

Asher parked the car next to an enormous stylized wrought iron cross intertwined with vines and grape clusters that mirrored the logo on the wine label. The building was pleasantly weathered, giving it an air of gravitas that suggested anything produced within must be very fine indeed, be it prayers or wine.

"I especially appreciate the bell," Asher agreed, pointing to a huge church bell suspended from a notch cut into the façade that rose higher than the roof in front.

As if they'd timed it, he and Benji opened their card doors in unison. As Asher gazed up at the impressive two-story stone building and the rolling hills behind it, he took a deep breath of sweet, mulchy nature. There was a tingle in his gut just like he had when he'd found the silk, the diamonds, and the caviar. A vineyard named after Heaven. By God, it was fate.

The rumbling engine of an old truck drew his attention, and he turned to see the only vehicle in the whole world that could have possibly fit into the tableau, as if a set designer had put together the whole scene. He wouldn't be surprised if he walked around the corner of the building only to find it was a façade propped up with two-by-fours into the ground and the backdrop of rolling vines was painted on canvas.

The perfectly cast truck rumbled to a stop and idled there for a moment. The sun hit the windshield just so, and he couldn't see inside the vehicle. Ashe held his breath with anticipation, waiting for the people inside to make themselves known. With a creak of old metal and ancient hinges, the driver's door to the old Ford opened and a woman emerged.

She used her hand to her forehead like a visor and called over the hood. "We don't have any tastings on Mondays. I'm sorry. If you'd like to come back tomorrow..."

Ashe put on his smoothest smile, a real panty-melter. He closed his own car door and strode across the drive towards her. "Good morning." He held her gaze. "What a beautiful place you have here."

Her smile was forced. "Thank you. Several other vineyards in the area are available. I can give you a map."

He extended a friendly hand. He could almost see her sigh before she took it. "I'm Asher Mephisto. This is my cousin, Benji." Benji pulled his gaze from the scenery and gave her a smile and a lazy salute.

She wasn't immediately forthcoming with her name and that had Ashe stymied. He kept her hand until she finally said, "Evangeline. Dashiell. Eva."

He allowed her hand to slip from his grasp, and yet she still maintained her inconvenienced expression. Unusually light blue eyes for someone with such dark hair and tanned skin regarded him in challenge.

"You look busy," he said, taking in her jeans and baseball cap. The truck bed was loaded with lumber and sheeting as evidence. A quick glance in the cab revealed a young man observing their conversation. "We don't want to pester you. We were hoping we could simply take a look around at your beautiful facility. We don't need a guide or anything."

She hesitated. Ashe sent her a blip, an atom's worth of lust, just to smooth her over. Instead, her eyes narrowed, and she put more space between them.

Wait, what?

"Would it be alright if I painted here?" Benji called from near the car. He made a wide gesture with his arm encompassing the buildings, the rolling vineyard in the background, the towering trees. "It's quite lovely."

Ashe blinked and consciously eased the frown lines on his forehead. "My cousin is an artist," he blurted out, not knowing what else to say.

Who was this woman?

She gave Benji a half-smile. She couldn't seem to muster anything more than a squinty-eyed stare for Asher.

"I guess so, but stay up here in the public areas," she said and swung the driver's door to her truck open again. In one swift move, she plopped herself back in the cab of the truck. She cranked over the engine and the put the truck in gear. Ashe stepped back to avoid having his toes run over.

"Thanks," he called at the departing truck. "We'll touch base again later."

What the hell just happened here?

He waited until the dust settled, then he trudged back across the road and snarled, "That was great."

Benji shrugged. "She's gonna let you look around."

"Yeah, but didn't you see that? It was like she hated me on sight. Do we know her or something?"

Benji grabbed a sketchbook from the dashboard and shoved some pencils in his back pocket. "I don't know her, but I've been gone for a while. You'd know better than me."

"I really don't think I do."

Esther would know for sure. His gargoyle had amazing recall. Still, it wasn't like him to have left a dissatisfied partner. That was the whole point. Everyone felt better after an encounter with him, regardless of the physicality of it.

"Do you still want to look around, or would you rather sit here and pout instead?" Benji collided their shoulders together with a hearty bump. "Come on."

Asher followed Benji around the side of the building and the whole valley opened up in front of them. His cousin issued a soft sigh at the sublimeness of it all.

A half an hour later, Ashe was lying under the shade of a huge elm tree while Benji bent over his pad, sketching away with pencils in his mouth, behind an ear, and in his left fist.

"What do you think that was all about?" Ashe asked his cousin.

Benji squinted into the distance. "What what was?"

"That woman?" Ashe had been musing over their exchange and couldn't fathom why she was so...bitchy.

"What woman?" Just like Benji to notice none of the important stuff.

"The woman in the truck."

Benji tilted his head, changing his perspective "Oh, yeah. The pretty one."

Not pretty. That was an insufficient descriptor for her. Gorgeous. Exquisite. Stunning.

Ashe could still conjure her electric blue eyes, which had fixed him with intoxicating intelligence. As if she could see through him, deep into his heart where he was anxious and unsure.

Even though she'd unnerved him, he could sense an obsession blooming.

"Yeah, the pretty one." He rose to his feet and dusted grass from his butt and hands. He came here to find out if Empyrean Vineyards was his next project and he wasn't going to make that determination lying around with Sloth all day. "You can stay here and draw, but I'm going to look around."

The old stone monastery seemed to be both a home and the business center for the winery. A magnificent stained-glass window graced the front. It looked like the office, tasting room, and a small shop were located in the lower area, and the living quarters were above.

Ashe left Benji sitting on a retaining wall, concentrating on the scenery and his notebook and observed the softly undulating hills of the actual vineyard. Perfect long rows of green leafy plants filled his gaze for what seemed like miles. He wondered how much of this land belonged to Empyrean or if some of it included the neighbors. He stood on a rise and took in the view, enjoying the pleasing way the patterns switched up and made a crazy quilt of textures. The early afternoon sun was high, making the light breeze warm across his skin. He'd taken off his cashmere sweater and tied it around his waist. He actually wished he could remove his shirt too, and feel the sun kiss his chest and feel the air move across his shoulders like a feather.

The place was just so damn picturesque.

There were several outbuildings which probably housed tools and such. And one more long stone building across a narrow meadow that looked out over a small pond. Huge double farm doors were locked at the entrance, but when he looked in the windows, he could tell this was the barrel storage.

Yes, this place needed him, his special touch to bring it to its full potential. That's what he had done for the silk merchant, the diamond dealer, and the caviar farmers. Asher used his special skills to make fortunes. When he handpicked a project, there was no end to what he could do.

He wanted Empyrean.

And the woman, he definitely wanted her, too. He would crack her and figure out what went wrong there. She might just need more of a push. He'd gone easy on her before. Next time he'd plop a whammy on her and the situation would be handled.

As he climbed back up the rise towards the monastery, he worked on a pitch for the owners. He found his cousin in the same place, but now he was just gazing into the distance. Up until then, he saw Benji had been busy. Ashe picked up his notebook and flipped through the pages. His cousin really was amazingly talented. Not only had he captured the beauty in his pencil drawings, but somehow the whimsy of the place as well.

"Here comes your pretty lady," Benji said with a nod towards the monastery.

Ashe turned and saw the dark-haired beauty coming towards them from the offices. Her long legs, wrapped in tight jeans, ate up the lawn at a pretty rapid pace. He removed his sunglasses to get a better look at her. The ball cap was off now and her long hair swung behind her in a graceful arc. She had a determined air, and Ashe felt a mini adrenalin rush at the thought of combat with her, even if it was only verbal sparring.

"Hello again," Ashe said with a smile as soon as she was close enough to avoid yelling. "Your place is stunning."

"I know," she said and matched his smile. "My many-great grandfather chose the most sumptuous place in the valley."

As she drew closer, Ashe sensed something different about her, but he wasn't sure what it was.

"Are you the Dashiell in charge?" Ashe couldn't help skimming his eyes over her body. Tall and lean, but still managing to have an excellent ass. Ashe imagined that bit of perfection could be attributed to yoga. The boobs were all genetic.

"I am." She tucked some silky hair behind her ear. "I suspect you have an agenda."

She didn't smell quite right, or something. He still couldn't put his finger on it. She looked the same. Her hair was the same and her captivating blue eyes hadn't changed.

"I might," he agreed. "I see tremendous untapped potential here."

Her gaze turned speculative. "We have lots of plans. Plans take time and money."

"I'd love to hear what you have in mind," he said and took a step toward her.

Her gaze slid down his body and back up. It was a quick, furtive movement but he was used to it and would have totally ignored it if she hadn't been so standoffish before. "Maybe we could go inside, out of the heat," she suggested.

"Great. Are you staying here?" he asked Benji.

His cousin nodded, already bored of Ashe and the woman's exchange.

Ashe extended his hand in the direction of the main building and threw her another mega-watt smile. "Lead the way."

Instinctively, he reached to place his hand at the small of her back but withdrew it immediately. She definitely wasn't the woman from the morning. It wasn't like his skin tingled or anything. He just *knew*. She was every bit as beautiful and certainly friendlier, but...

She was just wrong. Or rather, not right.

He realized that she'd been talking, and he refocused his attention on her.

"...kitchen and bathrooms, but the plumbing is an expense we didn't think we could handle right now."

"I'm sorry," he admitted, "I was captivated by the beauty of the place and missed what you said."

"That's alright. I was just saying that we have a lot of remodeling and updating to the old monastery to do, but until some of the other projects start bringing in the money, it will have to wait."

Ashe looked at the building with a more practical eye. Beyond the obvious esthetic of the place, it was easy to see it was in need of some love. They stepped onto the lawn and heard the slam of a car door. Seconds later, an exact duplicate of the woman by his side strode around the corner. Her step hitched when she saw him, and he could sense more than see her eyes narrow into a glare from across the yard.

And yet, he felt a pull from his core towards her. At the same time, he experienced a sense of relief that he wasn't crazy.

"Hey," the lady by his side called to the woman Ashe knew as Evangeline.

Ashe turned on the woman escorting him inside. "I am so sorry. I thought we'd already met when I mistook you for Evangeline." He stuck out his hand. "I am Asher Mephisto."

"People always confuse us." She shook his hand and replied, "Magdelena Dashiell, but you can call me Maggie and my sister Eva."

"What are you doing?" Eva inquired with some steel in her voice.

"Just going inside for a chat," Maggie answered. "How goes the erection?" Long pause. "Of the sunshade?"

Eva threw Asher a completely uncalled for scowl. He'd barely even focused in on Maggie. It's not like he'd debauched her or anything.

And wasn't that interesting? His mojo worked on Maggie but not on Eva. Hmm. He didn't quite know what to make of that. The only people he knew of who didn't respond to any of the Sin's influence were the Sins themselves and their gargoyle companions. Come to think of it, he recalled it didn't work on his cousin Wrath's fiancé either.

"It's coming together. We'll have it all done in the next couple of days." Eva stood at the door to their office, blocking the entrance. "What are you chatting about?"

He smiled at the evil twin. "We've barely had a chance to talk yet, but I'm looking forward to hearing about the plans you both have for your property."

He took a deep breath through his nose and filled his mind with Eva's scent: Fruit, honey, and summer. Just that alone was making him half hard. He sent a push of lust square at her. Not a blip, not a molecule. He sent her a focused gob of the stuff, careful not to let it spread around.

Eva fell back a step and tore her gaze away, as if looking at him was more than her senses could take.

As if she took no notice of the undercurrents, Maggie asked politely, "And why are you so interested in Empyrean?"

Asher kept his focus on Eva. "Because I have money and time to invest and I'm quite taken with your vineyard."

Eva closed her eyes for a moment and then her gaze met his again. There was a fission of awareness there, but when she opened her mouth to speak, Asher was gob smacked.

"We're not even a little bit interested." She pointed her index finger at his feet. "You can take your two-hundred-dollar shoes right back to your three-hundred-thousand-dollar car and go home."

Holy shit.

Asher had never wanted a woman so badly in his whole life.

Hell XII

N eil had trudged across all of Hell, found the Devil's mansion, skirted the demonic staff, and found the Dark Lord's grandmother. He was damned proud of himself.

He'd been expecting an enthusiastic greeting. Not a parade or anything 'cause this whole thing was being done on the down low, but maybe a little whoop of excitement was called for.

Rachel, however, responded to his greeting with hysterical tears.

He stood just inside the threshold of her room and blinked at her, not sure what he should do. He hadn't been good at women's feelings in life, and being dead hadn't given him more experience. He inched forward and grimaced at her with speculative confusion. She was exceptionally pretty with miles of wavy blonde hair and watery blue eyes. She didn't look much older than his own angel, Juliet, which made it hard to think of her as a granny.

The white Persian cat that was perched on the table littered with jigsaw puzzle pieces hissed at him with disdain. Rachel scooped him up and clutched him to her chest and sobbed. The cat didn't look any happier about this change in his circumstance than he did before, but he tolerated it.

Neil stepped forward into the room, making it all the way to Rachel through the sea of cats. He pushed a straight-backed chair towards her and urged her to sit.

"Can I get you something to drink?" he asked her after the worst of it seemed to have wound down.

She shook her head and hiccupped.

"So, you're Rachel, huh. I wasn't actually sure you were real." He wavered his hands in a spooky movement. "Woooo, like an urban legend or something, but here you are."

Rachel wiped her eyes on the cat.

In a voice raspy from all that blubbering, she asked him, "Who sent you? Did you say an angel?"

Neil nodded and thought of Juliet. He thought about what kind of reward he might get from her when he shared the news he'd found the woman. A kiss. A real kiss this time. Maybe with a little tongue.

"What angel?"

The instant she let up on her death grip on the cat, he wriggled free and darted across the room to give himself a bath.

"Juliet. You probably don't know her. She's really young, and I don't think she's been up there that long." Rachel simply stared at him, expectantly waiting for more information. "I met her on the stairs. I was going up and she was going down." He shrugged, trying to be cool about it.

"I guess I don't know how the world works anymore." She used her index fingers to swipe away the tears under her eyes. "Angels and demons together..."

"It'll be anarchy," he yelled and laughed. Rachel started in surprise. "Sorry. Just screwing around. The world's the same. Hell fucking sucks, and I assume Heaven is all cookies and puppies and snowball fights. I don't know. I never been there. I never even met an angel before her."

"I thought I'd been lost down here. Forgotten."

"Well, you know—" he shrugged again "urban legend. Juliet told me about the curse. She's the one who found Lucifer and everything. I said I'd look for you down here if she looked for Cerberus up there."

Rachel's back stiffened. "Lucifer. She found Lucifer?"

"Yeah."

A million emotions played across her face. She looked like she was going to say more only didn't know where to start, but there was a crash from the hallway and the door burst open. A devilry of gremlins crowded through the door, snarling and spitting.

Neil cringed away from their thrusting spears and looked for a way out. He shouldn't have let his guard down. Of course, he should have known this was coming. How long could a trespasser be expected to traipse around in the Devil's mansion before he got caught? There was nowhere to go, no back door or window from which to jump. Even while he was backpedaling and scanning the room for something to use as a weapon, he could feel their boney, grasping fingers plucking at his arms and legs.

"What are you doing in here?" Rachel demanded at them. She slapped at the littlest ones as they tugged on Neil's clothes. "Hey, what do you think you're doing? This is my room and I have immunity."

She was roughly pushed out of the way by the gremlin leader. "Yeess," the leader hissed. "But he not have."

"But you're not allowed in my room." For someone who'd just been hysterically crying, she certainly managed to pull off the air of indignant royalty awfully well. "This is my sanctuary. He's safe in my sanctuary."

Four of the nasty group were roughly binding Neil's hands behind his back, but they paused as if she might have merit.

"Whaaaat—" the captain narrowed his beady eyes at her "—you think this church? You break rules, too. Maybe Master will let us punish you some."

"He will not!" She still used that outraged tone, but even Neil could tell she was less sure of herself than she'd been before.

The rope cinched around Neil's hands and was jerked tight. One of the smallest of the corps was gnawing on his shin until he kicked it off. Neil didn't struggle though. This group was unfamiliar to him and he knew from experience that if he went quietly and didn't put up a fuss it was possible they would lose interest in him and he could get away. The lessers generally got bored quickly when their subjects didn't scream or beg.

"Where are you taking him?" Neil heard her ask over the grunts and chittering of the gremlins pushing him out the door. "Hey, don't you ignore me. Don't you dare. Hey, no. No!"

The door slammed behind them and the captain pocketed the key. He stood on tiptoe, still only coming up to Neil's belt buckle, and growled up at him. "You be so sorry we find you. I gets to discipline you." If it was possible for a gremlin to purr, that might have been the noise that came from its throat. Whatever, it sounded sexual, and Neil's balls crawled into his stomach.

Neil swallowed back a gag from the stench of its breath. "I'm just looking for the dog. Duke Valefor told me to find him." Neil threw out the name of the Demon in charge of Circle Three, like a schmuck who was trying to get a good table at a restaurant.

The tugging and shoving began anew, and he was dragged down the hallway. "Valefor no help you here," the captain cackled. "I finds you. The Master gives me you as reward."

"Reward, reward, reward" the horde chanted in a sing-song.

Neil knew he should be concerned about Rachel being left alone down here again. She didn't seem the most stable person. And Juliet, too. His little angel would be waiting for him and probably worrying. But God help him, the minute he was deposited in the dungeon his good intentions left him.

No one could help him down here.

Just like always, he was all on his own.

Chapter Four

E va was hot and tired. Her arms felt like heavy tubes of jelly from holding them above her head for so long while raising the heavy shade sails over the vines. Her shoulders ached and she had several cuts on her hands and forearms from the wire that poked right through her heavy gloves.

The real bitch of it was they'd only gotten a third of the way done. Damn all overly ambitious projects.

When both of their stomachs were growling for lunch, Eva had sent Ernie home to his cute wife and baby, and she turned the truck towards the monastery. What she wanted to do was fall face-first into the pond by the cellars and then drag her ass in for a tall glass of iced tea and a peanut butter sandwich. No luck. When she came around the corner from the southern fields, that damned Aston Martin was still parked in the lot, and she could see Maggie chatting the man up on the lawn.

Well, that was something. At least he hadn't been wandering around the estate alone doing God only knew what. As soon as she'd jumped back in the truck, she'd had Ernie text her sister to tell her about the lofty shyster walking around the grounds. Eva couldn't even begin to guess what he wanted with their small-time operation. There were plenty of larger growers in the area. Regardless, whatever it was, Eva wasn't interested. Unfortunately, she'd left the much nicer twin to shoo away wolves at the door. Maggie liked everyone, and generally, the feeling was mutual. Maggie got that from their grandfather, whereas Eva had acquired stubbornness and flagrant hostility.

Maggie tossed Eva a smile. "You remember Mr. Mephisto. We were just going inside, out of the sun." Her sister paused and raised an eyebrow that suggested Eva should shut her hole, stop being mean, and listen to the man with the money.

Eva tore her glare from her sister, made a concerted effort to quell the antagonism, and looked to the man. There was so much there to find annoying. He was entirely too good looking for her taste. His expensive clothes and shoes—shit, even his artfully tousled haircut that no doubt cost more than her pickup—implied that he knew exactly how attractive he was. Men like that, men from money, expected things to go their way. Generally, their way was at odds with her way.

"Of course, I remember your lovely sister." Mr. Mephisto oozed charm. "Please call me Ashe. All my friends do. You've been working out in the sun all day—"

"Yes, Mr. Mephisto, working's what we do—"

"Eva." Maggie harshly cut in before Eva could launch into a good rant. "No one wants a lecture on your work ethic. The Puritans are dead, for God's sake. Come inside and get some tea and cool off."

Maybe tea was what she needed. She'd woken up this morning full of anxiety and maybe some of this animosity was misplaced.

Mr. Mephisto quirked an eyebrow and she could almost hear him scratching a point in his favor on the tally board.

Or maybe that animosity was right where it was supposed to be.

Eva cast a suspicious glance at the other man still sitting in the shade, a notebook and pencils on the grass beside him. He nodded at her with a drowsy smile, and she found herself smiling back. Now why couldn't Mr. Mephisto be as noninvasive as his cousin?

She followed her sister and the man inside. The minute she stepped over the threshold, the cool of the building calmed her. One of the advantages of living in the old stone structure was that it stayed cool in the summer. A person needed a thick sweater in the winter, but that was hard to care about when the grapes were withering in the hot sun.

Maggie and Mr. Mephisto were gabbing away like old friends while Eva disappeared through a door into the private confines of the home she and her family had lived in for generations. She pulled her shirt over her head down to her sports bra and stuck her head under the kitchen faucet. The flirty sounds of her sister's giggling grated on her nerves. It was frustrating that her sister was so easy around people she didn't know.

She filled a glass with cool water. Her hair dripped down her shoulders and onto the floor. What she really wanted to know was what that man could possibly want with their little company.

You can play the game long enough to get the lowdown, Evangeline. Her grandfather's voice resonated in her head. *You're a smart girl. Act smart.*

She grabbed an apple and climbed the stairs to the family's apartments on the top floor of the monastery. When she came back down, she'd talked herself into a better mood helped by her favorite Empyrean Vineyards t-shirt. Across her chest read the words, "Of course size matters. No one wants a small glass of wine" with the family's logo on the back.

She took a deep breath and opened the door into the tasting room. Maggie was on her feet and had both a bottle of red and one of white in her hands. "This one got best in show in California Commercial Wine competition, and this one placed second the next year. We're very proud of our little operation." Maggie turned at the sound of Eve's entrance. "That apple wine that brought us to your attention was the brainchild of my sister." Eve dipped in a tiny sarcastic curtsey. "She's really brilliant with blending varietals. She created a whole line of fruit blends which have received lots of attention and accolades." Maggie beamed at her.

Eva felt Mephisto's eyes on her. She kept her own eyes trained on her sister, but her skin was warm from his gaze.

Maggie held up the bottles again. "Red or white?"

"Both," he said with a smile that Eva could hear in his voice.

"Get some glasses," Maggie said to her, "and join us."

When Eva's eyes darted to him almost of their own volition, he smirked and dropped his eyes to the writing on her chest. "I'll need a big one." The man's voice was like honey.

Eva could kick herself for supplying him the ammunition. Stupid shirt.

She threaded the stems of six wine glasses like Jenga blocks through her fingers and followed them to one of the tall tables in the tasting room. The large public room they used for sampling their products took advantage of the beautiful sanctuary at the front of the monastery. The enormous stained-glass window seen from the parking lot took up a large part of the eastern wall. The original pews lined the outer walls and were set up in little vignettes around the room. It was Eva's favorite place in the entire building. She loved the vibe she got when she was in here—not necessarily religious because Eva didn't really go in for organized religion—but it was peaceful.

And earthy. And she felt more at one with her ancestors in there. It didn't make any sense, but there it was. She didn't tell anyone else her hippy dippy philosophy, but Maggie probably already knew.

Mr. Mephisto uncorked the bottle of red like a professional and served the three of them while Maggie did the same with the white. He wrapped long manicured fingers around the bowl and swirled the liquid into the light, observed the legs of wine as they slipped down the glass. Next, he closed his eyes and his nose dipped into the glass and he inhaled deeply. Eyes still closed, he took a sip and pulled air into his mouth over the liquid.

Eva couldn't drag her gaze away from him. Wine tasting was a singularly unattractive endeavor. In her opinion, having seen it a zillion times, men always looked prissy while doing it.

Mr. Mephisto did not look prissy.

With his eyes closed, she could look her fill without his judgement. Thick, pitch-black hair and eyebrows framed his face. It was middle afternoon, and he already had the hint of a five o'clock shadow. All that darkness made him mysterious, until he opened his eyes and striking gray irises peered back at her in amusement and his lips curved up in a smirk.

Eva narrowed her own eyes in response. Smug bastard.

To make it worse, Maggie had noticed her watching him and her sister's knowing grin told her she knew exactly where Eva's thoughts had wandered off to. Eva finished her red in two swallows then set the glass down with a heavy clink.

She opened her mouth to propel this scene forward, but he started talking before she got her first word out.

"The finish is lovely; woodsy and smooth." His voice was at least an octave lower than it had been before, and Eva felt it in her chest. How annoying. He took another sip, and her gaze, like a laser beam, tracked the movement of his lips and the working of his throat as he swallowed. "Mmm. I very much enjoy the velvety mouth feel."

Eva jumped to her feet. She could not allow her lady parts to be distracted by this wolf in rich person's clothing. "So, what are you here for, Mr. Mephisto? What do you think you're going to get out of this seduction you have going on?"

Maggie pursed her lips. *You're going to ruin this, Evangeline. Shut up!*

A smirk still playing about his mouth, Mr. Mephisto leaned back in his chair. "What I offer is venture capital. I see a lot of potential here, and what you clearly need is an infusion of cash."

"Interesting," Maggie agreed. Beside the table where the man couldn't see, she very sternly pointed her index finger at Eva in warning. "Do you have other projects? Other companies you've taken an interest in?"

"Certainly. No other vineyards, but I have interest in a silk importer in India, and a diamond mine and caviar farm, both in Russia. Once I became involved, they proved to be immensely successful."

"Ah, and there's the rub." Eva couldn't keep the cynicism out of her voice. "You're going to expect to make all kinds of decisions about our business. Maggie and I inherited this from our family. No one but a Dashiell has ever run it, and we're not changing that now."

"Eva." Maggie was stern. "We're just listening to his ideas. Would you please calm down?"

Eva glared at them both even while she heard the groan of the ancient water heater on the other side of the wall. If she listened really hard, maybe she'd even hear the shingles on the roof rotting off. This building and what it represented meant everything to her, and yet it was crumbling apart at the seams. Everything hung on this harvest. A good crop and some skilled use of the fruit would be Empyrean's salvation. Or a misstep and it could all be over. Not even her preternatural understanding of the earth and vines could alter the weather or infestation or any other natural disaster prepared to destroy them.

"I don't want to own your vineyard," he said. His eyes flashed with sincerity. Or with a con man's genius. "What I enjoy the most is partnering with visionaries like yourselves to bring out the opportunities of whatever you do best. For example, the caviar I spoke of before is an impeccable product, but hardly anyone knew about it. I became involved, and now connoisseurs around the globe enjoy it."

Maggie leaned forward. "And you think you can do the same for our wine?"

The smug smile was back. "I live an epicurean lifestyle and I have many influential contacts. What I offer, even beyond money, can be immeasurably useful to you."

Her sister was nodding, taking in his whole line of shlock. "We have lots of ideas to turn this place into a destination. We'd like to be able to host weddings and other functions, but we have a lot to do before that's even viable."

Mr. Mephisto lifted the glass of white wine and began the slow, sensual dance of sampling the chardonnay just as he'd done the red. Eva regarded him over the rim of her own glass. She knew full well what the vintage tasted like, but she found her mouth moving in concert with his. She breathed over the wine in her mouth, inhaling the same buttery, oaky essence he did. And when he swallowed, her throat did the same. Then as he set the glass back on the table, he addressed Maggie.

"Can I convince you to give me a tour? I'd really love to see your vision."

Maggie's smile was genuine. "I'd be happy to."

The man rose from the chair. "Will you be joining us, Eva?" he asked her like he was inviting her to show him around her damn vineyard. Already he was acting like he owned the place.

"Unfortunately," Maggie said with a sad smile that was as fake as an alien autopsy, "Eva is so busy this afternoon, aren't you?" Maggie looked pointedly at Eva.

She did have plenty of things that would keep her busy around the vineyard, and she was just now cooling off from her hard day of work erecting that damn sunshade. Honestly, she wasn't sure how much longer she was going to be able to stay nice to this self-important jackass. While her sister was much too nice to deal with this guy in the long run, she couldn't make any decisions today, not without Eva signing off on them, too.

"No, Mr. Mephisto," Eva said with an ironic tilt of her head, "I'm terribly sorry. Maggie will have to squire you around today. She is an excellent tour guide."

"Please, if we're going to be in business together, you'll need to call me Asher." The way he captured her gaze and lowered his voice was magical. Like they were the only two people in a five-mile radius. "Alas, you will be missed today. Promise you'll tell me all your desires another time."

Eva swallowed and blinked out of the miasma that seemed to fill the room. "We'll see, Mr. Mephisto. Nothing has been decided yet." So unbelievably arrogant!

He only smiled, a smooth curve of his lips that made her stomach flutter.

"Hey," Maggie whispered to Eva as she ushered the man from their office. "Can you check on the air conditioner? I've noticed some cold spots in here, and we cannot afford that mess. Also, I heard some glasses shatter in the storeroom when we came in. Maybe we have mice in there?"

Eva nodded and exhaled in frustration. She took a deep cleansing breath to center herself, but it didn't work. The air still had the faintest hint of his cologne, and somehow she could still feel the buzzing in her chest from his baritone.

Through the window, she watched her sister lead the man towards the cellars. Maggie threw her head back and laughed while the man flirted shamelessly.

This was going to go badly. Eva could feel it—somehow that man was going to worm his way into their business, into their lives, no matter what she did to try and circumvent it. If only she could figure out what his game was.

Several hours later, Eva wandered back into the office. The Aston Martin was gone and so was all the mystical evidence that he'd ever been there. She took a tentative sniff, and she couldn't detect his cologne, so he'd been gone for a while.

"So, when did he finally clear out?" Eva asked Maggie.

Mags rolled her eyes. "A bit ago. I cannot understand what your problem is. We were just talking about how tight everything is and when a checkbook with legs—very fine legs, I might add—comes walking into our lives, you act like a shrew."

Eva couldn't believe Maggie didn't realize how dangerous he was. "This is our farm. Our family has worked it for so long." Eva let her shoulders droop. "I cannot fail them. Phineas would be so disappointed."

Maggie's tone softened. "Honey. All of this is not on you. We're in this together. And I'd like to point out that we are not failing. You know even Pops struggled sometimes. It's farming. So much of what happens here is beyond our control. We put up sunshades and protect from insects, but we can't control the weather or blight. And it's never been just Dashiells working here. Ernie and his family have been here two generations now."

"I know. And I love Ernie like a brother, but he doesn't own Empyrean." Eva clenched her fists and shook them for emphasis. "If we can just keep it together until harvest…"

"Everyone knows you're brilliant, but you can't control everything. But even then, we won't know for more than a year if your experiment worked. What will we do until then?"

Eva deflated again.

"Asher's capital could take the load off." Maggie squished her lips together and nodded knowingly. "All the work that needs to be done here is going to cost a small fortune."

Rubbing the frown on her forehead, Eva tried to sound reasonable. "We have no idea what he's going to demand once we take his money."

Another eyeroll and a sigh. "And we never will if you refuse to listen. We're morons if we don't at least hear out his proposition."

"Did he proposition you?" Eva asked, preparing to be scandalized.

"I wish." Maggie gave a little shiver of delight. "He wouldn't even have to complete his sentence before I ripped his clothes off. That man is yummy." She said that last word like she was describing him to frat brothers.

She wrinkled her nose. "Really? You think so?"

Maggie laughed. "You're so full of shit. I saw how you looked at him."

Eva raised her palms. "Okay. He is attractive in that obvious way, but I cannot get past his arrogance. He's such an asshat. It completely negates his face."

Her sister was still giggling like a pubescent girl. "He was very nice to me. Maybe the problem was you."

"Um hmm," Eva hummed. "Maybe you just need to get laid by someone who isn't trying to steal your family business out from under you."

"So long as I was underneath him when it happened." Maggie cackled.

Eva dropped her expression and stared at her sister. "That's not even a little funny."

Maggie made an effort to sober up. "I know. You know I didn't mean that." When Eva looked away, she changed the subject. "What was the situation with the air conditioner? Did you take a look?"

Eva shrugged. "I couldn't see anything wrong with it."

"Weird."

"The water heater, however, is on its last legs."

"And the roof," Maggie reminded her. "And your truck. And—"

"I know, I know. And a half a dozen glasses." That prickly ball of anxiety started to roll around in Eva's gut again.

Maggie collected Eva's hands and made her look at her. "He's coming back tomorrow. Promise me you'll be civil. We need to hear what he has to say. We don't have to accept anything, we can totally negotiate, but we have to hear it."

Eva sighed in resignation. This was not going to end well.

Chapter Five

A sher was all by himself this morning. He'd tried to round up Benji to accompany him to Empyrean Vineyards, but when he showed up at Benji's house at seven-fifteen in the morning, his cousin's gargoyle laughed at him. Judith was the exact opposite of Asher's gargoyle. Where Esther was tall and thin and oozed female-rock-star-superhero vibes, Judith was petite, sweet-faced, and acted and dressed like a kindergarten teacher. She suited Sloth perfectly. Still, no amount of coaxing was getting Benji out of bed before eleven two days in a row.

He pulled the Aston Martin into the parking area in front of the winery and observed the old building with a blossoming affection. The regal old structure set the tone for the entire estate and, with what Maggie had shown him of the other buildings, he could absolutely see the vision the sisters had for an expansion. Anyone looking to set an event in a rustic but classical setting wouldn't find somewhere more charming.

Once the place underwent some TLC. A little of his special style of fluffing.

The sisters had referred to the main building as "the monastery" and that had sent up some red flares when he'd first heard it, but strangely enough, he'd had no problem going inside. On the car ride home, Benji had reminded him that he himself had been in St. Peter's Basilica in Vatican City for the better part of six months the previous year and he'd ultimately been alright. Benji said he'd ruminated over it at length and decided it was because, although he had the potential to be the Devil, he wasn't yet. That wasn't to say he'd felt at ease. Benji described it as a constant state of queasiness. Like he'd had a six-month hangover.

However, that had not been Asher's experience. He'd hesitated at the door but, once he'd stepped inside, he'd felt no change at all. Nothing.

Benji considered that could be due to the fact that it hadn't been used as a monastery in over two hundred years. It wasn't consecrated ground anymore.

That little tidbit had only gone further into convincing Asher that finding this particular vineyard was kismet. It ticked off nearly every single one of his boxes. Empyrean Vineyards wasn't named for an angel as the others had been, but Heaven certainly fit into the celestial category. It was a luxury item. The bottles produced might not be blue chip status yet, but Eva was working very hard at that. And lastly, it was interesting.

More specifically, Eva was interesting.

Representing the Sin of Lust had plenty of challenges, but Ashe could ignore most of them because the pluses were so bountiful. Any night spent alone in his bed was a consciously made decision. Most of the time, he didn't have to expend any energy at all for company. A push was more often than not something he did simply to amuse himself. With Eva, he'd sent a push several times and nothing had happened. Nothing. Never in his entire life had that happened with anyone other than his cousins, the other Sins, or a gargoyle.

What the hell did that mean? He might have considered that he was broken except that her sister reacted perfectly as expected when some of the lust residue had filtered over to her.

It was perplexing. He could have discussed that, too, with Benji on the car ride home, but instead he'd mused over it on his own and Benji had slept. He'd pondered it all evening. Instead of his usual debauchery, he'd sat in front of the television and blindly watched nothing. He could have asked Esther what she'd heard about such a thing, but not while she was yelling out answers at game shows.

Sometime after midnight, he dragged his butt off to bed, threw his clothes on the floor, and climbed diagonally into his massive bed by himself. He dreamed of nothing, which in and of itself was not significant, but his very first waking thought—even before acknowledging the need to use the toilet—had been of Evangeline Dashiell, and that seemed full of import. His brain immediately picked up right where he'd left off.

What the hell was the deal with her?

Why was she so anti-him? No one was anti-lust. It literally wasn't a thing.

While he was brushing his teeth, he considered that maybe she wasn't attracted to him. Then he snorted out loud. Everyone, *everyone*, was attracted to him. That's how Lust worked. It didn't matter if she was attracted to men or women or My Little Pony, all lust would be directed at him.

What if she was asexual? Like with no sexual drive at all?

He spat toothpaste into the sink. Again, he reminded his reflection, that wouldn't matter. One of the finer points of lust was that it evoked a person's innermost desires. What they really wanted in the core of their being. Even if sex wasn't on the table, something else was. Still, he got nothing from her.

And when it came down to it, there were many reasons why this was not acceptable.

First, his entire being revolved around his identity as Lust. Since he was ten years old that was the only way he interacted with people. That didn't mean he started fucking everyone when he was ten, but it did mean that he was dialed in with people and their desires. His ego sort of morphed into what it was they wanted. Now that he was in his thirties, he'd come to rely on the ease his curse afforded him. The only people he had actual relationships with were his cousins. Just like his sin didn't affect them, their maledictions didn't bother him. He never had to use social skills, and now he wondered if he actually possessed any.

Number two was that he needed to get Eva on his side. He knew he didn't have to work on Maggie. She was sensible enough to see what he brought to the table was good for their company. Still, he wouldn't get Empyrean Vineyards without Eva's buy in.

With no other tools in his arsenal, he figured he'd best stay in front of her. Out of sight, out of mind was a very real concern. He'd just keep at her until eventually he'd wear her down and she'd choose him and what he had to offer.

Inside his closet that morning, he searched through his clothes for something that might penetrate her fortifications. Something casual seemed the least intimidating. He selected his favorite jeans. The denim was soft against his skin, and he liked the way they hugged his butt and legs without feeling tight. He pulled a turquoise cashmere tee-shirt from a stack. Lastly, a soft pair of merino wool socks laced inside of his favorite, well-worn leather, laced-up boots. A look in the mirror told him he looked disingenuously relaxed yet wealthy. A little too much like A Kennedy Goes to the Farm.

He ruffled his hair, but that wasn't enough. He found a baseball cap in the back of the closet which did the trick.

"Where are you going today?" Esther asked entering the walk-in with his coffee in her hand. She cast a glance at his outfit. "The home improvement store?"

"Not quite, but I'm glad I look the part." He took a rapturous sip and let the caffeine infuse him. "Back to the vineyard."

She grimaced. "I don't have to go, do I?"

He considered her as backup for only a moment before deciding that her getup of short hot-pink leather shorts, sheer black blouse, and thigh-high leather boots wasn't going to help him in any way, so he shook his head. "I'm having some trouble with the sisters."

His gargoyle raised an eyebrow. "What kind of trouble?"

Asher swallowed and scowled. "One of them hates me, and I have no idea why."

She shook her head. "She doesn't hate you."

"No, she definitely hates me." He sipped his coffee and adjusted the ball cap in his reflection. "She's mean and glares at me at every opportunity. I actually believe she thinks I'm stupid. She certainly assumes I have nefarious plans with her family's winery."

Esther ruffled through his shirts and pulled out a gray Burberry flannel he didn't even know was in there. "Here, this will help tone you down a bit. Now you go out there and send her a whammy."

He stroked a hand along the downy cotton. She was right. The shirt helped make him look more authentic.

"I already tried a whammy." He paused for effect. "It didn't work."

"What didn't work?"

"The whammy. I tried a couple times. It worked on the sister, Maggie, but not on Evangeline."

Esther put one manicured fist on her hip. "That is extremely interesting. It always works."

"Not on you. Not on my cousins. And not on Evangeline Dashiell." He nodded in the face of her disbelief. "I pushed hard at her and there wasn't even a blip that she felt anything. Just kept sending me bitchy vibes. What do you suppose that means?"

"Hmmm," Esther said. "Wrath had the same issue with the apple lady?"

"Mia?"

"Yes, Mia." She nodded in contemplation. "I'm going to call Jebediah and let him know."

Asher left Esther to her mission and, an hour on the highway later found him standing next to his Aston Martin contemplating his next course of action. He shoved his hands in his jean's pockets and plodded up the dirt track towards where he guessed she'd be working this morning. Coming over a small rise, he heard some old school country music and the sound of a woman singing along. He grinned as she didn't quite make the high note when Patsy Cline did.

He approached with quiet steps, not wanting to spook her like a mean junkyard dog. Pushing the bill of his cap back on his head, he maintained his friendly smile and waited for her to notice him.

"I'm crazy for feel—" She shrieked and dropped her staple gun. "Holy cow, you scared me."

"I'm so sorry," he said with a small bow. "I was specifically trying not to do that."

"A person trying not to scare people would announce their approach. Not creep up on them and ogle."

He held back a laugh. "I was not ogling." But maybe he was. She was perched on the third rung of a short ladder and leaning over the top of leafy vines hanging heavy with fruit and wrestling with some heavy material. Her ass jutted out and her shirt dipped low, generally giving him an unexpected pornographic pose.

She let the fabric go loose and climbed off the ladder in a huff. "What are you doing here?"

"I'm here to help."

Never taking her eyes off him, she bent for the staple gun. "Why?"

He lifted his shoulders in an easy shrug and let his smile go wider. "A show of good faith. I only want what's best for Empyrean. Saving this crop from the sun is what's best, isn't it?"

She looked at him for very long seconds before she said, "I sent Ernie into town for more supplies, so I do need help."

"I'm your man. Just tell me what to do."

A speculative eyebrow rose on her forehead. "You don't strike me as the kind of guy who does an awful lot of actual work. What can you do?"

"Hey." He pretended to take offense. "I work out five days a week."

She let her gaze travel his body. She paused on his arms hidden inside the flannel and his thighs wrapped in denim. It wasn't a flirty perusal, but Ashe found himself flexing inside his clothes just in case.

"I didn't say you looked weak," she clarified. "I said you didn't look like you work."

He stripped off the flannel shirt and tossed it across the vines behind him. "Consider this an audition then." "Crazy" had ended and Kenny Rogers started up. "Tell me where to start."

She stared at him for an uncomfortably long time, taking in his clothes and judging his ability to labor. Asher concentrated on not fidgeting. He smeared a smile on his face, and when his skin started to prickle under the scrutiny, he shoved his hands in his pockets and said, "We're burning the morning."

"We need more scaffolding." She turned and pointed to the long lengths of wood laid out in the dirt of the rows.

"Great. I'll start there then." He inspected how they'd build the framework to hold the shade material up over the vines. Didn't look too complicated. It wasn't like he'd ever worked construction or anything, but he'd built stuff before. The fort with his cousins when they were little came to mind. He found a hammer and a bucket of nails and got to assembling the structures and fitting them over the top of the vines. Together they'd pull the dark netting over the wooden skeletons and secure it from the sun and wind.

With the sun on his back and the weight of the hammer warming his muscles, he found himself humming along with the radio. They developed a nice rhythm. Using few words to communicate, they made good time moving down the row.

"Because you're mine," he sang with Johnny Cash, "I walk the line."

Eva looked up, and Asher was certain he saw a smile there before she wiped it away. Her cheeks were flushed from the morning sun and exertion. She was stunning.

"I love old Johnny Cash," he confessed, completely unapologetically. Then to fill the silence, he added, "And Willie. And Waylon. I always wanted to name a trio of hound dogs Johnny, Willie and Waylon."

She nodded. "I had a friend growing up who had dogs named Johnny and June."

"See, that's cute." He lifted the hem of his t-shirt to wipe the sweat from his brow. He caught her looking at his stomach before her gaze darted away. Well, that was interesting. "Do you have a dog?"

"My grandfather used to." Eva climbed down from her ladder and moved it several feet further down the row. "A little terrier name Velma. She was a maniac, used to run the rows and keep the varmints out."

He laughed. "Now that's a word that's not used enough. Varmints. Very Yosemite Sam."

"My grandfather was a big fan of shotguns and yelling, so I guess he was pretty Yosemite Sam-like in his own right."

She walked back several yards and came back with an enormous water jug. She unscrewed the cap and hoisted it up to take a long drink. Her face was turned to the sun and her eyes were closed. Ash watched her throat work as she swallowed and followed a steady stream of water that spilled out the side, down her chin and onto the vee of her work shirt. When she was done, she handed him the jug and he took a long drink, hoping he made as attractive a picture doing it as she had.

"We don't have a dog now, though," she said, completing her thoughts. "A shit-ton of bitchy cats, though, and they do the trick, varmint-wise."

"A clowder."

"A what?"

"Clowder. That's the collective noun for cats. Some people say it's a glaring of cats, but I like clowder better."

She nodded and scratched her nose contemplatively. "You should wait until you meet these cats. They do a lot of glaring."

Like someone else he knew. Still, that was encouraging. He could be reading a lot into nothing, but she did just imply that he would be around long enough to meet the cats. Encouraged, he got back to work and retrieved two more nails to hammer into the wood to complete the next section of scaffolding.

She reached over and helped him thread the wooden frame over the vines, all the while continuing on, "And they're pretty mean. All totally feral. Maggie and I trap them and get them fixed when we can. We put out food and stuff, but they're definitely not pets."

He pulled the shading tight and she used a staple gun to attach it. Before they knew it, they'd completed the second row and had used the last of the shading fabric.

"So, what do we do now?" Ash asked.

"I sent Ernie to get more shade cloth a while ago." She used her hand to extend the bill of her cap and looked up the dusty track for signs of her old red truck, but there was nothing.

"Alright then." Ashe shoved the hammer in his back pocket and bent to gather the nail bucket. "I'll just move all this stuff to the next row and start putting together the rest of the frames so at least that will be ready when he comes back."

She watched him with her forehead creased with thought. He ignored her and went back for the wood lying in the dirt.

"Why are you doing this?" Her voice was steady. She sounded curious instead of angry for a change.

"Aren't we also doing the next two rows?"

"Yes. But why are you doing it?"

"I want to show you I'm serious."

Her gaze narrowed. "Serious how exactly? Serious about swooping in here and taking over everything? Serious about leaving us high and dry when you get bored? What do you mean exactly?"

Ash took the lumber to the next alleyway between the vines, dropped them in the dirt by the bucket of nails, and then stalked back up the row she was standing in. Her hands on her hips and her expression earnest. "I have no intention of stealing anything. I will not leave you high and dry, as you put it. All I want to do is see your business succeed. I want to partner with you and your sister to make Empyrean better."

"That's what you say now. I've seen what happens when family vineyards go corporate. They're evil."

He sighed. "I am not corporate, Eva. I'm here helping in this field because I'm trying to prove to you that I'm sincere."

She pursed her lips together and snorted and turned on her heel. "We'll see." She marched up the row away from him as Hank Williams started in about cheatin' hearts.

Evangeline Dashiell was going to need more convincing. A lot more convincing. It would be a hell of a lot easier if he could just kiss her.

Or screw her until she saw the light.

Heaven & Hell XIII

"Reward. Reward. Reward."

The gremlin horde was still singing as they towed Neil down the seemingly endless miles of corridors. Now instead of just tuneless chanting, they'd switched to a three-part non-harmony that made Neil's ears itch.

"You guys are going to be in very serious trouble when—ow! Son of a bitch, that hurt." He kicked out at the gremlin who was gnawing on his shin. "If you eat my legs, how are you going to march me to the dungeon? Hmmm?"

The Captain of the group snarled at the lesser gremlin and slapped it with a bony four-fingered hand. "You, back of line."

Neil raised his eyebrows at the leader and shook his head. "It's impossible to find good help, huh? Back when I was topside, I never did find a trustworthy second."

"No one care," the creepy little thug growled and shoved him in the back.

So much for ingratiating himself with the little fuckers. He was quickly running out of ideas for escape. He didn't know any of the guards in this level's horde, but demons were demons and even if he was familiar with them there was no telling how much good that would do him.

All he knew for certain was that the longer he was locked up in here, the longer Rachel was left alone again. As crappy as he'd had it down here, she'd certainly had it worse. She didn't seem like she was all that stable either. Although considering how long she'd been down here, his assessment wasn't really fair. If he'd been held captive as long... Shit, he'd likely be chewing on his own toenails or something. So, she was a bit squirrely, but she'd likely be alright until he could get back to her. She had survival skills.

The parade of guards made a sharp turn. Several scabby little gremlins scrambled past him to the end of a short hall and pushed open a massive iron door to a small rough room seemingly carved out of the rock. With a grunt, the creature at his back shoved him hard, propelling Neil into the cell, and the door was slammed shut. The horde cheered a raucous chorus and tumbled off down the hall to celebrate.

Neil squinted around his new home. Thinking of it as a room was generous. It was really a cave. The space was dark and humid. Moisture came from a giant puddle near a gloomy corner so dark he couldn't see the wall behind it. He inched that direction until he realized by the pungent stench that the puddle was likely pee, which begged the question of a cellmate. Nose wrinkled in disgust, he shuffled back to the front of the cell.

Looking over the edges of the door and inspecting the hinges, he looked for a way out. The fortifications down on this level were sturdier than on Level Three. Duke Valefor and his horde were much more interested in the immediate torture and weren't so concerned about keeping their prisoners around for extended periods of time.

He grabbed the rusty bars and gave the door a good shake. Not even a millimeter. He tried lifting it too, because he'd seen an old western once where the guy got out of some old-timey jail by hoisting the door off the hinges. But not this one. He dug his fingernail into the rock around the iron hinge to see if there was any room to whittle away the wall holding it all together. Nope. The bars too, were solidly welded.

The way he came in was likely not the way he could sneak out. The door at least seemed fortified.

A recurring thought had him feeling frantic.

Juliet.

His innocent angel would be waiting for him, unprotected and fragile. He had to get out of here right fucking now.

Shifting slowly, he turned to face the shadows behind him again, thinking there might be a better chance of escape on the other end of the cage. Now that his eyes had fully adjusted to the darkness, it seemed that he could distinguish the back wall. The furthest corner was still murky enough that he couldn't be sure if he could actually see the wall or just imagined he could. He squinted and stared intently until something in the darkness moved.

"Oh, shit!" He jerked back so quickly he hit his head on the iron door. "What the fuck is that?"

The thing shuffled in the shadows. It sounded massive, but it was impossible to tell while it remained in the darkness.

Neil rubbed the back of his head and gulped down his knee-jerk panicky reaction. "Hey, you know, I'm perfectly happy to stay right here in this two-foot square and you can have the entire back. I won't bother you, and you won't eat me."

It gurgled a deep-throated groan that oozed torment. And it kept coming. The shuffling got closer and the putrescent stench was sharpening as if it was a creature of its own. The deep shadows shifted closer, and a form coalesced in the darkness.

"Oh fuck," Neil whispered on an exhale. "What is that?"

There was a thunk followed by the rhythmic strum of what was most certainly claws against the stone. A short pause, then the other foot duplicated the sound preceded by what seemed like the weight of a whale dragged across the floor.

Footsteps. Claws. Dragging.

Neil whirled around and clutched at the bars on the door. He shook, pushed, and pulled with all of his strength, but nothing budged.

"Hey," he hollered down the empty passage. "Hey!"

His eyes watered from the fetid air as the creature got closer. Neil turned to face his doom. The only chance he had at saving Juliet, or ever even seeing her again, was getting out of this intact. One humungous, hairy foot emerged into the light. As it hit the ground, it spread out to the size of a manhole cover, and the yellow three-inch claws drummed against the floor, one at a time, like a bored cop on the hood of his cruiser. A few more steps and the head emerged.

Neil didn't have a name for this creature. It had what might have been the head of a lion. The mangy hair was so patchy and matted it was hard to tell. Massive jaws and snout showed an epic underbite and fangs so decayed and discolored they looked like orange traffic cones. Shockingly, there were no eyes. Its head was all nose and mouth. Where eyes would have been was a dark, weeping void.

The beast swung its head from side to side. Neil wasn't sure if it was searching for him or what. Swallowing vomit, Neil edged further away, trying to make himself part of the rock wall. With a horrific undulation, another massive section of the animal came into view. The ratty hair tapered into gray, patchy skin that reminded him of an elephant. No, not an elephant, a walrus. The back half of the thing looked like a massive walrus with seeping, infectious sores.

Neil gagged and the sound brought him to the vile thing's attention. It snuffled blindly in his direction, then a black forked tongue slithered out and tested the air. Neil pressed against the wall and moved soundlessly a few feet further away. The creature bored of the lackluster hunt quickly and turned away.

Neil swallowed and exhaled as silently as a dead man.

He had no way of knowing how long he was trapped in that dungeon. There wasn't any way to track the passage of time. It was an eternity, or it was an hour. Neil stayed on the move, staying away from the monstrous jaws and avoiding the increasing piles of creature shit and puddles of piss.

He fretted and sent up prayers that Juliet would be safe until he could get out of there.

He searched every inch of the hole in which he found himself and couldn't find a chink in the rock or a fault in the construction.

Dozing slumped against the wall on his haunches, he heard the cacophony of a small gremlin horde in the passage.

"Comes and sees! Comes and sees!" they chanted as they rounded the corner.

Neil struggled to his feet, certain the monster would be roused by the singing. Along with a handful of imps, the captain of the guard who captured him from Rachel's room was leading a tall demon down the hall towards his cell.

"See!" the Captain screeched in excitement. "Gives me reward."

This demon was flashier than Duke Valefor who ran Three. A crown hung off one twisted goat horn and a full-length blue velvet cape swept behind him. Snake eyes appraised him from the other side of the bars.

"Aren't you the boy who watches the dog?"

Neil nodded. "Yeah. I'm supposed to." He checked for the monster over his shoulder.

Yellow eyes narrowed. "Where is that dog?"

He shook his head. "I don't know. I was looking for him when I was captured."

Slowly the demon turned his gaze to the captain. "Where is the dog?" it asked the captain.

"Don't know," the Captain squeaked, and shrank away out of slapping distance.

The demon's tone grew incredulous. "You put this boy in the dungeon, and you don't know where the dog is?"

The captain's entire body shook in terror, but it didn't answer.

"You know what I'm going to do?" The demon pointed a long boney finger at the captain. "When his majesty asks why no one knows where the dog is, I'll be sure to tell him it's your fault."

The captain wailed and moaned. The imps who'd tailed along behind them scattered like rats.

"Open. This. Door. Right. Now."

Not a moment too soon. The monster stirred from the back of the cell, drawn to the hysterical screeching. Neil could hear it slithering clumsily from the darkness and fidgeted in panic. It took forever for the clumsy captain to get a key in the lock and the door open. Finally, Neil threw himself out into the passage before the jaws could snap closed around his legs.

The Duke of Level Nine snapped his fingers in front of Neil's face, pulling his attention from the monster who had managed to capture the captain by a skinny arm and was dragging him, kicking and screaming, into the darkness. "I don't want to see you again until you have that dog. Is that clear?"

"Yes. Yes, sir." Neil nodded like a bobble head. "Absolutely."

"Go. Now."

Neil nearly flew back down the passage, fleeing the screams and nauseating bone crunching coming from the darkness.

Hang on Juliet. Hang on. I'm coming.

Chapter Six

The sun wasn't up yet when Eva rolled out of bed. She padded to the bathroom in the pinkish gray light of predawn and made sure to close the door with a silent click before turning on the light. She washed her face and combed through her hair.

"You're being stupid," she whispered to herself even while she scooped up the hair on either side of her face and secured it with a barrette on the top of her head. The style did something to her cheekbones and framed up her blue eyes nicely. "Dumb."

She swiped on some eyeliner and did a quick couple of flicks with a mascara wand. She didn't want to look like she'd tried at all, but she wanted to look... She struggled to define to herself what was motivating her this morning.

"You don't even know if he's going to come today," she reminded her reflection with stern frown. "Won't you feel like an idiot if he doesn't show?"

She held onto the counter with both hands and looked herself in the eye. Peering back at her, sky blue eyes admitted that if he did show up she wanted to be attractive.

"He's been here three days in a row. He'll be here," her reflection assured her.

Eva snorted at herself. "Yeah, because he hasn't gotten what he wants yet."

"Um hmm." Her smug self smirked back. "And what is it that *you* want now?

Eva didn't know exactly.

She'd spent the last two days with him and Ernie working on the sunshade. The Gewurztraminer grapes were covered at last, and Eva felt much better about their chances of getting the wine she was hoping for. She'd kept Ernie around as a buffer, but it didn't matter. She couldn't keep her eyes off Asher Mephisto. She'd lied to Maggie when she'd said she didn't find him attractive, but of course her sister knew that. Really, she hadn't been all that attracted in the beginning. That first day they'd met and even most of the second day, she'd found him too arrogant to even consider. Too perfect. Too full of himself.

But the simple fact was, his gray eyes were not something that could be denied. When she wasn't sneaking glances at his eyes, she was appreciating his beautiful skin. What the hell did he use on it? Maybe he sacrificed goats or something, because men shouldn't have skin that flawless. Yesterday, he'd shown up with a stubbly jaw, and she'd nearly creamed her jeans before she got control of herself. Scruffy was even better.

She'd sneered at him instead and suggested that he should find some other vintner to pillage. His lips had lifted in a practiced smirk, that razor sharp jaw blurred by the fuzz of short whiskers, before he turned to follow Ernie out to the rows of grapes. She had sure as hell watched him walk away, though. Long confident stride, tight little ass in soft, faded jeans.

Good grief, she was going to have to stay strong.

And yet, here she was looking through her panty drawer for something nonutilitarian. It said something about her sex life that the only underwear in her possession was old, faded and cotton. It was not a flattering commentary. She shoved the drawer shut, cursing at herself for even caring what underwear she had on for a man who was never, ever going to see them. It didn't even matter if she was wearing underwear.

No—it definitely mattered that she wore underwear.

"You're losing your mind," she told herself.

Once dressed in her regular work clothes of practical cargo shorts, tank top, and lightweight, long-sleeved chambray shirt to avoid sunburn, she glanced in the mirror and groaned. It was only too obvious that his flirting was a ruse to get into her filing cabinet and not into her pants. Even with the mascara and her hair pulled up, she was just boring old Eva, and by the end of the day, her shorts would be grungy, and her hands would be dirty. "Super sexy." She snorted.

This had never bothered her before. She loved their farm, and there was nothing in the world she loved more than coaxing grapes into wine. If she wanted sex, she never had any trouble finding it. Jeez, a woman could always get laid if she wanted it. All Eva would have to do is head out to one of the bars in town and find a likely candidate. Usually that would be someone from out of town. She saw the wisdom in not sleeping around with anyone who lived in town. It was a small community, and their vineyard didn't need any nasty gossip. This was wine county, and there were plenty of tourists to scratch an itch.

So, even though she cleaned up alright, she was still nowhere near the top-shelf girls Asher Mephisto was likely to pull in. Someone who looked like him surely had super models on his speed dial.

Pointing her finger at herself, she said sternly, "Stop this." Then she flipped herself off and left her room.

Successfully downstairs without waking Maggie, she made her way to the kitchen and started the coffee maker. She poked around the refrigerator for something to eat and finally settled on a blueberry muffin because it wouldn't be as loud as toast. While the coffee maker did its magic, she put the muffin in the microwave and waited until the countdown was at two seconds before snatching open the door to avoid the ding. She chopped the muffin in half and slathered it with butter, topped off the coffee cup with half and half, and headed out the door, having safely avoided her sister and whatever teasing questions Maggie would have had.

Pausing on the lawn, she closed her eyes and took a deep breath, soaking in the loamy smell of fertile earth. The breeze ruffled her hair and sent the aroma of summer flowers dancing across the lawn. The sky had evolved from night to dark blue dawn with light blue and pink rimming the eastern horizon showing the beginnings of fluffy clouds drifting above the fields.

It was like coming out of the monastery into Oz.

"Pops, this is one of those best days," she told the ghost of her grandfather. He'd always described prefect mornings that waydays when the weather was ideal and the feeling in the air was bountiful and generous. The heat was still a couple of hours away, but Eva knew it was coming. The plan for the day was backbreaking. Ideally, she'd like to hire some day workers to help out, but they didn't have the money to spread around, as Maggie reminded her last night.

She made her way across the lawn towards the tool sheet and loaded the utility wagon with rope, twine, leather gloves, and several pairs of garden nippers. She filled up the heavy water jug and settled it in the wagon. Using a heavy hand, she applied a liberal coating of SPF one hundred spray-on sunscreen to her legs, then smeared some on the back of her ears and neck, throat and face. She tossed the can in the wagon and added another full can for later. At the last minute, she tossed a straw hat in the wagon as well. Cute hair and hot investor be damned. She didn't need skin cancer on her nose.

Asher Mephisto was sitting on the retaining wall when she reemerged into the sunlight. He was alone, but next to him sat one of those cardboard trays with four to-go-cups of coffee.

"Good morning," he said, bright and chipper.

He had also worn shorts, but his cargos made him look like a model who'd just stepped out of one of those weird European perfume ads where everyone was on some jungle safari. She couldn't understand why those images implied those models smelled good and not like sweaty jungle. Regardless, Eva was certain if she allowed this man to get close enough to her, he'd smell exquisite. Just looking at him made her think of the smell of warm sheets and lazy mornings—and who was she kidding here? He'd smell like the best kind of sex. And the aroma of coffee.

No, the coffee was real. He'd brought coffee.

"I didn't expect you this early. Or at all." She stopped the wagon in front of him and propped her hand on her hip. Her tummy had that heavy swishing feeling it got every time she was near him. And her brain was just as helpful as a tub of vanilla pudding would have been in her head.

"I'm ready to work," he told her with a smile that, if she took at face value, said he was sincerely looking forward to it.

Well, today was the day she'd break him. Today she'd work him to the bone. *We're not thinking about bones, Evangeline.*

Oh, for crying out loud.

"Um hmm," she cast him a suspect look. "Drink your caffeine. Today is going to suck. You'll need all the energy you can get."

He took a sip of his drink and, like a hormonal teenager, she watched his lips kiss the rim, swallow, and then lick a drop that started to roll down the side. Then he plucked a cup from the tray and handed it to her. Thankful to have something to do with her hands, she took it eagerly.

"Latte, breve, no foam." He produced a straw with a flourish to poke through the hole in the lid. "Did I guess right?"

Well, he sure as hell did. Guess, my ass. No one guessed that you wanted a straw. Eva couldn't even remember when he would have heard her say her coffee order out loud. She took the straw with a speculative glance.

"Not really," he confessed. "I asked Maggie what you'd want. I have one for her, too, and for Ernie." He indicated the two remaining cups.

"Ernie'll be along shortly. We want an early start before it gets too muggy out." She took a begrudging sip, but the latte was perfect. Dammit. "We'll end around lunch, then we'll be opening up for tastings for the rest of the afternoon."

He nodded. "It would be awfully helpful if you could hire more help up here for the tastings and the shop."

"Sure." She resisted the urge to roll her eyes. Also, to check her hair. Now she resented that it was pulled away from her face and she didn't have her go-to fidget of messing with her hair to keep her fingers busy. "There are lots of things that are helpful. Like for instance today, you're helpfully supplying me free labor for Hell Week."

"Hell Week?" he asked with a bit of a smirk. "Does Hell Week usually start on a Wednesday?"

"It starts whenever I say it starts." She set her coffee down in the wagon and raised her arms high in the air, then leaned sideways, stretching out her back in an exaggerated fashion. "By the end of this week, you'll be lucky if you can even stand up straight."

Maggie appeared out of the office door already wearing her straw hat. "She's trying to scare you, but she's mostly right."

"I'm absolutely right." Eva grabbed the handle of the wagon, expecting everyone else to follow along. She eavesdropped on Maggie and Ash's pleasantries. It annoyed her to no end that Maggie could chat him up so easily when she always felt so exposed around him. Her default response was sarcastic and mean, and Eva hated that about herself.

"You're very ominous, Eva. What are we doing today?" Ash asked.

"We're starting at the west end." Eva indicated the furthest corner of their rows of vines. "We're going to look at every single vine. We're pruning them of excess leaves, plucking off any late-blooming fruit. We're looking for bugs or rot and any fungus."

"That doesn't sound so bad."

Eva's laugh was pure evil.

"You'll be fine," Maggie nodded with a smirk, "by next week sometime."

Asher had the good sense to look worried. "Well, I'm game. It's far, though. You want me to drive?"

"In your big red penis car?" Eva asked with a high eyebrow. "All of us and the wagon?"

"Eva!" Maggie hissed and backhanded Eva's shoulder. "Oh my God!"

Mercifully, Asher barked out a great belly laugh. "No one's ever called it that before. I will assure you that my choice of automobile is not a reflection of my sexual prowess." Then after a pregnant pause, he added, "Or my size."

Eva should not have been intrigued by that statement, but—God help her—she was. Of course, she couldn't let any of them know it.

"I'm sure," she noted dryly.

"Good morning, everyone." Ernie jogged up to the group from the little lane that lead to the house he shared with his wife. Ash handed him his coffee and Ernie's always cheerful face became jollier with gratitude. "Thanks, man."

Eva couldn't stop herself. "Ash here has offered to drive us to the field in his Aston Martin which he assures us does not accurately represent his penis."

She thought her sister was going to have a seizure based on the ferocious looks she was throwing and the twitching of her head. Eva ignored her.

Ernie ignored her, too. "Nah, we'll take the pickup. It's used to being abused. And you're not going to want us in there by the end of the day." He made a stinky face.

Eva already had the keys out and Ernie dropped the tailgate. He gave a low grunt and hoisted the wagon into the bed. He followed it up and sat on the tailgate with his feet dangling down. He patted the spot next to him and Ash hopped up beside him.

"All ready," Ash said, looking like an excited puppy. "Let's go."

Eva was pretty sure she heard him whistling.

His tune was considerably different four hours into the day. She and Ernie had shown him how to look for insects, which ones were benevolent, and which were bad news. There had been instruction on how to lift the leaves, crawl under the canopy and check for mold and fungus. They gave him gloves and garden pruners and directions on how to trim the leaves to create better air flow to quickly dry the morning dew.

It was impressed upon him that every single thing they did to every single vine would affect the way the wine tasted.

He went to work with gusto. Eva really had to give him credit. He kept steadfastly working even after he walked blindly into a massive vine trunk and ripped up his shin.

He kept plugging away even after he rubbed sulphur in his eye.

He didn't even whine when his hand spasmed after four hours of gripping the pruners.

On the way back to the truck after six hours of backbreaking work, he inquired if they'd be doing the same thing the next day.

Eva nodded, thinking this was it. This was when he bailed. He was definitely going to hightail it out of there now. Maggie would never let her hear the end of losing that much investment capital. Eva also knew that meant she was going to have to figure out a way to come up with that money to do all the needed repairs and remodels on her own.

How much money could they get if they all gave blood? Every day. And maybe sold a kidney.

But it was all worth it because the vineyard would stay in their family.

"Yes," she told him, grimly. "Tomorrow we pick up where we left off today." She swept her arm in the direction of the seemingly endless rows of vines. "We have to do all of these."

He bowed his head for a long beat. "What time tomorrow?"

"Same time. Sunup." Eva rubbed the small of her back. Bending over all day was brutal.

He sighed deeply. "Alright. I'll see you then."

"Good work today," Maggie called in encouragement after his limping form. He waved over his shoulder without looking back.

"Thanks again for the coffee," Eva called, unable to wipe the smile of victory from her face.

The thrill was dampened when a strange van rolled into their parking lot late that afternoon. Two women emerged from the cab and toted two giant cases into the tasting room.

"Hi," one of them said. "We're the massage therapists."

Eva came from behind the bar. "The what now?"

The second woman set her case on the stone floor. "Heavenly Touch Massage." She unfurled a folded page from her pocket. "Asher Mephisto sent us. You've got us for two hours. Where should we set up?"

Eva was gob smacked.

God damn him.

Chapter Seven

I t was the third day of what Evangeline Dashiell called Hell Week. Asher couldn't think of any name more fitting. It was possible that this specific activity had its very own circle in Hell. An especially tortuous punishment for the tall, all that bending. As sore as he was, he knew he'd feel fine in the morning. His quick-healing immortality was convenient like that, and the only real blessing of his curse.

Although to be sure, being Lust was a hell of a lot less tormenting than Wrath, say, or Envy. To spend almost all of one's life angry or jealous... He did not wish to be his cousins.

Supernaturally resilient or no, when he came home from the farm that first night, he could barely stand up straight. Esther had offered to bring him the rolling chair from his desk to help him in from the garage. That's not true. Actually, she'd done a miserable job of controlling her laughter long enough to call him Methuselah and threaten to go get the rolling chair.

Sending the massage therapists to Eva and Maggie had been inspired. He could imagine the look on Eva's face when they showed up. Oh, she would be so angry. He'd laughed out loud at the thought. Also, she was beautiful when she was angry. Her hydrangea blue eyes grew even more vivid, clashing against her tanned face and dark brown hair like some kind of avenging nature goddess.

Esther would find that description hilarious.

The second day they tackled the next block of vines, doing the same work and leaving at the end of the day hobbling and itchy, covered in bruises and scrapes, everyone annoyed with each other to distraction.

Now here they were on day three, bone weary. Eva took every opportunity to point out this kind of drudgery was the life of a vintner.

"It's hard work, Asher Mephisto," she told him while riding her metaphorical high horse. "Not very sexy or romantic, huh?"

Both Maggie and Ernie had opted to start walking back from the fields, tired of listening to the two of them, Ash teasing and Eva sniping. Even Asher was worn down by it.

"All good things are hard work," he'd countered. "See how hard I'm working to make you like me?" All of this was exhausting. His back was aching again, and he was going to have another bruise on his shin from walking into a broken vine trunk. This sucked.

"That's a fool's errand." She jerked the wagon out of the bed of the truck before he could get back there to help her. It came out faster than she expected, and she lost control of the weight. Her little scream of alarm set him running around the bed of the old Ford.

It happened in a heartbeat, but he still wasn't fast enough to catch her. Eva collapsed on the ground and the wagon landed hard on top of her. He grasped it by the sides and hurled it off her before kneeling next to her where she lay gasping.

"Are you alright?" He gently probed her leg where the bulk of the wagon had landed, then peered at her face. "Eva? Are you hurt?"

She tried to sit up and groaned. "No."

"Are you sure? That would have knocked the wind out of me." He went to slide his hand under her shoulders to assist her as she struggled to sit up.

"Let go," she hissed.

He removed his hand and leaned back on his heels. "You know what you're damn problem is?"

She groaned again and rubbed her shin. "You. You're my problem."

Shaking his head, he squinted hard at her. "No. You definitely have issues. Besides acting like a witch, you're completely unable to accept help." He got to his feet and stood over her. "It's pathological with you. You can't accept help."

"I let you help us with Hell Week," she spit out.

He grimaced at her. "No, you did your best to beat me down with Hell Week. You did everything you could think of to make me leave."

Her jaw dropped. "My God, just when I thought your ego couldn't get any bigger. Do you honestly think I sit around thinking about you all the time? I don't spend any energy at all trying to figure you out. You're not worth my time."

He barked out a laugh. "You're a liar, Evangeline Dashiell. I have a feeling you can't stop thinking about me and it's frustrating the hell out of you."

"Oh, please."

Now he smirked. "You'll have to ask me nicer than that."

She rolled her eyes. "Why does everything have to be a sexual innuendo with you?"

He dropped the smirk. "Just my base nature, I guess." Because that's all he was, wasn't he? How else could Lust be expected to be? If not sex, the only other thing he was good for was money. He kept offering her both and she wouldn't take either.

Damn them all to Hell.

He glowered down at her.

He was not giving up. He wanted this. He wasn't getting Eva, that much was plainly obvious, but he wanted this vineyard to add to his portfolio of things he'd built. Or rather helped build. He had nothing else but these few magnificent things that he could share with the world. These few partnerships he was proud of. Each one of them had caused a stirring in him that he'd not been able to let go of. This vineyard spoke to him the same way the silk, the caviar, and the diamonds had. Eva spoke to him that way, too. It confused him because she wasn't a thing he could fix or improve. It must just be that she was all mixed up with the wine, since she was the vintner.

He shook his finger and laughed harshly at her sitting on the ground. "You lose. I'm not quitting. You need my help." He swept his arm wide to encompass the fields, the battered old truck, the decrepit buildings, all of it. "All of this needs my help. You're drowning and not in wine. You need me, Eva."

He backed toward the Aston Marin while she glared at him. Her color was high, making her achingly gorgeous.

"What time in the morning?" he hollered back as he opened the driver's door.

"Don't bother," she yelled back.

"Damn it, woman. You're ridiculous. There's well more than half these vines left to work. What are you going to do by yourselves?"

"Sunup," came the call from the dirt track that circled the fields. Ernie and Maggie stood a ways off, observing the spectacle.

He saluted Maggie in acknowledgment and dropped into the butter-leather seat. His back wept at the lumbar support. In a very childish move, he gunned the car out of the parking area, spraying a plume of dust which he instantly regretted. Once he hit the highway though, he put the pedal down. He had a plan for the morning, and he needed Esther and her wizardry to make it work.

When he explained the plan to Esther, she'd been supportive right up until the time it was revealed he had no idea how to bring the plan to life.

"So, what you're telling me," his gargoyle had said, "is that it's really only half a plan."

"I guess. But it's a really good half a plan." He smiled encouragingly.

"And how long do I have to figure out how to do the other half?"

Ash had looked at his watch, did some quick calculations, then widened his smile. "By sunup. I have every faith in you and your little black book of contacts." On his way to take a shower, he hollered back, "We ride at dawn!"

Now he was sitting on the retaining wall on the front lawn of Empyrean before the first hint of daybreak had colored the eastern horizon. Esther had filled him a thermos with his special blend of coffee, and his surprise was due to arrive any minute.

He kept an eye on the monastery for Eva and Maggie to emerge and sipped from his thermos. The grand old building stood tall and imposing but also ramshackle and shabby. The back left corner was clearly sinking and the tiles on the entire west slope of the roof were cracking, slipping, or just plain missing. If the buildings could be made as beautiful as the setting, the Dashiells would have a venue to rival any place in the valley. And that wasn't even considering the wine. If Eva had the skill he thought she did, all of those things, the wine, the scenery, the atmosphere, would make for a sensational showcase for parties.

Something fluttered in the small windows of what he assumed was the attic. Was that a face? He squinted up at the top of the building. Something hovered there for an instant, seeming to look down at him, and when he blinked it was gone.

He didn't have time to ponder that because the sound of a vehicle intruded into the morning. A long white van, the kind that picks up twenty-some people and all their luggage at the airport and totes them to a far-flung resort, pulled into the parking lot by his Aston Martin. The driver's door opened and Esther emerged from the vehicle.

She was wearing what every rock-n-roll super model would wear to a photo shoot for a farm. Tiny daisy duke's and high-heeled Timberland booties combined to show off sixteen miles of her legs. She had on a plaid work shirt with the sleeves torn off tied at her waist. And to top it all off, a distressed straw cowboy hat was pulled low over her eyes.

Asher suppressed a snorting laugh. Eva was going to lose her shit when she got an eyeful of Esther. "Hey," he called to her. "You pick up everything we talked about?"

She tossed him two thumbs up before signaling the occupants of the van that it was time to disembark. "Come on. We're here. Out you go."

Ash watched with curiosity to see who would emerge. He hadn't given her very much time to work with, but he had faith in her. The gargoyles could make just about anything happen if they were inclined to help.

The passenger and sliding door opened on cue and out tumbled a motley assortment of characters. There was something about them that was off, but Ash couldn't put his finger on the issue right away. The group, ranging widely in size, huddled together outside the van like a chain gang eyeing the possibilities of escape.

"Listen up," Esther commanded with the slam of her door. "You're going to do whatever you're told, just like we talked about. No one here wants to hear any lip from you. In fact, let's just agree right now that you're not to talk to any of the humans."

Ash's jaw gaped. "Esther, who is this?" He waved his arm around to encompass the group.

She grinned, her flame red lipsticked lips spread wide. "I cashed in all my poker markers."

Sweet mother of God. "Are you telling me these are demons?"

She stood tall and nodded with obvious pride in her solution. "Not all of them. There's a couple of ogres and a gremlin."

"Esther." Ash's ground out her name in frustration. "What the actual fuck?"

"What?" she asked. "You gave me a matter of hours to figure out how to get day workers out here. Consider my sources? Besides, they owe me."

He closed his eyes and shook his head. "You couldn't just go to The Home Depot parking lot like everyone else?"

Esther pursed her lips and narrowed her eyes at him. "Look, Asher Mephisto, I don't shop for humans." She added fists to her hips in emphasis. "Anymore. I got you exactly what you wanted. You did not ask for skilled labor. They're perfect. They'll do anything they're told."

Ash rubbed his temples. Shit, this might have been a huge mistake.

Esther strode to stand next to him. "Calm down. No one is going to know. I used a load of guile on them. They just look ugly at this point, not supernatural."

Ash eyed the horde with scrutiny. He could tell there was something wrong with them, but maybe Esther was right and Eva, Maggie, and Ernie would just think they were weird. Unless they tried to talk.

As if she was reading his mind, she said, "I've already told them they're not to talk to the humans. It's gonna be fine. They're afraid of me and in awe of you. One of the Seven? They'll have something to brag about when they get home."

He wasn't convinced, but he didn't have time to fuss about it anymore because Eva and Maggie emerged from the monastery with their own cups of steaming coffee. The identical twins had very different expressions as they took in the scene. In fact, they could have been the drama masks—one with a broad smile, the other with an epic frown.

Maggie spoke first. "Mornin', Asher. What's going on out here?"

"I brought reinforcements." He cocked his head to the side. "With us and this group, we should be able to finish Hell Week up today."

"That's fantastic." Maggie beamed at him.

Ash darted a quick glance at Eva and, just as he expected, she did not look pleased. He answered the question he knew was foremost in their minds. "I'm covering their wages, so don't worry about that. Just tell them what you want them to do."

Maggie looked to her sister and shrugged. "He's covering the wages." Then she headed for the tool shed where Ernie had arrived to collect the wagon and dole out garden nippers.

It was obvious that Eva was annoyed at the arrival of the day laborers, but the greatest deal of her animosity seemed to be aimed at Esther. Ash watched her watching his gargoyle with bemusement. She glanced from Esther to him, and then back to Esther.

"Good morning, gorgeous," he said to Eva.

She rolled her eyes. "Who is that? I can't imagine your girlfriend will enjoy participating in Hell Week. What did you say to sell her on it? And how much work can she really do in that getup anyway. She looks ridiculous. I'll bet it takes more than sending her a massage at night to make her happy. Boy, we should have held out for a lot more." The words came out of her mouth like an express train with no breaks for him to slip in an answer.

"The massage made you happy?" he asked when she took a breath. "I'm willing to do that for you any time."

She snorted.

Jealous. What a fascinating turn of events. He loved that Esther was getting to her. How had he not thought of using the gargoyle in that way before?

Esther finished ushering the legion after Maggie to get their tools, whispering threats and instructions the whole way, before making her way back to where the two of them stood. Eva averted her gaze and stared out at the neat rows of vines striping the hills into the distance.

"You must be Evangeline Dashiell." Esther stuck out her hand. "I can definitely see why Asher is so taken with you."

Eva's eyes darted back to Esther, but both hands still gripped her mug. "And you are?"

Esther did not reel in her offer of a handshake. Her right hand remained steady, extended between them. "I'm Esther."

"You are quite the girlfriend. Coming out here this early, getting you to work all day."

Esther laughed and slugged Asher in the shoulder. He swayed a bit. "I'm not his girlfriend. Sooo not his girlfriend. I take care of his helpless ass."

Eva let go of the mug with her right hand. "Like an assistant?"

"Ummm, not really. More like lieutenant, babysitter, bail bondsman, majordomo, and bodyguard."

"Wow," Eva said, finally shaking the extended hand. "That's a heck of a job description. You must know how annoying he is then."

Another chuckle from Esther. "I surely do." The two of them turned in unison to look at Ash who gave them a quick grin in response. Esther elbowed Eva. "But he's cute though, isn't he?"

Eva only grunted. Then she used her index finger to indicate the long expanse of Esther's legs. "You're going to get scrapped up wearing those shorts out in the vines. And we should find you a long-sleeved shirt or you're going be a bloody mess by the end of the day."

"Aren't you adorable." Esther tightened the knotted shirt at her bellybutton. "I don't work. Not manual labor, anyway. I'm more in management." She turned the three of them towards the outfitted group assembling next to the old Ford. "Anything you'll need, I will have already taken care of. I'll have lunch for you when you're ready. Until then, I'll find some way to keep myself amused up here."

Esther smacked Asher on the butt and sent him on his way. She pointed her index finger at the group of demons, turned her hand to point two fingers at her own eyes, and then back to the demons. When she raised her eyebrows at them, they all nodded in quick acquiescence.

As they piled in the back of the old truck, she stood on the lawn and waved goodbye. "Everyone have fun!"

All morning long, they crouched and crawled and snipped until the cramp in Asher's back was damn near incapacitating. They stopped several times for a break but, to the demons' credit, they kept right on going. Ernie made an effort to chat them up while working near them, but they only grunted, pulled their mouths into unpracticed smiles, and moved on.

"Where in the world did you find these guys?" Ernie asked when he joined Ash, Eva, and Maggie for a glass of water in the shade. "They work like they're possessed or something."

"Well, not quite," Ash assured them. "They're Esther's doing. She's a wizard."

"And she's not your girlfriend?" Maggie asked.

"Nope. Never has been. I don't think I could handle Esther," Ash told her with a laugh.

Ernie's eyes grew round. "She seems very strict."

Asher answered with a solemn nod.

Changing the subject, Eva demanded, "How much is this going to cost?"

"I've got it." Ash flapped a hand at her.

"We need to know how much so we can pay you back. Maggie, tell him we'll pay him back."

Maggie's smile was strained. "We know 'you have it,' but at the risk of sounding rude, we haven't agreed to partner with you yet, so the vineyard will have to cover this cost. I'm not sure when we'll be able to do that though."

Eva cut in. "I've told you, we do this work ourselves because it's way beyond what we can afford—right now. We just have to live very lean until... Well, just a while longer. You don't have the right to barge in here with employees. And now we have this added expense to pay before we can start any of the repairs or construction."

Ash squared his shoulders. "Don't you see that when you do agree to what I'm offering, you get all this? I come with the added benefit that you don't have to work yourselves to death. Not only can you start construction immediately, but you can hire all the workers you need to. You can concentrate on big picture, not the minutia."

Maggie trained her eyes on Eva, and Asher watched as some weird twin conversation took place in front of him. He let them talk, hoping that Maggie could telepathically talk some sense into her. At this point, she was just being stupid and stubborn. Who wanted to work this hard all the time? What the hell was the point when there was an alternative?

Ernie trotted up to him a bit later while he was scratching bug bites. "You know Eva loves every minute she spends out here with the vines, don't you?"

"I guess so." Ash shrugged. "But every minute?"

Ernie nodded. "Pretty much."

"Even the horrible parts?" Ash couldn't believe it. He wasn't a lazy guy like Benji, but he didn't enjoy working himself into martyrdom.

"That's just it, she knows how important every single part of the process is and she takes it all very seriously."

Asher paused. She had explained to him how thinning the cover leaves provided more air to the grapes, reducing the risk of fungus and mold. That would change the taste. How more sun, less sun, rain, wind—everything changed the final product

Ernie continued, "I'm just saying that maybe you're going about this all wrong. Bullying her into submission might not be the way."

"Huh," Asher grunted. He turned to watch her working. Her straw hat was pushed back on her head, and she was cradling a bunch of grapes in her hands. She carefully brushed away debris before lowering her face and inhaling the aroma. She plucked one bluish grape from the cluster and popped it in her mouth. Her expression took on a faraway gaze as she contemplated the taste. She savored the flavor, raising her face to the sun, eyes closed. She was magnificent.

And brilliant.

He'd never wanted to march over there and kiss some sense into her so badly.

He could also appreciate that Ernie was likely correct. The current plan sure as hell wasn't working.

By the time lunch rolled around they'd had a long, exhausting day. Asher left her alone, deciding not to poke her until he'd come up with another tack.

Maggie and Ernie applauded when they all arrived back at the monastery and Esther had a lunch all laid out in the shade just like she'd promised. Even the demons seemed appreciative at the bag lunches she doled out to each of them as they piled back into the van.

"Asher," she hissed his name before she climbed into the driver's seat. "Come here."

He trotted over. "What do you think? Isn't this place perfect?"

"Oh yeah," she nodded, her tone filled with sarcasm. "It's perfect. What the hell is wrong with you?"

He was taken aback. "What do you mean?"

Esther's expression suggested he was an idiot. "The fields are scenic. The buildings are like a setting in a romcom—falling down but charming. It smells out of this world out here. The girl is fetching."

"Right. So, what's wrong? Can't you see the vision for when it's all restored?"

"Sure." She nodded. "But what are you going to do with all the holy ghosts?"

"What?"

Esther crossed her arms. "Why didn't you tell me this place was haunted? It's lousy with monks."

Heaven XIV

J uliet had arrived at the top landing of the stairwell to Hell. She propped her palm against the cool cement and panted for a moment. Somewhere along the way she'd lost her sweater, and her ponytail hung limply down her back with heavy strands loose and sticking to her neck. After a moment's rest, she straightened and pushed open the door to Heaven.

The cool breeze ruffled her hair, and she realized how stuffy the concrete stairwell had been. She took some deep breaths of yeast-y air wafting over from the kitchens. A sandwich would be nice, turkey with swiss and yellow mustard. Like her mom used to pack in her lunch when Juliet was a kid, before she'd been old enough to carry money and purchase something from the snack bar in high school. The memory gave her pause. How nice it would be to sit for a few minutes, rest her legs, and nibble a sandwich, maybe a glass of lemonade. Certainly, the cook would even cut her crusts off if she asked. Shortbread cookies for dessert. Mmm.

Except that Neil was downstairs. "In Hell," she whispered to herself.

He wouldn't be having a sandwich and cookies. It had almost broken her heart when she'd given him her potato chips. It was like he'd been starving and those chips were the best thing he'd ever had in his whole life. Just stupid boring potato chips mostly crushed from her pocket.

In a surreal moment of duh, it became clear exactly how lucky she was that she was in Heaven. She complained about the lamest stuff, and yet there was Neil, suffering and starving. Poor, poor Neil.

Holding her head high, she strode past the kitchen. She could sacrifice a sandwich in order to hurry back to meet him. She'd make sure she'd have loads of goodies in her pockets to share.

She just needed to find that dog.

She emerged out from the support buildings into the main thoroughfare. Scanning the village-like quire, she considered where to start looking for Cerberus. While she didn't see the dog, she did see evidence that he had been there. An overturned garbage can in front of the Messengers temple suggested that it hadn't been too long before.

The archangel Gabriel was in charge of the Messengers and, like all the Archangels, he was intimidating. Much more so than the dominions like Hashmal who ran the lower orders like her own. Her first instinct was not to linger there. But, when she thought back on their meeting, Lucifer hadn't been all that scary, and he was an Archangel, too. It might be worth the risk to hang around for a bit.

Watching from the corner, she noted the number of angels coming in and out of the building, most carrying scrolls or folded parchment. From there, they branched out to all of Heaven, some even heading towards the Narthex and down the grand staircase.

If anyone had seen Cerberus, surely it would be them.

A lady came out with a broom and got to work corralling the debris from the can. Juliet ran her hands over her hair to smooth her mussed ponytail and patted down her dress, making herself presentable. Or at least, less suspicious.

"Hi." Juliet smiled.

The woman glanced up at Juliet but continued sweeping.

Juliet lifted the can upright, hoping to be helpful. "What happened here? What a mess, huh?" The woman only grunted, so Juliet powered on. "Couldn't get anyone from janitorial to do this, eh?"

The woman snorted and handed Juliet the dustpan to hold while she swept the trash into it.

Juliet ferried the full dustpan to the can and dumped it in. "Who would make such a mess?" she said, as if thinking out loud. "I mean in Heaven, too. Crazy."

"It wasn't an angel," the lady complained. "It's that dratted dog."

Juliet gasped in surprise. "A dog? What heavenly dog would behave that way? The kennel master usually has them all well trained."

The Messenger angel snatched up a couple of stray scraps of paper from takeout boxes and crumpled them into a ball before tossing them in the bin. "It's not one of those adorable schnauzers or poodles who belong. No, it was that dreadful Hell hound running loose up here again. Total nuisance"

She shook her head in sympathy. "Which way did he go?"

The woman tossed her hand in a direction down the street as she turned to go back into the building. "Just follow the overturned trash cans."

Juliet took off at a trot, spying another can two blocks further down the street. She dodged a crowd of novitiates licking ice cream cones in the square. That's where she lost the trail. She slowed to a walk, looking for signs. Anything. Drool, trash, clumps of dog hair. Mingling among the loitering crowd, she listened in on conversations, hoping to overhear a lead.

"...all the gingersnaps I can eat!"

"...watching my grandkids the other day, and Jimmy did the cutest thing..."

"...sit by the pool and drink mimosas all day...

A commotion from the furthest corner had Juliet moving in that direction. The quire opened up at the end of the block into a long meadow which faded into a forest. Generally, the fields were full of angels enjoying their version of Heaven: picnicking, sunbathing, playing football, any activity their heart desired. For some it was sunny with a breeze, and for others there was a light sprinkle. It was Heaven after all, and it was constantly evolving perfection.

Except for the fluttering of cherubim along the edge, wailing and hysterical.

Juliet sidled up to the cadre of nanny dominion whose role it was to tend to the flying babies.

"What's all the fuss?" she asked. She'd never seen such a hullabaloo in Heaven all the time she'd been there.

"It's chaos," Zophiel answered, her usually tidy bun hanging from the back of her head. She had her hands full of baby angels, three of the fat, little fledglings calmed to the point of sniveling. They wiped their noses on the shoulder of her robes, but Zophiel didn't notice. Or maybe she didn't care. Juliet cringed.

"What set them off?" Juliet asked. She gave a flirty little smile to one of the babie,s who shyly hid her face against Zophiel's neck. Just the thought of smearing all that snot against her skin... Blech.

"That cursed dog."

Juliet was shocked at the level of venom in the Dominion's response. It was rare to hear an Angel of the Lord speak with violence in her heart. Nevertheless, it was a sure sign that Cerberus had been this way.

Zophiel continued. "I'd brought the little darlings out to play with the butterflies and the newborn lambs, and he burst out into the field and all three of those awful heads of his were barking at the babies." She thrust the calmest cherub into Juliet's arms, all the while shushing and bouncing the others. "I know, honey, he's gone now."

Juliet did her best to duplicate what the older angel was doing. She swayed at her hips and made soft noises, but at the same time she held the baby away from her far enough to avoid getting any fluids on her. The background noise was still a chorus of blubbering as the hysterical babies helicoptered above them. It was going to take forever to calm them all down. Like forever forever. As soon as one of the nannies got one calmed down enough to turn it loose, the cherub would just fly back up to join the rest of them and get itself all worked up again.

"Awful, awful creature," another one of the other nannies groused while patting babies' backs. "They need to—oh, honey, shush now—get that dog out of here!"

Juliet turned her cherub loose. "You tell your friends everything is better now," she called after him. Then she turned to Zophiel. "I'm actually looking for Cerberus."

"You're too late," one of the other nannies called to her. "He's already wreaked his havoc."

"Yeah, sorry about that." Juliet didn't know why she was apologizing. She didn't turn the dog loose. "Cerberus sort of just does what he wants, you know. But I am looking for him. In which direction did he run off?"

Zophiel waved her only free hand vaguely to the left. "Just follow the sound of chaos. He can't be far behind."

She felt bad leaving the nannie with all the mewling, flapping babies. On the other hand, who knew what kind of shenanigans Cerberus could be getting up to until he was found. She could hear the cacophony behind her for quite a while as she made her way across the meadow. Not a babysitter in life, she was immeasurably thankful that she wasn't assigned to the nursery now. She blanched at the thought.

Having made a huge circle around the quire, she found herself back at the edge of the service buildings,the kennels in one direction and the kitchens the other way. She debated heading to the kennels and checking in with Hugh again, but she considered how long it would take to extricate herself from the dog keeper once he got to chatting. There were always new puppies to snuggle and play with, and she had a job to focus on.

So, she turned to the right and made her way up the path towards the smell of cookies.

And yelling.

In French.

She picked up her pace. This had to be the right way. When she swung through the double doors into the massive kitchen, the view cinched it. There was flour everywhere, and giant canine footprints gave evidence that someone had been chasing an enormous dog all around the room. Under a worktable sat one of the sous chefs, hat in her lap and her apron askew.

"Emylia?" Juliet tiptoed through the debris, adding her own footprints to the collage. She kneeled down and peered at the cook at eyelevel. "Are you alright?"

"No," Emylia said, sounding defeated. "It's all ruined."

Juliet glanced around. Pretty much everything did look ruined. "What happened in here? Where's Chauncey?" she asked when she noticed the chef himself was missing.

"A cake," Emylia stared. "We're making a fifteen-tier cake for the festival tomorrow..." Her voice died away, and she stared straight in front of her like a zombie.

Juliet didn't even bother to ask what festival. There was always some religious event happening or another. "Uh huh," she said to encourage further explanation. She patted the cook's shoulder. Her hand came away with frosting on it.

"It was all done." Emylia continued. "The frosting was all smoothed and we were ready to start piping when the door burst open." A hiccupping sigh broke up the last few words.

"Oh, no." Juliet knew what was coming. Paw prints don't lie.

Emylia whispered the next bit. "It was the dog."

"Oh no," Juliet repeated. She didn't know what else to say. This just seemed so much worse than the hysterical cherubs. The babies would eventually calm down and be no worse for wear, but this cake was definitely destroyed. She glanced around the kitchen and there really wasn't that much cake left as evidence. Lumps of frosting polka dotted the floor and smeared the table, counters and Emylia.

Still whispering, the cook noted, "It's all gone. Gone."

Juliet stood and backed away from the babbling woman. She wasn't going to be any help finding Cerberus, and she really needed to track him down before there were any more disasters. She followed the trail of pawprints, frosting droplets, and drool out a swinging door and through a pantry. She paused a moment and listened for barking or shrieking—something that would send her in the right direction. It was soft, but she did hear something faintly canine further ahead.

She finally found the dog with all three heads down, snuffling loudly at the door of the walk-in refrigerator. On the other side of the super thick door, she could barely make out the sound of French outrage. One of the enormous heads let out a playful woof that only amped up the swearing from inside the fridge.

"Oh, puppy, get away from that door." Juliet tugged at the dog's collar. Two of his heads turned up in surprise. Surprise turned to glee when the dog recognized her. It was bad enough to be licked and slathered with drool from one slobbery mouth, but two was completely barfy. "Oh, gah!" She shoved away one head just to have the middle on wrap his tongue around her chin.

The accented voice from behind the door asked, "Is someone out there? I need to get out. It's very cold in here."

"Come here, dog." Juliet pulled on his collar. "I'll give you treats. Come on."

Cerberus wasn't a bad dog. He was really just an enormous puppy—or actually three enormous puppies in one massive puppy body. A tail as thick as a sapling wagged with excitement at seeing her, whopping the steel walk-in door with a steady hammering.

"Hello?" came the voice from behind the door. "Hello?"

"Just a minute, Chauncey. Come on, puppy. You're such a good puppy. Yes, you are."

Juliet managed to get the slobbery animal across the room before hollering to the chef that it was safe to come out. The heavy door opened tentatively, and eventually Chef Chauncey stuck his head out.

"Is he gone?" he asked.

"Not yet, but it's safe. Come on out."

Cerberus's right head woofed gleefully, causing the French angel to scream a little.

"Do you have any cookies left? I can lure him out with cookies." Juliet promised, holding tight to the dog's collar with both hands.

"There's hardly anything left." Chauncey waved his arms around the mess in kitchen.

"Nothing? I don't know how I'll entice him out without something."

"*Une minute*," he said and disappeared back into the refrigerator. A minute later he reemerged and thrust a bag with a loaf of bread, a hunk of wrapped roast beef, a wedge of cheese, three apples, an artichoke, some jerky, a sleeve of crackers, and a jar of peanut butter. "Voila. Now shoo, *mauvais chien*."

Juliet slung the bag over her shoulder and called for Cerberus to follow along—which he did with no trouble. She led him directly to the backdoor that led downstairs. "I'll let you have one stick of jerky," she told him. "The rest is for Neil. Think how excited he's gonna be."

Chapter Eight

Eva watched the taillights of the Aston Martin follow the minivan down the long tree-lined drive towards the highway.

"Wow, that Esther—"

When her sister spoke right behind her left shoulder, Eva jumped. "Holy cow!"

Maggie snorted. "Sorry. I was saying how unexpected Esther was."

Eva responded with a nod, her eyebrows high on her forehead. "Yeah. I did not see her coming."

Maggie stood next to her sister, hands in her back pockets while they both stared into the distance. "She and Asher aren't a thing. She told me they never have been. I asked her if she was a lesbian or something. I couldn't believe the question came out of my mouth—it was so rude, but I just couldn't understand how that was possible. I mean, a man like Asher and a woman who looks like Esther. Wow. Think of the children they'd make."

Eva was *not* going to think about those children. She didn't want to think about Asher at all, and definitely not about Asher having sex with Esther which would have been done if they'd had children. She didn't want to think about Asher having sex with anyone, but her brain was not on the same wavelength. Thinking about him was just about the only thing she did anymore.

Asher's ass as he leaned around a vine.

Asher staring up into the sky, eyes closed, jawline sharp enough to slice cheese.

Asher's long fingers, wide palms, cradling a cluster of grapes.

Dammit. Eva pushed out an irritated huff and pivoted on her heel. She marched towards the monastery, looking for something to occupy her mind or risk being wound up in fantasies all day. How hard could it be to find a project? This place was literally falling down around their ears.

"Hey," Maggie called behind her. "Wait up. Where are you going so fast?"

Eva adjusted her course and passed the monastery, heading instead to the cellars. "I've got stuff to do, Mags."

Her sister caught up with her as Eva swung open the heavy door and grabbed a clipboard from the wall. "Let's take the afternoon off." Maggie suggested with a mischievous twinkle.

"What? No way."

"Come on. Asher gave us a free afternoon off. It's like a gift. You don't want to hang around here all day, trying to avoid that sketchy cat." Maggie pointed out Diablo glaring at them from behind the casks of last year's white.

The dodgy grey tabby, easily the largest of the working cats that ran free on their farm, ruled the underworld of the cellars. He was equal parts handsome and terrifying with what looked like the softest fur. There was no way to know for sure, because if you got within five feet of him, he'd start that low growl in his throat and raise his hackles, sounding like the very worst kind of demon, and no one had been brave enough to try and pet him. He did his job, though, keeping the mice and other vermin out of the cellars, so the family had always just let him do his thing.

Eva shook her head and headed to the racks. "Or it's an opportunity to get more stuff done. If you can't find something, I have a long list of stuff."

Maggie tried to snatch the clipboard, but Eva moved her hand out of the way in a flash. Instead, Maggie grabbed her shirt tail and tugged. "Come on, let's go shopping."

"Where?" Eva scoffed and pulled her shirt loose. "The Dollar Store? We don't have any money to waste on shopping."

"We don't have to buy anything. We can window shop. That's just as much fun," Maggie cajoled. "More importantly, it's away from here."

Eva cast her sister an indulgent glance before consulting the clipboard. "Do you think we should rerack that red?"

Maggie gasped. "I know! Let's go to a movie. Something funny, and we'll eat a ton of popcorn and soda and Red Vines. Remember how we used to bite the ends off the licorice and use it as a straw? Gah, so much sugar." Maybe she saw a glimmer of weakness in Eva because she changed the timbre of her voice. "There's that new romcom with Chris Evans... I heard a rumor there's a shot of his butt."

Eva closed her eyes. She'd been killing herself for the last six months. There was always so much to do. When she threw herself in bed at night, there were lists of things left undone. She pulled her bottom lip between her teeth and thought of Chris Evans' butt. Also, these barrels really needed to be reracked in the next few days.

"I'll let you put the M&Ms in with the popcorn. Salty and sweet."

"It's only a couple of hours, right?" Eva asked, her resolve teetering. This work would still be here. The red could be reracked tomorrow. And, Chris Evan's butt. Maybe she'd be able to substitute Chris's butt for Ashe's fantasy one. "Okay."

Maggie whooped and shimmied her hips. "I knew the candy would do it."

Eva snorted. "No, it was the butt."

Her sister growled and looped her arm around Eva, steering her out the door. "If I could just take a little bite out of that..."

Several hours later, when they left the dark theater, the movie over and the popcorn demolished, Maggie was able to convince her to walk around the shopping center. "Just for a bit," Maggie told her.

They wandered into a few shops and touched pretty clothes. They had coffee and split an almond croissant at an outside bistro. They even saw a few friends out and about whom Eva hadn't seen in months.

"You know what?" Maggie bumped Eva's hip with her own. "You're smiling."

Eva wiped the smile from her face. "I smile."

"Yes, you do." Maggie confirmed. "But most of the time it's a feral showing of teeth more than an expression of happiness or contentment."

That wasn't true, was it? Eva was content. Most of the time. Wasn't she?

"No, you're anxious most of the time." Maggie responded to her thoughts. "This was a really good break for you today. We need to do this more. You know, work/life balance and all that."

Eva took a moment to do a self-evaluation. The pinchy feeling she was so used to at the top of her neck was missing. Also, the sense of impending doom that was her constant companion was absent.

"I can promise you that I'll take a break every time Chris Evans' butt is made cinematically available."

"Deal."

It was almost dark when they made it home. Still full from popcorn and pastries, they made salads for dinner and watched serial killer documentaries on Netflix late into the night.

It was a nearly perfect day.

Unfortunately, the morning dawned and she was frustrated all over again. Legs tangled in the sheets, sweaty, hot and bothered. Damn Asher invading her dreams. She didn't even remember what was happening in the movie in her head, only that she was almost there, so close, when she woke up.

She lay there, trying to slow her breaths and calm her girl parts. She recited grape varietals until things settled down.

Grenache. Merlot. Sémillon. Carménère. Pinot Noir.

An hour later, Eva stepped out into the sunshine with her coffee and an attitude much improved by the marked absence of Asher Mephisto waiting on the lawn. Excellent. Today might be a break from his perfection taunting her all day. Between yesterday's day off and his no-show today, she might get back to some sort of semi-normal.

The tops of her sneakers were damp from dew by the time she crossed the large lawn to the heavy stone cellars. The morning smelled like heaven, or at least heaven to a vintner – warm and vaguely floral. Poufy little dots of clouds far on the horizon. Despite waking up to yet another sex dream starring her personal tormentor, yesterday had been really good for her. The old place looked somehow brighter and more carefully tended than she'd come to regard it as of late. The cracked and missing tiles on the monastery roof seemed somehow picturesque rather than shabby. She smiled. Everything wasn't as dire as she'd convinced herself it was.

The old canvas gloves made a crisp sound when she slapped them against her jean-clad thigh with each stride. Today they'd get the racks rotated. Her fingers trailed along the stone wall of the cellar, her fingers fitting into the cracks and grooves that made the old building so stately.

"It's going to be a good day," she said aloud as she rounded the turn for the stairs down to the entrance.

"Good morning, gorgeous."

Eva screamed and threw her gloves at the man coming up the stairs as her fight or flight response kicked in.

Ash caught them easily, but his smile waned slightly. "I am so sorry. It seems like I'm always creeping up on you."

Eva put one hand on the banister and the other over her heart. "What the hell is with that? For God's sake. Esther ever considered putting a bell on you?"

"Don't give Esther ideas." He extended his hand to her and she gave him the one from the banister without thinking about it.

"What are you doing here?" Once at the bottom landing, she reached for the keys in her pocket, but the door was already open. She stared at the knob, trying to piece together the previous afternoon. Surely, she and Maggie had locked up. "How —? Why is this—?"

Asher's wide shoulders shrugged. "It was open when I got here."

She and Maggie were never this careless. My God, anything could have happened. She pushed the door wide and strode inside with Asher behind her. A quick glance around and nothing looked out of place or disheveled. No mess on the floor. Even the clipboards were hanging on their nails.

Maybe the ghosts...?

Shiny silver eyes peered at her from the third row. "Who was in here, Diablo?"

Asher whipped his head around to face her. "What?"

Eva pointed at the cat who prowled to the end of the aisle for some more personal intimidation. "Diablo."

"Oh!" Asher's laugh sounded edgy. "I get it. Hey buddy." He spoke directly to the cat. He even turned and walked in his direction. "What's happening?"

Eva opened her mouth to warn Ash off the evil feline but changed her mind and snapped her jaw shut.

"Man, you are a handsome fellow, aren't you?" Asher kept up the friendly tone as he got closer and closer. "Is this your castle?" Now he was close enough that Diablo could slash through his pants and gash his leg with those wicked nails. She felt a twinge of guilt, but she still let him continue forward unwarned. She winced when he stooped and extended his hand, watching for the split second when the cat sunk his teeth into Ash's hand. That's what he got for wheedling his way into where he didn't belong.

But that's not what happened.

Improbably, Diablo pushed up with his front legs and did a funny little hop, shoving his head into Ashe's hand. Then the four-legged bastard rubbed the man's leg, meowing up a storm. Eva stared down at it. Her mouth dropped open when Asher scooped the cat up and snuggled him against his chest.

It must not be Diablo. That was the only possible explanation, except that when Asher turned back to her and the animal saw her standing behind them, he hissed and yowled at her like a puma. Eva stepped back in haste.

"Hey now," Ash cooed at the diabolical beast. "There's no need for that."

Yeah, it was totally Diablo. And the satanic beast loved Asher. Basically all her nemeses were joining forces against her. Nemesi? Nemeseses?

"He likes you," Eva stated the obvious, but not understanding it.

Asher scratched under the cat's chin. "My family has a real way with cats. It's in my blood."

That was the stupidest thing she'd ever heard, and it returned her equilibrium. "You never said what you were doing here."

He set his grey gaze on her. "Working."

"We finished Hell Week early, thanks to you and your hired help."

"Yeah, but there's always something, right? And I'm here to help. What happens down here? Just tell me what to do. I love learning all this stuff."

Eva shook her head. She was never going to get rid of him, was she? Maggie wouldn't let her literally throw him out, and she was smart enough to know why. They needed what he offered, but Eva just couldn't bring herself to trust him. There was some hitch he wasn't disclosing. Some codicil in the contract he hadn't told them about. She knew in the deepest lizard part of her brain that there was a major, serious piece to his puzzle they didn't know yet. Something that could make her regret trusting him for the rest of her life.

Asher kissed the top of the cat's head, then set him on the floor before giving her all his attention. "Come on, Eva. At the very least, take advantage of a strong back and willing arms."

And why shouldn't she? Rotating barrels was hot, taxing work. Here he was, annoying as hell, looking like sex on a stick, with tight jeans and a form-fitting t-shirt, wooing demon cats. It wasn't like he'd leave if she didn't take his help. Short of calling the police on the man—her sister would beat her over the head with their bank statements if she did that—she didn't know how to get rid of him. She had already been as rude and nasty as she knew how. She might as well make use of free labor until she could suss out the catch in his offer.

"Fine." She skirted the cat with a wide arc and led Asher to the back of the big room. Along the back wall stood racks and racks of oak barrels, towering above them, three high.

She showed him the A-shaped ladder on wheels and explained how they each needed to climb up a side and work together to rotate the barrels one-hundred-eighty degrees.

"What's in here?" Asher asked as they maneuvered the ladder to the furthest and highest barrel.

"Wine," Eva said with a smirk. When he raised an eyebrow she added, "Red. Pinot Noir."

"Mmm," Asher hummed appreciatively. "When can we taste it?"

Eva took the last step to the top and came face to face with Asher over the last rung. His grey eyes sparkled with what she assumed was the idea of a hearty glass of wine. She stood there, transfixed, for a long moment before snapping to her senses. "It'll be a while. Still barrel aging. Maybe another year."

Asher made a disappointed noise as they turned the barrel to the right.

"Wine-making is not for the impatient."

He flashed that grin that kept her up at night. "I know that. While I'm certainly not a sommelier, I'm not a complete barbarian either."

They moved down the ladder to the middle rack and repeated the process. "After we're done here today, I'll buy you a glass of whatever you want." She hesitated, then added, "I know a guy."

Asher whipped his head to face her through the rungs. "Wait just a minute. Did you just tell a joke?"

Eva rolled her eyes but couldn't keep the smile from her lips. "I'm certainly not a stand-up comedian, but I'm not a killjoy either."

He gave her a brief nod and that sexy grin. "Noted."

They turned five more barrels without comment. Eva refused to look at him because when she did, she turned stupid. Climb the ladder. Avoid looking across the top. Hold your breath so you don't accidently inhale his Asherness.

"So how many—" he grunted with the effort to turn the current barrel "of these are from that same year?"

Dear. Lord.

That had to be the sexiest grunt she'd ever heard. Not even Chris Evans with the magic glutes could have grunted any hotter than that. She made the mistake of glancing over at him, and she got sucked into his orbit for a moment. She realized he was staring at her.

"What?" she asked. Why was her voice so high?

He squinted at her. "Are all of these barrels of pinot from the same year?"

She nodded, afraid of what squeaky nonsense would come out of her mouth.

He put his hands on his hips and took in the entirety of the cellar. "Wow, that's a lot of pinot."

She swallowed and ordered herself to sound normal. "No, just from here to here are the pinot from that year." Gesturing to the racks they were finishing up. "The others are different years or grapes or whatever." She sounded like a moron, but at least her voice sounded mostly normal.

He raised his eyebrows and looked around the room again, clearly impressed. He appeared to be counting. "This is a lot of wine. There's sixty-five barrels here just of the pinot. How many bottles in a barrel?"

"It depends. Somewhere between one-fifty and two hundred. It depends on the angel share." She used the back of her hand to push her bangs back.

"The what now?"

"The angel share? You lose a percentage of spirits when you age in oak. It evaporates, you know, sort of floats up to heaven. The angel share."

"Like an offering," he said, laughing more than she thought was really necessary for the level of joke they were talking about. And there was a weird since of *schadenfreude* when he added, "Wouldn't the Devil be pissed."

"Oh, he gets his share, too."

"Of course, he does. How does that work? You pour a barrel in the dirt, 'one for my homies.' That kind of thing?"

Eva snorted. "No. But there's a certain amount of alcohol that seeps into the oak. There's no way to avoid it either. It's called the devil's cut."

"Well, if there's one thing that's true, it's that the Devil gets his due." He shook his head ruefully. He clapped his hands twice and demanded, "Okay, what's next? Teach me more."

"Why?" She closed her eyes so she could ask the tough questions without being distracted. "Why do you want to know all these things?"

She felt him take a step closer to her, like the air got thicker or something.

"Because I find it seductive. This whole process is fascinating. I had no idea before I got involved how intricate the details were. I mean, I understood the basic concepts, but until you get into the thick of it with someone brilliant like you, someone who really knows the secrets, you have no concept of how one little thing can change everything. Like what would happen if we didn't rotate these?"

"Um, well, we're moving the sediments around. Mixing the fermenting juices with the grape skins and stuff. We're just making it a more well-rounded, fuller-bodied wine."

His smile filled his whole face and made her heart pick up its pace. "Enthralling."

"Okay. Enough of this. If we let you in... If I tell you everything, then what's to keep you from just taking over and kicking Maggie and I out on our asses once you own everything?"

The smile-wattage dimmed. "I don't want to own everything. I only want to contribute to the overall product. All I want to do is make it possible for your vision to come to life."

"Do you hear yourself? That sounds like the biggest load of horseshit imaginable. No investor in the world brings in all that money and then just sits there without trying to make changes."

A quick expression flashed in his eyes, but he blinked it away. "Oh, I want to make changes; don't get me wrong. I want to create a fan base for Empyrean wine. I want to develop this property into the destination it deserves to be. The grounds here are so beautiful, and the buildings are so authentic. I've seen Maggie's vision and, together, we can make that happen."

"And to my point, all of that just takes money. What use will you have for the Dashiell sisters? This is my family's legacy, not yours. Where will there be space for us?"

He moved toward her again. Two long strides and he was directly in front of her, in her space. "I want to build a sensation around your brilliance. I can't do any of this without you, Evangeline."

Oh man, she wanted to believe him. It had been a long struggle without her grandfather there to make sure everything turned out all right. He had been her mentor, her strength. He'd believed in her when she couldn't believe in herself. Of course, she'd always had Maggie, but her sister was simply an extension of herself. Maggie told her what she wanted, needed to hear, but she was sorry to say, Maggie wasn't always enough.

She swallowed hard and looked over his shoulder instead of meeting his gaze. "But you're just going to stay as long as you find us interesting, and then you'll disappear just like with all your other 'projects.'"

He reached forward and scooped up one hand in his. "What do you mean?"

She braved looking at him for an instant, but she was afraid he would be able to see right into her needy soul, and that was too much to bear. Moving her gaze to his shoes, she said, "I don't hear you going on about silk and caviar all the time."

"They don't need me." He gave her hand a little squeeze. "But that doesn't mean I don't know what's going on with them or help when asked. Neeraj runs Pheresata Silk with very little meddling from me. I've helped him find competent and trustworthy assistants, but I'm available any time he calls. Kolya runs Arkhangelsk like a military unit, but I was just there two months ago when they had trouble with a supply chain. And frankly, Sergei and his Ryba-angel are moving along swimmingly—pun intended. That was the last venture I worked on. Regardless, Sergei isn't as bewitching as you."

They'd never been this close before. Not even on the ladder. There had been wood between them then. Now, there was nothing but magnetically charged ions zipping between them, seemingly pulling them together.

"What is my vineyard to do when you become 'bewitched' with someone else?" What was she to do?

He gave her hand a gentle tug and, with the help of the ions, she stood with less than a breath between them. Asher was tall, but then so was she. She only had to lift her eyes to be level with his. All the years of tasting wine and teasing out the flavors and notes had given her a finely developed sense of taste and smell. On Asher she found his cologne, something a little wicked and musky, and an undernote of exertion from their work today. There was also the faintest hint of shea butter, cotton, and leather.

"Evangeline," he practically purred her name. "I have been here every single day. I haven't even invested yet and here I've been. Where else am I going to go?"

That question snapped her out of the trance she'd been leaning into. She righted her spine. "What do you mean, where will you go? Anywhere. But maybe that's not the right question. Maybe what I should be asking is where will we go? When you own all of this, how quickly will Maggie and I be edged out?"

Asher still clasped her hand in his. He brushed his thumb across her knuckles and gently tugged her back to his orbit. "I'm not trying to buy you out. I'm not even trying to be the principal owner. We'll have all the contracts drawn up to be very clear on that point." He tugged her a little nearer, and his voice dropped to just above a whisper. "I need you here. Empyrean would be lost without your genius. You are the heart and soul of this place. It's you I want to invest in."

Oh, that bastard.

It was like he reached into her brain and found the magic words she needed to hear. She could almost feel her spirit squealing and cooing. They stood so close that it took only the slightest pressure for Eva to tip into his arms. Their lips met and all the tension she had left melted away. This kiss had been weeks in coming.

Why had she fought it for so long?

He tasted faintly of chocolate and cherries. Because of course he did. It was only reasonable that he would taste of her favorite flavors. He slipped his long fingers into her hair and cradled her head.

Somehow, she'd thought if she ever allowed Asher Mephisto to kiss her it would have been done with scientific precision and perfectly done. Anyone who looked like him and talked as much bullshit and tossed out so many innuendos as he'd done was surely an expert in kissing. She also figured she'd like it. It only figured he would have done it enough times to know how to kiss a woman effectively.

Afterward, he'd be cool about it, maybe blasé. One kiss in a million. This wasn't like that. At all.

His lips settled lightly on hers, the pressure tender, a little hesitant, wholly unexpected. A sensual shiver tickled up her back and she arched into it. He raised their joined hands and settled her palm on his chest before moving his own hand around her waist. With his heart racing beneath her palm, she knew exactly how affected he was by this kiss, and it encouraged her to act on her instincts. She clutched a handful of the waistband of his jeans just over his hip.

Asher moved his lips over hers, learning the feel of her mouth. It was not wolfish or professional. It was possibly the sweetest kiss she'd ever had in her life. Not that she had a whole catalogue of kisses to refer to, but enough to know this one was different. He went slowly, testing each corner before opening his lips and encouraging hers to do the same.

And then he made a little sigh or a light moan. Whatever it was, it catapulted Eva's lust into overdrive. She swept her tongue into his mouth and answered with her own moan. Her entire body responded, as if suddenly her insides melted to molten pudding. He pulled her tightly against him, one hand on her back and the other against the nape of her neck, but she still needed closer. She hooked one ankle around his lower calf and pulled against his clothes.

Swept up in the smell of his skin and the feel of his body against hers, it was as if the whole world fell away and the only solid things in the universe were Asher Mephisto and Evangeline Dashiell. Time stopped and the ambient air grew warm, so warm. Hot, actually. And if she could pull back into herself, she might be able to name the unusual scent wafting around them.

Asher deepened the kiss and Eva let the last thread of her wits slip away. All that she knew was him and his muscles against her palms and the taste of him consuming her. This was the kiss that she'd known was coming, not the tentative one from seconds ago. She'd never experienced arousal before this. Every sexual encounter prior had been laughable in comparison. Both of his hands slid to her ass and, with an effortless lift, her feet left the floor and she felt barrels hit her back. His erection pressed against her core through his pants and hers and, holy shit, she was on fire. He pulled her head back with a fist full of hair and ravaged her mouth. Their teeth clashing and tongues stroking. She needed his skin against hers and—

Just as she wrenched the tail of his shirt from his jeans, he broke away from her mouth.

"Wait."

She panted, sounding desperate.

Asher's head bowed and he cleared his throat. "Hold on." His breath sounded ragged, too. After several deep breaths, he admitted. "That really got away from me."

Embarrassment washed over her, and the heat on her cheeks took on a new meaning. She wiped her hand across her mouth and cursed herself for being an idiot. Pushing at his shoulder, she tried to get past him, but he propped that arm against the oak behind her.

"Hey," he whispered, somehow still making their little scene as intimate as it had been only seconds before. "Don't run away. I just needed a moment. Things were going to happen... before we were ready."

"Oh." She said and allowed him to nuzzle her cheek and neck.

Actually, now that she had returned to her senses, it would probably be smart to put the brakes on this whole fiasco. If they were actually going to become business partners, they couldn't be doing this in the wine cellar.

"We're done in here anyway," she smiled at him so that he would let her out of his confines. "Let's get some air. I don't know why it's so hot. We're going to have to check the thermostats."

The strange smell she couldn't quite identify still hung in the air, and once they got up the steps and into the yard, she took a deep breath to clear it. Something was seriously wrong with the ventilation down there, and that needed to be sorted out real quick. How much would that cost? All of these emergencies she could focus on instead of the fact that Asher Mephisto had been mere inches from being inside her. And that she had wanted that desperately.

She headed off across the grass but paused when his fingers intertwined with hers. "Are you alright?" he asked.

"Umm, yeah." *Probably three thousand to do a deep cleaning of the ventilation.* "So how quickly can you get the contracts so Maggie and I can look at them?"

The clouds that had floated over the fields like marshmallows that morning had congregated through the course of the day and now hung, gray and heavy, over the valley. The wind was whipping up, and the humidity had risen.

"You're ready?" His grin was contagious. "By next week."

"Well, then, partner—"

He pulled her into another kiss, but before it had a chance to ignite, a screeching like a million rusty wagon wheels had them whipping their heads towards the monastery.

"Oh. My. God."

Eva let her jaw hang open in horror as the entire eastern side of the roof tore away from the building, caught on a gust of wind. Tiles slipped from the edge like water droplets as, incredibly, the roof undulated in the wind, hung aloft for seconds and then came crashing down on top of Asher's beautiful, red Aston Martin.

"How about tomorrow?" she asked. "Can you have the contract by tomorrow?"

Chapter Nine

A sher was speechless.

He stood witness as the last wheeze of his Aston Martin's theft alarm faded away, buried underneath the downed roof of the monastery. No one would ever try to steal his sexy sporty darling ever again. His gorgeous car was almost entirely squashed under hundreds of pounds of lumber and Spanish tiles.

The whole morning had been surreal.

First, he'd finally convinced Evangeline to let him invest in the vineyard.

Second, that kiss. That. Kiss.

Sweet mother in heaven, that kiss.

Being the personification of Lust, he'd kissed maybe a thousand people. Men, women, and those who didn't identify as either. He enjoyed kissing. He did it damn near all the time. Except he hadn't actually been kissing anyone since he'd embroiled himself with Empyrean Vineyards and the Dashiell sisters.

Since, according to Esther, he'd become obsessed with Evangeline.

He hardly thought he was obsessed, unless you counted thinking about someone nearly nonstop and dreaming about them every night. It wasn't obsession, it was fascination. A preoccupation. Esther was very dramatic, giving him some song and dance about how she might be the one.

The One.

Which was absurd. The minute he and his cousins, the rest of the Seven Deadly Sins, had had that weird collective fever dream with the gargoyles, everyone had lost their minds. Esther had either been on the phone with Wrath's gargoyle, Jebediah, or texting him during every free moment. Frankly, there'd been a lot of free moments since Ash had also not been hosting overnight guests that she needed to oust. He'd obviously also freed up the time she would have been endeavoring to return "forgotten" clothing. So now she kept staring at him with squinty eyes and noting Ash's "symptoms."

But the kiss.

That kiss could begin to sway him that Eva really was the one. He hadn't even thought of kissing her in the cellar. Well, that was a lie. He thought about it all the time, but he hadn't thought of actually trying to do it. There had been no plan. The countless times he'd tried to push her with Lust hadn't worked and he'd kinda stopped trying—at least supernaturally.

Then she was actually talking to him about a partnership, not yelling at him, not stomping away. She asked questions that led him to believe she was considering the possibility. By some sort of voodoo, he was holding her hand and then she was in him arms.

Asher had felt the air around him still and grow heavy, giving him a sense of pulling downward. When his lips touched hers, it was rapturous. For the first time in his life, he felt an emotion during a sensual joining. Something euphoric stirring in his soul instead of the base stirring of his dick. He wanted this feeling to never end, and he chased it deeper into the kiss.

Eva felt it too, at least he thought she did. He could sense her anger and fear melting away to be replaced with intoxication on whatever chemistry they floated in. They were on fire. Everywhere she touched him, every breath, every stoke of his tongue on hers brought palpable heat. His feet were burning in his boots, so he lifted her to the barrels to save her. He needed her desperately. Their brief connection had given him a glimpse of everything he'd been missing in every single other encounter of his life. What he'd thought had been passion was plainly only lust. That was the comical truth of his whole life. Lust had been his driving force, but to learn now, in the grand scheme of things, his previous feelings had been nothing significant all along, was overwhelming.

Their kiss was crazy, irresistible, exhilarating. He could have taken her on the spot if he'd let their passion run its course, but some sanity pierced that bubble, and he pulled back before the emotions swamped him and he blew his wad in his pants.

He'd held her in the circle of his arms and gasped for breath and hoped for clarity, for some kind of explanation of what had just happened.

Gob smacked. What was happening to him? For fuck's sake, tears pricked the back of his eyes, and he blinked them away. The sensations were too much and he wanted to pull back, but at the same time he clutched her closer. He wanted to finish what they'd started, just not against an oak barrel full of last year's chardonnay. He should talk to Esther about this because if anyone knew what the hell was happening to him, she would. But she would likely take it too far and start talking about omens and signs and bullshit, and all he wanted to know was whether he was having a heart attack. It wasn't possible for him to die before the next ceremony and he had a little over a decade before that happened, but it felt like he had a brain tumor or something.

Caught up inside his own head, he'd followed Eva out of the cellar and into the fresh air which would hopefully clear out his fog. In the span of seconds, she agreed to partner with him and his car was destroyed.

He goggled at the site of the wreckage. The roof of the monastery had literally separated from the building in one giant section, had hovered over his car for a moment, before falling directly downward on top of it. As if a giant hand had reached out of Heaven to cause him grief.

He tore his gaze away from the mess and stared up at the sky, half expecting to see an archangel or maybe actual God frowning down at him. Was he being punished? Just who the hell was Evangeline Dashiell? His gaze flipped back to Eva who was still gaping at the mess with her mouth hanging open. He'd thought she was human, but maybe she wasn't. Maybe she was some sort of angelic being that God would not like consorting with the Devil? Had he inadvertently fucked this up for all mankind?

"I... I... Wow, umm..." She sputtered. "Holy cow."

He blinked at her, trying to see beyond her façade to what could be underneath.

"I don't even know what to say," she continued. "Are you insured?" She barked out a nervous laugh and immediately rolled her lips to squelch a smile.

He turned back to the wreckage, still unable to form words. What had he done?

Across the expanse of the lawn, Maggie emerged from the building to stare at the pile of debris and then up at the roof and then back to the pile.

"What the hell was that?" Ernie called from outside one of the work sheds further across the fields. He broke into a panicky run, surely expecting that someone must be dead or injured.

That realization finally snapped Ashe out of his fugue, and he realized the bigger picture. "Oh shit, the roof!"

"'Oh shit' seems to cover it," Eva agreed with an unbelieving shake to her head.

"Is anyone in there?" He started a jog across the lawn, Eva following closely behind him. "Someone could have been killed."

Eva pointed out her sister as they jogged. "Maggie's alright and looks like Ernie's okay. No one else is in there. Jeez, that whole side is just...gone."

Ashe paused only briefly at the site of the Aston Martin's murder before joining the sisters and Ernie to stare up at the gaping hole in the roof of the building. Ernie stood there, slack-jawed and blinking, his arms hanging limp at his sides. Maggie had both of her hands over her nose and mouth as if trying to hold in a scream or keep in the hyperventilating. Every so often a muffled, "Oh my God," came from her direction.

Eva on the other hand, seemed to have tipped over into hysteria. It started as a laugh that just sort of burst out of her. And another. Followed by a snort which set off a whole stream of giggles that shook her entire body. Asher crossed his arms and furrowed his brow and starred at her.

"What's so damn funny?" Maggie demanded. "What the hell are we going to do now? There is no money for this." Maggie gestured wildly at the gaping hole in their roof. "Where are we going to live?"

Eva shrugged and laughed harder. She barely got out the words, "I don't know."

Ernie looked at Asher and wordlessly asked if he knew what was wrong with Eva, but Ashe just shrugged.

"And sweet lord, look at your car," Maggie wailed and pointed with a shaky finger. "Our insurance will probably cover it. Oh, my God, I'm so sorry, Mr. Mephisto."

"I'm Mr. Mephisto again?" Ashe rolled his eyes at the affront. "Your building assassinates my car and you insult me by acting like we're not even friends."

Eva erupted with another round of hysterical laughter. All three of their heads swiveled in her direction to watch for a second. Eva waved her hand in front of her, completely unable to form words. She was turning red and Asher was actually concerned that she might not be able to breathe.

Maggie turned back to Asher, her expression pure agony. "That's not what I meant. I'm just so sorry."

Asher turned his back on the car, too disgusted to look at it anymore. "Don't worry about it now. It's not like we can revive it with CPR. We need to do something about this roof before the rain comes."

As one, all four of them—even the still giggling Eva—tilted their faces to the sky. The clouds still hung low, but they didn't seem as ominous as they had only ten minutes before. And the wind that had been so destructive and threatening was nearly nonexistent now. As if the weather was controlled by sorcery. Or Heaven.

Asher whirled on Eva. "Who are you?" he demanded.

His anger hit her like a reset button and the giggles halted immediately. "What do you mean?" she asked.

"You know what I mean." He wagged his index finger of ire between the sisters. "Who are you two?"

Maggie and Eva looked at each other before turning their attention back to Asher. Eva spoke for both of them. "We are now homeless, surely soon to be bankrupt, miserable failures who have disappointed their entire family tree. We did not ruin your car on purpose." She narrowed her eyes at him. "Maybe you could focus on the fact that this—" she waved her arms wide "—isn't all about you"

Asher very dramatically pointed to the Aston Martin. "Really? Not at all?"

"Well, obviously some of it is about you," Maggie slapped Eva's shoulder.

Ernie clapped his hands together three times. "Hey! It's about all of you, okay? Look, it's gonna rain eventually, and we need to cover this hole. Maggie, where do you have the insurance paperwork?"

With that call to action, Maggie went into the office, which was mostly unharmed by the freak windstorm, to locate the insurance information and Ernie left in the truck to check the vines. While Eva walked around assessing the damage, Asher pulled out his cell phone. He kept an eye on her as he waited for Esther to answer the phone.

"My liege," Esther purred into the phone.

"Not in the mood today," he told her. "When you were out here at the Empyrean, did you notice anything?"

There was a pause. "You're going to have to be more specific."

"You know." Asher grasped at what he was trying to ask, but he really didn't know. "Besides the ghosts, was there anything...weird."

Esther snorted. "Specificity is your friend here, Asher. What are you asking me?"

"Are the sisters..." He hesitated. It sounded sort of insane when he tried to say it out loud. But then again, what had just happened was insane. "Do you think they are preternatural?"

"I do not. Totally human." Esther was not indecisive in her reply. "Why do you think this?"

"Some very weird shit went down here today." He walked diagonally across the lawn so as to keep Eva in his eyeline while she continued her inspection. "I don't know what to think. It's crazy shit. Or maybe I'm going crazy."

"Are you willing to tell me what happened, or do I have to guess?"

Eva was heading back his way, her expression grim. He signaled he was on his cell, so she diverted towards the wine cellar. He tracked her with his eyes, searching her departing form for some sign that she was otherworldly.

"There was a freak storm here. Like, out of nowhere the wind ripped the roof right off the monastery and crushed the Aston Martin." Esther gasped. "Then the storm just stopped. Nothing else is damaged. Not even tree limbs are down and, from what we can tell, the vines all look fine."

"Is she totalled?" Esther asked.

Asher looked back at his poor baby and sighed. "Oh yeah. Squashed."

"No one was hurt?"

"No," he confirmed.

Ernie and the ancient red farm truck were making their way back up the dirt road followed by a brown cloud of dust.

"So, it's a storm. I don't understand why this would make you think there was something going on with Eva and Maggie," said Esther, the interminable voice of reason.

"Because I kissed her and then BOOM," he shouted for effect.

"Kissed whom?"

"Eva

"Hmmm," Esther hummed. "Just a kiss? I don't see how those two things equate."

"It was a hell of a fucking kiss," he admitted. Truth be told, he still felt a bit tingly and wobbly from it. The object of his desire was now talking to Ernie at the driver's side door of the Ford. She glanced up and met his gaze as if she could hear what he was saying, like she, too, was a bit woozy from all that had happened in the cellar.

"Oooh." Ester's voice oozed knowingly.

"Stop it. I'm serious." He dropped his eyes to his toes and lowered his voice. "I've never... There has never been... I'm just saying..."

"Uh huh." He could hear the smugness of Esther's smile over the line.

"What if she's an angel or something and God doesn't want Devil spawn kissing her?"

Esther chuckled. "That's not a thing."

"Oh, really." All the Sins hated how their gargoyles seemed to always know so much more than they did. "How would you know? All kinds of things could be happening out there that you don't know about."

"I would have heard some chatter if that were the case. I've already told you my theory."

"Right." The *one*. "But that doesn't explain this weird storm taking out my car."

"Yeah," Esther conceded. "I wonder if that was the ghosts. I'll know for sure when I get out there. I'm on my way."

"Okay, thanks. I'm calling Luke next. We'll need that roof fixed and we might as well get the remodel underway now. Oh, that reminds me, bring the contract and my laptop. Eva finally gave me the go ahead."

"Was that before or after the kiss?"

"I don't even know," he admitted.

Chapter Ten

Esther was coming and bringing the cavalry with her. Ashe's cousin Luke, the architect, also answered his call and would be arriving soon. Ernie had left for town to buy rolls of plastic to cover the hole in the roof. Maggie was on hold with the insurance company.

Asher lingered at the site of the murder of his car. He should call his insurance agent, but all of the paperwork was in the glove box and the glove box was under hundreds of pounds of roof. He grimaced, not relishing the thought of getting filthy to exhume her. He'd wait until Esther got here. She'd take care of it.

Eva came around the corner and stood next to him. She gave a deep sigh before placing her hand on his shoulder. "She had a good run."

Ashe snorted. "But she had so much more life to live."

"A very wise man once said, 'Only the good die young.'" Eva eyed him with mock sadness. "Seriously, though, I am really very sorry about this. And I'm sorry about all the laughing. I was just so...stunned."

He shook his head as a way of accepting her sentiments, but without quoting Billy Joel lyrics. After a long pause, he turned away from the rubble. "Now what?"

Eva started across the lawn towards the door to the residence portion of the monastery. "I'm going in. I need to see how bad it is."

"No, don't go in there," he protested. "Let the professionals do it when they get here."

She glared over her shoulder, but she didn't stop walking. "You mean the men."

"No. The professionals could be women or chimpanzees, for all I care." Quite possibly demons if Esther has any say in hiring the work crews. "It's dangerous in there."

She rolled her eyes at him but kept eating up the lawn with purposeful strides.

"All right then." He caught up with her and used his most authoritative voice. "As your business partner, I forbid it."

Her response was to throw her head back and laugh, which frankly was a better response than he had hoped for. He hadn't expected such highhandedness to actually work. He'd hoped by the time she got through yelling at him, Luke would have arrived and Eva would listen to him. Luke was scary.

Eva stopped walking so abruptly that Asher passed her and had to backtrack two strides. "Look here, you," she said. "Just because you have the money to rescue us—and just because you're the sexiest thing to breathe air—does not mean you get to tell me what to do."

Wait, what? "You think I'm sexy?"

She rolled her eyes again. "Oh, for God's sake." She set off across the grass again.

He paused long enough to grin madly at her back before he ran to catch up to her. "I'm coming with you." He knew he'd never be able to stop her.

"I'll be fine," she said,

"You can't go in there alone."

"Sure, I can. I'm a big girl. This is my house."

"That is clearly falling apart at the seams." He put his hand against the door to keep her from pulling it open.

She scoffed. "It's made of stone. This building isn't going anywhere."

"Tell that to the Aston Martin. No, seriously. Who knows how much damage the top floors have sustained? You saw how easily the roof just rolled off like some sort of celestial can opener went at it."

"Look, I need to know how bad it is. This is more than just my business we're talking about." She gave him a placating smile. "Nothing's going to happen to me."

"You can't possibly know that. Who knows what catastrophe could befall you in there? The ceiling could collapse. Or another freak storm could whip up and shatter all the windows."

Her eyes grew wide in mock horror. "Or a gaping hole could open up in the floor and suck us all down to hell."

He grabbed her wrist and stared into her eyes. "Why would you say that? That's not even funny. Don't joke about that kind of thing."

She pulled free. "Mm-kay. That's not at all weird." She gave him a look and pulled open the door. "Come with me if you want."

As it turned out, no catastrophes occurred. In fact, it was difficult to tell anything was wrong until you got to the second floor where the family apartments were located. They walked into the first bedroom at the top of the stairs to find visible sky shining through the ceiling, through the attic and to the outside.

"Oh, man," she moaned and dropped her head backwards to stare upwards. "I can't believe this."

"Well, that's bad," he said, noting the obvious. He let his eyes skim the trinkets on the dresser. "Is this your room?"

"Yeah." Her hands rested on her hips while she continued to stare at the sky through the enormous gap in the ceiling directly over her bed.

"At least it didn't rain." He nudged her with his elbow. "It's kinda crazy that there isn't more mess in here, though, don't you think? A hole that big, you'd expect debris and stuff, wouldn't you?"

Eva scanned the room. "Yeah. Be right back."

While she was out of the room, Asher reverted to sixteen and scoped out her room. It was mostly tidy. A hamper stood in the corner by what he assumed was the closet. The teenager in him spied a pink bra dangling over the side. He went closer to her dresser to look at the picture framed in silver. A slightly younger Eva and an older man laughed out at him. They both wore straw hats and Ash recognized the grape fields in the background. Her grandfather, he presumed. Another showed an even younger Eva and Maggie with two other women. The age gap and resemblance suggested their mother and grandmother.

He sniffed her perfume bottle, and the scent went straight to his cock. The flotsam of a lifetime lived in the same bedroom that surrounded him. Besides the womanly effects of bras and perfume, there were also a few stuffed animals—a teddy bear and what was probably once a pink unicorn were nestled in a patchwork upholstered chair, giving evidence a little girl had lived here, too. A bookcase crammed with paperback novels sat under the window.

The covers were pulled up neatly on the queen-size bed. He wondered if it had been added as an adult. A child with a queen-size bed seemed odd, but what did he know. His knowledge of raising children was exactly nil. He lifted a pillow to his face and deeply inhaled. The unmistakable scent of Evangeline filled his head: that perfume from the dresser, her shampoo, and wildness from working outside. He breathed in again, filling his lungs.

When he pulled the pillow away from his face, Eva was watching him from the doorway, wearing a bemused expression.

"What are you doing?" she asked, a smile playing around her lips.

He tossed the pillow back on the bed and strode towards her. "Thinking about you. In this bed." He slipped his arms around her waist. "And I'm still thinking about that kiss."

"It was a hell of a kiss." She agreed and circled her arms around his neck.

Asher slid his nose along the nape of her neck and smelled her skin and hair. "That pillow smells exactly like you."

"I hope so." Eva tilted her neck to the left giving him better access.

"I'd like to circle back to your earlier statement." He nibbled her earlobe.

"Huh?"

He kissed down her neck, tilting her head backwards with a thumb to her chin, and settled his lips briefly into the divot of her throat. He spoke breathy words against her skin. "You said I was sexy. 'The sexiest thing to breath air,' you said."

"Mm hum." She hummed.

With both of her palms on his cheeks, she tried to maneuver him to her lips for a kiss, but he evaded her. He wanted her lips free to answer his question.

"How long?" He kissed her chin.

"How long what?" She sounded frustrated. He kissed the corner of her mouth and chuckled.

"Have you thought that?" His mouth was a hair's breadth away from her lips. He could feel the energy coming off them.

She pulled back far enough where they could focus on each other. "I don't know. Since the first day, I guess."

Since the first day? That didn't make sense. Why had she been so distant? Angry? Mean? He didn't understand. If she'd been attracted from the start, then it had to have been Lust that caught her attention. But, if that was so, why wasn't she affected by his push? None of this was making any sense.

"What difference does it make. Stop thinking and kiss me." Her lips met his with determination and it was only an instant before Asher's mind was swept clean and he wasn't able to think anymore at all.

Eva's fingers tangled in his hair, tugging with delicious urgency. Arms still around her waist, it was two steps before he had her back against the wall. He filled his hand with an ass cheek and pressed his body against the length of hers. Eva gasped, a throaty, needy sound that made him desperate to touch her skin. She must have needed the contact, too, because her hands slipped underneath his shirt sliding up his belly, leaving a trail of fire in their wake. His free hand cupped her breast only to have Eva arch her back to press tighter against him. His hips moved against her pelvis, anticipating the rhythm they both needed.

Her bed was mere feet away. If he could just—

Like before with the barrels, he scooped her up and she wrapped her legs around him. He knew the way to the bed by memory or instinct or by divine guidance. Or, more likely, the devil showed him the way.

Eva's lips crashed down against his again, her tongue gliding across his, her fingernails scraping across his bare back. His cock thrummed to be set fee.

"Guess what those bastards at the insurance company said," Maggie's voice boomed up the staircase.

Eva reared her head back and wiggled to be released. Her toes met the floor just as Maggie's footfalls hit the upstairs landing. Asher whirled away from the door and righted his shirt over his stomach. Thrusting his chin to the sky, he looked out the hole in the ceiling as if it was the most perplexing thing in the world.

"What's going on in here?" Maggie asked.

Any fool would be able to tell something was up. He was still panting and was certain Eva was doing the same. Their hair was ruffled and their faces flushed. The only thing missing was the smell of sex, and that was only because she was seconds too early.

"Look at this hole," Eva pointed at the ceiling. Or lack of ceiling.

Maggie took a moment before responding, giving them both the eye before tilting her own face upward. "Guess what the insurance company said. Just guess. I don't know why we've been paying insurance premiums for all these years."

"What did they say?" Eva asked, pulling her hair back and smoothing it down.

"They're sending an adjuster out right away, but the jerk on the phone mentioned acts of God. Can you believe that shit?"

Asher snorted. "Yeah. That sounds about right."

Eva pointed to the sky. "The hole is this big in your room, too. We haven't even been up to the attic yet to see what that looks like."

Maggie craned her neck to see past the limits of ceiling in the bedroom to the attic roof. "Well, based on how much blew off, it can't be good. Who knows what the trusses look like up there. We should wait to go up, though, until—"

"That's what I said," Asher gave Eva a pointed look. "My cousin will be here shortly. He's the architect and he'll know what do next."

Eva threw up her hands and spun on her heel. "You people are such chickens."

Ashe looked to Maggie for some sort of answer why her sister was so difficult. "I just don't want you to get hurt."

The two of them followed Eva to the doorway that led to the attic stairs. Short of tackling her on the ancient carpet in the hall, there was no way to stop her. It took both hands on the doorknob and some considerable yanking for Eva to get the door to open, which Ashe certainly thought was an omen of things ahead. A flood of light poured down the staircase.

"I don't remember there being dormer windows up there," he said to the sisters.

Maggie clucked her tongue. "They were very recent installments."

Eva snorted with laughter. "Our contractor was An Act of God."

The roof over the attic had been rolled back like an old sardines can from a cartoon. The section over the family bedrooms gaped through sections of the attic floor, and when Ashe approached on gentle feet, he could clearly see Eva's bed. The contents held in storage were exposed to the elements and scattered about. How nothing had fallen through the holes to the quarters below was unfathomable.

"Wow, this is so much worse than I thought," Maggie sounded close to tears.

Eva clasped her sister's hand in both of hers. "Yeah, but it's going to be okay. Don't panic. We'll make it better than it was before."

Asher approached the edge of the hole where he could peek around to the front of the building. Except for the spectacular disaster of his car, the yard was spotless. "I just can't get over the fact that there's no real debris. Where are the branches and leaves and stuff? It's like, literally, the only thing that blew was the roof."

"And some of the attic," Maggie added. "And the ceiling plaster."

"Yeah," Eva agreed. "There's nothing in here but two hundred years of dust and old furniture."

The hole also gave a clear view of the road and the little parade of calvary that was zooming to his rescue: Luke in his classic hotrod, his gargoyle, Jeb, following behind in his Mercedes Cabriolet convertible, Esther in her black

Porsche bringing up the rear, and Ernie in the vineyard pickup back from town.

Asher clapped his hands together. Thank God Luke was here. Now he was going to get some damn answers.

Heaven XV

N eil's chest burned. He'd been running through the warren of corridors in the dungeon as if the monster was on his heels. It probably wasn't. Probably still snacking on the goblin guard it snatched instead of him, but it was a good idea to keep up the pace at least until he got outside.

At the next juncture he took the corridor to the left, the decision made because there was a torch on the wall in the distance and he could at least see the floor and walls where he was running. Quickly, this corridor opened into a spacious room acting as a juncture for four new hallways.

For fuck's sake, was there no way out of here?

He stood in the middle for a long moment, wheezing, hands on his knees and waiting for his breath to catch up to him. After several minutes he righted himself and surveyed the options. He sidled up to the first passage and squinted into the grayness. He sniffed and didn't detect anything repugnant, but that didn't necessarily mean anything. No noises, either. He sucked on his teeth in contemplation but moved on to the next option.

The second hallway was ruled out immediately when he paused in front of the threshold and a shrill scream emanated from somewhere deep inside.

Moving quickly to the third option, he noted with dismay that there was a hard turn about forty feet in, effectively slamming shut any opportunity for reconnaissance. But still, there was something familiar about it. The stonework and dirt making up the walls was exactly the same as every other wall in the dungeon, but something tickled at the back of his mind. In life, Neil had firmly believed in following hunches to see where they went. Sometimes that ended badly—case in point, he was in Hell—but that tickle was persistent, so without a backward glance, he strode into option three. He paused at the dogleg turn and poked his head around the corner. It just seemed prudent, tickle or no. The air down there was certainly more humid. Was that a good sign?

Even more upsetting, there was another sharp turn just ahead.

He rumbled off a stream of curses, but ventured forward, putting faith in the tickle. Once again, he peered around the corner. The only thing between him and another cursed turn in the corridor was a fat sewer rat.

Rats he wasn't afraid of. It scurried forward ahead of him, something Neil considered a good sign. The rat wasn't stupid enough to run straight into danger, was he? He followed the squeaky tour guide around eight or nine more right angles and then, suddenly, a massive wood and iron door stood ajar before him.

The rat scurried through the gap. The tickle was a full-on scratch now, so Neil threw caution to the wind and followed him.

Son of a bitch. The outside stretched before him. Acreage of sulfurous lake as far as the eye could see.

"Thanks, buddy," he told the rat, before it ran off around the side of the building.

The stench was magnificent, rolling off the fetid lake in putrid clouds. He didn't remember this scenery when he got off the elevator at the Devil's Mansion, but Hell was squirrely like that. Actually, it was impossible to tell if he was even on the same level, there had been so many rises and stairs and ramps as he wound his through the dungeon.

He moved as close to the water's edge as he could get before his eyes started watering. He looked for that sweet spot between the caustic water and what could be lurking in the depths, and the wide-open steppes outside the dungeon where he was on display to all the denizens of Hell. He needed to move away from the dungeon and any platoons of gremlin guards who were out to find him and drag him back inside. No matter that the Duke of Nine had set him free. Gremlins were greedy idiots, and once they got something in their mind, they held on to it like a crackhead and his pipe.

He kept to a slow jog, this time. Unlike the dungeon when he had no idea how far he had to go and no idea where the monsters were in the darkness, out here he could visually follow the beach around the lake for miles.

And miles. And miles.

In theory, he could also see anything approaching him, so there wasn't the fear of a sneak attack or stumbling upon something that wanted to eat him.

Nevertheless, there was an urgency pushing him on. Juliet was coming, and he was terrified of her encountering anything Hellish. Or of anything Hellish encountering her.

So, he pressed on. At some point during the circumnavigation of the lake, he was bound to encounter the elevator platform and from there it would be short work to trade Charon something on his person to take him up to the top level. Though, he was quickly running out of valuable trade items.

He looked over his shoulder and was pleased to see how far he'd run from the dungeon. He relaxed his shoulders and shook out his arms and hands.

"So, Neil, what's the game plan? And here I am talking to myself again." He moved his head from side to side as if he was more than one person. "You're excellent company, Neil. Why thank you, Neil."

A small splash of water caught his attention out of the corner of his eye. He gave the lake a quick once over but didn't see anything besides a vast expanse of toxic water and a fire or two on the surface. You know, a very standard Hellscape.

"Back to the plan. What are we going to do? Besides obviously get the fuck off of this level."

This time he heard the splash rather than saw it. It gave him pause. Again, he saw no evidence, except for the concentric rings rippling outward caused when something large disturbed the water. Neil stopped and turned to face the lake, narrowing his eyes and staring out over the deceptively placid water. He couldn't see anything, but who knew how deep that lake went and what sort of hellish monsters thrived in the pestilent waters.

Regardless of what was in there, he needed to get off this level A.S.A. fucking P., so he needed to make tracks. Still, in deference to the unknown, he moved a little further from the water. He gave it two long beats, then returned to his trek—but this time at a faster pace.

"All right, listen up, Neil. Juliet is going to get to the meeting spot before you and that means your sweet little angel is going to be all alone in there. Something horrible is going to find her and that will be all your fault for screwing around down here."

The splash was bigger this time and Neil knew if he turned around to look it would be more than just ripples of water.

"Quick feet, dude," Neil encouraged and broke into a run. It never occurred to him that whatever was in the water was benign. Nothing in Hell was benign. Literally everything in Hell was out to get you.

Running full out, he angled his trajectory further away from the water line and more towards the open tundra-like flatland. By his estimation, he'd made it a little less than halfway around the lake. The dungeon had receded into the background and, with the exception of an ominous mountain in the foreground, there wasn't much by way of scenery. Low prickly grass covered the ground with intermittent sticker bushes and nasty clumps of nettles spaced just close enough together to make running through them a steeplechase.

"Where is that damn elevator?" The sulfurous air made his lungs burn worse than unusual. If there was ever an opportunity to chat up his younger self, he'd make sure to tell that punk to stop smoking. And maybe get some more cardio in.

The splash was alarmingly close this time with water droplets landing near his feet and sizzling on the dead grass. He yelped and dodged to the left, running through a sticker bush that yanked at his pants leg.

He considered climbing back up to the steppes and away from the lake but changed his mind when a quick glance revealed a garrison of trolls camped out on the ridge above him. So far, they hadn't noticed him, but they surely would if he got any closer. Back down to the packed, silty beach, he pumped his legs and swung his arms as if he was racing in the Olympics.

"Run, you fucker, run," he chanted over and over, adrenaline rushing through him till it felt like his heart would burst.

When the tentacle grabbed his foot, he faceplanted, hard. It was so unexpected his body didn't have the chance to get his hands out in front of him to stop the forward momentum. He flipped over on his back and kicked at the long squid-like arm while it dragged him towards the water. About ten feet out he could see a whole bunch of arms waving out of the water—not sure how many, but it was way more than the expected eight. He scrabbled at the ground, groping for anything to anchor him to shore, but there was only dirt and worthless clumps of dead grass.

"Let go. Let go. LET GO." He kicked as hard as he could while pulling back on the captured leg. He tried wedging the toe of his boot against the dinner plate sized suckers and peeling them back, but no luck.

"Help!" he screamed but he didn't know who would show up to do that. No one, that's who. The only person he had on his side was a sweet, beautiful angel he was never going to see again.

The roiling water was only a few feet away now. As the terrible creature splashed its massive arms, singeing droplets landed on Neil's chest and neck, making holes in his shirt and burning his skin. Another massive tentacle landed on the ground next to him. He was able to push the inky black arm away from him with his free foot before he went back to chopping at the one holding him captive.

"You bastard!" he screamed. With a massive grunt, he yanked his foot free of his boot. In a flash, he scrambled backwards like a crab, one foot booted and the other in only a sock.

With a horrific, angry scream, the creature lifted Neil's empty leather boot high in the air, held in the curled end of a massive, black-speckled arm. The splashing just offshore upgraded to churning, frothy soup with the monster's arms writhing in fury.

Neil got to his feet and ran through the pricker bushes like a freight train doing a serpentine pattern. He had no idea how far the reach was on that abomination, but he knew he stood a better chance if he was further away and unpredictable. Of course, all the commotion attracted the attention of the trolls and there was a line of them running an intercept pattern. He turned back towards the water, risking his own danger in the hopes that he would also lure the dimwitted trolls to the—what was that fucking thing?

Lungs on fire, fresh acid burns on his exposed skin, and one bloody foot, Neil kept up the pace and was gratified to see the elevator platform appear as he came over a rise. With an earth- trembling thump, a colossal, sucker-covered arm landed in front of him. He hurdled it and kept running the zigzag pattern.

"Charon!" he screamed. "Open the doors."

A troll flew over his head with a slimy tentacle around his neck. The battle axe dangling from its hand nicked Neil's ear as it passed.

"Charon!" Neil used all the air left in his lungs to catch the attention of the elevator operator. "Open the fucking door."

Neil was only twenty yards away when Charon finally lifted his head and acknowledged the urgency of the situation. "What do you have to offer?"

"Anything!" Neil screamed. "I'll give you anything you want."

He didn't have much left so whatever Charon wanted was going to hurt. Or he could be digested for an eternity by an honest to God Kraken living in a sulfurous lake. Neil ducked another swipe from the battle axe. That troll had some stamina considering the sea monster was actively choking it while swinging it around like a rag doll. The rest of the trolls were closing in on Neil, their rattletrap armor clanging louder and nearer.

"I want the phone." Charon demanded, the doors to the elevator still maddeningly closed.

"Fine. Fine," Neil screamed and put on an unlikely burst of speed. "Just open the damn door before this thing gets me, or you get nothing."

Charon opened the door and Neil leapt to the platform, sliding into the elevator on one bloody sock. He turned with his back to the wall and watched in fascinated horror as the monster dropped the screeching troll into its gaping maw.

Just before the doors slid shut, Neil's lost boot whizzed through the gap and hit him right in the forehead.

Chapter Eleven

Four cars converged in the monastery parking lot at the same time. Esther unfolded herself out of a sporty black Porsche and joined with a smaller, very pretty young man. They headed over to the Aston Martin, clucking in dismay like two hens. Ernie continued through the parking area in the vineyard's old Ford and followed the unofficial lane to the side of the monastery.

Asher, the man who until fifteen minutes ago had been passionately kissing Eva as if his life depended on it, threw his arms around a cute young woman who'd emerged from the passenger side of a classic muscle car. He hugged her tight while swinging her in a quick circle. "Mia, you gorgeous thing!" he exclaimed.

"Mia" giggled and swatted at his shoulder, but the woman certainly seemed pleased to see him, too. "Hey, hot stuff. You here causing trouble?"

Eva was disgusted by her body's visceral jealous reaction and swallowed hard, clenched her jaw, and exhaled through her nose. *Don't be stupid,* she told herself. *You always knew he was a flirt and philanderer, what the hell did you expect? In truth, you're the one with the desperate kisses.*

"Always," Asher said with a grin. He put her back on her feet and planted a soft kiss on her cheek.

Eva disliked her on sight.

"Get your bloody hands off my wife." This was said in a low, menacing growl that set Eva's fight or flight instinct on alert. The speaker was a very tall, very broad, very handsome man who stalked towards Asher with brutal intent.

As annoyed as Eva was with Asher, she didn't want to see him hurt, that was unless she was doing it. She took a step forward considering if she should intervene, not even knowing if it was possible to stop that huge man from anything. Asher clearly had no sense of self-preservation. He looked the giant in the eye, gave a brilliant smile, then wrapped an arm around the woman, tucking her in tight next to his side.

"Mia, I'd love you to meet the ladies of Empyrean Vineyards." Asher steered Mia towards Eva and Maggie, who was also watching the drama unfold with rapt attention. The huge, angry man followed closely behind. "This is the business mind behind the label, Magdalena Dashiell."

Mia extended her hand with a friendly smile. "So nice to meet you. I'm already a fan of your wine."

"How nice of you to say," Maggie smiled back, and they shook hands. "Please call me Maggie."

"And this fetching beauty," Asher said, meeting Eva's gaze, "is Evangeline Dashiell, the exceptional mind behind the wine."

Eva rolled her eyes at the complement, but inside she glowed. "Hello," she said with a nod.

Asher finished the introductions. "Eva, Maggie, this is Mia, my cousin-in-law. She's a genius with plants, absolutely brilliant biologist who's done miracles with apples."

"Oh?" Eva's gaze flipped back to Mia with interest. The woman was considerably shorter than herself, but Eva was taller than most. She wore boyfriend cut jeans, loose and soft and cuffed at the ankle with an old pair of canvas sneakers. Daisy Duck smiled coquettishly from her pink tee-shirt. She was exceptionally pretty but didn't use it in an intimidating way. Eva felt herself warming to the woman.

"We're not married yet," Mia divulged as a clarification.

Asher continued, "And this wrathful bastard is my cousin and her soulmate, Luke Mephisto. He's not much to look at, but he is a talented architect and I've brought him to help with all our plans."

The scary man gave Asher a withering look of annoyance, but when he turned his attention to Eva and Maggie, the threatening expression was gone. Instantly, the forbidding aspect softened to a pleasant expression and the bestial quality totally vanished when he smiled.

"Hello," he said, ignoring his cousin completely. He tossed his head over to the pile of rubble at the side of the monastery. Esther and her friend were staring up at the gaping hole and gesturing. "So, you've had a bit of weather?"

"I'll say," Maggie agreed. "Craziest damn thing."

Maggie and Luke turned towards the building, already chatting about repairs and God knows what. When Eva turned back to Asher and Mia, she found the woman gazing at her curiously.

Mia extricated herself from Asher and crooked her arm through Eva's. "Would you mind terribly showing me your fields? Or would you feel better staying here to discuss the details of the repairs?"

Despite her initial kneejerk reaction, Eva thought she was going to like her, regardless of the greeting she'd received from Asher. Mia's smile was straight forward and friendly. She didn't get any mean-girl vibe from her at all. "I'm sure Maggie and Asher have this." She turned them towards the eastern vines, leaving Asher to do whatever Asher did when not following Eva around and pestering her. "Anything special you want to see?"

"I'm fascinated with what techniques you use. I'm not really familiar with grapes, necessarily," Mia explained. "I'm an apple detective—"

"No!," Eva exclaimed. "Really? That's so fascinating. I'd heard about someone who'd found a whole grove of Pensley's Jewels in the Puget Sound area. My grandma would wax poetic about the applesauce they'd make when she was a kid. I picked a few up at the farmer's market last winter, and they were everything she said they were."

Mia grinned from ear to ear. "That was me. I found that old grove in the woods when I was on a camping expedition."

"Shut up." Eva came to a stop, dragging Mia with her. "That's so awesome. You're sort of famous then."

Mia chortled. "Only in the apple community which, let's be honest, is a very specific subset of weirdos."

"Whatever." Eva continued them on the pathway to the chardonnay vines. "There was a write-up in the paper and everything."

"Okay, but it's not like *People* magazine is doing an exposé or CNN invites me to chat up John King about my discovery. Most people have no idea apple detecting is even a thing."

"I love John King," Eva confessed. "I would totally snuggle up in bed with him and tell him all about grafting grape vines."

That elicited a giggle from both of them.

"Aren't smart men the hottest?" Mia nudged her with an elbow.

Eva thought of Asher with his dark hair and smoky eyes and outstanding ass. He was also no dummy as evidenced by the international conglomeration of investments he ran. Having a conversation with him was stimulating and exciting in ways that didn't always start in her pants. Clever and witty all wrapped up in that beautiful package.

"The Mephisto cousins are a lot." They stood at the top of the first row of Chardonnay. Mia clasped a grape leaf between her fingers and rubbed gently. "But, every damn one of them is hot as sin." She laughed as if it was an inside joke. "That's funny," she said as an aside to herself.

Eva lifted a cluster of grapes in her palm and weighed the heft. "How many cousins are there?"

Mia was squatting now, looking underneath the vine's canopy. "Seven. All gorgeous and smart and totally fucked up."

Oh, that boded well, Eva thought with an internal eyeroll. *What have we gotten ourselves into?* "Then why are you with Luke?"

Mia rose from her crouch and sighed. "Well, you've seen him, right? That's what started the whole thing. Six-foot-four of luscious muscles and crabbiness, the worst attitude you've ever seen. We did nothing but fight for weeks."

Sounds familiar. "How did that evolve."

"I saw him boxing. Not boxing, I always get that wrong. Ultimate fighting, they call it."

"Like in the cage?" Eva thought back to the giant man. Yeah, she could see it.

"Exactly," Mia nodded. Her gaze drifted to the sky, and she seemed to be somewhere else for second. "He was so hot. He has some anger issues he controls with the boxing–not boxing, you know what I mean," she waved her hand dismissively. "But in the other part of his life, he's a brilliant architect. That's how we met. He designed my father's building, and I was in charge of the project. I gave him impossible demands, and he met them," she said with a shrug.

"Sounds interesting," Eva said with a smile. "Maybe perfect."

"Interesting, yes. Perfect, no, but close," Mia admitted. "Believe me, Mephisto men come with challenges you'd never believe. But when it's right, it's right." She started down the path between the vines, and Eva joined her. "So how long have you been with Ashe?"

"Oh, I'm not *with* Ashe." Was she? Did she want to be? She was going to explode if they didn't get some sexual release soon, but how much more did she want out of him? He didn't really feel like relationship material, and she certainly didn't possess the quality stuff relationships were made of. Besides, she had enough on her plate without adding a full-time man, and one that clearly would take a lot of work.

"Oh, I thought... I mean, I'd heard about you from Jeb, and I just figured since we'd never heard anything about any of Ashe's other people, you must be the one."

"The one," Eva repeated. "What do you mean, 'the one'? And who the hell is Jeb?"

Mia's eyes grew wide as if she recognized she'd stepped in a big ole pile of Oh Shit. "Jeb is Luke's Esther. You've met Esther, right? Gorgeous Amazon, little bit scary? She concierges Ashe's life. All the si– cousins have an Esther. And they all talk amongst themselves, a lot."

Eva sent an annoyed puff of air out into the world. "That's just fucking great."

"It's not bad, really. I adore Jeb."

They walked a bit in silence, but Eva could feel tension from Mia. It was obvious there was more she wanted to say.

"What did Esther say about me?" Eva prompted, not sure that she really wanted to know if it was bad.

"Esther likes you," Mia assured her, but Eva could see that she was choosing her words carefully. "The talk was really more about how much Ashe likes you. Look, I'm going to guess there's a lot you don't know about Asher and his family, and I'm definitely not the one to tell you about it." Eva went to interrupt, but Mia stopped her. "No, really. That's a conversation you need to have with him."

This sounded ominous and certainly not worth it. "Wow, alright then."

Mia pulled Eva to a stop in the middle of the row. On either side of them were parallel rows of Chardonnay stretching for rolling acres. They were far away from anyone else. In fact, they could only see the chimney of the monastery from there.

"Look, I'm not trying to scare you off. Not at all. I think Asher is one of the greatest people I know. He loves his family and is loyal to a fault. I love him like a brother. He's generous and smart and affectionate, but he doesn't affect me the way he does most everyone else. I think that's true of you, too, and that's a very significant thing you don't even understand right now. If you're having feelings for him, you should investigate them. See where they take you." Mia grabbed Eva's hand. "All that being said, when you need to talk to someone afterwards, and you will, I'll be here."

Eva blinked at her, overwhelmed and a little bit horrified. "Um, okay. This sounds like a lot more than I was bargaining for just to get laid. Now I'm not sure I even should."

Mia's eyes grew wide, and she damn near yelled, "You haven't had sex yet?"

Confirming that there was no one around to hear and be mortified, Eva shook her head. "No. Not yet. Pretty close, but not all the way. Yet."

The woman threw her head back and cackled at the sky. "Holy. Shit. Oh my God! Lust must be dying. That is so rich. I wonder if Jeb knows that."

"I'm not real crazy about everyone knowing my sex life, or lack thereof."

She regained her composure and wiped the laughter from her eyes. "Your secret is safe with me. And my offer is still good when you need someone who understands."

"I feel like I'm in Mission Impossible." Eva made her voice lower. "Your mission, should you choose to accept it, is to sleep with Asher Mephisto. It's all rather cloak and dagger."

"But, honey, I'll bet it will be worth it." Mia linked arms with her again. "Enough about sex. I have serious biology questions."

"That's what she said." Eva smirked. "Come let me show you some of my experiments."

An hour later, they were still chatting about biology and fertilizers and new irrigation systems when they crested the last hill to the main buildings. There was a small crowd gathered on the lawn and raised voices, but Eva couldn't make out the words.

Mia stopped dead in her tracks and her face was ashen. "Oh, fuck. Luke's dad is here."

Chapter Twelve

"W hat are you doing here?" Luke was seething and the words came out low and methodical.

Asher understood where his cousin was coming from. Why indeed? He couldn't understand why the Devil would show up at Empyrean for any reason other than to make things difficult for him and Luke.

The Devil's grin was slow and sly, spreading across his face until he showed his teeth. His suit was charcoal and expertly tailored. Asher knew if he slipped the lapel between his fingers, he'd find lustrous silk, probably Italian. The same with the loafers.

The Devil fooled no one with his affable tone. "Why not? It's a beautiful day topside."

Luke was clearly making an effort to hold his Wrath in check. The Devil loved to needle his son, poking at the bear. Ashe placed his hand on Luke's shoulder as a reminder he was there and that he had his back. As much as that was even possible.

Wrath closed his eyes and breathed deeply through his nose. "I have asked you repeatedly not to frighten Mia. She doesn't deserve that."

The Devil turned his head, taking in the empty lawn in a silky-smooth motion. "Is she here? Where is my beautiful girl? I'm not here for Mia, but I always love to see her."

Ashe added pressure to the hand on Luke's shoulder, silently urging him not to take the bait. "Mia is out in the fields. What can I do for you, sir?"

When the Devil turned his attention full force on Asher, his stomach dropped. He'd not spent any significant amount of time with the man since the ceremony when he, Luke and the rest of the Sins were ten and Aaron Mephisto was chosen as his generation's Devil. There'd never really been a reason before. Why now?

"Asher, my boy." The Devil raised an elegant eyebrow. When Ashe thought about this scene later, he would swear the Devil actually sniffed the air before pronouncing, "I don't know that I've ever known Lust to have blue balls before." His laugh was low and nasty. "I'm simply dying to meet the woman who has set you on a dry streak."

He wanted to deny it, but what was the point. He could lie, but the Devil would know otherwise. "Also, not here," Ashe said and forced himself to smile.

"I'll wait." The Devil said in a lazy drawl. He looked exactly like his cousin's father, Aaron Mephisto, and indeed he was once that man, but it would not do to forget, that time was over. "I've got all the time in the world."

With the kind of timing that only happened in movies, Maggie emerged out of the office door with arms full of paperwork. She took in the new addition to their group for only a moment before she juggled the papers and reached out to shake Aaron's hand.

"Hello." Aaron took her hand in both of his. "Magdalena Dashiell. Charmed."

Maggie smiled at the Devil while Ashe's pulse rate skyrocketed. Why did he know her? What the hell was happening here.

"Thank you." Maggie blushed. "I'm afraid I don't know your name."

Luke growled out an introduction before his father could muck it up. "This is my father, Aaron Mephisto."

"Very nice to meet you." She seemed almost in a trance.

"And where is your lovely sister?" The Devil drawled these words, and Asher couldn't ignore the sense they were on a roller coaster that was careening madly off the tracks.

As if bewitched, Maggie replied, "She's giving a tour of the vines, but she'll be back shortly. I'm surprised you could tell me and my sister apart. Most people can't."

The Devil's chuckle was low and conspiratorial, and Ashe didn't like the sound of it at all. The man finally relinquished her hand. "Darling, I'm not most people. There is much about you to set you apart from your sister.

"May I offer you a glass of wine?" she asked, her arms still laden down with papers and rolled-up tubes of blueprints.

"Well, this is a winery." The Devil oozed charm. "Are those plans for the monastery? Luke, take those from her, for crying out loud. You'd think I raised you to be a barbarian."

Luke narrowed his eyes at his father even more and ground down on his molars, but he relieved her of the plans she'd dug up for the old buildings. Now that her hands were empty, the Devil reclaimed one and tucked it close to his chest, the result being she was within whispering distance. With a raised eyebrow tossed over his shoulder at the Sins, the Devil turned Maggie towards the tasting room.

Asher threw Luke a panicked look. "What do we do?"

"What can we do?" Luke shrugged. "He's gonna do whatever he wants. It's best not to make a big deal about it or he'll be even worse. He's like a bratty child. He's Damien."

That did not make Asher feel better. "Maggie," he called, making an effort to keep his voice level. When she turned, he said, "Don't sell him anything."

Her eyebrows met over her nose. "Of course not. We're just tasting."

"Okay. Just don't sell him *anything*," he emphasized.

Maggie laughed. "What? Like my soul? Why are you being so weird?"

"Yes, Asher," the Devil said with a deadly smirk. "Why are you being so weird?"

Ashe couldn't allow the Devil to run off with Maggie. Even if Luke didn't think he'd hurt her, it seemed like an extraordinarily bad idea. "I'll come with—"

"No." The Devil said with finality that Asher felt powerless against.

"Ashe, we'll just be over here." Maggie indicated the patio with the *al fresco* tasting bar. "We won't go inside the building, so don't worry. We won't get hurt."

They turned their backs on Luke and Asher and he could no longer hear what the Devil was saying to her, but at least they were in visual range. If anything happened, well Ashe guessed there wasn't a damn thing he could do about it anyway.

He let his head drop backwards. "I'm going to have a heart attack. Holy shit, seriously Luke." He placed two fingers over the pulse in his wrist and then to the spot under his jaw. "My heart is going a million miles an hour. What the hell are we going to do?" He followed his cousin around the building to his car where Luke popped the trunk and tossed the rolls of plans and stacks of paper inside. "What do you suppose he wants? Is he here for us? Or Mia? He asked about Eva. What do you suppose that means?"

Luke's tone was short and gruff. Nothing new. "How the fuck should I know what he wants? Whatever it is will be bad. That's a promise. If he knows about Eva, then it's doubly bad for you. I'd be asking myself why he even knows anything about her."

Asher was definitely going to throw up. "Why? What does that mean?"

Rolling his eyes, Luke took off across the parking lot towards the rows of vines where Eva and Mia had disappeared before. Ashe tagged along. "Because he knew Mia and you know how that turned out."

Asher shook his head. He felt like he was missing something very important. "What do you mean? How did it turn out?"

"She's my... I don't know, my *one*. She loves me even though I'm Wrath. And the push doesn't work on her."

"The push doesn't work on Eva, either."

"Uh huh, that's what Esther told Jeb. You need to do some soul searching and realize what that means. There they are." Luke waved at the women and signaled for them to hurry up. "I'm taking Mia and getting the fuck out of here. I hope she didn't see him, but the look on her face tells me she did." They paused on the lawn and Luke took Ashe's arm, forcing him to look him in the eyes for what Luke said next. "I have a feeling he's here to meet Eva. As terrifying as that is, it cannot be stopped. He used to visit Mia in her dreams so there's not really anything you can do to protect her. I don't think he'll hurt her, just scare her. But she's going to need some answers, soon."

The ladies had just crested the rise to join them on the lawn. Asher searched Eva's face for—he didn't know what. His cousin's words rang in his ears. Luke and Mia falling in love had been a huge event in the lives of all the Sins. Each one of them understood their part in the family curse. Mostly, they didn't have to actively do anything. They were assigned a Sin and they embodied it. At some point they all had a son in the course of one year. It didn't matter if they were with the mother romantically or not. Until the most recent generations, it would be apt to say most times the Sin wasn't in a relationship with the mother of his child, merely a donated womb. Slowly that changed. When Luke and Mia fell hard for each other, there was a shift somewhere in the universe. The cosmos was aligning or something. All of the Sins were brought to the great cathedral where Notre Dame, the gargoyle queen, lived and they heard for the first time that perhaps the curse could be broken.

Somehow, they all had a part to play, but Asher had no idea what his role was. The instructions had been very vague. Apparently, Luke seemed to think being in love had something to do with it, but Asher wasn't in love with Eva. And Eva certainly wasn't in love with him.

And yet the Devil was here.

And he wanted to see Eva.

And that seemed like an incredibly bad idea to Asher.

Grim-faced, Luke took his lady's arm at the elbow and pulled her towards his car. "Come on, I'm getting you out of here."

"Wait." Mia dug her heels in after they'd gone only a few steps. "I'm not leaving Eva here to deal with this alone."

"Deal with what?" Eva was only steps behind Mia.

Mia wouldn't really tell her anything, would she? Ashe narrowed his eyes at Mia for a second. She caught his eye and shook her head almost imperceptibly. No, he didn't think so. There was no bigger "in" secret in the world.

Mia did the gameshow hostess move. "All of this disaster. You need all the help you can get." Luke appeared to want to cart her off caveman-style, but Mia would kick his ass and he knew it.

With a gentle arm around her waist, Asher turned Eva towards the side of the building with the gaping hole and away from the patio across the lawn where the Devil was sweet talking her sister.

Eva's shoulders sagged a bit. "Yeah, what the hell are we going to do with that."

As if summoned because there wasn't enough trouble, Esther and Jeb swung open the residence door and marched outside. They wore matching dour expressions and Jeb looked to be in his usual tizzy.

"We'd gotten them all calmed down and then this." Jeb threw up his hands.

"Gotten who calmed down?" Eva asked.

Esther's lips curved up on one side as if letting her in on a joke. "The ghosts." And then she winked.

"Ghosts." Eva just said the one word, but it incapsulated much more. All at once, she denied their existence and demanded an introduction.

"There are multitudes, darling." Jeb stepped forward. He was wearing what Asher assumed was "gardening chic": a short-sleeved plaid button-down, a pair of creased olive green Burmuda shorts, and some sort of complicated men's sandal. He also carried a straw hat with an excessively wide brim. He stuck out his hand and gave Eva a wide grin. "I'm Jebidiah, Luke's boy Friday, but please call me Jeb. Aren't you just the most resplendent, statuesque thing. Blue eyes with that dark hair, sublime."

Eva's smile made her even more beautiful. "Um, thank you."

"So, the monks ripped the roof off," Esther blurted to the rest of them in her no-nonsense way. "Apparently, they've been working up to it since Asher arrived. Pretty big deal, you know, for noncorporeal beings. Jeb and I got them calmed down before the big guy arrived. Now, though, they're in a total tizzy and will be, at least while he's here."

"What monks? Who are the monks?" Eva asked. She looked to Ashe, so he smiled vaguely and blinked at Esther to pass back the baton.

Everything about this day had him in a mild panic, from the near sex, to the supernatural destruction of his car, to the Devil showing up. He wasn't in any condition to try to explain anything to anyone.

"You've known you have ghosts, right?" Esther asked. "Funny things happening in the house, stuff like that."

Eva giggled nervously. "This is a surreal conversation."

Oh, you have no idea, Asher thought to himself. He glanced back over to the tasting patio and counted seven cats winding their way through the Devil's legs, lying on the counter, and generally basking in his glorious evil. Ashe had only ever seen one cat on this entire property and now they were legion.

Eva continued, "We've always said we have ghosts, like 'hahahaha, who moved the spoons', and I guess we believed that on a very benign level. We never believed we had ghosts like **GHOST** ghosts. How do you know?"

Jeb clasped her hand again in one of his own and patted it with the other. "Esther and I are able to chat them up." He gave a diminutive shrug and added with modest flair, "It's one of our superpowers."

It was obvious from Eva's expression that she didn't believe any of this. Why would she? This was entirely insane. His life was insane.

"Okay." She humored them. "Why monks? And why make a fuss now?"

Jeb leaned forward and whispered. "Monks because they all died in the original fire."

"Oh sure, that makes sense." Eva nodded vigorously.

"And now," Esther continued, "because they don't like Asher being here. They have some crazy idea that he's bad news."

"One hundred percent," Eva agreed. She tossed a flirty, one shouldered shrug to Asher, whose stomach fluttered in response. "I've been saying that since he first got here. But they really screwed themselves, didn't they? I mean if they didn't want him here, they certainly made that impossible by destroying the roof. Now we need his investment more desperately than before."

"They're monks," Esther explained to all of them. "Not astrophysicists. And we explained that to them. They seemed to grasp the idea, even accepting Luke was here to make the whole place better. Then the Dark Lord showed up, and all bets are off."

"Are we talking about Voldemort here? I think I've lost the thread of this conversation." Eva looked to the others for help, but all attention had swung back to Luke's father and Maggie and the multitude of cats. They were up to eleven now.

Maggie uncorked a new bottle and poured the red liquid into fresh glasses. They had several lined up already. The Devil did all the pretty and expected things: he put his nose to the glass, swirled the liquid, watched the 'legs' run down the inside. Maggie took a sip and promptly spit it on the ground. She grabbed the bottle and peered at the label before shifting to the side to look around the man to Eva. There was fear in her eyes. Ashe could see it from all the way across the lawn.

"What fresh hell is this?" Eva closed her eyes for an instant in what looked like a silent prayer. For all the good that would do her.

Maggie and the Devil were halfway across the lawn already when Asher grasped Eva's hand in a protective gesture, gently pulling her flush to his body, as if he could keep her safe from the Devil's attentions. They were followed by a clowder of twelve mewling cats.

"Eva, this wine is vinegar." Maggie thrust the bottle at her sister. "I just uncorked it and it's undrinkable."

"It can't all be that way," Eva assured her, staring at the label much the same way her sister had. "I uncorked one yesterday that was just fine."

The Devil, however, only had eyes for Eva. His gait was so smooth as to appear that he was gliding. His smile was warm, making Aaron Mephisto's eyes twinkle as if he was nothing more villainous than a movie star playing the devil in some blockbuster summer movie.

"Here she is," the Devil crooned, all seductive and charming. "Evangeline. Aren't you just the thing. I see why the boy is so taken with you."

Asher tightened his grip on her hand. Fear curled around the base of his spine, winding its way upwards until it felt as though his hair stood straight with it.

The wine bottle forgotten, Eva blinked at the man. "Mia said you're Luke's father?"

"That and so much more." He didn't enlighten anyone on that cryptic statement. "I've so enjoyed talking with your sister, but you're the one I'm here to meet."

"Why?" Asher's voice croaked. He cleared his throat and tried again. "Why?"

When the Devil's gaze traveled to Asher, everything in those dark eyes changed. No longer was he a harmless, flirtatious gentleman. Asher would swear later that he saw Hellfire burning in their depths. Fear froze him to his spot.

"I always know when one of the boys has met *the one*. Nothing you do goes without my knowing. We're connected, you Seven and me."

Asher swallowed hard, pushing the need to vomit back down. He registered a gasp he thought might have come from Mia, and a guttural growl that certainly came from Luke. Asher himself could make no sound. He was unable to protect anyone, certainly not the woman beside him. That realization shamed him beyond belief.

Attention back to Eva, the Devil suggested an alternative. "Since tasting is off the table, how about a tour?"

Diablo the cat had wandered over from the cellars, answering the feline siren call, which brought the number of cats to thirteen. He sat on the grass at the Devil's feet and gazed upon him adoringly.

"Not much to see right now," Eva pulled her hand from Ashe's grip, but it took effort. He couldn't seem to release the tension in his fingers. "Not until the repairs are done, but I'm happy to show you around."

Right on cue, the door Esther and Jeb had left open to the kitchen slammed shut, along with every window along the side of the house.

"Well then," Jeb noted. "If it wasn't consecrated ground before, I'll bet it shortly will be."

The Devil laughed, low and sinister. "Alright, maybe no tour right now. No worries. We'll let the friars think they've won this round." He turned to Eva. He kissed both cheeks. "I'm afraid I have too much to do while I'm up here and can't entertain the ghosts all day. I'll be back to visit soon. I'm interested to see what you do with the place."

Maggie joined Eva's side. "We look forward to seeing you again. Don't be a stranger."

The Devil nodded in acknowledgement at the Sins. "Boys. Miss Mia." With a lazy salute he turned and strode across the lawn towards the main road.

Asher felt the tension leave his body like the air coming out of a balloon, in one big whoosh. "Wow, I need a drink." He took the bottle from Maggie without thinking about it and drank directly from it.

"No—" both of the Dashiell sisters yelled.

He swallowed. "Tastes fine to me."

Maggie sniffed the neck, then took a tentative sip of her own. "Well, that's really weird. I'm telling you it was vinegar." The entire group of them swiveled their heads to get confirmation from the only other person who'd drunk the wine, but he was gone. The only thing left in his place was a mess of cats wandering around the meadow.

"This whole day has been really weird," Eva admitted. "Your father seems really nice, though, Luke. We'll have to invite him back when we get the remodel done." Luke merely growled.

"Esther, come on." Jeb called. "Let's see what kind of damage control we can accomplish with the monks."

"Monks?" Maggie asked.

Eva shook her head. "Oh, have I got a story for you."

Chapter Thirteen

Evangeline peered at the upper level of the monastery. She searched the attic windows for faces. What she expected to find she wasn't sure. They'd said ghost monks. She found herself looking for Friar Tuck from the Robin Hood movies; fat and jolly, complete with a funny ring of hair around his otherwise bald head. She saw nothing like that.

The appearance of Luke's father had set everyone else on edge. Mia, who had defied all of Eva's misgivings, turned out to be someone she thought might actually be a good friend. It was rare, even in the farming community they lived in, to find someone so in tuned with her wavelength. But now, Mia and her fiancé stood several feet away having a very quiet argument that Mia appeared to be winning, even though the man towered over her and had the most fearsome scowl Eva had ever seen on an actual human. With a final hissing "No," Mia slashed her hand in the air between them and walked away.

Luke turned his scowling face to Asher and growled, "If anything happens, this is your fault."

"Screw you, man. This isn't on me any more than it's on you. It's not like I invited him here." Asher crossed his arms over his chest and scowled right back at his cousin. Granted it rated a six to Luke's ten on the fierce meter, but it still wasn't bad. "Besides, I didn't see you making any brilliant moves to get him out of here. What the Hell was I supposed to do exactly?"

Eva tossed a glance at her sister. *What's the dynamic here?*

Maggie raised her eyebrows and curled in her lips. *I don't know but it's crazy balls.*

Figuring she'd try to get more out of Mia later, Eva called after Esther and Jeb before they disappeared back into the house. "Hey, you're going back up to see the ghosts?"

Esther paused. She didn't look like a ghost hunter in her shiny red leggings, baby-doll t-shirt with the word "discipline" across her boobs, and Frye motorcycle boots. The cast of this reality show was really playing against type. "Yes. We'll calm them down all over again somehow. I love repeating myself."

"I'm coming, too. If I own ghosts, I should get to meet them." Also, as curious as she was about Asher and his family, she didn't want to be a witness when Luke lost his shit and ate Ashe alive.

"You don't own ghosts, honey," Jeb told her. "Ghosts own you."

Esther gave him a perplexed look. "What the hell does that even mean? How can a ghost own you?"

Jeb giggled. "I don't know, but I don't think they'd appreciate the idea of being owned, either. We don't want to piss them off any more than they already are. They were freaked out enough with Lus–, eh, Asher. It was a miracle they settled down with Luke here, too. And now that the big guy showed up..." He threw up his hands in a dramatic flourish.

"Maybe I can help?" Eva flashed them a hopeful grin. "I don't know what you're talking about, but I'm dying to meet my spectral overlords. Maybe my presence will help. I've lived with them all my life. They must know and trust me, eh?"

The thought of seeing ghosts made her giddy. She didn't think it would actually happen, but what if? What if there actually were ghosts in her house. That'd be pretty fucking cool. She'd bet Maggie was already mulling over ways to work that into a marketing scheme.

Esther narrowed her eyes thoughtfully at Eva before saying to Jeb, "It could work."

Jeb waved them both ahead of him. "Sure. Come on."

"You're not going in there," Asher called from the far side of the lawn. "It's still dangerous."

Shaking her head, Esther responded, "Nah, it's safe. The monks didn't want to wreck the place, just get rid of you." She finished with a huge, smarmy grin.

"Well, damn." Eva said. "If I'd known that's what it took to get rid of him, I'd have chatted up my ghosts weeks ago."

Asher was trotting across the lawn towards them. "Didn't work, though, did it?" he asked Eva. He slipped an arm around her waist, gave a squeeze, and walked inside with her. "I'm still here, and now we have to fix a roof."

Eva following behind, the four of them trouped up the stairs after Jeb like ducklings. She saw nothing in the attic besides old furniture, dust, and mouse droppings. Clearly the cats weren't doing their jobs as well as they should. Most of the furniture was covered in tarps or old sheets and, while they looked spooky if you squinted at them in the dim light, they were clearly not ghostly.

Truth be told, she never believed for a minute that she'd see these monks. It had been fun blaming little things around the house on ghosts, but she never actually thought it was true. Did she? That was ridiculous, right?

But sometimes it really did feel like her grandfather was with her, especially when she was out among the vines. She desperately wanted that to be true, although it was most likely only because she missed him so much. She felt like she was floundering without him, so she'd made up something comforting. There weren't really any such things as spirits. She knew this to be true.

And yet...

Esther and Jeb, who came across as perfectly competent people, seemed to believe in this ghost business one hundred percent. Asher didn't seem thrown by it either. Frankly, neither did Luke or Mia, and they were serious professional people. Luke was a really well-known architect; Eva had Googled him on the walk back up with Mia. Mia was a brilliant biologist, a scientist, and she didn't seem to bat an eye at this lunacy. Maybe she and Maggie were going to have to expand their horizons.

Ghosts. Pshaw. And yet, she really wanted to see them and was incredibly disappointed when she couldn't. Esther and Jeb made a hell of a show of having conversations with them. Either they were gifted or putting on a hell of a con.

Eva and Asher left the ghost talkers in the attic to do whatever the hell it was they did and went down to find Luke and Maggie to discuss repairs and remodels.

"Can you see them?" she asked Asher on the way down. "The monks?"

"No. I don't think they really want to be seen." Asher twisted his lips into a wry smile. "I know what you're thinking."

"No, you don't." She pulled her chin into a frown and shook her head.

He hauled her to a stop at the second-floor landing and into a darker recess. "You think these people are all insane, don't you?"

"'These people'?" she teased. "But not you, huh? You're not included in this folly?"

He laughed low and husky, and she felt it in her belly. And lower. It was a sound she needed to figure out how to make him do again. "Not me. I'm as steady and well-grounded as they come." He brushed his lips over hers in a teasing kiss. "I know my people are...unique, but it's all going to work out in an amazing way. You'll see."

"Since you're our partner now, I have no choice but to believe you." She draped her arms around his neck. "I'm very confused by what happened today."

Asher ran his lips feather soft along her jaw line. "Apparently there are heavenly poltergeists living in your attic who dislike me." He deposited a gentle kiss on her chin, and then skated up her jaw line on the opposite side to whisper in her ear. "Clearly because they haven't met me."

She was a mess. A simple stroke of his lips against her skin and she was melting and on fire at the same time. She shivered from his breath against her neck. Instead of tilting her head to give him better access, she hunched her shoulders. As much as she wanted to give him free run of her body, she was tired of getting interrupted, and that was bound to happen any moment.

"Luke's dad seemed nice. Why all the weirdness?" she asked.

That cooled him down right quick. He pulled away and instead settled both hands on her upper arms so he could hold her rapt attention. "Aaron Mephisto is not what he seems. If he comes back here when I'm not here or none of my cousins are here, I don't want you to have anything to do with him." His gray eyes implored her with intensity. "You'll just go inside, or better yet you'll get in your old truck and drive away. Promise me."

His gaze was so vehement that Eva didn't even protest, she simply nodded.

Seriously, what was the dynamic going on here? As much as Asher and his cousin fought, it was obvious that they were close. After all, the man had dropped everything and come running when Ashe called him. And hey, she'd met that other cousin once before. What was his name? Brad? Bart? Benji. It was Benji. He had none of the intensity of his cousins, but he had a good rapport with Ashe-they seemed to enjoy hanging out together. She was going to have to get Mia on her own with a bottle of red and get her to dish on just what the hell was happening here.

"Promise me," he implored. His grey-eyed gaze, blazing and intense, filled her with a rush of squishy heat. The tense lines of his face only emphasizing his beauty. It almost took her breath away.

His concern unsettled her equilibrium. It was almost as if he actually cared about what happened to her. Was it possible he was concerned about her and not only his investment?

"Yes, I promise." She nodded while holding his gaze.

Ashe pulled her into a fierce hug, flush against his body, his arms banding tightly around her. He placed a tender kiss on top of her head, and she melted a tiny bit more. The feels swamped her. This wasn't fair. How had she not seen this coming? She clung to him, both of them huddled in the shaded corner near the stairs.

"You have our word on it." The sound of Jeb's voice filtered down the stairs.

Eva sighed and lifted her cheek from Ashe's shoulder. They met Jeb and Esther at the landing. The three of them exchanged a look that Eva couldn't interpret, but they seemed comfortable with whatever solution they'd come up with, and so she didn't ask for an explanation. She had the feeling whatever they told her wouldn't be the truth, certainly not the whole truth, anyway. Later she was going to have to decide exactly how she felt about that.

Esther spied them in the corner and held out her hand for Eva. "Shall we pack you a bag?"

She stepped away from Asher and his seductive warmth. "Why?"

With a hand on her hip, Esther stated the obvious, "Um, your house doesn't have a roof."

"Well, the attic doesn't, but the main floors are all covered." Eva felt like she was stating the obvious.

Jeb stopped in his tracks halfway down the final flight of stairs. "There's a hole directly over your bed, honey."

"Yeah," Eva conceded, "but I can sleep on the sofa in the living room. That way I can keep an eye on the place. I wouldn't want to leave the house empty for something worse to happen."

Esther cocked her head. "What worse things do you imagine happening? Elephant stampede?"

A laugh escaped Eva's lips at the absurdity. "Maybe."

Esther smirked in response. "I'd love to see you stop that."

"Honey," Jeb said and climbed back up the stairs. "The ghosts aren't going to do anything else. They're cool now, at least for the time being. Don't worry about the building; worry about yourself and your sister."

These people's obsession with ghosts would be amusing if everything wasn't such a mess. "There are other things to worry about besides these supposed ghosts. Any manner of things could happen. Burglars. Rain." Eva listed them off on one hand starting with her thumb. "Raccoons. Meteors. Wrath of God."

A guffaw burst from Esther like a shaken soda bottle. "Is that in order of likelihood?"

Asher reclaimed her hand. "There's not much we can do about meteors or wrath of God." He gave Esther a quelling look. "But we can do something. Esther, will you call in your markers again. Get some of that same crew in to guard the place tonight?" Esther pulled out her cell phone and started texting without a word. Asher continued, "They'll definitely keep out raccoons and burglars. I think Ernie is handling the rain with tarps. I'm afraid there's not much we can do about meteors. I'm going to check in with Luke. I'll see you in a few." He gave her a quick kiss and then trotted down the stairs, and they heard the door close behind him.

Sighing hard, Eva turned to Jeb and Esther to protest again. "I'll be fine on the couch. Really. I promise you."

Jeb scoffed. "That sounds miserable."

It did. The couch was a thousand years old and lumpy as hell. Also, it wasn't quite long enough so she'll either have to fold her long frame in half or have her legs hang off from the shins down. "It'll be fine. We don't really have the funds to stay in a hotel, so-"

Esther tucked her phone into her bra. "Don't be ridiculous. You'll stay at Asher's house. It's huge and he's just rambling around in there."

Oh, no. Oh, shit. That seemed too soon. Right? Too soon? On the other hand, maybe they could finally take one of those toe-curling kisses to its natural conclusion. It was tempting, but ultimately likely a bad idea.

She shook her head.

Esther dealt her a dominatrix look that made Eva's butt clench. "I'm not discussing this with you. You are not sleeping on the couch. I'm going to go pack you a bag. Why don't you go touch base with your sister?"

"No," Jeb actually yelled and raised both palms to stop her. "I'll go pack a bag. If you let her do it, she'll forget important stuff like panties and your toothbrush. Don't look at me like that, Esther. You know you'll just pack weird stuff like thigh-high boots and vinyl bustiers."

Eva laughed. "I don't have any of those things."

With a fresh light in her eyes, Esther suggested, "Maybe we need to schedule a shopping trip."

That thought both terrified and thrilled her. "I don't think so."

Esther's smirk was back. She wore it like a prom dress, sparkly and revealing. "We'll see." Then over her shoulder as she towed Eva outside, she said, "Alright, Jeb, you go pack sufficient panties. Come on, Eva."

Eva tagged along behind, wondering when she lost control of this situation. Maybe when all the backup appeared today? Or earlier when Asher had kissed her this morning? In all reality, it was probably when Asher showed up to tour the vineyard that very first time. Nothing seemed to be normal ever since he'd showed up in her life. The control she wielded over her simple life was crumbling.

To prove her point, Maggie and Luke seemed to have come up with an entire plan of attack without her. Ernie was finishing up with the plastic sheeting on the roof to keep the outside out. Improbably, that same white van from before was making its way down the long driveway, presumably filled with the workers Esther had recalled. Where the hell had they come from? They had to have been close, but if they were local, how had she never seen or met any of them before?

Eva stood in the middle of the grassy lawn, unsure what to do with herself. When Mia broke away from Maggie and Luke to approach her, Eva felt the oddest sensation like she might cry.

"Hey, sweetie. How are you hanging in there?" Mia handed her a bottled water. "Drink this."

Eva tried to thank her, but the words were caught in a bubble in her throat.

"Oh no," Mia exclaimed. "Drink, drink. It's all so much worse if you don't stay hydrated." She rubbed Eva's back in slow circles. "It's going to be alright, hon. We'll all help. I see more help is arriving already."

Eva nodded and swallowed. "I don't know what's wrong with me. I'm not normally like this."

"Meh," Mia dismissed Eva's statement with a wave of her wrist. "We're a lot. And the roof coming off like that. Apparently ghosts you didn't know about. I guess you'll just have to let us take care of you."

Maybe that was it. She'd never been good at letting other people do stuff for her. Eva was a self-contained person. Wasn't it enough that she let her sister and her grandfather in? Now she'll feel like she owes all these people something. Eva finished her water and got a grip on herself. She watched Maggie shake Luke's hand before heading across the lawn.

"It's all going to be fine," Maggie declared, using the words that Eva usually said. "I talked with Ernie and Yesenia. I'm going to bunk with them. There's no room for you, too, but Asher said you're going to his place."

Eva shrugged. She still wasn't sure about the intelligence of this plan. Her sister narrowed her eyes at her.

Is everything okay?

Nothing is okay?

Are you afraid of Asher? Do you feel safe?

Eva didn't hesitate. *Yes. That's not the problem.*

"It's gonna work out. In fact, I'm kinda convinced that this was the best thing that could have happened. Now we'll get all the repairs done that have to happen and the build-outs we were hoping to finish in the next couple of years done in one fell swoop." Maggie couldn't hide her enthusiasm, and that helped Eva put a better spin on it in her own mind. "I know you were concerned about taking on an investor." Maggie's glance shifted to Asher instructing the new work crew with Esther. "But I think it's ideal. Grandpa would have agreed, you know. He was all for progress. He'd tell us to jump at this opportunity."

Eva nodded her head. She knew Maggie was right, but she was torn. She couldn't seem to reconcile her growing feelings for Asher with the dread she felt at giving up control at the vineyard. Maggie would tell her to stop being so difficult and let things happen.

Let things happen.

Let things happen. It felt like a whisper in the back of her mind. Let things happen. She closed her eyes and listened. Was it the voice of her grandfather or of something darker? Soothing and compelling, she let the voice persuade her.

When Jeb came out of the monastery with a duffle, she took it from him with a grateful smile. She thought to place it in Asher's car, but then remembered it was currently under a ton of rubble.

"Are you ready?" His voice low and from behind her as if he knew she'd been thinking of him. He relieved her of her bag. "I have the keys to Esther's Porsche, since clearly we're not going home in the Aston."

She let his honeyed voice smooth over the last of her nerves. Let things happen.

"How will Esther get home?" she asked.

"Jeb will drop her off."

"Are you sure it's all right that I stay over?"

Asher wrapped his free hand around her waist and pulled her against this body. He kissed the tender patch behind her ear before whispering, "I would love you to come over so long as it's all right with you."

It was all right with her.

Let things happen.

Heaven & Hell XVI

Juliet leaned against the enormous mutt and popped a cheesy cracker in her mouth.

"How far do you think we've already gone?" she asked Cerberus. There was no way to tell how many flights of stairs they'd already descended. She'd stopped counting long before. One thing that was certain, she was further down than she'd been the first time, the time when she'd met Neil. She could tell because it was hot as heck in this stairwell and that last time, she'd been only warmly uncomfortable.

Cerberus's right head snuffled against the cracker box and Juliet handed him one. He took it gently from her fingers with his front teeth before swallowing it whole.

"Why do you just woof them down like that? How do you even know you like them if you can't taste them? You know, this could explain your gas problem. If you're not chewing properly, then you're likely experiencing gastric distress."

The three-headed dog thumped his singular tail against the stairs and offered a gentle woof from the middle head in response.

Juliet rose with a sigh. "Onward, doggy. Let's go."

Down. Down. Down.

Would this ugly stairwell ever end? She hummed the tunes to commercials and cartoons for twenty turns down or so, and then broke into a full voice to finish the last line of an old favorite from her childhood.

"Can you tell me how to get, how to get to Sesame Streeeet?"

Whew, it was really getting unbearably hot. A line of sweat trickled down her spine. Her knapsack weighed heavily on her shoulders. If it didn't hold snacks for Neil, she would have abandoned it hundreds of levels above. She pulled the straps up and away from her skin, hoping for a little air circulation on her back, but hot air didn't do the trick.

Down, down. All three of the dog heads were panting, so it wasn't just Juliet having a low tolerance for heat. She dropped her hand on the head closest to her.

"Oh doggie, how do you ever deal with this heat? It must be miserable wearing hair all over your body. At this point, I'd be willing to shave my head to just not to have to deal with this anymore."

Early on in the descent, there had been a near catastrophe when her hair tie had snapped. The thought of her hair hanging long against her back brought her close to crying. She had braided two long lengths and then tied them in a knot on the top of her head, and so far, that was working—as long as she didn't move her head around too much.

Cerberus arrived at the landing for the next turn and threw himself on the floor with a massive exhale.

"Oh, come on, puppy. We can't rest again so soon. I know it's miserable, but Neil will be waiting." A heavy drop of sweat slipped down the slope of her nose and plopped audibly on the concrete. She pulled on the middle head's collar, but he didn't budge. She patted the left head and massaged his ears. "Come on puppy, please."

When it was apparent the dog wasn't moving for a bit, she sunk to the floor. If she expected, or hoped, the concrete might be cool against her skin, she was mistaken. It felt more like sitting on a sidewalk that had been in the summer sun for hours. Heat radiated from the ground and the walls and, she assumed, the ceiling. She felt like a roasting duck.

Inside the backpack, she dug around until she found a juice pouch. "I'm so sorry I don't have any water for you. I'll remember next time to bring you a canteen full of cool, heavenly water." She punched the straw into the pouch and took a hearty sip of hot fruit punch. It was refreshing even though it was as warm as soup.

Cerberus's left head eyed her balefully while all three tongues hung limply from their mouths while they panted. Swamped with guilt, she tilted the pouch towards Right Head and squeezed a bit of juice inside. The giant dog smacked his lips appreciatively. She tipped the rest of the pouch in the other two mouths, then patted him on his heads.

"Is that enough to get you moving again?"

There was a chorus of enthusiastic woofs and he actually did lumber to his feet and begin trodding further down the stairs. Excellent. She was tired and hot and pissy, too, it was hard not to be, but she didn't have any idea how much further down they'd have to go to find the end. They needed to keep moving. She didn't want Neil to have to wait for her down there.

Maybe he wouldn't wait.

Maybe he wouldn't show up at all.

That thought made her stomach hurt for a couple of reasons. The most important one being that she needed his help. She didn't know any way she could find Rachel without him. She was depending on him. And Lucifer was depending on her.

Also, she really wanted to see the cute demon again.

She'd once seen a really old movie on television–so old it was in black and white–with a super cute guy named James Dean. He was like the big heartthrob when her mom was young. He had been troubled and afraid and tried to look cool to fit in. Juliet had seen through all that posturing and had just really wanted to give him hug.

Juliet wondered if Neil had been like that boy in the movie. They dressed alike with dark jeans, motorcycle jacket, and big, heavy boots. Maybe that's all Neil had needed in life, too. Someone to love him and tell him everything was going to be alright. Would that have been the difference between him going to Hell or coming up to Heaven? Someone who loved him?

"How much further do you think?" she asked the dog. He shook two heads and drool flung around them in a wide arc, whapping against the concrete walls, ceiling, and floor. She was pretty sure she heard a responding sizzle. "Gah! Gross. Shouldn't you keep that inside you? I'm sure it only speeds along the dehydration."

Many, many flights later, as they were rising to their feet again from another pit stop, Juliet could not find the enthusiasm to hook the straps of the hot, heavy backpack around her shoulders again. A quick glance at the dog gave her an idea. She pulled the straps out as far as they could go and looped one around Cerberus's left head and the other over the right. The dog didn't mind, especially when she scratched behind his ears, all six of them.

With the bag of goodies thumping along the dog's massive back, they moved down the stairway and deeper into the furnace. The heat was tangible now, something she could almost touch as she moved through the stairwell. It lay heavy on her skin, making her flesh feel stretched tight against her bones. Her eyes kept watering, losing precious liquid against the ceaseless burning sensation. Or perhaps it was from the odor that had begun to permeate the air. The inside of her nose felt singed. She'd never smelled anything like it before.

"Gosh, I hope the end isn't too much further. Like, how much worse can this get?" The dog snorted. "I don't know why I ask. You're never going to answer."

"Not much further." The voice came from below, drifting up the stairwell, riding the scorching waves of stench. "But a lot worse."

"Neil?" she shrieked and somehow found the energy to sprint down the last five flights. She passed Cerberus who'd found a burst of energy of his own.

When she rounded the final corner, she saw him and squealed in glee. Neil looked impossibly handsome, leaning against the filthy concrete wall. He did look just like a modern-day James Dean; one hand in his pocket, one knee bent with the boot kicked back against the wall. He shoved away from the support and used his free hand to push his ebony hair away from his face. He licked his lips and smiled at her, a ridiculously cool, butterfly-inducing half-grin that made his eyes sparkle and emphasized his sharp cheekbones.

She couldn't stop herself. Juliet launched herself at him.

"I'm so relieved to see you." She wrapped her arms around his neck and squeezed him tight.

He chuckled and wrapped his arms around her waist, matching her squeeze with his own. "Me, too," he confessed. "I was worried you wouldn't come back."

Juliet let go of his neck, and he set her back on her feet. "Of course, I'd come back. I promised, right? I even brought snacks." She turned to Cerberus to get the backpack but he had already launched himself at Neil. Her beautiful rebellious demon was pinned to the floor with the giant dog licking him with all three heads.

"Okay, okay, okay." Neil pleaded and pushed against the massive, furry chest, but he was laughing, so she didn't make an effort to save him.

Finally, the dog let him up.

"I don't suppose you brought any towels with you?" When she shook her head, he lifted up the hem of his t-shirt and wiped his drooly face.

Juliet spied a swath of naked skin across his belly and quickly averted her eyes. Almost immediately, her gaze darted back, but she was sad to see it was gone. She turned her attention to the backpack which she retrieved from Cerberus. With a giant grin, she unzipped it and peeled back the material to reveal the bounty of junk food it contained. Neil's smile morphed into a blank expression of awe.

"Is that a Twinkie?" He reached in and plucked the yellow snack cake from the pile with reverence.

Juliet beamed. "Yup. There's all kinds of stuff in here."

Neil had her in his arms so fast she didn't even have time to gasp.

And then he kissed her. His lips pressed against hers while his hands cupped the sides of her face. She clutched a fistful of his t-shirt with her free hand and returned the pressure of her lips on his. Her eyes fluttered closed and she sighed. When he finally pulled away, her lips tingled and she made an involuntary hum.

"This is amazing," he said, indicating the backpack. "Wow."

"Thank you for helping me and Lucifer." She smiled. "Oh, and of course Rachel, too."

"Oh yeah. I got so excited with the goodies, I forgot to tell you I saw her."

Juliet pushed against his shoulder with both hands. "You didn't!"

He grinned, and it made his face so beautiful she almost lost her train of thought. *And he kissed me.*

"I did," he assured her. "I talked to her and everything." Then he grimaced. "But then the goblins arrested me and threw me in a dungeon."

"Oh, no!"

"When I got out, I came right back here, so I don't know where she is now." He shrugged. "She might still be in his palace–"

"Who's palace?"

"The Devil's," he explained. "At the bottom."

She lowered her eyebrows in confusion. "The Devil has a palace?"

Neil lifted his shoulder in a lopsided shrug. "Well, sure. He's the king down here."

"Alright then," Juliet said with finality. She zipped up the backpack and slung it over her shoulders. "Let's go to the palace, then."

He pursed his lips and scowled at her. "It's on the bottom of Hell?"

"Okay." She started for the doorway that she assumed led out to Hell proper with Cerberus on her heels.

"You're an angel," he said, patiently. "I'm pretty sure you can't set foot in Hell."

She swung the door open and the blast of heat and stench threatened to set fire to her hair. "Whoooo! That's brutal." She wiped her face. It felt grimy already. *You don't get acne when you're dead, right?*

Neil arrived at her side, and the two of them stared out into the Devil's dark abyss.

She tried to sound decisive, but her voice was tepid. "What are we going to do? I came all the way down here. I'm not gonna send you back in there to do this all alone."

Her beautiful rebel needed her help and support and love. She could not expect him to do all the work without taking risks of her own.

"No, you can't go in. You don't belong down here. There's rules for a reason."

Cerberus padded across the threshold and disappeared from view into the smog from the smokestacks and chimneys.

Juliet screwed up her courage and took a step out the doorway, but Neil was right. Her shoe wouldn't alight on the sooty ground. Some unseen force repelled her foot, refusing to allow it to touch the ground. When she tried again, there was the inexorable pressure pushing back like reverse gravity. Frustrated tears filled her eyes, and that only fueled her desire to figure out a way in.

"Hmm, I wonder," Neil pondered out loud. "Here, climb on." He crouched down and she scrambled on, piggyback style. "Here goes nothing."

Juliet took a deep breath and Neil took a step out the door. His boot landed flat on the charred ground, a puff of silt clouding around each step.

She cheered and pointed forward. "Onward to the palace."

Like a twisted version of the Wizard of Oz, a demon, an angel, and a three-headed dog took off across the wasteland of Hell heading for the Devil's palace. What could go wrong?

Chapter Fourteen

A sher was inexplicably nervous.

It was just him and Evangeline in Esther's Porsche cruising back into the city. Per his gargoyle's instructions, he had both sweaty hands on ten and two. It wasn't the car that had him on edge. It wasn't residual sadness from the unceremonious murdering of his Aston Martin. He didn't even think it was from the stress of seeing the Devil, and that had made his blood pressure skyrocket.

No. This unnecessary anxiety was entirely sexual. Ashe had never been nervous about sex before. Never. Not even the first time but he'd likely not really known what was happening that time. He had been thirteen and it had been sort of a blur with a happy ending.

On the other hand, this time he was one hundred percent present. He knew where all the parts went and what was expected of all parties. This time, unlike all the zillion times he'd had sex before, this encounter was for him not for his sin. He couldn't really explain the distinction, not even to himself.

Usually when he had a sexual encounter, it was almost like the sin took over his body and he was just along for the ride. He was there, obviously, but sort of in automation. He'd tried to explain it to Benji and Ethan once, and neither of them could fathom the concept.

"You don't like it?" Benji asked, after he picked up his jaw from the floor. It was the most energetic reaction he'd seen from Sloth in months.

"Of course, I like it, you idiot." Asher responded in consternation.

"This is fucked up," Ethan noted. "You live all my fantasies, and you don't even care."

"I care," Asher protested. But did he? Or was that just what he was supposed to do?

Ethan flung his head back and howled at the ceiling. The rest of the patrons at their favorite bar, Jugheads, gave them a glance but not much else. The regular rabble at Jugheads was rowdy and tended to mind their own business. Ethan howling was probably the least weird thing that went on in there that night.

Benji took a pull on his beer and gave Asher a speculative eye.

Ethan signaled the waitress for another round, and then leaned across the table towards Asher. "Look, I get laid plenty, so I'm not jealous about the amount of ass, or dick, or whatever you get. I say, 'good for you.' It's what you were built for, right? But don't try to tell us—" he motioned to himself and Benji "—that you're not really into it, because your Sin says otherwise."

Asher rolled his eyes. "That's not what I'm saying, asshole. You know this proclivity of mine is just as onerous as yours, right? Or Benji's or any of the other five of us. Of course, at the time, I'm enjoying it. My dick is happy, and someone else's sexual itch is getting scratched at the same time. But is it really that hard to believe I don't enjoy being a slave to my Sin?"

Benji held his beer by the long neck and twirled it lazily along the table. "Nah, man. I get that. I'm not gonna get in a pissing contest with you like Envy over here." He side-eyed Ethan. "But, in the grand scheme of things, you must realize that you do get some nice fringe benefits from yours. All I get is a wasted life."

He didn't know how he'd ever get them to see his point of view. Besides dealing with Sloth, Envy, Pride, Wrath and the rest of them, they were also healthy, youngish men with healthy libidos. The idea that Asher got to stick it in anyone who was willing probably seemed like a dream come true to them.

Instead of continuing the debate, he went and got himself a shot of tequila. Along with the double shot, he also got a wink and an unsolicited napkin with Garrett the bartender's phone number. Sigh. He most likely wasn't going to ever allow Garrett's proclivities a free run. Either Asher would have to stop coming to Jugheads afterwards or he'd have to get Garrett fired. Best not to fuck where you drink.

Back in the Porsche, the sliver of nerves had turned into an angry tumor at the base of his spine. He'd never used his Sin against Eva. Or rather, he'd never successfully used his Sin against her. There had been no loosening of morals. No magical temptations. No hint of darkest fantasies to be realized. This entire encounter was mundane–no supernatural whammies had fucked with the natural order. Their sexual attraction was all animal, chemical, and emotional.

Never in his life had Asher had sex under these circumstances. Or at least never that he knew of. No one wanted to fuck Asher Mephisto. His many, many conquests had fucked Lust. It was entirely different.

Thus, the panic.

Asher glanced down at the speedometer and backed off the throttle when he realized they were racing down the highway at a buck ten.

What's the hurry man? Slow the fuck down.

"You barely feel it in this car, huh?" Eva said with a flick of her eyes to the ones and zeros on the gauge. "German engineering for you. Believe you me, you go one-ten in the vineyard Ford and you'd leave half the engine on the asphalt. Poor old girl," she finished with a chuckle.

Ashe took a calming breath. "Maybe it's time to look into investing in a more reliable vehicle for the vineyard then."

"What? No!" Eva gave him a look between the tiny space between their bucket seats. "I love that truck. She was my grandfather's. I can't believe you'd even say that about Miriam."

He chuckled. "Miriam? You named her Miriam?"

"I didn't. My grandmother did. She said any woman that her husband spent that much time with deserved to be sworn at by a Christian name. Gram was a feisty woman."

Eva's voice was laced with affection any time she spoke of her grandparents. It occurred to him he'd never heard mention of her parents. The vineyard seemed to have skipped an entire generation, swallowed whole with no trace.

"How about your mom? Is she feisty?" *Is she? Was she?* He didn't even know what the right verb tense was for her parents.

A grunt then a sigh. "Feisty isn't the word for Mom. Free-spirited seems too romantic. Selfish, too basic."

"Ah," Asher said, sounding stupid. "So, she's not around?"

"Only when it's convenient. It's never convenient."

Her answer was clipped and there was none of the warmth for her grandparents left in her tone, but he found he couldn't stop himself from prodding further. "And your dad?"

She turned in the seat, fitting herself into the corner near the door and faced him as much as the bucket seat would allow. There was a false brightness about her smile and energy that made him strangely sad. "How about your parents? I see how well Luke got along with his father. How about yours?"

"My parents are dead," he told her matter-of-factly, letting her diversion slide. The scenery whipping past was becoming more suburban as the rural attractions of wine country merged with consumerism. They passed both an outlet mall and a tractor dealership. "They died when I was twenty-two. They were on vacation in the Caribbean. I'd like to be able to say their yacht disappeared in the Bermuda Triangle, but it wasn't anything that exciting."

"What then?" Eva's voice was soft.

He shrugged with one shoulder. "Just a freak storm."

"I'm sorry," she said. "You were really young. What did you do? Did your family step up?"

"I was already living on my own by then. Well, not exactly, Benji and I shared an apartment. Of course, I had Esther and the rest of my cousins, so I was alright."

"How long have you and Esther been together?"

He signaled and merged onto another freeway heading into the heart of the city. "Esther and I are not together. You understand that, right? Never have been. Esther is... Well, she's been in my life since we were ten. She doesn't just work for me, she runs my whole life. Any other relationship with her would be impossible."

Eva bunched up her eyebrows and nodded. "You trust her."

"Implicitly."

"I like her," Eva admitted. "She's a little scary, but she's also straightforward. It's a bit disconcerting. Still, I think she's super cool."

Asher raised his eyebrows and stated emphatically, "Esther is fucking terrifying. But if you ever need anything, she'll take care of you. She knows everyone. Sometimes I think the phrase, 'I know a guy' was invented by her."

They both laughed and he realized his anxiety had lessoned its death grip on his bowels. The tall buildings of downtown filled the windshield. They passed the site where Luke's latest building was going up. The billboards on the grounds still showed the artist's images of what the finished product would look like. He pointed it out to Eva with pride for what his cousin had created.

"I was reading about it in the Google search I did on him. It's going to be so amazing. The writer in *Time* likened it to the Hanging Gardens of Babylon."

"No, Eden," Asher corrected her. "It's apple trees and Eden and Sin."

"Either way, I can't wait to see it when it's done."

Ashe wanted to twine his fingers in hers. They lay there lightly on her leg, and he had an intense desire to ground himself with her solidity. Instead, he poked her knee gently with his index finger. "I'll make sure you're invited to the grand opening," he said.

A moment of silence stretched, and they both spoke at the same time.

"Again, I'm really sorry about your car."

"I'm really sorry about your roof."

Eva snorted. Asher loved the sound. "It's not your fault the roof flew off," she reminded him.

They passed over a bridge, and his apartment was only blocks away now. "The car isn't your fault either."

She raised her finger to correct him. "Apparently, it's my ill-behaved ghosts who started this whole thing, so in some way I feel responsible. Even though I didn't know they were real. Or why they'd take issue with you. Or that I had so many cats," she ended with a snort.

Unfortunately, Asher did know why they took issue with him. And why Aaron Mephisto's appearance only ratcheted up the situation to apocalyptic levels as far as a bunch of ghost monks were concerned. None of which he could explain to her.

"Esther will get it all taken care of," he assured her. "She and Jeb are miracle workers."

"Is this where you live?" Eva leaned forward and peered up through the windshield at the facade of the old hotel that had been remodeled into luxury condominiums. "Wow."

He pulled the Porsche into the parking garage and wound around to his assigned spot near the elevator. Once they got out, he pulled her bag from behind the seat and chirped the alarm. He watched her eyeing the other expensive cars while they waited for the elevator and then her hiccup of surprise when he used his special keycard to select the penthouse suite from the list of available floors.

"The top?" she croaked.

He grinned. "The best view. Wait until you see it."

When the doors silently slid open into his foyer, Eva giggled and covered her mouth. "Wow. Our old monastery looks like a shit pile next to this."

Asher shook his head modestly. "Your home has character and style and I love it as much as you do. We'll restore it to its old glory. You'll see."

He followed her into his living room, her bag slung over his shoulder, and watched her expression as she took in his home. Her fingers trailed along the arm of his snow-white contemporary suede sofa before perching lightly on a blue velvet chair. "No pets, huh?"

"Why do you say so?"

"White suede and velvet? It would attract hair like nobody's business."

"I have a cleaner."

Again, she snorted. Why did he find that so arousing? "Of course, you do," she said.

On the far wall, she paused in front of an eight-foot canvas done in the style of the old masters; something from the renaissance, maybe Leonardo da Vinci or Caravaggio, using chiaroscuro techniques of light and dark. It showed the fall of Lucifer as he was dramatically cast out of Heaven, but in this portrait he was not cast out alone. Holding tight to his hand as the two figures plummeted down to the fires was his lover, Rachel. The face of the fallen angel was masked in anguish as one would expect. However, the calm adoration portrayed on the face of his bride was mesmerizing to behold. Asher gazed at Eva as the panting's subject matter captivated her.

"This is amazing. I've never stood this close to one of the masters before. Whose is this?"

Again, pride filled Asher as he confessed, "That is actually my cousin Benji's work. He's breathtakingly talented. He did an extended study at the Vatican last year."

Her breath came out in a soft, wondering sigh. "Wow."

"Indeed," he agreed. "Someday, maybe I'll explain the story behind it."

She smiled at him and ignored the staircase as she traveled further into his home. Thank heaven. He wasn't ready for the upstairs. Not yet. If he could just get his heartbeat under control...

"Kitchen's this way?" she asked and strolled past the dining room and into his giant kitchen. "Do you actually cook in here?" She was clearly full of skepticism. Pulling one red tulip from the vase on the counter, she traced it along her lower lip and raised an eyebrow at him.

He swallowed a groan and broke eye contact as a grasp at self-preservation. "Absolutely. Are you hungry? Esther usually has the place pretty well-stocked." The refrigerator revealed steaks and fresh veggies. He would make her a meal that would demonstrate how much he thought of her. He wanted to impress her. Prove that he could take care of her in more ways than just rescuing the vineyard. "Have a seat and let me feed you."

Eva kicked off her shoes and hopped onto a bar stool. "I was thinking you'd want to work up an appetite first."

"Or," he said as he set two balloon wine glasses and a bottle of Empyrean merlot in front of her. "We fortify ourselves." He flashed her a toothy grin and a flirty eyebrow wiggle.

"Well, when put that way…"

He held up his glass, "To being fortified."

Eva clinked their glasses together, then leaned across the bar counter and pulled him to her by his collar and feathered her lips across his. He opened his mouth to deepen the kiss, but she was gone. When he opened his eyes, she was sitting back on the stool and sipping from her glass.

"So, fortify me, big guy." Her teasing grin was sexy, but more importantly there was a sheen of wine on her bottom lip for him to fixate on. When her tongue came out and swiped it off, he almost came undone.

And yet he didn't know what to do about it. This was a new situation, and he felt like an untouched boy. As Lust, he represented other people's fantasies. Honestly, he didn't even know what his own fantasies were. Did he have any? He was so in over his head, here.

What he did know for sure is that he wanted this to mean something. This wasn't just Lust-sex, it was Asher-sex. Nothing about Evangeline Dashiell was throwaway, but fucking had never been about emotional fulfillment before.

He swallowed hard and turned back to the dinner fix-ins. "How do you like your steak?"

The clink of glass on marble was followed by, "Rare. What can I do to help?"

"Nothing. You sit there and talk to me." He didn't want her anywhere near him while he was working with knives and flame. He was skittish enough.

While he sliced portobellos she told him what back story she knew of the monastery. "When he found it, there wasn't much more than a shell, as I understand it. Some of the outbuildings are original. Also, that amazing stained-glass window, that is rumored to have come all the way from France."

By the time he lay a plate with a rare filet mignon steak with butter sauteed baby portobellos and thin, juicy grilled asparagus spears in front of her, Asher's anxiety had barely leveled off. As much as he took pleasure in hearing Eva's brilliant theories on botany, in fact, just listening to the hum of her voice while she talked with such enthusiasm usually acted as an opiate, he spent this time while cooking giving himself a pep talk, which had probably been a mistake.

It's just sex, and you're way overthinking this. You're the ultimate Sin of pleasure—you got this. She's only one woman. You've had way more than one person at once before. Maybe that's a problem. When was the last time you concentrated on one person at a time? You're totally fucked. Hahaha—you may not get fucked at all at this rate. Oh, won't Benji love the irony. Maybe you should call him. Maybe he'll talk you down. Or make fun of your pathetic ass. Esther. Call Esther. She always has your back. You're a grown-ass man! Get control of your cock and calm down before you humiliate yourself.

"Hey." Eva's voice broke through his internal dialogue. "Are you alright? You're looking a little gray."

"Uh, yeah. I'm fine. You start and I'll be right back." He backed out of the kitchen. "Pour yourself another glass of wine, and one for me, too, and, and, okay, I'll just be a second." He literally sprinted up the back stairs to the second floor down the hallway and into this bathroom where he locked the door.

The cell only rang once before Esther picked up. "Why are you calling me?" she asked. The background noise was outrageous.

"I need your help."

"What?"

"I need your help."

"Yes, on the rocks. Thanks." Then to Asher, "You want what now?"

"Where are you?" He was inappropriately annoyed that she was busy having fun while he was in crisis.

"Out." Then her voice was away from the speaker, but he still clearly heard her yelling for Mordechai and Judith, the gargoyles for Envy and Sloth respectively. "Over here. Jeb just went for another pitcher of margaritas." Then back to him, "What do you need? Why are you talking to me instead of your beautiful lady?"

"I'm freaking out."

"Breaking out? With hives?"

"No. Freaking out. I'm fucking freaking out here. I don't know what to do. You need to help me." He saw a glimpse of himself in the mirror and he was pathetic; wide, round eyes, disheveled hair and not artfully so, chapped lips and cottonmouth.

"Save my chair, guys. I'll be right back." The din diminished followed by the sound of an industrial door opening and closing. "Alright now, what are you telling me?"

"She's here. In the house and I don't know what to do with her."

There was silence on the other end and then she said, "Asher Mephisto?"

"Yeah, it's me. Who the hell do you think this is?"

Esther chuckled. "I wasn't sure. So, start from the beginning. What have you done so far?"

"Took her on a tour of the downstairs and then I made her dinner."

"Um hmm. And where is she now?"

"In the kitchen." Probably assuming he was a complete maniac.

"And where are you?"

Sigh. This was humiliating. "I locked myself in the bathroom upstairs."

He could imagine her standing there, hip cocked to the side, fist on that hip, staring into the phone, confused. "Ashe, what is the problem, exactly."

He whispered it. "I'm scared. I really want her to like me because I really like her, and I feel like this is going too fast and it's really important."

Another long pause. "Oh, honey. You're going to be fine. Just go back down there and let nature take its course. Tale as old as time, right? I promise you; instincts will kick right in when it all comes down to it."

"Are you sure, I just feel–wait. What was that?"

Someone rapped softly on the bathroom door. "Asher? Are you in there? Who are you talking to?"

Chapter Fifteen

Well, this was humiliating. Asher shoved his cellphone into his back pocket, took a deep breath, and opened the bathroom door full of false bravado. "Hi, sorry. Esther had a thing." He waved his hand in a throwaway gesture to signal that it was unimportant. "All good now. Let's eat."

"Umkay," Eva's eyebrows were still knotted together. "Can I ask about this room real quick?"

He plastered on a smile that he hoped looked sure, friendly, and not at all creepy. He still kept a pretty sure grip on her hand, though, and tugged inexorably toward the hallway. "Sure."

"Holy cow." She pulled him to a stop with her hand gripped on the bathroom door jamb. "How many people does that shower hold? I guess as many as that bed does, huh?" Now she was pointing at his enormous bed.

He shouldn't have brought her here. His life was just too much for a normal person. How could he ever explain all this so he didn't sound like a deviant? Who was he kidding? He was a deviant. This stuff was bound to repel her.

Asher closed his eyes for a second and regrouped. "Can we go downstairs and eat and talk?"

The look she gave him was speculative but curious. "Still planning to fortify me? By the looks of what you've got going on here, I'm going to need all the energy I can get."

"I can explain," he assured her as he tried to get her started back down the stairs to the kitchen.

"Explain what? Do you think I'm a country bumpkin or something?" Her hands were on her hips now and she looked adorably put out. "I've had sex. Lots of sex. One time in my twenties there was more than one person."

"Two people, huh?" He nodded. "At once?" Yeah, he was a total deviant. Two people, how quaint.

She stared at him for several heartbeats. "Mostly. We were all pretty drunk, and my friend sort of just passed out on the bed. She never even got her clothes off, but technically she was there, so it counts." She paused another long moment and peered at him with a million questions skittering across her face. "I don't think I understand what's going on here. You were so...I don't want to say aggressive before, but you were coming on to me, right? Am I making a complete fool of myself? Oh, for fuck's sake, you're not into this anymore, are you? if you ever were."

She tried to pull away, but Asher gripped her hand firmly. "Slow down." He gentled his voice like he was speaking to a spooked cat. "I want you. I *really* want you. I promise."

Her jaw was set and her eyebrows indicated she was calling bullshit. He tugged her into his space and wrapped his free hand around the nape of her neck and kissed her. He wasn't gentle. He didn't go in softly and feather her lips. No, he funneled his anxiety and apprehension into it. He didn't want her to feel one speck of the inadequacy he was riddled with. He knew he wanted *her*, Evangeline Dashiell. He didn't ever have any fear when Lust was driving him towards anonymous sex. But this time, now with her, there wasn't any possibility that what he was feeling wasn't honest.

The same couldn't be said about whatever was driving her. There was every chance she was being compelled by his sin and not for actual feeling for him.

She remained irritated for about three seconds before a needy groan belied her stiff shoulders. Clutching a fistful of his shirt in each hand, her tongue met his with greedy swipes. He wanted to devour her, their tongues and teeth clashed in urgency. He pushed the hand at her nape upward and delved into her hair. Tugging a handful of hair, he tipped her head back and to the side, got the angle he wanted. He plundered her mouth. Pressed his body against hers. Rocked his hips aggressively against hers so she could feel the powerful proof of his desire in his erection.

Except his cock was not hard. The life of the party was a useless, flaccid lump in his pants. How could his brain be on fire, and his penis not even show up? What the ever-loving fuck?

He let his dick do anything it wanted and the one time he asked it to show up, it pulls this shit?

Eva stepped away, gasping for breath, her lovely breasts heaving under her t-shirt. She dragged her teeth over her lip while slipping a hand around his belt buckle and started to pull him towards the bed. Walking backwards, gorgeous mouth spread in a seductive smile.

"This bed of yours," she teased. "Like it's got its own zip code."

He let her tow him forward, dread compounding with each step. She climbed onto the mattress, kicked off her sneakers, and rose to her feet. She bounced gingerly, testing the bounce-ability.

"This is outrageous. I didn't even know they made beds this big." Every time she jumped her shirt rose higher, showing increasingly larger swaths of her torso. When she raised her arms over her head, the lace on the bottom of her bra peeked out. His head said, "Woo!" but his dick said... Nada. Said not a fucking thing.

He didn't understand what was happening.

She stopped jumping in the middle of the bed. Standing there with her hands on her hips and smirking, she had never been sexier. God, he wanted her so much.

"Why is your bed this big?"

"I'm a big guy."

She turned a slow circle in the bed, one eyebrow raised. "Not this big."

"You haven't seen all of me." Good line, but she wouldn't be seeing all of him at this point.

Her guffaw was both adorable and hot. "Okay, I'm pretty sure that if your penis required this entire bed we'd have heard about you by now. There's no way Jerry Springer wouldn't have had you on his show."

He wanted her. More than anything he could ever remember. He wanted her—not Lust. Asher David Mephisto wanted her in every way imaginable. But until he figured out what was going on with his equipment malfunction, he needed to get her off his bed.

With his hand extended in a courtly gesture of assistance, he said, "Why don't you come down from there and we'll finish dinner."

Ignoring his hand, Eva whipped her t-shirt over her head to reveal a lacy whisp of a hot pink bra. The contrast from her every-day, working-farm uniform to this hyper-feminine display got his mental juices bubbling. She'd worn that with him in mind; he knew it in the basest, testosterone-soaked swamp of his soul. His fingers itched to touch it. To feel the heat of her body through the lace.

"You know what I think?" she asked while unbuttoning her jeans. "I think we should section off this bed into quadrants and debauch each one differently. Maybe name each after a specific sex act, what do you think?"

He wasn't able to form an opinion while she was shimmying out of her jeans.

"You know—" she paused while her jeans were near her knees "—I think we need more than just quadrants. I want to do lots of wicked things to you, Mr. Mephisto." She literally did the stripper move and pushed the denim to her ankles without bending her knees so that her heart-shaped ass wiggled in the air. He couldn't take his eyes off the hot-pink, lacey boy shorts. The lace framed her ass perfectly.

His breath shuddered from his chest and he was unable to form words.

Leaving her jeans at her ankles, she rolled up to her full height. Knowing his eyes were on her, she ran her fingers under the bottom lace gently, caressing her own ass cheeks. "What do you think?" she asked, her voice unexpectedly kittenish. "Maybe eight sections?"

Asher's mouth watered. Standing tall, she looked down on him from on high. When he extended his helpful hand to her again, she touched her fingertips to his palm and he pulled her toward him. When she reached the edge of the mattress, he lay his palms on the backs of her calves. She radiated strength and sensuality.

She was Aphrodite and Athena. Lithe. Magnificent.

He stroked his hands up her powerful legs, behind her knees, spanning his fingers around the backs of her thighs and rubbing his thumbs over the front. She swayed towards him, and he used the opportunity to press his lips to the satin skin of her belly. On a deep inhale, he tongued her navel then kissed a trail down to the lace of her panties.

"What shall we call the first section?" she asked on a husky whisper.

None of this was going the way he'd expected. He had to think at some point Lust would kick in, things would come alive, and his reputation would be saved. Right? *Right?* But, if Lust really had forsaken him, then he would have to impress her with other skills. Fortunately, his resume was packed with skills. New plan: deflect her into submissiveness with multiple orgasms thanks to his prodigious skills.

The height of the bed and his long legs put her belly right at face level. He kissed her pubic bone over the lace and squeezed both globes of her ass. "Lady's choice," he told her.

Eva's increased breathing was lovely to behold from below, her pink lace-covered breasts rising and falling. When he bit her hip and then soothed the bite with his tongue, she squeaked. He followed up with little nibbles and kisses along the edges of the lace. When he looked up again, her mouth was agape and her eyes were heavy-lidded. Holding her gaze, he slipped his hand behind her right knee and lifted her leg and settled it across his left shoulder. She squeaked again—a noise he was beginning to love—and grabbed his head with both hands to steady herself.

Asher turned his face and kissed the inside of her thigh just past her knee. She gave a little hum of encouragement. He smoothed his hand along the outside of her thigh until it was back to her ass and clamped the other one on the opposite hip. He squeezed to anchor her and then he used tongue and teeth to make his way towards her center.

He halted a breath away and turned his face up to her. She licked her lips, and he smirked. Holding her gaze, he squeezed her butt cheek again before letting go and running his knuckles from the top of her lace, down her pubic bone, and along her silk-covered slit. Her panties were damp and, when he tucked his finger inside the fabric, she was slick.

"Ashe," she whispered.

He rubbed his afternoon whiskers along the inside of her thigh. Running his fingers along her damp flesh, he closed his eyes and breathed in her scent.

"Ashe," she whispered again and tugged his hair.

This was the ticket. Whatever had been holding him back, he felt his body start to come alive.

He opened his eyes to see her panting and trembling. A quick kiss on her silk covered center, then he shrugged her leg off his shoulder to clasp her by the hips and lower her down to the bed. When she reached for him, he deflected her away.

"But you have all your clothes on," she protested.

He plucked an ankle from the bed and lifted a naked foot to his mouth and kissed the instep. "So I do." He pressed his lips to the inside of her knee. "And you still have on too many."

He crawled up the bed between her legs, smoothing his hands up the marble-smooth skin of her toned muscles. She raised her hips in invitation, but he bypassed that lacy triangle of promise and continued mapping her body with his hands, over her hips and along the indent of her waist, tracing the ridge of her ribs. He worshiped her body made strong from work. He ran his thumbs along the bottom of her bra and gave each breast a light squeeze to test the size in his palm. He was rewarded with a gasping breath and an arch of her back.

"Asher," she whispered, breathlessly. His name on her lips...glorious.

He pinched a nipple through the lace and her flesh responded immediately by pebbling up into a hard knot of nerves. A tender kiss between her breasts, then he licked a fine line straight up her breastbone to the divot in her throat. His body was stretched over hers, but they weren't touching. Braced on either side of her shoulders, he bent his elbows and lowered his lips to hers. Parting her lips immediately, she let him in and his tongue met hers. He couldn't suppress his moan; she tasted so good that he abandoned himself to her mouth.

Until her hands crept under his shirt. Deft fingers kneaded his sides and abdomen, and Asher swallowed hard.

He took a hiccupping breath and nerves skittered down his spine.

Fingertips slipped beneath the waistband of his jeans and just like that, the anxiety was back. Like a shot, he scrambled to his knees and clutched at her hands. He took a calming breath before kissing each palm, then tucking them into one hand and holding them above her head.

"Not yet," he told her and exhaled a nervous chuckle.

It looked like she was going to protest, but he silenced her with another kiss. He could feel her body revving up underneath him. Her hips rose up, mindlessly seeking the pressure of his. Alternately her chest arching as if to encourage him. Her legs moved restlessly in concert with her arms tugging against his hold over her head.

So long as she didn't touch him, his body cooperated. He could fake his way through this and figure out his problem after. But for now, she was the priority. She couldn't find out just how epically screwed up he was—Lust who couldn't fuck.

Oh, the irony.

He broke the kiss, leaving them both panting. "If I let go of your hands, you can't move them unless I tell you, understand?"

Her eyes were glazed over and her lips were swollen and wet. "Um hmm."

With a hand underneath her back, he pinched her bra clasp open and tossed the lacy pink thing to the floor. He filled his hands and used his mouth to tease her nipples to attention. Sucking hard then soothing with a soft tongue, he teased gasps and moans from her. She swore when he nipped his teeth on the underside of her breast.

He caught her hands trying to reach for him, but brought them up over her head again. "Am I going to have to tie these up, or can you behave?"

The look she gave him was both thrilled and spooked. "I don't know," she whispered.

"How about—" he pulled at a nipple with his teeth "—if I promise—" he switched to the other nipple and spun his tongue around it "—you will come harder if you obey me."

She straightened her arms over her head and grinned. "I'll be good."

He turned a commanding gaze on her, hoping it disguised his disability. He held her eye as he ministered to her breasts, paying attention to her sweet noises and frustrated movements. When he headed south again, her arms twitched but she left them up there.

"Raise your hips for me, gorgeous." He tucked his fingers inside her panties and pulled them over her hips and down her magnificent legs. He stepped away from her just far enough that he could take in her entire exquisite body. Sublime.

When she tensed her abdomen to sit up, he raised a supercilious eyebrow, and she lay back down.

"Evangeline." His voice, husky and raw, belied the façade that he was in control. My God, she was just so gorgeous it made his soul ache. "You are Joan of Arc. Cleopatra. Helen of Troy."

She snorted, which on her was still sexy as hell. "Don't tease."

"It is a crime that you don't see it. A true disgrace there isn't poetry and ballads written in your honor."

"Okay. A little overkill."

He grasped a shapely ankle. "You're the most beautiful woman I've ever known."

Covering her face with one hand, she groaned. "Please."

"I'll prove it."

He licked, kissed, and nibbled up her legs, draping her knees over his shoulders until he found her center. Pink and glistening with her arousal, he blew against her skin until she quivered. When he parted her folds and massaged her clit with the flat of his tongue, she lifted her hips and groaned. He took advantage of years of experience to move her to a squirming, writhing wanton in moments.

A crooked finger slipped inside her and she brought her hand down to wind in his hair. He allowed it because, regardless of the rules he'd made, he was desperate for her touch. When he added a second finger and sucked lightly on that bundle of nerves, he knew an instant before she was going over the edge.

Her muscles seized him tightly and she keened his name. A light kiss on her mons before he crawled up the bed to pull her spent, naked body into his. He wrapped his arms around her and held her while she returned to this world.

"Holy shit," she said, finally. She snuggled up against him, her arms trapped between their bodies where she could do no harm.

Planting a kiss on her temple, he marveled at the tender experience. One thing about Lust, there wasn't a lot of cuddling after. Unconscious passing out, yes, but not snuggling and petting when it was over. When was the last time he'd held a lover? Stroked their back? Enjoyed postcoital affection?

Maybe never.

He'd never known what he was missing.

"You're an amazing man, Asher Mephisto." Her hot breath caressed his neck before she kissed him there. "You're handsome and generous and you make me feel things."

"Things?" he asked and rubbed a slow circle on her back.

"I thought you just wanted my vineyard. And then I thought you just wanted sex." She took a play from his book and bit his neck where the tendon met his shoulder. "The only reason I'm here now is because you want me."

"I do," he whispered because it was true. True and terrifying. "I want you every way imaginable."

"I want you, too." She'd managed to move her arm free and it circled behind him and hugged him to her. "But I don't want you to think it's just for your money."

Asher laughed, a guffaw that turned into a belly laugh. Oh, that she should only want him for his money and not just for sex. An interesting role reversal from the usual romantic problems.

"I'm not afraid you want me for my money," he confessed, no longer thinking her mistake was so amusing. At this rate she wasn't getting him for his dick either. He surreptitiously moved his hips backwards and away from their twinned bodies.

She pulled away from him at the waist, backing up to see his face. Her eyebrows scrunched together in concern. "Hey, did I say something wrong?" Her gaze moved from eye to eye, trying to discern what he was trying to hide. After a long pause, she suggested. "How about we go down and finish that dinner, huh? We have plenty of time to get around to finishing up here. If you want to, I mean."

Now was his turn to be perplexed. "Why?"

"Because as outstanding as that was—" she waved her free hand around her nether regions "—you seem strangely disconnected, and I'm not sure what I've done wrong. So maybe if we go downstairs and eat and flirt and talk like friends again, I can figure it out."

"You want to eat and talk?" He was flummoxed. He never ate with his lovers either, unless it was off of each other's body parts in a fetishy way.

"I want to be friends again. Or become friends. Or something."

Guess what else he'd never been with sex partners. That's right. And Evangeline Dashiell wanted to be his friend.

And just like that, his dick showed up to the party.

Chapter Sixteen

E va hadn't been sure what to expect when they finally got down and dirty, but a shy and hesitant lover was not it. Especially when she got a look at his house. That bed was fucking ridiculous. Twelve people could romp around on that thing, no problem.

And then when they were done, the whole squad could report to the giant shower for a spray down.

She wasn't going to tell him, because for some reason he was really freaked out, but when she'd followed him up the stairs, she'd taken the liberty of looking in a few doorways before finding him in the master bedroom.

There was a walk-in closet in the hallway that, swear to God, was shelf after shelf of condoms. Large, extra-large, Magnum. You know, in case you have a Clydesdale up in this bitch. Some were textured. Some were studded. She didn't even know that was a thing. There was something called a "tingling pleasure condom", which frankly sounded iffy. Of course, the tacky edible and glow-in-the-dark ones. Kiss of Mint condoms. Why? Organic condoms. Is that really necessary? She felt like she'd walked into an AP Sex Ed class.

She fully expected to find a sex dungeon behind one of these doors.

But the way he was acting, she almost wondered if this wasn't his house at all. Or that he had an identical twin brother who wasn't aware of their near copulation all over her vineyard. Something had changed in him, and she couldn't for the life of her figure out what it was. He'd gone from red-hot-libido-frat-boy to over-tired-dad-with-a-tummy-ache. Confounding. He'd been all over her for weeks and when they're finally at a place where sex could reasonably happen, he spends the whole time trying to keep her in a kitchen and feed her.

There had even been a horrifying moment when she thought he'd been trying to brush her off. But then he was kissing her. Honestly, he had her pinballing all over their conversation. It was massively confusing.

Then, woohoo, he laid her out and stiped her naked. And the man could use his tongue. Good lord. She couldn't wait to tell her sister. She and Maggie always had a debriefing afterwards, and she finally had a story worth telling. And not just oral sex, but also the crazy bed and shower. Oh, and holy shit, the COC—she pronounced it "cock" in her head—Closet of Condoms. Her sister was never going to believe this.

Asher was a cuddler, too. Not something she would have predicted, but it was nice. She'd kind of thought he would be one of those "oh hey, I got an early meeting tomorrow" sort of guy. What a pleasant surprise. When he wrapped her up in his arms, he smelled like warm grass and juniper. It sounded unlikely, but it reminded her of a few magical weeks she, Maggie, and their grandfather had spent in Provence.

She couldn't figure out what had changed to make him so uncomfortable, but she felt really bad about it. Certainly not interested in convincing him to do anything he wasn't totally into, she tamped down her lascivious thoughts, and pondered how the evening could be salvaged. Maybe it couldn't. Maybe she'd read him all wrong. Had she'd done something to kill his attraction? Maybe he was one of those guys who weren't interested once they'd gotten what they wanted. But they hadn't even had sex. Maybe all he'd wanted was the vineyard and she was a total schmuck. Maybe she was going completely insane.

He brightened up immediately when she suggested they backpedal this date.

Untangling their legs, she slid out from under him. "Come on. Let's finish making that dinner."

He gripped her hip, staying her movement, and said, "I'm not hungry." His voice was thick and when she turned back to look at him it was easy to tell he was hungry, just not for anything in the kitchen.

Huh. Things were looking up. She was going to get whiplash.

"Oh really?" She raised her eyebrows in disbelief and took in his long form laid out on his bed. "What are you thinking?"

"I'm tired of thinking," he told her and reached for her hand. "Been doing way too much thinking."

"Oh, is that what has been happening here?" She gazed into his hazel eyes. There was definite heat in them now, where before she'd seen nothing but doubt. "What conclusions have you come up with?"

"You want me." Curiously, he put the emphasis on the last word. *Me.*

"No, actually, I want the other fifteen naked people you can fit in this bed. What are you talking about?" How had she never noticed how odd he was before. She'd noticed his ego and confidence and other annoying traits plenty of times, but this weird talking in circles thing was new.

He chuckled in a self-deprecating way that tickled her skin with goosebumps. "Nothing I say is going to make sense outside my head. But, it's a good thing. A really good thing."

"You're a very unusual man," she told him.

This time his chuckle furled her nipples and she breathed in a sharp gasp.

"Oh honey," he told her as he pulled her back to him. "You have no idea."

She landed sprawled across his chest and his lips were on hers a heartbeat later. She didn't know who she'd been kissing earlier this evening, but it seemed like the old Asher was back. These were the toe-curling, spine-tingling kisses that had gotten her so revved up in the cask room. Even though he was underneath her, he definitely controlled this kiss. He had one hand wound through her hair, holding her at the angle he preferred. The other wide palm skated down her back to rest on her ass, squeezing her butt cheek. The part of him that had been so eager during their earlier trysts, the same part which had been so absent from tonight's festivities, made itself known by pressing up to her stomach with great enthusiasm.

She maneuvered over him until her she straddled him, freeing up her hands so she could explore. She nuzzled his whiskered cheeks with her own, traced the line of his jaw with her mouth, and nibbled his chin. Moving back onto her heels, she encouraged him to sit up with her and she dragged his shirt over his head without unbuttoning it. In hindsight, it would have been easier to have done it more conventionally, but her brain was all foggy with lust. He had to roll his shoulders and there was grunting involved, but she finally got it over his head.

Now his hair was all tousled, wavy locks hanging over his forehead. When she brushed the hair from his face, his gaze back at her was reverent.

"I want you so much," he rasped, his hands framing her face.

"Okay," she said and leaned in to kiss him again.

He filled his hands with her breasts, massaging and caressing each as he licked and sucked her nipples. She let her head hang back and soaked in his intensity. With her hands roaming his back and ribcage, she took in the warmth that seemed to seep from his body. When he pulled hard on her nipple, her hips rocked against him. The heat spiked from where his body strained to meet hers.

"I need you," he whispered against her throat.

She nodded and pulled his hair to bring his mouth back to hers. Their tongues stroking each other only made the need greater, and soon grinding against the fly of his jeans was not enough for her. Asher slid his palms underneath her butt again and she wrapped her legs around his middle. In one graceful movement, he turned them both and lay her back against the bed.

Gasping at his withdrawal of her, she feared the worst, but his gaze was still fervent and charged with emotions she didn't have the mental acuity to sort through just then. She watched as he yanked at his zipper and shoved his pants down. Sweet Lord. Asher Mephisto stood there, chest heaving, muscles all defined like an anatomy lesson, black, wavy hair wild on his head. He was like a fantasy, the way he looked at her as if she was the most beautiful woman in the world. It was so...much.

"Why are you looking at me like that?" she asked.

"You're so beautiful. The most amazing woman I've ever known." He wasn't smiling or wiggling his eyebrows or anything. He didn't seem to be teasing.

"Um, okay." She swallowed hard and looked away, suddenly wishing she had on even a scrap of clothing. When her gaze darted back at him, he was still looking at her the same way. Heady stuff, that. None of this was going the way she'd expected. This was supposed to have been a sexy romp with a player. All indications had suggested a no-strings-attached-don't-involve-your-heart kind of deal.

"I mean it, Evangeline." He crawled back to her. Stretched out his naked length alongside hers, he kissed her shoulder, her nearest breast, the curve of her jaw. "You are a wonderous creature."

She turned into him, dazzled by his pretty words and adoring expression. Supported on one elbow, he smoothed his hand across her cheek, softly kissing her lips, then her nose. He ran his fingers through her hair and kissed her lips again. Down his hand went, smoothed over her shoulder and along her back and side until he was cupping her ass again.

"I never knew I was missing you until I found you." The words were whispered, almost as if he was thinking out loud.

They were going to have to unpack that statement later, but right now she was too distracted by his lips on hers and his thumb rubbing circles on the inside of her thigh. She grabbed his face with both hands and brought him back for a kiss. As the tip of his tongue slipped into her mouth and teased hers, one finger slid inside her. She almost flew off the bed when a second finger joined it. Sweet Sauvignon, she was finding it hard to breath.

Mapping his back with her fingers and squeezing his hips between her thighs, she moved her body in the rhythm he'd set with his tongue and fingers. His kisses were worshipful, softly stroking the inside of her mouth, feathering her cheeks, and nibbling on her earlobes. All the while breathing words of adoration against her skin.

Tension curled in her body, winding tighter with the pressure of his thumb on her clit and his fingers curling against the tender spot inside her. He swallowed her gasp when he did some magical move that sent dazzling sparks of sensation twinkling throughout her body, and the orgasm surprised her.

Barely competent to form words, she noticed when he left but he was back quickly with the crinkling of a wrapper, stroking and kissing her again.

Settling between her legs, his cock edging her entrance, he crooned, "Eva. Honey, look at me."

When she opened her eyes, his smile was soft but tight with control. She lifted her hand to stroke his face. Had he always been this intense? This gorgeous? His hazel gaze held hers as he slid inside her, filled her. The sensation was so intense, so much, that she closed her eyes and breathed through, trying not to come again so quickly.

"Love," he said, his voice straining, "Look at me."

Eyes open once again, he started to move. Long, smooth, even strokes, she raised her knees to allow him deeper access.

"Oh God, Asher" She grasped at his shoulders and the back of his neck.

Holding himself over her with the strength of one arm, he drew her knee over his hip. Withdrawing almost to the point of pulling out then with a swift, sure flex of his hips, he drove all the way home. He grunted and took a steady, shaking breath, but his gaze never left hers.

She couldn't look away. It was as if there was a tether connecting them from behind his eyes through hers. Was it too hokey to say it seemed like his soul was mating with hers? God help her, she held his gaze while he filled her. He drove them higher together—and she encouraged him, pressing her heels into his ass, moving in concert with his body, and finally crying his name when their stars exploded.

They lay there together, chests heaving in unison. When she wrapped her arms around him, he was shaking.

"Asher?" She stroked his hair and whispered against his shoulder. "Baby?"

His response was to hold her tighter and sink his face into the crook of her neck.

"Are you alright?" she asked and caressed his warm skin. When he said nothing, merely nodded his head, she hugged her arms and legs around him and held him tight until the trembling stopped.

Eventually he settled and turned his face to her. His eyes were soft and some of the intensity had left them but, if it was possible, he was even more gorgeous than before. He smiled and her heart gave a little squeeze.

She had so many things she wanted to say. Once again, Asher had surprised her. Expecting ribald, dirty sex and instead she was made love to. It was breathtaking, sure, but... So many questions, but she was afraid to break the spell. At this moment, it felt like they were in a bubble where none of her insecurities belonged.

Until her stomach growled.

Asher laughed. "I never did feed you." He pulled away and slipped his legs into his jeans, then pulled her to her feet. "Come downstairs with me and we'll do that fortifying thing." He pulled her naked body flush with his and kissed her breathless. "We're going to need it."

Locating her underwear, she put them on and then slipped her arms into Ashe's shirt, tying the tails into a knot at her waist. "Promise?" she teased.

He swatted her butt sending her giggling down the same back stairs they'd come up. She came to a halt at the bottom of the stairs. Asher somehow managed to avoid mowing her down. The center island held a huge platter of crushed ice with oysters on the half shell. There were bowls of strawberries and some obscenely large bananas. A couple of pomegranates had been split and the arils spilled out onto the counter. A crock of golden honey sat by a basket of figs and ginger. There was chocolate and several bottles of both champagne and red wine.

"Where did all this come from?" Eva asked in awe. None of the dinner fixin's were visible anymore, just this bountiful display of...sex food.

Asher snorted a bawdy laugh. "Esther must have been here." He popped a strawberry in his mouth and grinned.

Eva didn't think she actually needed any aphrodisiacs, and based on the bulge in Ashe's jean's he didn't either. He turned his back to pull champagne glasses down when she saw his tattoo. She ran her fingers over his back along his shoulder blade. A handsome, red-skinned devil with horns and a tail was bowing and kissing the hand of a lovely maiden. A trick of the light made it seem for a second that the devil winked at her.

Whether they needed it or not, they ate their way through the feast. Well, at least to the point where they could use the counter for other recreation.

Heaven & Hell XVII

"Let me know if I get too heavy."

Juliet riding piggyback weighed no more than a sweatshirt hanging around his neck. And Neil got to enjoy the feel of her thighs hugging his waist. "Nah, you're as light as a feather."

She gave his shoulders a squeeze. "Eventually I'll get heavier though, and you'll need to put me down for a bit."

He had no idea how that was going to work. She couldn't touch the ground in Hell, so it wasn't like they had any options. Neil took off across the sooty ground following the dog. Juliet's head peered around his shoulders, taking in the horrific scenery.

"It doesn't look so bad down here," she declared. "It's not like Heaven, by any means, but it's not so awful. It's definitely hot, that's for sure." She emphasized her point by dripping sweat down her nose onto his shoulder.

"Don't get too comfortable," he said over his shoulder. "We're basically in Hell's lobby. It definitely gets worse as we go down."

"How far down are we going?"

"All the way." He dodged a floor vent, shooting caustic steam. "To the last place I saw Rachel—the Devil's mansion."

Juliet waved her hand in front of her face, and Neil knew if he could see it her cute little nose would be wrinkled from the stench. "The mansion?"

"Oh, sure," he said, like *everyone* knew there was a mansion down here. "The Devil has a mansion."

"That sounds...nice."

"It's not nice," he warned her. "It's awful, and I want you to know that every step we take, every level, is going to get worse and worse."

"I know," she said.

But she didn't. There was no way she could imagine what was in store for them. Juliet had obviously come from a nice middle-class family in the suburbs. He was willing to bet she didn't even share a bedroom with brothers and sisters. She'd likely never known horror in real life, so this was going to be a hell of a shock.

They followed Cerberus around the back of the squat cinderblock buildings, trying to keep off the main drag where there was a better chance of keeping Juliet under the radar. There was no way to hide her forever, but Neil was in no hurry to let Hell at large know what was going on.

What kind of explanation were they going to come up with for her presence when they inevitably ran into someone? It had never happened before. Ever. The only angel that had ever been in Hell was Lucifer himself.

"So, how far is it to the mansion?"

"A bit further until we get to the elevator. We'll get Charon to take us all the way down. It'll be a lot faster than when I went down level by level."

Her breath puffed against his ear. "How many levels are there?"

His arms broke out in goosebumps—in Hell. "Nine."

She was quiet for a few moments, and then asked, "What is that smell?"

"Well—" Neil took an exploratory sniff. "It's hard to say. Most obviously I'd say brimstone, but it's possible you're smelling rotten garbage."

"Eww. Garbage? Really?"

"Yeah, definitely sulphur. And probably burning hair." He didn't want to tell her that the smell-soup probably also included charcoaled flesh, because that was just too awful. They were going to have to take baby steps introducing her to Hell.

"Oh." She was quiet for a few more moments. "Does this smell not bother you?"

Cerberus disappeared around the end of a smokestack.

"No, it definitely bothers me." He gave her knee a squeeze. "I guess I'm just sorta used to it."

She hugged him again. "Oh Neil, that's the saddest thing."

"What is?"

"That you're used to this horrible place."

He couldn't help it. He milked it the tiniest bit with a long, deep sigh. "Yeah. The beatings are the worst."

"Beatings," she shrieked. If he wasn't already dead, she'd have burst his eardrum. "What do you mean, beatings? How often does that happen? What are they beating you with? This is unconscionable."

He snickered. "Hey doll, I'm in Hell, remember. I did bad stuff, and now I reap the whirlwind."

"It couldn't have been that awfully bad, could it?" she asked, her soft voice behind him sounding unsure.

"Bad enough. I never killed anyone myself, but I certainly did things that caused other people to die." He'd had plenty of time to ponder his lamentable life choices in the time he'd spent down here. He'd even narrowed down the pivot points when choices were made that sent him in very specific directions. If he could do it all again...

Well, he couldn't so there was no point in that fantasy. Besides, Hell was no place for that bullshit. What was done was done. Now it's time to suck it up.

Juliet patted him on the shoulder. "When we're all done and we've got Rachel and Lucifer back together, then we can figure out a way to get you out of here."

This time he snorted. "I wouldn't count on it, babe. Us bad guys are down here where we belong." He wasn't going to spend any time hoping for that. That was a fast train to insanity town. He'd seen people down here who'd let hope get to them, and it was fucking grisly.

"We'll see."

Thankfully, she dropped the subject once she got distracted by five cats sitting on the side of the path. She made kissing noises at them, but they responded with disdain.

"Psspsspss." She tried again. "Kitty, kitty, kitty."

Three of the furry bastards totally ignored her, but one of those naked, wrinkly fuckers got up and walked away with a sneer on his face. A long-haired, white Persian bared his claws and hissed at her.

"Rude," she declared.

"Honestly, you should ignore them. Even if one let you get close enough to pet, it would just rip you to shreds. The cats here are horrible monsters." Neil picked up the pace, giving the cats a wide berth. Even still, he could feel her looking backward at the mangy crowd.

"It makes me sad. I had cats when I was alive. My tabby even had kittens once. There were six of them. All gray stripped like their mom and one random orange one. He was my favorite."

"This bunch of cats are not like yours. Just think of them as fuzzy demons."

They were nearing the main square which would likely be much more crowded with demons and other hellish denizens. There was no way to predict how they were going to react to an angel in their midst, but it certainly wasn't going to be good.

"Juliet, listen to me. We're getting close to where the elevator is. We're probably going to see some demons there. Just be quiet and let me do the talking, okay."

"Okay. What will they...?"

When she trailed off, he knew what she was thinking. "I really don't know. You're pretty unprecedented. Also, they don't all look like me. Like, I was originally a human dude, but there's a lot of heinous creatures down here that are not and never were human."

He didn't feel her leaning into his back anymore. "You're telling me they're scary, right?"

Oh man. Scary didn't even begin to cover it. He squeezed her knee again. "Scary is a really simplistic take on it, babe. There is nothing you've ever imagined that even comes close to what's happening down here."

She took a deep breath and patted his arm. "Let's just take it as it comes, okay? We're going to find Rachel."

Man, she was something else. This was an insane quest they were on, and she was brave to even come down here. So, his plan was to get to the elevator, down to nine, and into the mansion before they ran into anyone—or anything—really horrible. They'd collect Rachel and get her the hell out of there. The whole thing would be over. Easy-peasy.

The elevator loomed in front of them on a small rise. The platform was empty. In fact, the whole square was vacant. What in the Hell?

"Where is everyone?" he wondered aloud. He circled the platform, looking out over the wretched vista. There was no sign of Scourge or any of his legion. None of the ghouls that generally lingered in the area. No one.

This was weird.

"So far, it doesn't seem so bad," she said from over his shoulder.

"I don't know what's going on," he confessed. He pressed the down button on the elevator. "But it's kinda freaking me out."

He felt her shrug. "My dad would say not to look a gift horse in the mouth."

Shaking his head, he told her, "Don't look anything in the mouth down here. Seriously."

She giggled. Actually giggled. He really hoped the misery of this place didn't ruin her. She was so perfect just as she was. Cerberus woofed from behind them and hopped up on the dais.

"Hi puppy!" Juliet chirped at him and reached down to pat the closest head.

There was a ding and the elevator doors slid opened. Charon peered around the door, saw the angel hanging on his back, and his eyes grew to the size of hubcaps.

"Hey, man." Neil adopted that cool, breezy tone he resorted to when he was going to try to con someone into something. "How have you been?"

"What is that?" Charon's voice rasped like an old muffler. He raised his arm and a chicken bone-like finger extended and pointed at Juliet.

"A friend." He thought it was best to move off the subject right away. "How much to take us to nine?"

The ancient elevator man couldn't tear his eyes from Juliet, but like he asked, she remained mute. So, the three of them stared at each other and the three-headed-dog scratched behind the left head's ear.

Neil couldn't take it. "We have all kinds of things to trade for a ride," he prompted.

Cerberus shook a head, snorted, then got up and wandered into the elevator. That distracted Charon and he jerked back to life. "That dog's not coming in here," he insisted.

"It looks like he thinks he is." Neil shrugged.

Bones creaking like a haunted house, Charon turned to eye the dog. "I don't like that dog."

"No one likes that dog," Neil repeated his regular mantra when the dog was mentioned. There was a squeak from Juliet, but nothing else. "We'll pay extra for the dog."

"It's gonna cost you." Charon's rheumy eyes twinkled with greed. "For you, the dog, and that—" he pointed at Juliet again "—there's no way you can afford it."

Neil pulled a king-sized Snickers bar from his pocket. The ferryman's jaw dropped open, giving him and Juliet a full shot of the horrific state of his teeth. Another gasp came from behind his head. Neil had to chuckle. He'd warned her.

Faster than Neil thought the decrepit old man could move, a skeletal hand shot out and snatched the candy bar from his fist. He had the wrapping open in a flash and sank his rotten teeth into the coated nougat.

"Get in," he croaked, his lips dripping melted chocolate.

Neil walked the angel into the elevator and the doors slid shut behind them. "Here we go, babe."

"Here we go," she whispered in his ear.

Chapter Seventeen

Asher was in Heaven.

There was no other explanation. He lingered on the cusp of asleep and awake with no hurry to spoil the bliss. Eva's warm, naked body little-spooned with his. When he smoothed his hand down her hip, she felt like the softest velvet. He flexed his spine, curving around her even tighter, and buried his face in her hair.

He would happily stay here until he died. Probably from starvation.

But eventually they'd have to pee. Stupid body functions.

Eva sighed in her sleep, and in response, Asher's heart squeezed. He roused her further by kissing her shoulder.

"Hmmm." She snuggled backwards. "Mornin'."

He lifted the hair from her neck and feathered her hairline with kisses. "Mornin', gorgeous."

"What time is it?" she mumbled.

"Who cares." he answered. He filled a palm with her breast. She arched her back, pressing her chest into his hand in sleepy encouragement which served to press her butt deliciously into his morning wood. "This bed is where we live now. Everything we need can be brought in. You can consider Esther at our beck and call."

"Does Esther know that?" Eva giggled into the pillow. "Doesn't seem like something she'd be real keen on. She's not really a beck and call kinda gal."

He ran his nose along her nape then took a small bite of her shoulder. "Actually, you'd be surprised. Esther has a smooshy center."

Letting his hands roam along the silky skin of her chest and along her torso, he found the thatch of hair between her legs. She shifted her limbs to invite his knee to slip between them. He could feel she was already damp in anticipation. He patted the mattress behind him until he found the string of condoms they'd been resolutely working their way through. He rolled away from her just far enough to roll one on and then slid his impatient cock inside her.

She moaned his name when he rocked against her, moving slowly so she couldn't climb too high, too quickly. He set the rhythm for a nice, leisurely fuck. They had all day. There was no hurry. He wanted nothing more than to stay inside Evangeline Dashiell for the rest of their lives.

Fingers clamped tight on her hip, he undulated his pelvis in slow controlled movements, all the way out to the tip and back in until his groin was flush with her ass. Slow, deliberate, and steady. He slipped his bottom arm underneath her to wrap around her chest, pressing her whole body to his. Together they moved, straining away from each other, then their bodies merging again. He released her hip and delved his fingers between her legs. Eva threw her head back against his shoulder and it sounded like she'd quit breathing. Finally, she gasped. Her muscles pulsated and embraced him, and then he let himself go.

His face deep in her hair, he breathed her in, inhaled her like a drug. They lay there for a long, quiet moment with Asher's arms wrapped around her, and her arms wrapped around his. He basked in euphoria.

Is this what other people got from sex? Lust was mighty good at sex, but even with all his otherworldly skills, he didn't think he'd ever been transported to this level of rapture. Eva made a contented noise and Asher understood the difference from every other sexual experience and this one.

He cared about her. Perhaps she cared a bit about him, as well. If he was lucky.

She removed her arms from the awkward embrace and then reluctantly pulled away. "I really need to use the bathroom," she whispered as if she didn't want to break the spell either.

He let her go, but not before kissing her shoulder. When she crossed the room in all her naked glory, he leaned up on one elbow to enjoy the view. He flopped back on the pillow with a grin on his face.

"Hey," he called. "Are you hungry? I'm starving."

"Yeah, what are you thinking?" The toilet flushed and the water ran in the sink. "Coffee?"

Eva's head appeared around the doorway. "Can we take a shower first? I mean this thing is amazing. There's like seven shower heads in here."

He threw the covers off and hopped out of bed. "Just wait until I show you what that middle one can do."

Some time later, they were in the kitchen nibbling on fresh berries and beignets from a pink box on the counter. Even the coffee machine had been set up for his extravagant brew. All he'd had to do was hit the button. God bless Esther.

"Wow, this is a tough existence you have here." Eva met his eyes over her coffee cup. "I don't know how you manage to be such a charming fellow living in these austere conditions."

"It's rough." He grinned back at her and tossed a blueberry in his mouth.

"Whatever you're paying Esther, it isn't enough."

He dismissed her comment with a small shrug. He couldn't possibly explain to Eva that Esther neither expected nor received any compensation. Their relationship, as with all the Sins and their gargoyles, was a complicated but immemorial one. It was only recently that the Sins had come to understand that their association with the gargoyles was as a guardianship rather than a punishment. Until they'd all met the leader of the gargoyle order, Notre Dame, and she'd explained the true nature of their job, the Sins had believed the gargoyles acted as spies for the Devil.

No, indeed, Esther took exceptionally good care of Asher.

Eva set her cup down and Asher watched with singular interest as she dipped a strawberry in powdered sugar before wrapping her lips around it and sucking. She chortled when he made a strangled noise and dribbled coffee down his chin.

She popped the berry in her mouth and said, "What are you going to do today?"

Asher contemplated the wording of this sentence. Curious that she said you and not we. "Well, I thought about trying a few more positions in my giant bed." He shrugged his naked shoulders and tried to look coy. "Maybe introduce to you a few toys. Make our way through that closet you found so interesting."

Her eyebrows rose suggestively. "Toys? Is there another closet I don't know about? You're a man of mystery and unexpected charms, Asher Mephisto."

He snorted. If only. "Not so much, honey. There are some who'd say I'm really rather single-minded."

"No way." She scoffed and ate a blueberry. "International luxury brand investor. New vineyard co-owner. Matchless sexual dynamo. White knight in a red sports car."

She was wearing her pink lace bra and his black boxer briefs she'd stolen when they'd emerged from the shower. He wasn't sure what she'd expected—that he'd be forced to go naked in his own home if she stole his underwear? He'd held her gaze in unmitigated challenge as he'd pulled her pink lace cheekie-shorts over his own hips. Things weren't actually well-contained in there, but her aghast giggles were reward enough.

"Well." He said it all breathy like a 1960's sex kitten which was obviously especially seductive while in pink panties.

"Seriously though," she said and straightened on her stool. "There's a zillion things to do at the vineyard. Now more than ever. As much as I'd like to, I can't sit around all day in each other's underwear."

Coffee cup in the sink, Ashe stuck his thumbs on either side of the lacy underwear and pulled them off. "I'm also happy to sit around in no underwear. Whatever makes you happy, honey."

Peels of laughter rang through his kitchen, making him grin. God, he loved her laugh. She got off the stool and in one quick movement dropped his boxers on the counter and took off to the living room. By the time he got around the counter and into the other room, all he saw of her was disappearing up the staircase to the second floor. Bless those mile-long legs of hers.

The sun through the windows suggested early afternoon and they were eating grilled peanut butter and banana sandwiches on the carpet in the living room.

"This is so yummy," Asher told her and licked the melting goo from his thumb. "I haven't had one of these since I was a kid."

She grinned at him with peanut butter on her teeth. "My grandfather's favorite."

"So, my favorite vintner, what wine pairs best with this?"

It took her a moment to respond. He could see her mouth working against the peanut butter, and then finally she said, "Hmm. Do you want a red or white?"

"I don't know. You tell me."

"A sauvignon banc wouldn't be overpowered by the peanut butter if you want a white, but I think a cab sauvignon would be even better. Oh! Or maybe a Malbec."

Asher hopped up. "I'll be right back." Inside the pantry there was a secret door leading to a hidden wine closet. Floor to ceiling space for fifteen hundred bottles, but it only housed a third of that now. Now that he'd found Eva's vineyard, it should fill up quickly. He reemerged with a bottle and grabbed an opener and glasses on the way back to the picnic. "I got a case of this the last time I was in South America."

He popped the cork and gave her a glass.

"Oh yeah. This is perfect." She grinned around her glass. "I knew it would be."

Man, her confidence was such a turn-on. "You know what I wanna' do?"

Eva stopped midchew. "Holy cow, your stamina is like Olympic level. Probably higher. Maybe God-like."

Bending down to kiss her, he said. "Definitely more of that, but right now I want to go buy a new truck. I'm going to need something more appropriate. I really loved that car, but she wasn't really a farm vehicle, you know."

Eva popped the last of her sandwich in her mouth and chewed while she gazed up at him contemplatively. "Exactly how much farming are you expecting to be doing?"

He shrugged. "I don't know, but you have to admit, the Aston Martin wasn't smart at the vineyard."

"Smart enough. You're not hauling materials or anything."

He narrowed his eyes at her playfully. "It's a moot point, don't you think? Since the Aston is deceased."

"Touché."

"So, let's go buy a truck." He rubbed his hands together.

She set her empty wine glass on an ottoman and made a pointed look at their bodies. "We'll have to wear pants."

As much as he loved her wearing nothing but her panties and bra, they couldn't stay that way forever. "How about it I promise we can make out in it later?"

With that promise hanging in the air, Eva dug through the bag Luke's gargoyle had packed for her and he went to his closet to find truck-buying clothes. Not long after, they took Esther's Porsche to a dealer and wandered into a showroom. Eva held back, lingering by the door until he laced her fingers in his and towed her into the building. "Come on. This is going to be fun."

She shook her head. "You don't need to buy a truck. I don't know why you're doing this. Buy another cute little car."

Asher snorted. "The Aston Martin was not 'a cute little car.' That car was hot as fuck. Believe me. I know these things."

"You're right. It was a hot car. So buy another one." She was almost pleading.

Right in the middle of the showroom, he pulled her into his arms. "Evangeline," he said her name low and serious. "What's the problem?" She looked away and chewed her cheek for a moment. Then it occurred to him. "Is this about my involvement in the vineyard? You're still nervous, aren't you?"

She shook her head and exhaled, sort of deflating her shoulders. "No. Yeah, but not really. I trust you. It's just... It's been me and Maggie and Ernie on our own, struggling for the last few years, and we were surviving. I guess I'm just nervous about relaxing my guard. That maybe your money will make us, me, soft. And I'm still concerned that another person's involvement will dilute my control."

"First, soft? No way." He spread his lips in a wide grin. "I'm investing my money so you better not think you can slack off. I fully expect a large return on my investment. I don't give my money and time to losing propositions." He ducked his head to regain her gaze. "Second, you're the vintner. You're the one who has to make the wine. It all depends on you. I'm just going to drive around the place in a big-ass truck and throw money at all the problems."

Despite herself, Eva snickered at that remark. "Then be smart and get a used one. Don't waste your money on a new truck."

"Oh, I am smart," he assured her, reclaiming her hand and leading her into the dealership. "I snagged you, didn't I? And the things that fascinate me in the world have made me tons of money. Diamonds. Silk. Cavier. And now wine. But I also, don't drive around in used trucks."

"You drove around in mine." She pointed out.

"Let's call Miriam a classic, shall we?"

An archetypal car salesman presented himself in their path. He stuck out his hand. "Henry Swanson at your service."

Ash extended his own and made introductions, then launched right into it. "Nice to meet you, Henry. We're here to buy a truck."

"Then you've come to the right place." Henry beamed at them as they headed out to the lot. "What are you looking for this truck to do for you?"

"Towing. Hauling. Looking manly. Pretty standard truck stuff, Henry." Asher squeezed Eva's hand and gave her a broad grin. "I'm new to the agricultural game, and my previous vehicle fell pretty flat."

Eva groaned. "Here we go."

It didn't bother Asher that Henry looked at him like a whale with a commission check. Regardless of Eva's doubts, this was going to be fun. He might actually be one of the few people on the planet who loved buying cars. Since money wasn't an object and he fully admitted that his taste ran to bougie, he was not intimidated by salespeople. "Lead the way to the big—"

Eva cut in, "To the most reasonable pickups."

Asher raised his eyebrow at her but allowed Henry to lead the way. The salesman must have taken one look at them, and probably took the sportscar they drove up in into account and started across the lot. "This model is very reliable."

He stopped them in front of a smallish mini-truck in white. White! Could you imagine? Never in a million years would he a) be caught dead in a mini anything and b) sure as hell not in a white one. It didn't even have a pearlescent coating.

Asher hooked his thumbs in the belt loops of his cashmere jeans and struck a cowboy-ish stance. "There's no way we could haul pigs in this tiny truck."

Eva guffawed then slammed her jaw shut. She nodded her head seriously and crossed her arms over her chest. "No. There's no way fifteen hogs are fitting in there."

Henry was not ruffled at all, although he did another longer assessment of Ashe's outfit. Dark wash cashmere jeans, cognac alligator loafers, and cotton/silk blend Henley. Asher kept a straight face as the salesman struggled to figure out exactly what their story was. A pig farmer wearing a five-thousand-dollar outfit?

"What's our budget?" Henry asked.

"To be determined when I find the truck we want." Asher knew better than to lay out all his cards. There might not be a budget but telling Henry would seriously hinder their negotiations later.

"So, something bigger then?"

"Maybe a king cab, unless Eva here plans to ride in the bed of the truck." Eva rolled her eyes. "She does not."

"Of course not, gorgeous. And you smell infinitely better than the pigs." He planted a kiss on her lips. "Onward, Henry."

They stopped at a midsize pickup. "This here is called a super cab. You can see there is more room but still a manageable vehicle." Unfortunately, it was blah.

Eva walked around it and nodded her head. "This is good. This one will work." She studied the sticker on the window

Asher tilted his head to the side and gave her a look. Then he made a point of opening the door and assessing the back seat. It was a half size bench seat. Anyone with knees would be uncomfortable here. "Mmm, it's gonna need to be bigger."

Eva raised her eyebrows and smirked. "That's what she said."

"We could test it out." Ashe pushed on the seat, testing out the cushion.

Eva giggled and Ashe's libido roused itself from its recovery nap. Henry looked from Asher to Eva and back again with a strained smile.

With a slam of the super cab door, Asher told Henry, "Bigger."

The next truck, while bigger, still wasn't what Asher wanted. His vision was grander. More opulent. He liked a cushy ride, hence the Aston Martin and the Audi before it.

He let his face dissolve into a frown. "You're disappointing me, Henry."

"We have something over here," Henry said and pointed to the far side of the lot. "It's a special order that didn't sell. It's a bit extreme, but I think it might be big enough—" he coughed "—for what you're looking for."

They rounded a bend into a tucked-away corner of the lot. There, gleaming in the afternoon light, sat the big-ass truck of his dreams. Hulking and yet beautiful. Capable of all manner of vineyard-related tasks. And other things. Topping it off, it was sumptuous merlot-colored red. Almost as if this beauty was sent by God himself.

"Now you're talking." Asher couldn't hide his enthusiasm.

"Are you kidding me?" Eva pointed at the truck. "This thing is a monster. Why in heaven's name do you think you need something this big? There is no scenario I can think of where you'd need a dually. None. We've worked all those years with Miriam, and she's held together with bailing wire and hope."

Asher wasn't listening. He'd already climbed into the Ford King Ranch F350. "Smell that leather?" he asked.

Eva's hands landed on her hips. "Perfect. You'll be able to wipe the pig shit right off."

He laughed and climbed back down. Opening the back door, he tossed her a flirty look. "Come on, you like it."

Henry wisely hung back. She stared at Ashe in response, giving him nothing back. He wrapped her in his arms, his hands lingering on her perfect little butt, and gave her a solid kiss.

Pulling back but still in the circle of his arms, she said, "This is a stupid, excessive waste of your money."

He tightened his grip around her waist and lifted her off her feet. "Will it make you feel better if we paint the logo on the side? That way it'll also count as advertisement, too. Dashiell Vineyard and Pig Farm."

"You're such an idiot," she said, but it was clear she was trying not to laugh.

He tossed her on the back seat and crawled in on top of her. "We can check the gewurztraminer vines and then fuck right there in the rows. Just think how convenient it'll be." He ground his hips into her as a reminder.

"Fine," she conceded sounding a bit breathy. "But do me a favor and don't park next to anything with a roof, huh?"

Chapter Eighteen

Eva was so hot. That was one of the hallmarks of this dream. This was the third time she'd had it in the last ten days, and every single time that was the first thing she noticed—humid, skin-bubbling heat. It made her lungs ache with its burning intensity.

She looked around for the man, but he wasn't immediately with her as he'd been in the previous dreams. She scanned the wasteland around her, but she didn't spy him as far as the horizon. This was the best look she'd had at her surroundings as the previous dreams she'd been too captivated by the man to notice anything but the heat. Squinting at the barren scenery, she likened it in her mind to a set piece from a Mad Max movie. Everything looked as if it had once been alive but was now charred and withered. A decrepit tree seemed to have been torn in half based on the jagged quality of the stump. Otherwise, there was just nothing. Barren.

Surely this was what Earth would look like after a nuclear bombing. A scorching breeze brought with it a stench that made her eyes water. Hearing a rustling behind her, she whirled around fast enough to see the tail end of some unknown creature disappear into a sandy hole. All she'd spied was a foot. A hoof? Then it was gone.

"Evangeline." Her name skittered across her skin, raising goosebumps of unease, yet the voice was strangely melodious. She turned her head, looking for the owner, but no one was there.

Another movement in her peripheral vision sent her spinning back around. This time the man was walking towards her. He hadn't been there only moments before, she was certain. His lips spread in a felicitous grin that was at odds with the scenery. As was his attire. A bespoke slate-gray, flannel suit with a dark blue waistcoat. He was handsome and familiar, and she wanted to relax. His attitude was one of ease, but she couldn't quite get there.

Maybe that was because she couldn't make out his face. She'd had a variation on this dream time and again, and she still was never able to clearly make out his features. It was more what she just intuitively knew. She understood that he was handsome. She would have been able to verify that he was clean-shaven and the shape of his face was pleasing. She could testify that he had a straight nose and his mouth was often shaped into an easy grin, but if asked to describe the color of his eyes, she would only have been able to aver that there were two. If asked to pick him out of a lineup, she would have said it was impossible.

As he drew nearer, he stretched out both his hands in greeting. Her instinct was to refuse. To simply not allow him to take her hands. But then as if she was unable to deny him, her hands rose to slide into his.

"Evangeline." He nearly purred her name. She closed her eyes when he came in to kiss her European-style. His cheek and lips were soft against her own. "Delighted to see you again."

Eva forced herself to smile. "Where is this place?" She'd asked before and he'd never said.

His look was placating. "As I've said before, it's nowhere. Neither here nor there."

Tucking her hand into the crook of his elbow, he drew her into the vast expanse of nothing. His suit was thick, textured, soft, sort of like her grandfather's suits had been. How he managed to look so put together in this heat, she had no idea.

Where she thought before there had been vast emptiness around her, she began to realize she was surrounded by hundreds of creatures who all ducked out of sight as they advanced. Primarily insects, there appeared to be grotesque combinations of scorpions and spiders. Some seemed to have the ability to jump where others skittered across the sandy earth sideways like crabs. None of their parts seemed to go together. A grasshopper with massive scorpion pinchers and tentacles. A spider with dozens of legs.

Eva snapped her eyes closed before she could scream and went rigid.

"Come along," he said and patted her hand. "Nothing will bother you here. Not when you're with me." She opened her eyes, keeping her gaze well above the horizon to avoid accidentally seeing anything hellish. "Good girl."

They walked several more paces before the man spoke again. "Tell me more about your vineyard."

"Oh, you know it? Yes, we've talked about it before, haven't we." She tried to remember specifics about their previous encounters, but they were as murky as her description of him. "It's very good. My experiments are finally coming to fruition. I'm very proud of them."

"Um hum," he prompted. His interest excited her even when other parts of her seemed wary of his attentions. "What of your other plans?"

"There've been some setbacks," she admitted. She gasped when a larger animal burst forth from the ground and snatched a horrible beetle-esque insect and dragged it back into its den. The bug emitted an almost human screech and clawed at the sandy ground, but it was no match for the creature's slimy tongue when wrapped around it and seemed to squeeze before they both disappeared back into the earth.

"Tell me about your young man."

Eva sensed this was where the conversation was really heading. She turned her gaze back to him and tried to focus her attention on his face.

"He's very handsome."

The man chuckled. "Of course. Tell me more."

"He's incredible in bed. Like, an amazing lay." She should be blushing, with anyone else she wouldn't even be having this conversation. In fact, she wasn't even sure how those uncharacteristic words were coming out of her mouth. They were true, certainly, but not confessions she'd felt form in her mind.

Now his laugh was raucous. "That's Lust for you."

Eva didn't understand what that meant. The stranger frightened her, but also made her feel wicked.

"Besides fucking, I'm more curious how your relationship is progressing."

Reluctant to share since she still hadn't come to terms with all these feelings herself, she hesitated. She'd come to learn the hard lesson about saying wishes out loud, as they inevitably fell apart right before your eyes. If you don't speak them, then you don't give them life. Then they can't hurt you when they wither and die.

You can wish for your mother to come home with every ounce of hope you possess, but she won't.

When he paused their walk and turned towards her, she stopped breathing.

"Come now." His regard weighed heavy on her. "You know you're dying to tell someone." She couldn't meet his gaze, so he chucked a finger under her chin. His voice was gentle but firm. "I can compel you, but you'll be happier if you tell me yourself."

She swallowed hard, and a wave of nausea passed through her. "I don't know how I feel. He seems like a bird, migrating from one project to another. If he leaves—when he leaves, I don't want to be left broken. Besides, he's a golden child and I'm just Evangeline."

"Interesting." The handsome man held one hand by her fingers and brought it to his lips, like Cary Grant or something. "Until we meet again."

And then he walked away. He didn't look at her as he left, he simply strode off into the desert.

When Eva woke up, Asher wasn't in the bed. She heard the shower running so, she flopped back onto the pillow for a moment to get her bearings. She tried to clasp onto the threads of a dream that were drifting away, but they were so fine she knew she'd never catch them. She'd had several dreams like that lately. She'd never been much of a dreamer, or at least she didn't remember them in the past. But these had all been odd, what she could recall of them, anyway.

She rubbed her eyes, then threw off the covers. She had a busy day ahead of her, and she couldn't lay around in Asher's bed for all of it, although it was tempting. The bathroom was all steamy when she walked in. She could just make out Asher's shape behind the glass wall. She didn't hesitate to join him in there.

"Good morning," he said, nearly purring and pulled her flush with his soapy body.

That's the way it had been for the last week. Luke wouldn't let them stay in the monastery, so Maggie was still holed up at Ernie's house and Eva at Asher's until the engineering reports came back. They'd barely left Asher's apartment. They'd barely even worn clothes. Since all the work with Hell Week was wrapped up early, the vines were on autopilot for a bit. Ernie kept her posted, but nothing really needed to be done. Eva hadn't seen her twin in over seven days. They hadn't even talked in four. The reality was that Eva had been so wrapped up in Ashe that even their twin-sense was feeling a little rusty.

While she dried off and slipped on her underwear, she vowed to do better today. She'd find Maggie and they'd sit and have some coffee and chat. There was so much to tell her.

That random thought had her harken back to the dream. It was just an elusive sliver, but it seemed like she'd been talking about Asher with someone. She closed her eyes and sought to catch the ephemera before it vanished, but she was so startled when a wave of dread slipped over her that she let the thread go with a gasp.

"Hey, you okay?" Asher asked as he emerged from his closet. He slipped a silk t-shirt over his head.

"Oh, yeah," she assured him and smiled. She slid her palms across his pecs, stroking the fine material. "All your clothes are so soft and sensuous. I can't keep my hands off them. Even your sheets and towels. They must all cost a fortune. This is how you use your money, isn't it?"

He pulled her flush with his body and tucked his fingers down the back of her panties. "What can I say? I love beautiful things. Would you rather have scratchy shirts—" he ran his stubbly chin up the side of her neck "—or the softest material against your skin?" He eased the burn with his lips. "If I can't find what I want, I go help someone make it."

"Hmmm," she stretched and purred at his ministrations. "I'm not complaining."

"We all have our way. The way we handle things," he continued, but he was no longer kissing her. It felt suddenly as if the words he was saying had weight. She opened her eyes and met his gaze. "I surround myself with sensuous pleasures. Luke does cage fighting. Benji paints."

Eva understood the words, but taken as a whole, they didn't make sense in her world. People had hobbies and careers. Wasn't that everyone?

"And you like nice things." She shrugged. "I get it."

He held her gaze for a heartbeat. "No. I like sensual things. Carnal things. There's a distinction."

"Okay." She pulled him in for a tight hug.

"I want you to know me," he said into her hair, and she squeezed a little tighter and held on for a heartbeat longer.

She didn't know how to reply to that. Should she divulge something about herself? Was this a tit for tat situation? She wasn't sure if there was anything about herself that held the same kind of reciprocal energy he was giving off. This information from him didn't seem like a big deal, but clearly he thought it was, and she didn't want to make light of it.

It must have taken her too long to come up with something, because he pulled away and turned his back on her to walk out the door, saying, "We should get a move on. Luke texted he has something important to discuss."

She stood there a second, feeling bereft that she might have disappointed him or hurt him in some way she didn't really understand.

"I'm coming," she said and grabbed her pants.

She really needed some twin time with Maggie. No one knew her better, and if there was something weird about herself that she could share with Ashe, Maggie would certainly know it.

When the huge Ford pulled up into the parking area at the vineyard, it was already crowded. There was a classic hot rod parked way far away from any structures. She also noticed the cute little convertible Luke's assistant drove was parked next to the van Esther had driven that day she'd brought out all the dayworkers to help during Hell Week.

A giant temporary shipping container had been parked on the near side of the parking lot and a hulking, ugly roll-off dumpster had been left right next to the monastery. A parade of laborers were exiting the old building with dollies and hand trucks loaded up with boxes and steering them into the storage container.

"Holy cow," Eva said and jumped from the cab. She hustled toward all the activity, not liking that all of this was happening and she didn't even know about it. Well, she knew on a basic level that all of this would be occurring, but she'd been in that Asher-centric bubble for days and days. Damn it.

She found Maggie on the lawn with her cell phone to her ear. Eva threw up her hands in the universal sign for 'what the hell?' and Maggie held up one finger and pointed to the phone.

Eva headed for the old building where they'd lived all their lives. She intended to go inside and supervise the dismantling of her home, but she was stopped by Luke's assistant. He was also on the phone tucked between his shoulder and his ear. In his hands was a iPad and an electronic pencil. He stepped in front of her and shook his pencil in a no-go motion. There was no getting around him.

"Uh huh," the pretty little man said into the cell. "No later than Wednesday, understood? I have to go. Another call is coming in." He gave her an apologetic smile and switched to the other call. "This is Jeb."

She left him to his business and went in search of someone else who could explain. Luke was around the corner with his back to her. She recognized him by the enormous width of his shoulders. Also, she sure as hell hoped he was using a headset to talk on his phone, because if not, he was standing there, all alone, yelling at a tree.

"Maybe I should call you people on my own phone," she growled out loud. "Then I can talk to someone."

Throwing her hands down in frustration, she headed back to her sister.

Maggie mouthed *one more second* and rolled her eyes. Eva had no choice but to watch the strange workers trail out of her home like mutant ants. The container looked to be well over half full, so they'd been at it for a while. She should have been out here, helping deal with this. If her sister hung up the phone and chewed her ass out, she would deserve it.

"Sorry," Maggie said and gave her a one-armed hug. "It's crazy around here."

Eva gestured to all the comings and goings. "What's happening?"

"Oh my God!" Maggie gushed. "So much. Luke has been working on the plans to renovate the monastery, and I've been talking with his assistant, Jeb, about our ideas for the party space and stuff. He's brilliant. So many great ideas. Oh, and apparently Luke and Asher have another cousin in publicity who can help with promotions. I guess there's a whole ton of cousins lined up to help. This is going to be so amazing. I wish Pops was here to see it all."

Eva blinked at her. Guess Asher really was going to save them. This was all their dreams happening, and she hadn't even been here to help.

"I'm sorry I've been a little absentee." She gave Maggie puppy eyes. "You've had to do this all alone, but I'm here now. I'm gonna start by supervising the packing of our stuff." She made to go in the house, but Maggie stopped her with a hand on her arm.

"No. Luke won't let us inside. Something to do with the foundations of the building. He's all freaked out about it."

"But the problem is the roof, not the foundation."

"I know. I don't get it, but he's gonna explain it all to us shortly. I'm so glad you're here 'cause I didn't want to be responsible for explaining all this to you later. Don't worry about boxing and sorting. Esther brought the workers from before, and basically they're just boxing up every single thing in the building and moving it over there."

They both watched the workers going in and out. Eva lowered her voice. "They're really weird."

"I know," Maggie whispered back. "They never speak. Never make eye contact."

They silently watched the trudging parade.

"As a redeeming factor, they do work like the devil," Eva noted.

Esther exited the building, spied the sisters and smiled. "Here." She thrust the box in her arms at the nearest empty-handed grunt. "Hi. Look who's up and walking around," Esther teased with a pointed look at Eva.

"Funny." Eva was certain her expression suggested the opposite. "I'm here to help."

"Not inside, you don't." Esther shook her head. "Not until Luke gives the go-ahead. Don't worry. I have everything under control."

Before Maggie could insist, Jeb rounded the corner and joined them. "Howdy!" he called. "I've been on the phone with some of the designers I was talking about to put together some bids. The cellar is going to be gorgeous for parties. Oh, and Eva, Maggie and I were talking about cleaning up the pond for gazebo events and such. It's all going to be marvelous. Once we get the monastery back together—that's really the cornerstone for the whole vision. To be able to sell the age and history of the building and the vineyard. No other place will hold a candle to it."

Maggie grabbed her hands and she and Jeb squealed. Eva wanted to roll her eyes at their display, but their excitement was contagious. When Asher walked up with a sour-faced Luke, she couldn't help but beam at him.

"So, Luke," Eva said and transferred her smile to him. "What's going on with the monastery? When can we get in there?"

"Not anytime soon, I'm afraid. The roof is the least of our problems." Luke's expression was grim. "I've called in an engineer I know to consult. Frankly, I don't understand how this building is still standing. It may very well be a total tear-down."

Chapter Nineteen

W hen Luke told them the awful scenario of a possible teardown, Asher thought the sisters were going to faint. Instead, Maggie sat down hard on the grass and Eva bent over like she was going to hyperventilate. Asher moved to stand behind Eva and rubbed slow, supportive circles on her back.

"What do you mean exactly?" Eva managed to stammer out.

Luke had the good grace to look miserable delivering the news. "I mean I question its soundness as a building. I can't figure what's holding it up. I have concerns about the damage inflicted over the years due to neglect, earthquakes, insects, even that original fire."

"Neglect?" Maggie asked. "You mean it's our fault?"

Asher shook his head. "Not you guys. Neglect takes that form over generations, right Luke?"

"Oh, sure." Luke agreed. "This building has taken some hard knocks from nature that has nothing to do with the owners. This part of the county gets tremors all the time and that does a number on load-bearing beams. Forest fires and floods have all impacted this area in the last several hundred years. Those natural events always disturb the integrity of structures. Buildings need constant care."

"This is just freaking great." Eva stood straight and moved away from Asher's comforting hand. "What the hell do we do now?"

Asher put his lonely hand in his jeans pocket.

"Like I said," Luke continued. "I've asked my colleague to evaluate the foundation." He ended in a shrug. "We'll see where we go from there."

Jeb scowled at Luke before rushing to Eva's side. "Don't panic, honey. He's terrible at delivering bad news." The gargoyle stroked Maggie's hair. "It's possible he's wrong. While he is very smart, he doesn't know everything."

Eva crossed her arms and glowered at the old building. "I thought he was the best architect ever."

Asher snorted.

Luke raised his palm as if he was swearing in court. "I'm an excellent architect. I am not, however, the most brilliant structural engineer, so I called one. Jeb's right. Let's not panic until we know what's happening."

Asher needed to touch Eva. He needed the reassurance maybe as much as she did, but when he took Eva's hand and kissed it, she took it back immediately.

"It'll be fine. Really," he said. When she didn't respond, he asked, "What are your biggest concerns?" Hoping he could address each one and soothe her panic.

Eva turned that glower on him. "Are you serious?"

"When is this engineer coming?" Maggie was getting to her feet. "We need to rethink our plans and everything."

All eyes turned to Luke. "Monday."

"Alright then." Maggie brushed off her butt and hands. "It's only Thursday. I say we finish cleaning out the monastery like we're already doing. Either way, all that stuff has to come out."

"There's plenty of vine-related work I need to catch up on, too," Eva agreed, but Asher thought she still sounded angry. He had hoped the advent of a list of tasks would distract her, but clearly not.

Maggie clapped her hands together as if to rouse the troops. "Alright – back to work. I need to wrap this up by four today because I'm tired. This whole thing has been exhausting." She lowered her voice and spoke to Eva, "Oh hey, guess who came by earlier while you were all messing around behind the monastery."

Eva tossed her hands in the air as if to suggest the whole world was possible. "Who?"

The sisters did that thing where they have an entire conversation without words. Maggie shrugged and grinned and Eva responded with wide eyes.

Asher brightened by the turn in her mood. He welcomed any topic that drew her out of the dark funk of worry.

Maggie's tone altered conspiratorially. "You remember the older man who came by the other day, Aaron Mephisto? Luke's father."

Luke and Asher spoke in unison not even pretending they hadn't been listening. "What?" "Who?"

The sisters ignored their reaction. "He said he came by to offer assistance. I guess he heard about the mess and..." She shrugged. "He seems really interested in your work. He asked such insightful questions."

Eva grinned at her sister. "No, Maggie, I think he was just back here to flirt with you some more. He's really handsome."

Asher couldn't even form words. He turned to his cousin who looked positively apoplectic. Ashe opened and closed his mouth several times, but was still unable to stammer out his biggest concerns—which were legion. His impotence didn't matter. You didn't have to be supernatural to sense the thundercloud forming over his cousin's head. It was nearly visible to the human eye.

"WHAT?" Luke roared, letting Wrath loose and ignoring the flapping arms of his assistant. Several sets of startled eyes settled on him, and he must have realized he needed to take it down several notches. "Who did you say?"

Maggie blinked at him. "Your father. He was here for about ten minutes. He asked a bunch of questions. We chatted a bit. No big deal."

Jeb rushed in front of Luke and put a hand on his chest, but it was swatted away. Instead, Jeb used all his granite strength to push at Luke's midsection, as if to push him backwards several feet. Luke didn't budge, but he also didn't come any further. Regardless of their disparate sizes, both were as solid and massive as the Colossus of Rhodes, which was ironic since the statue had been toppled and no longer existed.

Asher wasn't thinking straight. This scenario wasn't possible, and obviously he'd heard wrong. And Luke had heard wrong. Or maybe Maggie had just said it wrong. It was inconceivable that she was chatting up Luke's father.

The Devil.

Disbelief was what came out of Asher's mouth. "No." He shook his head vehemently, refusing to believe that this was a thing. The Devil flirting with his girlfriend's sister, her *twin* sister. "No."

Eva's smile faded. "He just came by to talk, be helpful. She's not marrying him. What's the problem?"

Luke had marched away across the lawn and was pacing frenetically around the dirt lane that led down to the vineyard terraces while Jeb whispered frantically at him.

"What's the problem?" Asher repeated her question like a moron. He didn't have any idea what he could say here. Everything would make him sound like an insane person. "He's the Devil."

Esther laughed out loud. "Well, that's one way to go."

"Is he dangerous?" Maggie asked.

Once more, Asher couldn't speak. Appropriate words had left his vocabulary. All he could do was open and close his mouth.

Maggie turned to Esther. "Is he dangerous?"

Esther closed her mouth tight and frowned. Then she blew out a heavy exhale through her nose like she was trying to decide what to say. "I do not believe he would hurt you," she said. "But I understand why the idea of him coming around here so often is upsetting to Asher and Luke. I assure you, he wasn't here to be helpful."

Maggie put her hands on her hips and her expression grew darker by the moment. "It's because I'm not good enough for your rich dad?"

Esther shook her head, still frowning. "Certainly not."

"Is he a criminal?" she demanded, her voice rising.

"No, but he is a proper villain."

Eva raised her eyebrows, then shrugged at her sister. "What does that even mean? A 'proper villain'? Does he tie maidens to railroad tracks and twirl a mustache on the weekends?"

More than twenty yards away, facing into the rows and rows of vines, Luke roared unintelligible words. Asher recognized it as what it was, a desperate attempt to shed some Wrath. The sisters startled and whirled in his direction.

"What in the hell..." Eva's hand clapped to her chest, alarmed by this raw display.

Maggie on the other hand, stood taller, and her eyes flashed. "What is his problem?" she demanded.

"I don't want Aaron around here, and you are absolutely not allowed to conduct any business with that man. Do you understand?" Asher told Maggie. He shook his head repeatedly. It was as if since he couldn't find the right words, he could convey the horror of the situation with the repetitive motion.

Her face flushed with...fury? Maggie's fists settled on her hips. "I'm going to need a damn good reason why we should turn down other investors. All he wanted was to talk about business opportunities. Something about including our wines in his restaurants, which seems like a damn fine thing to me. You guys are full of bullshit."

Eva's eyes darted from her sister to Luke. Esther wasn't helping, and Jeb was way over on the other side of the yard trying to settle Luke. When her gaze settled on Asher, he lifted a hand in frustration, completely impotent to deescalate the situation.

"This seems like an overreaction." Eva raised both hands in a supplicating gesture.

Suddenly it was clear as day how this situation had gone completely bonkers. Luke's cast off Wrath wouldn't affect Asher or the gargoyles. Obviously, Esther was right about the Sins not affecting Eva as she was unchanged. But Maggie on the other hand was drowning in a tsunami of Wrath. He might be able to convince her not to see the Devil if he could get rid of Luke. Right now though, they were awash in preternatural rage, and she was completely irrational because of it.

He turned to Jeb and Esther. "You guys have to get him out of here."

"Don't worry about it," Maggie spat out. "I'm leaving." She threw her clipboard and notes on the ground and stormed away.

"Oh, for crying out loud. Like we don't have enough problems." Eva glared at Asher and Luke as she followed in her sister's wake.

Asher rarely got angry, and he never showed temper. It wasn't in his nature. Nevertheless, he stomped across the grass towards his cousin. "This is all your fault, you asshole." Jeb dashed between the two of them, arms outstretched to keep them apart. "If you could just have kept your cool, we could have squashed any awful scenarios."

Asher turned back towards the direction of Eva's exit in time to see them disappear into the cellar.

"You did this." Asher accused. "Now what the hell are we going to do?"

"It's not my fault he's my father and it's not my fault that he has the audacity to linger around your girlfriend and her sister." Luke was calming down. Asher could hear it in his breathing.

"No," Asher pointed out and scrubbed his hands over his face, "but it's your fault that you spewed Wrath everywhere and this all went apeshit. Oh my god, what a disaster."

"I'll fix it." Luke laid a hand on Asher's shoulder, but Ashe shrugged it off. "I will."

Asher threw his hands in the air and demanded, "How? How?"

"I have no idea. I'll call Mia."

Asher should have asked Luke how long his pushes usually lasted. He loitered around the yard, pretended to supervise the demon work crew, and eavesdropped when Luke called his fiancée. He wanted to give Maggie plenty of time to calm down and come to her senses before he tried to talk to her. He suspected Eva would be no help. She was likely to take her sister's side on the matter. Under normal circumstances, he and Luke had no leg to stand on. Any lie they told would be obviously disproved.

This was not normal circumstances.

He was ruminating on this matter, looking for options when Jeb and Esther approached him.

"We need to talk with you." Esther was wearing her serious face. "In private."

Ashe looked around and, except for the demons toting furniture, there was no one around. "Okay. Go ahead."

Jeb pointed to the rows of vines. "Let's take a walk away from all the ears."

Neither of them spoke until they were well away from the buildings.

"We have a problem." Jeb's eyebrows suggested this was bad news.

Asher closed his eyes and dipped his chin in defeat. "What now?"

Esther crossed her arms. "In a nutshell, if the old monastery is demolished, we think it's the end for this vineyard."

His eyes snapped open. "That's absurd. We're talking about a building. Obviously, Dashiell Vineyards would be easier to market if there is a monastery, but if we lose it, we'll figure something else out."

"Well," Esther continued. "It's more than that. The ghosts are irrevocably tied to the monastery. If it goes, it's likely they'll go, too."

"I fail to see the problem with that. We're not marketing a haunted monastery."

Jeb cut in. "Remember, the ghosts are monks who lived and died here. There's reason to believe that they are tied to the vines."

Asher was skeptical. "The original Dashiell brought the vines here from France. That was well after the fire. The monks were all long gone by then. Probably already haunting the ruins. How could they be tied to something that came after they died?"

Esther held up a finger. "That's what we thought. But we were chatting up the old dead dudes today because they were freaking out about the demons being in their house. It was one thing when they were upset about the Sins, but actual demons in their house? Holy shit, they were losing their minds."

"The abbot was almost hysterical," Jeb added with a nod.

"Right," Esther continued. "We were explaining how Luke was going to fix up the place better than new. That the demons weren't staying. The abbot kept going on about some pit or doorway or something—he was hard to understand. Regardless, once the basement was cleared out and the crew went to the upper floors, we were able to reason with him."

"I started asking him some history questions about the place to distract him." Jeb absently stroked the grape leaves near him as he continued. "He said the Frenchman started his root stock in the old cemetery where the soil was most fertile."

Asher raised a skeptical eyebrow. "You're telling me the monks are actually in the vines?"

Jeb shrugged his dainty shoulders. "The abbot seemed to think so."

Esther seemed more sure of herself. "If the fledgling vines used the monks as nutrients is it so hard to believe the monks are tied to the vines? I mean, spirits get tied to things for lesser reasons that that."

Asher didn't know anything about spirits or what tied them to stuff. As much as possible, he tried to steer clear of the most absurd facets of his supernatural life. Wasn't it enough that he had to deal with Lust without concerning himself with ghost origin stories?

"I have no idea if that's plausible or not," Asher said. "Have you talked to any of your cronies about it? Oh, or asked your Lady about any of this?" Surly, the leader of the Order of the Gargoyle would know about this stuff.

"No. We'll go there next. We're telling you now because we're just learning of it," Jeb explained.

Esther laid her hand on Asher's shoulder and held his gaze intently. "Listen to me. I think this is a real thing. I think if the building gets demolished and the ghosts are severed from their ties here, the vines will very likely die as well. No ghosts, no vines, no wine."

No wine.

This morning everything had been perfect. And now...Well, shit.

He told the gargoyles to keep this development to themselves until it was an actual problem. Or at least until they had concrete information.

Surely there was some way to fix this.

Heaven & Hell XVIII

T he icky old man in the elevator did not like her. Juliet had trouble coming to terms with this as old people generally did like her. She was smart and well-spoken, something her grandparents' generation seemed to appreciate. Not this guy, though. He kept chomping on his Snickers bar and eyeing her while she hung on Neil's back. She did as she was told and she didn't speak to him, which was fine by her because she didn't want to be the cause of him opening that gaping maw of a mouth again.

The ride down didn't take very long, but what did she know? The summer she'd ridden the elevator in the Empire State Building it had only taken one minute, and that was eighty-six floors. Neil said this was only nine.

Also, the music had been much better in the Empire State building elevator. For this ride, they were subjected to children's nursery rhymes as played over and over by squeaky clarinets. Juliet remembered the noise from the school concerts when she was in elementary school. Neither Neil nor the elevator man seemed to notice, but it made Juliet want to cry.

When the doors slid open, she was not only relieved but insanely curious about what was out there. A mansion for the Devil. That was so intriguing. She'd heard of mansions in Heaven before, but in Hell? Hell was supposed to be...hellish, right?

Except that outside the elevator, beyond the platform, there was a lawn. With grass. Granted, it wasn't as lush as Heaven, or even her old schoolyard, but it was still a lawn. And the house was huge. Albeit, a bit spooky, like maybe the Addams family house. Still, we were talking about a giant house. She craned around Neil's head and shoulders to get a better look.

"Out with you and the mutt." The old man pointed a bony finger.

"We're going to run in there and run back out." Neil told the elevator man. "Will you wait here?"

Juliet shuddered a dry heave when the ancient man cackled.

"Wait?" The noxious fumes from his mouth were almost visible. He punched the close door button, and they were left with the mechanical sound of the elevator leaving.

Juliet felt like maybe someone had been bullshitting her all along. She wasn't saying Heaven wasn't the most wonderful place in all of imagination, but the Devil's mansion on Nine didn't look so awfully bad. You know, a mansion is a mansion. Even Cerberus seemed to appreciate the landscaping since he was already a ways off with all three noses snuffling on the ground.

"Okay, listen." Neil hopped off the platform and took off across the grass at a trot. "We need to get inside and find her right away without anyone seeing us."

Juliet thought he might be talking to himself because there wasn't really anything she could do about it.

"Umm, hey, is there any chance I could try and touch the grass? I just wanna see what grass in Hell feels like."

His trot slowed a bit but didn't stop. "We don't really have time for that. We don't want to be caught down here."

"Oh," she said, peppering the word with disappointment. "Okay. It's just I doubt I'm ever gonna get this opportunity to feel Hell's grass again."

Neil stopped abruptly and knelt on the ground. "Quick, feel it."

Juliet extended her leg and pointed her toes. She placed her foot on the ground. Only she didn't. It felt like hot air blowing up against her foot, propelling her away from the surface.

Darn.

"Nothing?" he asked.

"Nope. Still can't touch it. I guess that means everywhere, huh?" As far as experiments go, it was unexciting.

Neil stood and began the loping dash across the lawn again. Juliet had never ridden a horse, but this had to be what it felt like. Bouncing around on his back made her feel nauseous until she crossed her feet around his middle and squeezed her arms tight around his neck to ground herself.

Neil made a garbled noise and didn't stop running, but definitely slowed down.

"What?" she asked. He repeated himself, but she still couldn't understand him. "Huh?"

"I can't breathe," he gasped and started to lean.

Which made Juliet wonder, since they were dead, did they really need to breathe at all? Regardless, she loosened her grip and his posture improved immensely.

"I'm so sorry." She patted his chest.

They arrived at the porch without incident. Though Neil seems relieved by this, Juliet didn't understand why. She'd still not seen a single goblin, demon, or boogeyman. With the exception of that awful man in the elevator, she'd hadn't felt in any danger. Not what she'd expected from Hell. This had to be a fluke, right?

"This is it," Neil said, needlessly. His nervousness was palpable, and Juliet tried to take him seriously. "I don't know what we're going to find inside. It's really weird that we haven't seen anyone. It's kinda freaking me out."

He'd said that before. She shrugged in response, but realized afterwards that he couldn't possibly know since she was behind him.

"Let's just go in," she suggested. "We can't accomplish anything out here." She reached around him to press the doorbell.

"No!" He let go of her left thigh in order to swat her hand down. "If anyone's in there, we don't want them to know we're here."

"Makes sense."

"Right." He hesitated for a moment, hand hovering over the doorknob, then he quickly turned it and thrust the door open. It banged hard against the opposite wall and rebounded in their direction.

More of a SWAT team entry than a quiet, covert one, she thought. She didn't have a chance to say anything because she got a load of the mansion's entry way.

"This is where the Devil lives?" she asked Neil. "Really?"

With the exception of the dark colors, this place wouldn't have been unreasonable in Heaven. She'd read a book about the robber baron John D. Rockefeller in the fourth grade. There had been glossy pictures in the middle, and they'd looked just like this. Thick patterned rugs and dark wood floor and paneling gave the place a grandiose feel. What she could see of the furniture was all swanky in an old-fashioned way.

"Holy moly," she breathed past Neil's ear.

He nodded. "That's what I thought the first time I was here. It gets even better."

"It's just..."

"Not what you expected, right? Like, way too posh or something."

He started them deeper into the house. They went down a long corridor lined with paintings she was certain would have been in the finest galleries on Earth.

"Where do you think these came from?" she asked, tailing her fingers along the bottom of the frames as Neil traveled down the hall.

"I actually thought about this," he told her and paused in front of a particularly elaborate oil painting. "I think these are all from people who sold their souls or made some kind of deal with the Devil."

"Oh!" She peered at an artist's signature but couldn't make it out. "I guess that makes sense. There's so many of them though." She cast her gaze down the rest of the hallway and into each room as they passed it.

"You know, Jules, there's a lot of people in Hell, right?" He paused, raised a finger to silence her, and appeared to be listening intently. Apparently, whatever he thought he heard wasn't anything to worry about. He continued, "Lots of people. Not only regular people like me, but also famous people. Artists—" he gestured along the hallway at all the frames "—musicians, writers. Do you know who Hunter S. Thompson is?"

Juliet thought for a moment, thinking there might have been an inkling in the back of her mind, but no. "Huh uh," she said.

"Oh," he said, clearly disappointed. "Well, pretty famous dude. Anyway, he's here."

He picked up the pace again, moving them quickly down the corridor. She kept peeking in the rooms as they passed and was not disappointed. This really was a magnificent home. Wait until she told Hashmal about it. He wouldn't believe it any more than she did.

The end of the corridor was a dead end. With unfailing confidence, Neil turned left and headed quickly down the new corridor. Most of the doors were closed this way, so all she could see was the lush carpet and the paintings, which were still magnificent. He slowed down just before another junction and stopped completely before a closed door.

"This is it," he said in a loud whisper. There was no one to hear, but he seemed nervous anyway. "Her room is behind this door."

Juliet's breath caught. All of their hard work was going to come to fruition in mere seconds. She wondered if Heaven would know when they found her.

Would there be a ripple through the ether or something? Would the Heralds ring out? This was an epic moment.

"Open it," she whispered back and squeezed his shoulder.

She could feel him take a deep breath, then he twisted the doorknob. The room was dim and quiet. Also, as she'd come to expect, the room was lush and well appointed. A stately four poster bed stood against the far wall complete with comforters and a multitude of pillows. An overstuffed chair with books piled next to it settled against the opposite wall. In the center of the room stood a large round table covered with puzzle pieces. The floor was littered with even more. The only movement in the entire space came from cats roused by their entry. An enormous gray Persian was draped across the table and, as it rose to its feet, jigsaw pieces rained down to the floor. A Siamese wandered out from under the bed and a pair of massive orange tabbies morphed from one hairy lump into two hissing felines from the coverlet.

What she didn't see was a woman.

Neil ventured further into the room. "Rachel?" he called out.

While the room was large, it wasn't so large that an entire person was hiding in plain sight. There weren't even curtains for her to duck behind, since there weren't any windows. In fact, she was sure she'd not noticed a single window the whole time they'd been inside the house. Had there been windows on the outside? She couldn't remember, but there must have been, hadn't there? Surely, she'd have noticed if the house had no windows at all.

Neil stood in the middle of the room by the puzzle table and spun in a slow circle. "I'm certain this is the right room."

"I don't think she's here." Juliet whispered the words behind his head. She scrunched her fingers to entice the Persian for a scritch. He snubbed her and pushed another couple of puzzle pieces to the floor. "Maybe she went to get something to eat?"

He shook his head. "I don't think so." Juliet couldn't see it of course, but Neil sounded like he was frowning. "I kinda got the impression that she wasn't free to walk around the place."

"If that's the case, then where do you suppose she is?"

Neil sighed and his shoulders slumped a bit in defeat. "Don't know. They took me right to a dungeon when they caught me here."

Juliet gasped. "You don't think they took her to a dungeon too, do you?"

"It hadn't occurred to me until now." He turned them around until they were heading back out the door.

"Well, so much for this being a piece of cake, huh?" Juliet sighed and patted his shoulder, hoping to convey sympathy. "I'm sure we'll find her quickly, though."

The noise he made wasn't really a laugh. It sounded bitter actually, and Juliet hadn't expected it.

"We're in Hell, Juliet. This place is indescribably horrible, and everything is always harder than it needs to be. We've been really fucking lucky so far. I can't explain it, but there's no way things are going to stay this easy."

They made their way back the way they came. As they approached the intersection of the entrance hall, Neil nearly ran over the ugliest creature Juliet had ever seen. About half as tall as Neil, with gray skin covered with oozing sores and pustules, the thing was wearing an old-fashioned maid's uniform. Improbably, there was even a little white and black hat perched atop its scraggly hair.

Instinctively, Juliet shrunk down and did her best to hide behind Neil. It occurred to her that her legs and sandled feet were wrapped around his middle and the creature would certainly notice them at its eye level.

"Hey!" Neil said, really loud and maneuvered to keep the beastie in front of him. "Where is everyone?"

It crossed its spindly, boil-covered arms, a skimpy feather duster tapping against an elbow. "I don't know. I never hear jack shit down here."

"Well, the other levels are practically empty." Neil kept sidling to the side as the goblin or whatever it was continued on its own way down the hall. "No one's around at all."

The goblin snorted. "Probably another training or in service or something. Last I heard, they were planning those every quarter."

Training? For what? Hell was really not what she expected.

Neil stood with his fists on his hips, maybe trying to make himself larger to hide her better. "I'm looking for Rachel. She's not in her room."

Juliet peeked around between his bicep and his side and regretted it immediately. The thing was idly picking at a scab and thick yellow fluid oozed down its arm.

"Not for a while," it agreed and used the apron to wipe the slime from its arm. It sounded bored.

"I really need to find her. Any idea where she might be?" Neil pressed.

"Maybe." The repulsive thing swiped its feather duster along the baseboards. "But it'll cost you."

Oh no. The backpack full of goodies was still on Cerberus. She should have thought of that before they let him run off.

"I figured as much," Neil agreed. "What do you want?"

The gremlin's red eyes had a greedy glint to them now. "That damned writer cleaned us out."

"Hunter?"

"Crazy bastard," the creature mumbled. "He's one of the big guy's favorites. Can't imagine why. You go see Jose, Jack, Johnny, and Jim and refill the bar. I've already been there twice this month."

"That's it?" Neil sounded hopeful. "Really?"

When the beast smiled, revealing several rows of sharp little teeth, Juliet let out a little, "Eep!" and ducked back behind Neil.

"Not as easy as you think, dog-boy. You get that done and I'll tell you where the old lady is."

Chapter Twenty

D amn it. Eva hated crying. She hated feeling weak and not in control of her emotions. Even worse was having a witness to her outburst.

Her sister had just stormed out of the wine cellar still in the throes of a fit like Eva'd never seen from her sister before. Actually, from anyone ever, short of an over-stimulated toddler at a Walmart. Eva didn't try to soothe her or calm her down either. These fireworks felt like something more than an unusual outburst. It was remarkable not only because Maggie was generally an easy-going person who wasn't quick to anger, but also because in their entire lives, Eva had never seen her sister out of control.

Maggie's fury had come out of nowhere. Eva couldn't figure out what set the whole thing off, except that Luke and Asher seemed dead set against them having any sort of relationship with the elder Mephisto, not even a working one.

Eva didn't get it. The two of them had one, maybe two, brief conversations. It had seemed mostly business anyway. Granted, the man was an unrepentant flirt. He was handsome, certainly, but no one was that handsome. Not even Asher. Nevertheless, Maggie was immovable on the subject.

Even if keeping up a dialogue meant Asher would pull out of their deal.

Even if that meant losing the vineyard.

Eva let her sister storm away, assuming that at some point Maggie would come to her senses. But if she didn't, if this was the hill Maggie wanted to die on, then Eva would die with her. Maggie was more than her twin; she was her other half. She didn't think it would happen, but she also never thought she'd see her sister this angry. She'd also never seen her act like this, and she didn't understand how Maggie's feelings had gotten to this point. Was it the flirtatious banter that changed the dynamic?

The possibility that everything they'd worked so hard for could go up in smoke made Eva's stomach roil. She'd only just come to peace with Asher being involved in their company, with being thankful that he was going to save them all. And now he could yank it all away and they'd be in a worse place than they'd ever been before.

Worse yet, she mused ruefully, if-when-he withdrew his support of the vineyard over the participation with his cousin's father, he would leave her as well. In the most unlikely of scenarios, Eva had fallen in love with a player. God damned her to a life of misery. How could she have been so stupid? She knew better than to count on anyone who wasn't family. And now, even the family was iffy.

Thus, she was sitting crossed legged on an oak barrel of chardonnay wiping snot on her t-shirt hem when Asher crept to the back of the cellar looking for her. He stopped at the end of the row, hands in his jeans pockets, looking unbearably handsome.

"There you are," he said, his voice just above a whisper. "Why are you crying?"

"I'm not," she lied. Wiping a brusque hand across her cheeks, she smeared away the evidence of tears.

His forehead creased like he didn't believe her. "But you are upset. At the risk of sounding obtuse, please explain to me why? This feels like more than just Luke's explanation."

She didn't give him the satisfaction of an answer. She felt her old ally, righteous anger, simmer to life in disguise of how disheartened she was. She made her voice flat. "I'm fine."

More silence in the cellar. She hated that she'd lied to him as a test. If he believed her, if he didn't care enough about her to dig a bit... She was being the cliché she despised.

He didn't speak. His forehead smoothed out when he swallowed hard. He crossed the distance until he was standing directly in front of the barrel. She set her mouth in a brave line she didn't feel and looked at her lap.

"You don't look fine," he told her and pushed back hair from her face. Knuckle under her chin, he raised her face. "I know why Luke is upset. I have a very good idea why Maggie is upset. But you are a mystery."

That actually made her angry. "How can I not be upset? I'm preparing to lose everything that means anything to me, and I just keep thinking how disappointed my grandfather would be with me."

He was winding his index finger in a long bit of her hair. She tried to ignore how good the tension felt against her scalp. The headache was another reason why crying was never worth it.

"I think you're being very hard on yourself," he said. "I imagine your grandfather would be very proud of you."

She scoffed. "You know nothing, Asher. Carrying on this family legacy was the only thing that mattered to him."

"Well," he said with measured slowness. "If that's the case, he probably should have taken better care of it then."

The earlier helpful anger spiked into a righteous fury, and she yanked her hair free of his caress. "What an asshole thing to say! I shouldn't be surprised, coming from a person with such obscene privilege. My grandfather couldn't have known about the problems Luke described."

Asher seemed completely nonplussed by her anger. He reached for her again and paused when she flinched. "But you're telling me that you should have known about all these things from the instant you and Maggie inherited the property? Did you ignore an angelic messenger from Heaven with all the important information? Did an owl deliver you a golden letter that you assumed was some frivolous correspondence and you threw it away?"

"No." She heard how petulant she sounded and wanted to lean into his hand. It hovered there just to the right of her temple, waiting for permission to pet her again. She knew how soothing his fingers would feel tangled in her hair, the pad of his thumb stroking her cheek.

"So why are you more responsible than your grandfather or any other Dashiell in history?" He waited patiently, but she didn't answer, nor did she move away from him.

Oh God, she wanted the comfort he offered, more than anything, but she couldn't bring herself to move that tiny bit to accept what he was giving. Was it pride? She didn't know, but it was that same rotten instinct that had her refusing help when it was offered and solace from the man she was coming to love.

With great care, like a foolish person attempting to pet a wild animal, Asher's fingertips gently stroked down the back of her head. "Sweetheart, please don't do this. Don't pull away from me. This is only a bump in the road. Everything will work out."

Her heart sank. "How can you say that?" The tears had slowed, but her voice was still rough with emotion.

Bravery obviously making him bold, he stepped up to her and simultaneously cradled the back of her head with both hands. Pressing her forehead into his chest, he kissed the top of her head. "Because whatever it is, we'll overcome it." When she didn't relax, he asked, "Let's look at it this way. What's the absolute worst-case scenario."

She raised her face and stared at him a moment. "The worst thing?"

"Yeah. Let me hear it. What is your absolute worst fear here?"

"I can think of a lot."

He shrugged and settled his hands on her shoulders. "Lay it on me."

"That engineer guy comes in and says the whole building is a tear down, that there's literally nothing holding that building up. To make matters worse, there's black mold and massive termites and wood rot. As he tells us this dire diagnosis the entire building crumbles to the ground. Then in some sort of weird flash, the cellar catches fire and we lose all these barrels, too. Everything is ruined. The bills are skyrocketing and now we have nothing to offer. Nothing. And now we're not worth your time anymore, so you make a bunch of excuses or actually you just say fuck this and leave. You leave the vineyard and me. Alone with nothing."

Asher blinked at her for several heartbeats. "That's the worst you've got?"

Eva narrowed her eyes at him. Was he seriously making fun of her? When he barked out a laugh, she considered punching him.

"Oh, love." He kissed her forehead. "That's not the worst that could happen. How about if Luke's bleak warnings are indeed true. What if the monastery is a complete teardown but that causes the monk ghosts to be banished and then all the vines shrivel up and die? I mean really die. Like there's no grafting them to bring them back. Maybe they all fall into dust and the ground starts weeping blood or something. And the barrels down here all turn to vinegar because demons from Hell are streaming into the vineyard from some ancient hole in the ground and the Devil himself decides to make this his home or some such shit. All the beauty of this valley basically turns into a Hellscape. By then you'll realize that I bring you nothing but misery and grief and you try to throw me away, but I won't leave."

Eva watched him with her mouth agape.

"Well?" he asked.

"Holy shit, Asher. That's awful."

"Agreed." He lay a gentle kiss on her lips. "If the monastery has to come down, we'll rebuild it. We'll use the same stones and timber from these woods."

She added in a whisper, "That will cost an obscene amount of money."

"And, I have access to obscene amounts of money and I'm not going anywhere."

That's what he said, and she wanted to believe him more than anything.

"What about Maggie? She's pretty adamant about hearing his offer out."

Asher closed his eyes and took a deep breath. "I believe that Devil is just doing it to vex us, Luke and me. Esther assures me they'll keep an eye on the situation."

"They?"

"Her and Jeb."

"Well, they seem to be in control of what they put themselves in charge of, so..."

He snort-laughed. "Yeah. Wait until you meet the rest of them."

She unwound her legs and draped them over the sides of the barrel, creating a space for Asher to step into. His horrifying take on the worse that could happen game had actually gone a long way to settling her mind. If he was willing to stay through that shit show... The man was so rational. She'd always had Maggie to be the stalwart one before, but based on new evidence, Maggie had a dramatic side to rival Eva's own. It's seemed that the world and most of the people in it were destined to disappoint her.

"The rest of whom?" she asked.

Stepping into the triangle she'd created for him, he wrapped his arms around her and pulled her close. "All of my cousins have overly competent assistants. You'll meet them all, sooner or later."

Her heart settled a bit more. "Okay." She breathed in his scent and slid her hands around his middle. He was still making plans with her. That was a good sign.

"Eva, you need to stop worrying that I'm going to leave you in the lurch. I'm here—not just for you, but for the vineyard. I'm committed. The more likely scenario is that you're going to want to be rid of me before this plays out."

She hugged him tight. "Nah."

He inhaled a deep breath and let it out slowly. "We'll see. I come with a whole host of issues you've never imagined."

Circling her long legs around his hips and clasping her ankles together, she squeezed him, hoping to impart the promise of a strong and steady heart, just as he'd done for her. She couldn't imagine what kind of a mess he would bring to the table. She already had crumbling infrastructure, cantankerous ghosts, and a sister who was hopefully only momentarily off the rails.

When Eva and Asher emerged from the cellar, Esther's enterprising workers had nearly finished clearing out the monastery. The PODs were near capacity, stacked neatly with rows and rows of boxes and draped furniture. It was astounding.

Asher wandered off to find his cousin. Eva stood on the lawn and stared at the massive stone building that had been the centerpiece of her life. She still felt like this was somehow her fault and that she was betraying her family

Jeb sidled up next to her, iPad in hand. "I have a specialist coming out to look at the stained glass. They'll give us an estimate to safely pull those out and preserve them if we have to dismantle the building."

She looked at the handsome young man who seemed to be reading her mind. "Thanks for thinking of that. I would have eventually, but probably too late."

He wiggled his iPad. "I make an effort to think of everything."

Eva nodded. "I've noticed. Esther's the same way. You guys really should think of setting up an agency, or something."

He gave her a polite smile and a cryptic assurance. "We've got that covered."

Knowing from experience that he wouldn't actually explain anything if she asked him what he meant, she merely nodded. "Since you've got all of this under control, I'm gonna go find my sister."

It seemed like Jeb wanted to say something else, but in the end, he just stared at his notes and nodded.

"Words of advice? Comments? Nothing?" Eva prodded. He obviously knew something, probably everything based on her knowledge about Esther and Jeb's relationships with their employers. "Come on. If there's anything Maggie needs to know about negotiating with him..."

Again, he opened and closed his mouth several times, but only exhaled forcefully though his nose.

Eva wanted to narrow her eyes and put her hands on her hips. She towered over the man, but so did his boss. Luke was a thousand times scarier than she was and Jeb wasn't cowed by him in the least. She'd never be able to bully him into telling her anything. She changed her tactic.

"How about you just assure me that everything is going to work out. Put my mind at ease, eh?" She punctuated with a smile.

Jeb tucked the iPad under his arm. The competent expression was back. "I do not believe that Maggie will be in any danger tonight. I cannot promise anything, but rest assured that Esther and I and the others will be keeping an eye out."

Though cryptic, Eva did feel calmed by his words. "Alright then. Thank you."

She found Maggie at Ernie's house. He was out, probably in the lower rows tending to the Chardonnay vines—where she would be if everything up here wasn't completely insane. His wife, Yesenia, and daughter, Isla, had gone into town for groceries and errands so she and Maggie were alone. When Eva stuck her head around the door jamb of the back bedroom, her sister was standing at the end of the guest bed staring at her personal belongings recovered from the monastery piled up on the bed.

"Hey," Eva said, testing the waters. "How are you doing? Is it safe to come in?"

Maggie acknowledged her with a nod and a wave of her hand to enter. "I don't feel good."

When Eva peered at her, she saw her own face looking back at her but with a dazed expression. "For real? Are you okay?"

Maggie nodded. "Yeah. No." She sank on the guest bed and pulled the pillow in her lap. "I just feel weird. Like I've been on a three-hundred-and-six-ty-degree rollercoaster."

Eva leaned her butt against the dresser and crossed her arms. "Well, you sorta went bonkers out there."

She squeezed the pillow. "Yeah. I'm not really sure what that was all about."

Eva chuckled with absolutely no mirth. "You seemed damn set on accepting Luke's dad's help and money and Ashe and Luke are dead set against it."

"No, I remember that part. I'm just not sure why I was so angry."

"Well, you were," Eva noted. "What exactly happened during this discussion with Aaron?"

"The whole conversation is fuzzy in my head. I couldn't tell you what we said even if I had to do it in court." She raised the pillow with both hands and smooshed her face into it. "All I can say for sure is that he's ridiculously charming and outrageously handsome."

Eva had seen the man. Maggie wasn't lying. Aaron was elegant and sophisticated. Asher was, in a word, gorgeous. Luke was a giant, beautiful man. And Benji, though quiet, had a lazy, graceful allure to him. "That whole family, right? I wonder what the rest of them look like."

"The rest of whom?"

"The cousins." Eva nudged the clothes on the floor with her toe. "Asher said there are seven of them. I guess they're all really close."

Maggie's gaze turned speculative. "I remember hearing that some of the others might also be willing to help put our vineyard back together. Special skills or something."

Eva heard the crunch of gravel outside. She looked out the window to see an obscenely fancy sports car coming down the drive. The sleek black car pulled into the lot, parked next to Luke's classic car, and two men emerged. One of them she recognized as Asher's cousin, Benji, but she'd never seen the other guy before. Another cousin, maybe?

Back at her sister, Eva wondered if some of her earlier display had been enhanced by jealousy. They hardly spent any time together now that Eva was basically obsessed with Asher. Maggie deserved attention in her own right. Having just spent countless hours in Asher's bed (and kitchen, shower, living room rug, backseat of the new truck), she thought Maggie was overdue for some grown up happy time.

"Hey," Eva began. "I'm really sorry I haven't been around much. I feel really guilty about it."

Maggie tossed the pillow back to the top of the bed. "This wasn't about you."

Eva looked at her shoes. "Okay."

"It's not about you," Maggie repeated. "I am not jealous of Asher and I'm not projecting any envy of your situation with him on Aaron. I'm thrilled for you, so stop it." She made solid eye contact, and Eva felt the sincerity of her emotions matching her words. She pulled her sister into a fierce hug.

Outside the window, Eva saw another car pull up. "Holy shit. Is that a Rolls Royce?"

Maggie snapped a clutch purse closed. "Oh God, that's Aaron again. Lord help us."

The car pulled to a stop and a driver exited to open the door. Asher, Luke, Benji and the other man strode across the lawn to speak with him. Eva couldn't see their expressions in the twilight, though the distance would probably have been a hinderance even at noon. Based on their tense stride, things were likely to get dicey. They looked like four cowboys heading to a showdown. She hurried Maggie down the hall and out of the house, hoping their appearance would provide a chaperone-like presence.

"Oh look, Mia's here, too." Maggie pointed out Luke's fiancée standing alone away from everyone at the far side of the grass and waved. The normally bubbly Mia merely lifted a hand in weak greeting. Why was everyone acting so damn weird?

"Come on," Eva said. "Let's get out there before anything more happens."

As they got closer, the men's voices sounded edgy and troubled, and the conversation ceased immediately before Eva and Maggie got close enough to hear the words.

Aaron Mephisto turned an entrancing smile Maggie's way. "Lovely as ever, Magdalena." He kissed her cheek while Luke scowled deeply enough to cause a sink hole where he stood. Aaron continued, "And Evangeline—" he went in to kiss her cheek too, but Asher took her hand and pulled her tight to his side "—the two of you have such a remarkable resemblance, a person could easily mistake one for the other."

Asher grimaced. "Not really."

Eva squeezed his hand. "People do it all the time."

Aaron turned that lethal smile's full wattage on Maggie. "I was just telling the boys that I popped back around to invite you to dinner before I left town. How about Paris? I know a fabulous bistro right on the Champs Elysees."

"Paris? France?" Maggie sputtered. "I don't know where my passport is. And I don't have a jacket."

"If you think you need a jacket, I'll have the Hermés store open, and we'll get one."

"The Hermés store." Maggie giggled in disbelief.

Aaron's shoulder lifted ever so slightly in an elegant shrug. "Someone owes me a favor."

Next to her, Asher snorted. "Right. I'm sure."

"It doesn't matter, I really don't know where my passport is. Somewhere in those storage units." Maggie pointed at the huge roll off containers.

"I could take care of that for you, too," Aaron assured her. The sound of Luke's teeth grinding seemed to amuse him immensely. Benji lay a hand heavily on Luke's shoulder. "But we'll stay domestic this time. My favorite French restaurant in the States is just outside of Chicago."

"Really?" Maggie was breathless, like she was channeling Pamela Anderson or something. Honestly, Eva had never seen her like this before. "Sounds sexy."

"Sexy," Luke finally spit out. He jabbed Ashe in the side with a finger the size of a dill pickle. "This is your fault."

Asher shook his head and held up one hand. "Nope. I was very, very careful. This is not on me."

Then Maggie surprised them all. "Actually, as exciting as that all sounds, I'm going to have to ask for a raincheck. I've got the fiercest headache and I think I'm just going to turn in early tonight."

Aaron Mephisto kissed her hand like an old Hollywood movie star. "Of course. I hope you're feeling better soon. I'll be back around and we'll do it another time." He turned to the guys and gave them a cocky smile and a salute. "Boys. It has been fun." Then he ducked back in his car and was gone in a cloud of dust. The whole episode took on a surreal quality that made Eva slightly dizzy.

"Okay, Luke, exhale," Benji said. "You did an awesome job, man."

When Eva turned around, Luke had grabbed Mia up in a massive hug. She was whispering something in his ear and literally stroking his arms and hair as if to soothe a fierce animal. Eva looked away from the display, feeling like she was intruding on something very personal.

"Wow," the unknown man said, making no effort to hide the fact that he was staring at the couple. "She can really bring him down like that? That's amazing. Seriously. No wonder he's not at the gym as much anymore." He turned towards her and Asher. He grinned at them. "I'm betting that doesn't work the same way with you, too, huh?"

"Funny," Asher said, dryly. "Eva, this jerk is my cousin Ethan. Ethan, meet Evangeline and Magdalena Dashiell, the genius vintner and her business whiz sister."

The introduction confirmed two theories. First, he was indeed another of the cousins, and second, he was just as implausibly good looking as the rest of them.

"Nice to meet you," Maggie said before excusing herself. "I really am going to go lie down for a bit. I think I'm just exhausted."

Eva kissed her on the cheek as she passed before turning to the new cousin. "Hi," Eva said and shook his offered hand. "Is that your car? Is it a Bugatti? Wow, I'm so envious."

Ethan chuckled and gave her a knowing wink. "Of course you are."

Chapter Twenty-One

A sher let Ethan draw Eva away to go look at his sports car. When she was out of earshot, he turned to Luke and Mia. "Paris? He was going to take her to freaking Paris?"

"It's a good thing she didn't know where her passport is, huh?" Mia was back on her feet, her hand firmly engulfed in Luke's massive palm.

Luke snorted. "Like that would have made a difference. He's the Devil, honey. If he really wanted to get Maggie into France, a stupid passport wouldn't have stopped him."

Of course, Luke was correct. The Devil had every means necessary. There literally wasn't a thing on Earth that could stop him if he wanted to do something, and the Seven held very little faith of any kind of intervention from the opposition upstairs. Heaven had never been on their side before, and it was extremely doubtful they were going to take an interest in this generation of Sins. Why would they bother all of a sudden?

"He could have anyone in the world. Literally anyone. Why does he need Maggie? Why does he need to be involved with this vineyard. He's never expressed any interest in any other company I've owned. What the fuck is he up to?" Asher clenched his fists and roared into the vineyard in frustration.

"Hey." Luke bumped his shoulder with his own. "I really understand how you're feeling right now. You know I do, but I've learned the best way to deal with him is to try and let it go. I know it sounds impossible, but you're never going to get him to change his course of action. You'll likely never even figure out his motivations."

Asher looked at his cousin Wrath like he was insane. "How can you say that? Earlier today you almost gave yourself a stroke freaking out about him being here. He tosses one look at Mia and you're like a pressure cooker exploding."

Luke grimaced. "I know. I know. But I think that's mostly my sin and not me."

"Uh huh." Asher snorted. "This moment of Zen brought to you by Wrath and the letters B and S."

"Dude, getting bitchy is not going to help." Benji intervened. "Luke is right about one thing. You can't stop him. Try not to fret—" he held up a staying hand when Ashe started to protest "—I know, but try not to. Esther has your best interests at heart. Maggie will be fine."

Across the expanse of yard and parking lot, Ethan was showing Eva the interior of his sexy little car. They were chatting amiably, and when Eva threw her head back and laughed, Ethan grinned over the top of the car at him and nodded appreciatively. Apparently, his cousin approved.

Obviously.

She was spectacular.

He wanted to crush her to his chest, hold her there forever, and promise that everything would be all right. He wanted to protect her from every horror he would bring to the table if she entangled herself with him. He wanted to apologize for ever darkening her door with his presence in the first place, but he wasn't strong enough to do the thing he should, which was leave her be.

He couldn't do it. The thought of walking away made him want to throw up. He'd never realized he was such a weak man. When it came down to it, was it actually surprising, though? Really? His entire existence was a representation of weakness. He was Lust. He was the personification of an egregious character flaw.

Evangeline deserved so much better.

Benji continued, oblivious to Asher's existential crisis. "When it comes to us, you have to assume the Devil's plans are not really nefarious. He was one of us—he remembers how it is. At least, I think he does."

Asher rounded on him, completely exasperated. "How the hell do you know? You haven't had any contact with him. You've been off galivanting in Italy."

A raised eyebrow suggested Benji thought that remark was uncalled for. "You know damn good and well, I've never galivanted a day in my life. I'm simply trying to make you feel better. Try to look at it as if from a disinterested party."

Right hand up, pointer finger extended, Asher said, "You should be happy I'm not Wrath right now, dude." Benji trained that patented unconcerned gaze on him. "One of these days you're going to find someone to care about, and he's gonna come sniffing around, and you're going to lose your shit, just like the rest of us."

Benji snorted. "If that ever happens, you may feel free to call me on it. For now though, let's try to manage what we can control, huh?"

"Boys." Mia's voice wasn't commanding enough to intercede.

"What are you even doing here?" Asher tried to keep his volume down, but really, Benji's attitude was so inciting. How could he not even care?

Sarcasm dripped from Benji's every word. "Esther called Judith and Mordecai. She thought you might need a little support tonight. Stupid gargoyles, giving a shit and everything. I put on pants for you, asshole."

Mia tried to politely interrupt again, but Asher wouldn't let her. "Boys." This time Mia whisper-yelled. "She's on her way back."

The four of them whirled around and faced the approaching twosome. Asher did his best to subdue his aggressive expression.

"Wow, Ashe, that car is something else. It's so sleek and, sorta wicked looking," Eva gushed, her cheeks flushed with excitement and her eyes sparkling. "I told Ethan not to park it anywhere near the monastery. God forbid."

At that, Ethan hung his head in mock sympathy. He even clutched his chest as if in grief. "That poor, poor Aston. She had so much life left in her. What are you going to replace her with?"

"Already did," Asher said, completely capable of purchasing a car on his own.

Ethan looked around the parking area. "With what?"

Eva and Asher pointed at the humongous red truck at the same time.

Ethan did a double take and then sputtered. "That?"

"Yeah. That's a perfect truck for a vineyard co-owner." Ashe loved his new truck. He'd named her Betty, which gave Eva a good laugh. "Don't make that face. What can you haul around in that two-seater you've got?"

Ethan laughed from his belly. He grabbed Eva around the waist and pulled her flush to his side. "I'm only looking at hauling pretty girls around." Eva giggled.

"Ah, you fool!" Asher crowed. "But what are you going to do with her once you get her in there?" He held his hand out to his lovely woman in a courtly gesture. Eva came back to him with a sultry smile. "I've got a very plush backseat as my darling already knows. You try anything in yours and you're going to end up with cramps in all kinds of uncomfortable places."

Still chuckling good naturedly, Ethan bowed his head in defeat. "Trust you to buy an automobile based on ease of fucking."

"We all have our talents, cousin."

Mia watched the conversation and shook her head. "I'm starving. Can we eat?"

Eva described a restaurant in town that specialized in wild game. Luke and Mia nodded. Ethan even remembered hearing about it—either from social media or their cousin, Seth. It was agreed. Mia went with Eva back to Ernie's house so Eva could put on some clean clothes and check on Maggie.

Asher made a point of catching Benji's eye. He mouthed a contrite *sorry*. Benji nodded and just like that, everything felt right between them again.

"I'll drive," Asher offered. "I've got the big truck. We can easily all fit."

"No way in hell I'm sitting in that backseat now," Benji noted with a shake of his head.

"Eww!" Luke and Ethan shuddered in unison.

Everything seemed back to normal on Monday. There was a crowd of them milling about on the lawn when Luke showed up with the structural engineer to start the work on the monastery. Esther and Jeb were comparing notes about something in whispers at the far edge of the yard. It occurred to Asher that whatever it is might be something to be concerned about, but frankly, he was tired of all the histrionics. After the roof crushing the car and the ghosts and then *the date* with all the melodrama surrounding it which turned out to be absolutely nothing, he craved normalcy. One quiet day where nothing blew up or got unbearably weird. Was that too much to ask for?

He looked to the human manifestation of his heart. Eva stood with her sister, Ernie, and Mia. They were discussing fertilizers or mulch or bug infestations. It didn't matter. The subject didn't interest him, but the gorgeous brunette in well-worn jeans and old tee-shirt reading "Lady Farmer" did. From the bottom of her purple rubber boots to the top of her ratty straw hat, he'd never known anyone more fascinating.

Luke introduced everyone to the structural engineer, but Asher couldn't concentrate on the conversation. His eyes trained on Eva's mouth watching her lips caress each word as she chatted with the engineer. And how her brilliant blue eyes sparkled with intelligence. How, even dressed for farm work with her exquisite sable hair plaited into two thick braids, she was more luscious and desirable than any person he'd ever encountered.

Mitchell, the engineer, was outlining the plan. He was talking about geotechnical soil sampling and impact echoes and ultrasonic-pulse velocity. Asher tuned back out and watched the way the morning light and her eyelashes made oval shadows against her cheeks.

"We're going to need to pull the soil away from the foundation all the way around." Mitchell started a parade of interested parties towards the monastery, Luke next to him followed by Maggie, Eva, and Ernie. Asher brought up the rear, hands behind his back so as to not reach up and touch her as he so badly wanted to do, but it would distract her, and this was important stuff.

Luke signaled and Esther and Jeb joined them, Jeb with iPad and ePencil ready. They needed to arrange for workers—no worries, Esther had that covered—to come and start digging around the foundation. The two gargoyles took off just as quickly with Jeb barking orders into a phone and Esther presumably off to rustle up some more demons to do the dirty work.

Maggie asked about the time frame of the project, and the engineer's answer was vague. When Eva pointed out the situation with the roof and raised the point about weather and wildlife, Mitchell reminded them that everything depended on what they found.

"So, we'll hurry, eh?" Asher noted from the back of the small crowd.

"Right," Luke agreed with a terse nod. "Michell will get started right away." Then he and the engineer disappeared into the building, leaving the Dashiells, Ernie, and Asher to mill anxiously on the grass.

"Well, I've had enough of this. The waiting is only going to make me crazy," Eva announced. "I'm going down to the cabernet. Who's coming with me?"

Ernie and Maggie both raised their hands. "Idle hands are the devil's workshop," Maggie said, and Asher snorted.

"Or something like that," he said.

Ernie split off from them to grab tools from the shed which he'd drive down in the old farm truck. When Maggie followed him, Eva called out that she was going to walk and would meet them down there. Of course, Asher joined her. He threaded his fingers through hers as they began the sloping trek down the old dirt road that led to the lower steppes where the cabernet grew. She gave him a sweet smile and squeezed his fingers, but her forehead and distant expression said she was elsewhere.

"Are you still worried about the monastery?" he asked. It was a stupid question, and he knew it, but her silence made him nervous.

"Yeah, of course, but that's just a drop in the bucket of my worries."

"Can you tell me? Maybe I can help." He would literally give her anything she needed. If it wasn't in his power, surely Esther knew someone who knew someone. Esther was only like three degrees of separation from *anything*.

Eva laughed. "That list is pretty unwieldy. I don't think you know what you're asking."

"Try me."

"You promised you are in this for keeps, right? I'm not going to tell you all my nonsense and you're going to run screaming back to the city, right?" Her lips curved ever so slightly, easing Asher's mind that she was not so mired in despair that he needed to be worried. Only slightly concerned, not call-in-the-troops concerned.

He crossed his heart then raised their joined hand and brushed his lips over her knuckles.

"Alright, you asked for it." They paused at the rise of a hill and gazed out over the valley. Acres and acres of farmland stretched out before them, as far as the eye could see, well past the boundaries of Dashiell Vineyards. The morning fog hadn't completely burned off in the lowest areas, giving the whole bucolic scene a bit of a mystical fairy touch. "God, I love this place."

"I know you do. It's stunning."

"Yeah, but even more than that, I feel rooted here. I've never wanted to be somewhere else. Not like my mom who literally left the minute no one was looking. She was withering here, but not me. All of this—" she swept her arm across the valley "gives me life. Does that sound weird? I don't even care. It just means that everything that happens here, to this land, to my grapes, to my home, feels like it's happening to me." She thumped her chest lightly. "I spend a lot of time fretting about everything. Literally everything. It's exhausting."

That broke his heart. All he wanted to do was protect and hold her. "How can I help you?'

She graced him with a smile and wrapped her arms around his neck. "You already have. You're going to save us all."

"Anything," he told her and kissed her like his life depended on it so she wouldn't sense his desperation.

All she needed from him was money. He would give her all that he had if it would make her happy, but would his money be enough when she found out who he was?

Could he keep her innocent a little longer? Just long enough to find an enduring reason for her to need him like he needed her? He had to find a way to show his presence brought enough merit for her to accept the darkness of his world.

He held her tight and tried to keep the panic at bay.

Hell XIX

When Rachel wasn't in her room in the Devil's mansion, Neil wanted to scream and throw things. If Juliet hadn't been with him, he might have gone berserk. It would have been so satisfying to overturn that stupid jigsaw table, scattering the pieces everywhere, and slam a chair into the wall, bashing a hole in the plaster and splintering the chair at the same time.

But Juliet was there, clinging to his back, and voicing a running commentary the whole time. He couldn't scare her like that. They'd been very lucky, but that was bound to run out now. There was no way they were getting up to Six and getting in and out of Scorchy's bar without Juliet being found out. It wasn't possible.

He'd been delighted when he found out about the place. A bar? In Hell? It had seemed too good to be true, and to some degree that was the case. The beer was warm and the bar snacks had been revolting, but still, it smelled like a neighborhood bar, and the crowd had been similar. Instead of the local garbagemen and plumbers and mechanics, there was a hodgepodge of worker bee villains in the form of gremlins, goblins, and lesser demons.

And they were all going to see Juliet.

He needed a new plan but was at a total loss on what to do.

As they waited for Charon and the elevator again, he listened to Juliet's stream of consciousness.

"Where do you suppose Cerberus has gotten to," she asked, the words delivered with sweet little puffs of breath against his ear. "I'm still reeling from the art in that house. I'm telling you, no one in Heaven knows about that mansion. That's not at all how Hell was represented. All squishy soft furniture and classy decorations. Even then, it does have a haunted house vibe. I don't know what to think about it, actually."

Where the Hell was that gross old man? Neil pushed the call button several times in rapid succession. It was oddly sticky, and he wiped his index finger on his jeans. "The dog will show up. Don't worry."

"Okay," she said, and he felt the pressure of her front leave his back when she leaned away to glance behind them. "Hey, did you know there's someone, something, coming out of the house?"

Neil wheeled around to see what she was talking about and sure enough a lower demon had emerged from the mansion. He could tell it wasn't very tall, even from their distance across the lawn, but that was made up for by its thick muscular arms and shoulders. It paused outside the door, seemed to search the air, then turned to face them. It took off in their direction with a weirdly loping gait that covered ground quickly. One fist held a clumsy looking club as big as a dinosaur bone.

Nail cursed and spun back around to frantically jam his finger down on the call button.

"It's coming really fast," Juliet squeaked from behind him. Her legs and arms squeezed him tightly. "Neil!"

The beast let out a merciless roar that rang in his ears. Juliet screamed and covered her own ears. Her trembling spurred Neil into banging on the elevator doors with both fists. "Open up! Charon!"

He looked over his shoulder again to find the beast was little more than halfway across the grass and gaining. Its mottled green skin was broken up by spikey horns encompassing its entire body, even its tail ending in a mace-like ball of sharp horns. When its mouth opened wide to bleat the battle cry again, Neil realized the thing's mouth made up the entirety of its head. No eyes. No ears. No nose. The head simply split in half, exposing rows and rows of drool-covered fangs. Another terrifying howl filled the air. The atmosphere seeming to vibrate with it.

Juliet screamed again, this time in Neil's ear as she tried to hide her face in the crook of his neck and shoulder. She clutched at his arms and hair as if scrabbling to get inside his skin.

"Charon!" Neil yelled again, panic making his voice reedy and thin. "Charon."

Another glance backwards and the thing was three quarters of the way there. Even with that quick of a glance, Neil could see definition in those teeth— discolored, razor sharp, and dripping with slime.

Unbelievably, over all the commotion, he heard the elevator ding, but still the door didn't open. The seconds between the bell indicating the arrival and the actual sliding of the door was interminable. Neil jammed his fingertips into the seam where the door would open and tried to pry it apart. He even lifted his leg and pushed against the jamb for leverage.

He heard the panting breaths; the beast was so close. Neil could barely move his own head with Juliet's buried so deeply into his neck. Each grunt from the creature brought another terrified scream from her and she'd claw her way higher and tighter.

Finally, the door began its creaky slide open. Neil thrust his shoulder between the jamb and the panel and shoved to make enough room for them to slide in.

"Hey! Whoa, whoa there." Charon flapped his skeletal arms to ward them back, but Neil ignored him. He planted one palm flat on the old man's concave chest and pushed him backwards like that old Heisman trophy. Once inside the elevator box, he whirled back around and ran his hand down the number panel lighting up every single floor, then slammed his palm flat on the door close button.

Neil glanced up to check on the progress of the beast. Holy fuck! It was maybe fifty feet away. Juliet wasn't even screaming anymore. When he looked over his shoulder, her mouth and eyes were wide open in a pantomime of a scream but there were no sounds. Time slowed as Neil banged on the elevator button and the monster continued to close in on them. Huge chunks of grass flew up behind it with each footfall and ropes of drool slathered out of its mouth and tailed behind in glistening streams.

From behind them, Charon said, "What the hell is that?"

"Make this elevator move, old man," Neil commanded, though he couldn't look away from the charging fiend.

Oh, fuck, it was close. So close he could make out tufts of black hair around the bases of the many horns. The three of them stared because they had no choice. Juliet started to cry behind him, and he could still feel her whole body shaking. Neil futilely hammered the close button. It couldn't be more than five galloping steps away when it raised the massive club over its head.

"I'm so sorry, Juliet," was all he could say. He never should have let her down here.

The demon took a giant breath like he was winding up for another horrific howl when from out of nowhere the body of a giant three-headed dog slammed into it from the left. The monster went down hard with Cerberus on top of it. Two heads were already tearing at its mottled flesh while the third middle head snarled and barked with matched ferocity.

The door slid shut.

"Holy shit," Charon muttered.

Neil turned his body and brought one arm behind him to swing Juliet around until she had her arms and legs wrapped around him from the front like a horrified koala bear. She was weeping in earnest now, great gulping sobs that he could feel all the way down to the bottom of his inky black soul. He circled his arms around her and held her tight.

"Shh," he whispered. "He's gone. Cerberus got him. He's gone, baby."

He repeated himself over and over, murmuring nonsense until her sobbing slowed. He stroked her hair and rubbed tiny circles on her back like Sister Agnus used to do when the children were upset.

He held her tight when the door to Nine opened up. Charon wisely said nothing. No new passengers were waiting, and the door closed quickly. Juliet didn't even notice the horrors outside.

"We're okay," he assured her. "He's gone."

"Actually," Charon piped up from the corner. "I think it was female. It had boobs. Four. Did you notice?"

Neil glared from over Juliet's shoulder and redoubled his efforts to soothe her. He kissed her temple and smoothed a thumb over one cheek, catching the tears and wiping them away. The same thing happened with the landing on Eight. The door opened, Charon kicked a snake back into the fray, and the door slid quietly shut.

He pulled away slightly, just far enough that he could look down into her face. He smoothed her long hair from her face, unsticking the strands from her wet cheeks, and tucked it behind her ear. "Baby, can you take a couple of breaths for me?"

She complied, hiccupping. He used a finger under her chin to lift her face so he could see her eyes. "You're alright," he assured her then pulled her back in for another hug.

Nodding against his chest, she whispered, "I'm okay. We're okay."

He kissed her temple again, marveling at the fact that they actually were unharmed.

The doors slid open on Seven. The scent of burning flesh wafted in, but again Charon let the door slide closed. Neil couldn't believe the ancient ferryman was being so cool about this.

"What about Cerberus?"

Neil smiled. "I'm sure he's fine. He's a tough one."

"Where are we going now?" her voice was small but steady.

"We'll have Charon take us back to the top and I'll get you back to the staircase."

Juliet jerked away from him and looked at him with her red, puffy eyes. "Why? No."

"Look, babe, you don't belong down here. We've been so lucky, but that fucking thing could have gotten us. I'm taking you back and you need to go home."

She wiggled furiously until her legs were loose. She dropped them down until she was standing on the toes of his boots. Clutching the leather of his lapels, she peered up at him. "We're in this together. I started this whole mission and I'm going to finish it—with you."

Neil shook his head. "Nah. You aren't supposed to be down here. I can't even think about what will happen if... I'll find her."

"Not by yourself." When he continued shaking his head, she added, "I'm not leaving. You'll take care of me. And we always have Cerberus."

This was a stupid conversation. There's no way he could have protected her against that monster alone. This was luck, pure and simple, and they were bound to run out of it quickly down here. Luck wasn't something that existed in Hell.

"Juliet," he used his firmest voice and steeled his expression. "It's not really up to you. You're not staying here."

She narrowed her eyes and stared up at him. Then out of the blue, she stood on her tiptoes on the front of his boots, raised one hand to his nape and pulled him down for a kiss. She was young and so sweetly innocent. Pressing her lips to his firmly, her eyelids fluttered closed, but the kiss stayed sweet. No tongue or sexy noises. Just a pretty girl kissing a condemned guy. Neil would be a liar if he said it didn't affect him, though. When he breathed her in, his mind and heart were filled with a lightness he'd never felt before. Not even in life. Even when she ended the kiss and withdrew, a fraction of that bliss remained. ˑ

Hope?

"I'm staying here. I'll be with you, and we'll do this together."

Neil couldn't refuse her. He knew it was wrong and he would spend the rest of his eternity regretting letting her stay after something horrific inevitably happened, but hope was a powerful thing.

He blinked his eyes against defeat and said to Charon, "Six, please."

The ferryman raised his eyebrows and pursed his lips, conveying in a soundless way how stupid Neil was to let her push him around like that. When the doors opened on Six, he extended his spindly arm in front of the door to hold it for their exit. "That thing was pretty awful so maybe you forgot. It's all right. This ride was on me."

Neil moved Juliet to her previous piggyback position, and they stepped out onto the platform with grateful nods.

"What are we doing here?" she asked. Oh, she could insist all she wanted, but he heard the trepidation in her voice. She might be brave and determined, but she wasn't stupid. Now that she'd seen what Hell had to offer, she'd likely treat it warily and with some earned respect.

"Scorchy's." Neil took the first steps off the platform and recalled how hot the ground was on this circle. He picked up his pace, noting that the buildings and trees and everything that had been on fire on his previous visit still burned. There were sinners far in the distance, digging burning ground, but the flaming demon he expected to see manning the desk was absent.

"What's Scorchy's?" she asked.

"A bar."

"I don't have ID," she admitted.

He shook his head and wondered how the universe had ever paired them up together. "We're in Hell, babe. We don't need ID."

"Oh, right." Her head bobbed in his peripheral vision. "This will be my first time in a bar. Hopefully it will be fun."

But she didn't sound like she believed it.

Chapter Twenty-Two

Asher was admiring the pop-up canopy tent he'd bought to go over Maggie's worktable. She'd declared the weather was too nice to sit indoors and since she couldn't go in the office in the monastery until the engineering report came back, she'd set up a little office in the yard. She was using a picnic table as a desk and Ernie had run a couple of extension cords from the shed to power her computer and printer. The tent was perfect for the short term. It even had screen covering all sides to keep the flying insects out. It was kind of brilliant, because even if a breeze came up, her papers would be stopped by the screen.

Esther had shown up with a lawn chair complete with cup holders which she'd plunked down in one corner for when she needed a place to set up.

When Maggie had seen it, she'd given him a high five. "Look at you! This is great."

Eva had blessed him with a kiss. "Brilliant," she'd decreed.

Asher was still reveling in the praise, so desperate was he to prove his value to the operation beyond paying the bills. In the days since the engineer had been out to inspect the property, he'd spent daytime hours working among the vines with Eva or muscling the casks based on her behest in the cellar. Evenings, however, were spent at his place in the city. Mostly naked. If he needed direction at the vineyard, he relied on his expertise at home. After that first magical time with her, Ashe had relaxed and let his instincts propel him. He'd had a lifetime of experience and a supernatural proclivity towards pleasure to guide him, and he was one hundred percent certain she was satisfied. And even more miraculous, so was he.

Lust was sated.

The thought of being with anyone but Eva was ludicrous. When he considered that she might not feel the same way... He didn't even want to flesh that idea out. The oddest feeling of wanting to be "owned" by her had settled over him like the fog that blanketed the rolling hills every morning. It wasn't a suffocating sensation, but soft and peaceful. It felt like home. Like she was home.

He had never known a feeling like this was even possible. Did other people get this? Did his cousins know about it? He'd have to ask Luke if he had something similar with Mia.

Thinking about Luke must have conjured him because his phone trilled the sound of a text coming in from his cousin.

We're on our way there. We have the results of the preliminary inspection.
Asher responded with a thumb's up emoji. *Good or bad news?*
Then he grimaced at the response. *We'll talk about it when we get there.*

It would take them at least forty-five minutes to get out to the vineyard from the city, so Asher decided to walk down to the Cabernet vines where Eva and Ernie were concentrating their attention this week. It was a warm day, and the fog had long since burned off. The bugs were enjoying a balmy day so he spent much of the walk down swatting at flying things. About halfway he wished he'd taken the truck because the walk back up was going to be wretched. It wasn't a "nice day." It was hot. Was it supposed to be this hot for the grapes? They'd put up shade where Eva thought it was necessary, but still. Was air conditioning next? He'd pay for it because this was too hot to comfortably work in. He wished he had a hat like Eva did. That cute straw hat that shaded her face and shoulders. He should call Esther and have her bring one in from town. And maybe some of those work shirts that were made for being out in the sun. They had some sort of built-in UV protection or something and were designed to keep you cool and dry. He wondered if they even worked. Hopefully the fabric was soft because if he had to wear a cottony t-shirt underneath it to avoid scratchy material against his skin, that would defeat the purpose of them being airy.

He was lost in an internet search on his phone when he heard his name.

"Ash," Eva called. When he looked up, he realized he'd actually made it all the way down the hill without realizing it. "What are you doing?"

He noticed that Ernie was actually several rows away and probably couldn't hear their voices if they spoke low. "Coming to fetch you," he said with a lazy drawl.

Eva's laugh was low and that's exactly where Asher felt it. "What for?" she asked.

"I just wanted to catch another glimpse of you in those jeans." Slipping a hand on her waist, he turned her back to him. He took a moment to appreciate her perfect heart-shaped ass before pulling her flush against his front and sliding that hand around her middle. He flipped her long braid over a shoulder, ducked his head under the broad rim of her straw hat, and nuzzled her neck. He didn't even care that it was a bit sweaty. She didn't mind either, even when he sank his teeth into the tendon at her neck and gave a nibble.

"You're gorgeous," he whispered into her ear. "Wanna go find a shady row where we can lose our pants?"

Her laugh was louder this time, and she smacked his arm with her gloved hands. "Asher."

"I'm serious. We can be quick. Ernie won't even know." He rocked his hips against her rear. There was no way she could ignore what was happening in there.

She pulled away and straightened her hat. When she turned around, her appreciative gaze over the length of his body was sexy as hell. "Seriously, what are you doing down here?"

He kept his voice light. "Luke said they have some stuff to discuss. They're coming out now."

"Oh." She pulled off her gloves and tossed them in her wagon amongst the other tools. "How did it sound?"

Asher shrugged. He had a bad feeling, but he didn't want to upset her, so he didn't share those thoughts. "Whatever it is, we'll figure it out."

Trying to get up the motivation to climb back up the hill, he whooped with joy when she took him to her old truck parked at the bottom of the rows. He had to admit the old beater had some charm to it, with the oxidized red paint and the almost illegibly faded vineyard logo on the door. He and Ernie hoisted the wagons in the bed, then sat on the open tailgate while Eva turned the truck around and ferried them back to the monastery.

All the usual suspects were converging on the lawn and milling around Maggie's makeshift office. He recognized Luke, his assistant, Jeb, and Mitchell from the back, all with their hands on their hips staring at the monastery.

Esther met them as they hopped out of the truck with bottles of ice-cold water and one enormously wide brimmed hat that smelled of fresh straw and outdoors.

"Nice," he told Esther with appreciation. "This is excellent." It fit perfectly when he plopped it on his head. The brim stretched wide across his shoulders. He felt cooler already. How she always managed these things mystified him.

Maggie finished a call on her cell and joined their group. With anxious glances and shuffling feet, they waited for the verdict from the engineer. Unable to wait any longer, Eva gave Asher a shove towards his cousin and thrust her chin forward, offering him up as tribute.

"So," Asher drew up between the two men as the engineer talked and Luke grunted in agreement. "You've got some anxious people here. Are you ready to share?"

"Oh, yeah. Sorry." Luke pivoted towards them. "So what we have here is kind of a mixed bag. Mitchell here—" he indicated the engineer who gave a small wave "—actually thinks the building supports are fine and they don't propose any risk to the building coming down."

Their group sigh of relief was audible. Ashe squeezed Eva's hand and whispered, "I told you."

"But." Luke paused for effect. "There is still an issue."

"I knew it," Eva said under her breath and sighed deeply.

Asher squeezed her hand again. "Whatever it is—"

Eva shook her head. "Shhh."

"Hold on." Maggie held up her hand. "Let's hear what it is before we freak out."

Eva scowled at her sister. "I'm not freaking out."

"Okay, I'm just saying don't."

Maggie and Eva stared at each other for several heartbeats. A Russian-length novel of weighted silence passed between them. When they did this, it was utterly fascinating. Asher and his cousins were exceptionally close, but this was a whole other level.

Finally, Eva spoke out loud, "Actually, it sounds like you're freaking out."

"Can we just agree that neither of us will freak out?" Maggie asked. "We'll just hear what Luke and Mitchell have to say and then we'll come up with a new plan."

Asher nodded emphatically. "That's what I've been saying."

"Honey, shhh," Eva said with reproach. "We're just gonna listen right now."

Esther rolled her lip to keep from laughing at him. He clamped his mouth shut and raised an eyebrow at his gargoyle, daring her to make a peep.

Maggie spoke to Luke and Mitchell next. "Gentlemen, we're ready. What's wrong now?"

Luke indicated that Michell should fill them in, so the completely nondescript man spoke up. "As Luke said, the structure looks to be sound enough. I don't believe the beams and supports will cause any trouble in the future barring any new developments like seismic activity or something. A new roof will not bring any undue stress. But the foundation has me concerned. There is some indication of settling in the basement. Luke thought there was some possibility that there was a cemetery underneath the building. Ultimately, that can be a huge problem, and since you're looking at doing work on the property, Luke and I feel that this should be addressed right away. I brought out some technology that will be able to tell us what the ground underneath the building is doing without causing any wear and tear on the structure."

Eva nodded, concentration showing on her face. "What kind of technology?"

"LiDAR, Light Detection and Ranging." He directed them to the collection of equipment on the ground. There was a laptop and several open hardcases containing things that looked like ray guns and super expensive cameras. "We're able to use this to map the area underneath. We can do the entire vineyard with it if we hook it up to a drone."

Maggie perked up and noted with interest. "Oh, I saw that archeology guy on the Discovery Channel use this stuff. It's really cool."

Mitchell grinned at her. "It really is. The technology is amazing. We're going to take virtual pictures of the ground underneath the building and see what's happening down there."

Eva didn't look as convinced. "So when will we get the results of this scan?"

"Right away." "Today." Maggie and Mitchell said at the same time.

Luke agreed. "That's one thing that's so great about it. We'll be able to download everything to the laptop and see it almost in real time. And—" he acknowledged Asher "because it's so portable, it's not outrageously expensive."

"Thank God." "That's not a problem." This time it was Eva and Asher who spoke together.

"Cool," Luke cast him a weird look. "We're going to get started then."

It was only a couple of hours later, when they all reconverged in Maggie's little tent office to watch as the radar came up in grids on the laptop. To be fair, the monastery was large and they had to be patient while the whole thing loaded. Asher didn't pretend to know anything about archeology or architecture or even dirt, but the feed that came up was easy enough to read. To Asher it seemed uneventful, and he dared to be hopeful that nothing was going to come up. Everything seemed steady. Over a black field that he took to represent the floor of the monastery, a series of ghostly green images lay below like a lumpy mattress under a smooth duvet. However, in the very middle of the building the steady green was interrupted by a slightly oval circle of pitch black. It looked pretty big, but it was hard to put it into perspective on the screen.

Mitchell made some adjustments to the resolution, and the view sharpened slightly. Using the arrow keys like a joystick, the engineer moved the focus of the center of the screen to the black void. Another adjustment and edges of the circle gained definition. It looked to Asher like there was literally a giant beam in the center of the floor.

Jeb, who was standing on the edge of the viewing party, took a step backwards. "Umm," he said. "Esther."

There was a sharpness to his tone that was not easily ignored. Esther tore her eyes from the screen and nodded.

With a quick glance at Mitchell, Esther pointed at her own chest and then at Jeb. "We're going to go check on something. We'll be back shortly."

Luke nodded, too busy staring at the screen and suggesting adjustments to Mitchell to pay much attention, but Asher instantly recognized the gravity of the situation.

Squinting at the screen, he peered at it as if it was one of those weird optical illusions on the internet. One of those was-the-cat-going-up-the-stairs-or-down kind of things. He closed his eyes and tried to make his memory of what was on the screen go blank. Then he opened them again and refocused on the screen.

Oh, holy shit.

Was that an unfathomably deep hole?

Chapter Twenty-Three

E va stared at the anomaly on the engineer's laptop and tried to imagine what it could represent. She'd been in that basement a million times and, when she closed her eyes and visualized the space, she couldn't picture anything. Well, whatever. She was a farmer and vintner, not a structural engineer or architect.

She stepped back from the table where they'd all crowded, planning to get back to work. Regardless of this bizarre development, there were always ways to productively fill her days. As soon as there was a plan, Eva knew they'd let her know what it was.

Now that Asher was here, she didn't feel the obsessive need to be on top of every little thing in the way that had consumed her since her grandfather's death. She could worry about her vines and leave the rest of the world to spin on its axis knowing that Asher's capable hands could handle it. This was such a novel feeling. One would have thought the close relationship with her sister would have given her that peace of mind, but it hadn't. Probably because Maggie and she were almost the same person. If she didn't have faith in herself, then it probably made sense that feeling carried over to include her other half. However Asher had done it, she was grateful.

Asher had proved himself to be a steady, calming influence. Constant. Trustworthy. She wanted to add devoted to that list, but she felt like letting her mind get too comfortable with a word like that was bad luck. For now, she was going to enjoy the sentiment without naming it.

He had filled in her space at the table and was staring intently at the screen. Damn, he was so freaking cute with his eyebrows knit together and his lips slightly parted in concentration. He'd taken to wearing outfits Esther was calling "Rural Chic," and honestly, it was everything she could do to avoid tumbling him to the ground every time she saw him. Nothing looked accidental, but at the same time she didn't believe he cultivated the stylish farmer look he had going on. Somehow it all seemed to come naturally to him. Soft cotton jeans with a threadbare patch over one knee. Burgundy leather lace-up boots worn to butter-softness. A tee-shirt with fabric the consistency of butterfly wings. Honestly, where does a person get material that soft?

She lay her hand on the back of his neck and tucked her fingers down the collar of his shirt. His skin was warm from the sun, and when she leaned in to murmur in his ear, she got a whiff of his shampoo/fabric softener/chemistry that made her think of bed sheets and firm mattresses.

Her lips brushed his artfully stubbled cheek as she laid out an invitation. "I'm going to the cellars."

"Um hmm," he hummed, not taking his eyes from the laptop as Mitchell manipulated the image in various ways.

"You'll come and let me know what you guys find out, right?"

"Sure, babe." Asher swiveled his head on his neck, eyes on the screen, and absently kissed the air around her.

Maggie caught her eye and laughed. "I'll come and keep you company."

Not really the company she was hoping for, but she hadn't had a real conversation with her sister in ages.

"It's high time we had some wine and sisterly gabbing, don't you think?" Maggie asked.

"Just what I was thinking,"

Down in the cellar, Eva pulled two stools from the front counter and towed them behind her towards the back of the cavernous room.

"Why do you suppose Asher and Luke were so adamant about his dad? What do you think that's all about?"

Eva lifted her shoulders in a gimpy version of a shrug while she dragged the stools. "I don't know. Maybe 'cause he's so much older?" Leaving the stools at a counter, she glanced up at the casks. "To be honest, I didn't ask him because the topic made them all so crazy."

"Okay, you saw him, right? Even if he is Luke's dad, he doesn't look a day over forty. And it's a well-preserved forty at that. Besides, when a man comes to pick you up in an honest to God Rolls Royce, you get in the freaking car."

She gazed into nothingness and tried to remember the details of what Aaron Mephisto looked like. He'd had an odd familiarity about him. She assumed it was because he did look somewhat like his son, Luke, but she also had a nagging sensation that wasn't exactly it. The man had the sort of handsome that came packaged in spy movies from the 'sixties. A very *James Bond* and *Man From Uncle* sort of manliness in a fine suit and pretty manners.

Eva raised an eyebrow. "You didn't get in the car, though."

"I know." Maggie crossed her arms and cocked her hip. "And I cannot really explain that. I was all set to do it, and then all of a sudden, I was just like, no. Like I literally heard a voice in my head that said, 'no.'"

Eva stared at her. "I don't even know what to say about that. I guess you follow your gut. That's what Grams always said anyway."

Maggie shrugged. "So, I didn't go. I was legit wiped out, though, so I wasn't really lying. I didn't even go out with you guys to dinner."

"Before you say anymore, hold on." Eva climbed a step ladder and opened the hatch on one of the huge oak barrels. Gently slipping a glass wine thief inside, she extracted a length of ruby red liquid and filled two glasses with the unfinished wine. She climbed back down and perched herself on one of the stools and handed the other glass to Maggie.

"What are you going to do if he comes back and asks again?"

Maggie giggled, and Eva rejoiced in the sound. Maggie was much more stoic than she was. While Eva had a tendency to dramatics, Maggie was collected and unflappable. But that didn't mean she was apathetic or vacant. Maggie felt all the things, she just seemed to be playing a long game of poker and was the master at impassivity.

Her shoulders rose and fell in a shrug. "Well, he said he'd call the next time he's in town. I'm a grownup and he's a grown up, and why shouldn't I have some fun once in a while? You're having plenty of fun, and there's certainly nothing wrong with that. I wasn't lying when I said I haven't been jealous, but I've been a little jealous, you know what I mean? I can feel how happy you are, and I'm so pleased and excited for you. I mean, this thing with Aaron won't ever go the long haul, but my ego could use a little stroking."

"Oh, I get that. I mean, if he was going to take you to Paris this time, who knows where he'd take you next time." In amusement, she snorted into the glass as she went in to sniff the wine.

"I don't know, but I really should find my passport before this whole thing blows over. I could still get a trip to Paris out of it."

When she took her own sip of the wine, Eva was pleased. This vintage was coming along nicely. Still a bit green, a little too tart. A bit more time and it would be excellent.

"I hope you do," Eva told her sincerely. "Then I won't have to feel bad about being away with Asher all the time."

Now her sister was rolling her eyes. "We don't have to have the same life all the time. It's okay if you have found someone and I haven't. It's stupid to feel guilty." She nudged Eva with her foot. "Asher's the one, huh?"

Was Asher the one? It had only been weeks since they met, but the whole thing had been intense. It all felt so good and not comfortable exactly, maybe easy was a better word. Sometimes she felt like she'd been transported right into the middle of a relationship.

"Maybe," she said. "I can't describe what it is about him. I mean, he just drove me batshit crazy in the beginning. Rubbed all my nerves wrong. So full of himself and obnoxious. But at the same time, he's also genuine and real and honest."

Maggie smiled indulgently. "I can see that about him."

"Yeah." Eva smiled, too, because Asher really was all those things and so much more. It was funny that she couldn't really put into words for her sister the way he made her feel. Usually all of this communication was wordless between them.

"You're so much...softer with him. Do you know what I mean? For the first time since Pops died, you're not right on the edge of a freak-out. It's awesome. Even Ernie has noticed. That's Asher's influence, I'm sure of it."

Eva never realized she telegraphed her emotions that much. Here she thought she'd been keeping her feelings close to her chest. She was such a dope. Of course the people who knew her best would notice these things.

Inexplicably, she felt a little choked up. She swallowed hard and looked away from her sister until the stupid feeling passed. "Do you think... I mean... Does he..."

"Do I think Asher feels the same? I barely know him but, honey, the man moons over you. It's freaking adorable."

Eva let the grin bloom across her face. She could hardly resist it. The idea that a person as spectacular as Asher Mephisto would moon over her was thrilling. Now she wanted to go find him and kiss the life out of him.

And maybe lure him to a cozy, leafy corner and tumble him to the ground. She'd never in her life been so lusty.

She didn't regret a single hormonal moment of it.

Heaven & Hell XX

Scorchy's looked dirty. At least from the outside. Not dirty like grimy, which it certainly was. The stone walls looked coated with soot from the interminable fires on Six. What she meant was dirty like naughty. There was a giant arrow on the outside pointing to the nondescript door that blinked with salacious neon. This was the kind of place the police frequented and where there were always shootings.

"Well, that's new," Neil said and pointed at the sign. "At least I don't remember it being there before."

"Makes it hard to miss, though, huh?" Juliet recalled that there had been a place just like this in the city where she'd grown up, but the neon had blinked GIRLS in all caps. "Have you been here a lot?"

Neil shook his head. "Nah. Only the one other time. It's pretty gross inside. I should find a way to leave you out here."

Juliet looked around. There was nothing but desolation around the building. Across the street, a tree was burning. It looked like it had been burning for a really, really long time. Like forever. Through the ball of flames, it was naked of leaves and the trunk and limbs were black. And yet it burned anyway. Similar trees and bushes dotted the hellscape in the same manner. The ground beneath them smoldered. The whole place looked like a forest after a devastating fire.

There was literally nowhere available for her to sit. And to be honest, she didn't want to wait out here alone. Cerberus hadn't gotten on the elevator with them—they'd left him chewing on that awful creature—so he wasn't even here to keep her company.

Or to protect her from horrific creatures who wanted to eat her.

Holy Moley! Thank goodness Neil couldn't see her face anymore. A person didn't recover from a horror like that straightaway. She'd clung to him like a spider monkey in the elevator for several levels, trembling like a bowl of Jell-o, trying to stave off hysteria.

If she still had nightmares, that fiendish beast would have fueled them for an eternity. And, it certainly opened her eyes to what Neil had been saying all along. They had been very lucky so far.

Another reason why she didn't want to stay outside all by herself.

"I don't see how we can do that. There's nowhere for me to sit, and I can't get down."

Neil paused at the corner of the building. She could feel him thinking, running through what options they had—which were slim to none. She couldn't put her feet down. They knew that for sure.

He smirked at her over this shoulder. "There's an old nail on the wall. I could just hang you up there for a bit."

There was indeed an old rusty nail poking out of the wall. Her mouth fell open. She was appalled at the thought. "You can't," she squeaked.

"Why not?" She imagined his grin was unrepentant, making him look like a pirate. "It would keep you out of danger and your halo wouldn't get dirty in a roadhouse."

"That's not fair," she protested. "Besides halos are a myth. Also, I've never been in a bar before."

"Do you really think a bar in Hell is where you should start?"

"There aren't any bars in Heaven. If I don't go in this one, I'm never going to get to at all." She was whining, not a good look for her, but darn it. She wanted to see inside. She'd always wondered about that glowing Girls bar, and obviously that was a lost cause. Then she was struck with the obvious. "Besides, my wings would get in the way."

"Oh shit! Your wings. Jeez, I'm so stupid. Why don't you just fly?"

Well, poop. This was embarrassing. "I can't," she whispered.

"What do you mean, you can't?"

She hesitated. It was a mortifying reason and she didn't want to explain to this staggeringly cool guy that she was so pathetically hopeless. "I don't have a license."

"Wait, what?" he asked.

She sighed a big breath. The hair over his ear fluttered and he twitched. "I don't have a license. Hashmal won't let me have one."

He twisted his neck as far as he could to look at her, and she leaned down to the left to meet his gaze. "Who the hell is Hashmal?"

"He's my Dominion supervisor," she told him. It was clear from Neil's expression he had no idea what she was talking about. "He's like the principal of my school. In Heaven. I haven't been able to pass the practical exam."

Now it was Neil's turn to let his jaw drop. "There's an exam? In Heaven? For flying? You have got to be shitting me."

"No. You have to take it to get your license. You don't do that down here?" Neil shook his head slowly.

"What? There's just indiscriminate flying down here?" This was either madness or the best thing ever.

"Nah. Actually most things down here don't have wings. I have them; you saw, but I don't fly though because I'm not Hell-born." He shrugged. "I can sort of glide a little, but not really fly. Only the Hell-born fly. I think they give wings to some of us as a punishment. So you can see a way to escape, but you can't use it."

Juliet hugged him around the back and pressed her cheek against his shoulder blade. His own leathery wings were folded up tight against his jacket. "That's awful."

He did that cool maneuver where he circled her around his side and settled her tiptoes on the front of his boots. She grasped his jacket lapels with both hands and leaned backwards so she could see his handsome face.

"So now explain this test to me," he said.

"There's the written part, where I did fine, of course. I can study like nobody's business. The practical part is way harder. I can't get the liftoff quite right and I keep crashing on the landings," she admitted sheepishly. When his gaze turned speculative, she insisted, "It's really much harder than you think it will be."

He nodded with a knavish smile, then he surprised her by ducking his head and dropping a kiss on her nose. "You're so freaking cute."

How she could feel her skin growing warmer under a blush with all the heat from Six, she had no idea, but she could.

"You're not going to hang me up outside, are you?"

His laugh was raucous. "No, babe. I'm not going to hang you up outside." He wrapped his arms around her and pulled her in for a hug. Juliet felt deliciously safe in his embrace—even in front of a sketchy bar on the Sixth

Circle of Hell. Just like she had after that terrifying thing had come after them.

When he released her, she climbed back around to the piggyback position she was getting used to. The second Neil knocked on the bar door, a window opened in the middle, and a pair of shifty orange eyes glared out at them.

"What?" it growled.

"Hey, man. Here to see Jose, Jack, and Jim," Neil told it.

"So."

Juliet giggled. Probably nerves.

"So, the mansion sent me on the errand. Don't worry about it. I'll just tell them you wouldn't let me in." He backed up as if he was going to leave, but without turning his back and exposing her.

The tiny window slammed shut, and the heavy door yanked open. A wave of smoke billowed out with a gust of stale air. "Come in," the ogre said grudgingly. "I don't need any trouble from that guy down there. That boney little bastard thinks he's in charge of everything. I guess I'd rather have you than him."

As Neil maneuvered them through the door, shifting so his back stayed away from the ogre, Juliet tried to be invisible.

"Hey, wait," the door-ogre said, and she and Neil froze. "Aren't you the dog keeper?"

Neil cleared his throat. "Yeah."

The ogre peered back outside the bar. "That dog can't come in here."

Neil sighed with obvious relief. "He's not here right now."

"Fine, just know, I don't care what the mansion says, that dog ain't coming in here."

"Noted." Neil nodded with emphasis.

"And who's this?" The ogre pointed a warty finger at Juliet who tried to press herself even flatter against Neil's back.

Neil squeezed her leg. "She's my guest."

The creature narrowed its eyes to study her, even going so far as to grasp Neil's arm and twist him to the side to see her better. Juliet tried to smile, but heaven knows what it came out looking like. In her nervousness it was probably like a chimpanzee showing all its teeth.

"Look." The ogre lowered his voice to something that implied conspiracy. "We get all kinds in here. I don't know what you have going on here, or what she even is, but I don't want any trouble inside and that's—" he gestured with a circular motion at Juliet — "trouble."

"Sir," Juliet squeaked out. He was gross and smelled of rotten food, but he was nowhere near as terrifying as the beast who'd come after them at the mansion. He wasn't even as vile as the old man in the elevator. "I'll be as quiet as a church mouse. I promise."

"A church mouse?" He repeated.

Neil spoke up then, turning to face the door-ogre full on so she was in the shadows again. Except that she was giving off a faint glow; something she hadn't noticed before. Obviously, Neil hadn't notice either, since he couldn't see behind himself.

"She just means no one will know she's here, is all," Neil said.

"A church mouse," the ogre groused. "I'd eat a church mouse."

Juliet remonstrated herself for speaking. Neil had told her time and again to let him do the talking. *Fool*.

"Besides," Neil added, "we're not going to be here long. In. Out. Gone before you know it."

With a sneer, the ogre let them pass, echoing the last sentiment in a stage whisper that she wouldn't forget anytime soon, "I eat church mice."

Once past the doors, she gazed over Neil's shoulder as the bar came into view. Dark just as she'd always expected a bar would be, there was a large open room dotted with tables and a large counter-height bar at the back with stools surrounding it. Most of the tables and stools were occupied by various denizens of Hell, all of them facing a stage at the opposite end. A handsome young man in an old-fashioned suit was playing guitar and singing some song she didn't recognize, but she wasn't very familiar with blues anyway. So far, no one had noticed her hanging on Neil's back, but it was bound to happen eventually.

Neil paused, taking in the room and, Juliet guessed, looking for the guys they'd come to meet. She hadn't asked who Jose, Jack, and Jim were. Odds were good that she wouldn't know who they were even if someone told her. But the way he was searching the darkness made her wonder if Neil knew who they were either.

"What do they look like?" she whispered in his ear.

Neil absently shook his head. "I'm not sure. I'm guessing they were human, though, so that's what I'm looking for."

Juliet peered into the smokey interior, running her gaze over gremlins and ogres and wraiths and a whole bunch of things she couldn't begin to identify. Creatures that were weird hodgepodges of animal parts, none of them natural, skittered along on the floor or hung from the ceiling. In the furthest part of the room, she spied four actual men at a table littered with glasses. She pointed and Neil patted her leg to indicate she'd done well as he started across the room.

"What's that?" A gremlin the color of old guacamole jumped in front of Neil and pointed his finger at her.

"What's what?" Neil asked. Juliet wisely remained silent.

The gremlin stabbed at the air with a twisted finger and insisted, "That. What is that?"

"None of your business," Neil told it. He swept it aside with a flat palm to it head. It hit the edge of a table, but it bounced right back and skittered along next to them.

"What is it?" the Gremlin yanked on Neil's jacket hem. "Can I touch it?"

Juliet pulled herself as far up Neil as was physically possible to avoid its wrinkled fingers.

Another small monster tugged at him from the other side. This one was covered in matted hair that was so filthy as to be an unidentifiable color. "What's it?"

"Let go." Neil violently shook his leg, and the thing slipped off.

Juliet glanced behind them and spied six or seven more demons trailing in their wake. Every one of them was staring up at her, some with multiple eyes, others with only one. One fiend clambered over the others to get closer. It was shaped like a plucked chicken but instead of wings, it had scrawny arms that ended in two sharp claws. Its head was somewhat too big for its body, probably because of two horns weighing it down. When it opened its mouth, she saw a jaw full of razor-sharp teeth. It trotted close behind on a pair of human-like feet.

"Neil, we have a crowd forming back here."

"Let me touch it." The first gremlin was still stretching up to pluck at Juliet's clothes or anything else it could reach.

Neil whirled around to face the devilry of gremlins behind them. "Back off," he roared and kicked out with his heavy motorcycle boot. He connected with the chicken demon, and it hurtled across the room and thudded against the wall. The rest of the mob stopped short.

He picked up the pace to the table in the corner, but the damage had already been done. Any hope of them skating through the bar under the radar was lost.

Chapter Twenty-Four

"Well, whatever it is, it's under the floor," Mitchell the engineer said. "That sort of anomaly in the readout usually suggests a void of some kind."

Asher didn't like the sound of that. He rubbed his forehead vigorously a couple of times. What he did know for sure was they weren't going to figure it out from the tent in the yard.

"I'm going to go inside and look," he said and pushed away from the picnic table.

Eva and Maggie had disappeared into the cellar some time ago, which was good. He really didn't want them around while they sorted this out. Whatever it ended up being, it would be easier if he was able to explain to all to them once they had a plan to fix it. He didn't want a new disaster to upend Eva's calm. Anything he could do to make her life easier so she could concentrate on the things that brought her joy. The light that shone in her when she talked about her wines and the vineyard was inspiring. It was whenever she got caught up in the minutia of running the vineyard and its struggles that she let anxiety overtake her. He was happy to run interference in that regard and help Maggie with the business end of things.

The old monastery was preternaturally quiet inside. With a family legacy worth of belongings moved out and in storage, even the air seemed vacant.

Having never seen the ghosts himself, Asher wondered if even they had abandoned the place.

Using the stairs in the kitchen, Asher went down into the bowels of the old house. The basement was cavernous, spreading out under the entirety of the main house's floor plan. What he could see of it was dark and musty, as all basements must be, and just as vacuous as the upstairs had been. The area was broken up into spaces he assumed made use of the load-bearing walls. It had occurred to him that when the demons had been boxing up the contents down there, they likely unearthed some fantastic finds relating to the monastery, the monks, and Eva's family that would make for interesting lore to include in the establishment of the place as an event facility. He'd tossed some initial ideas about it around with his cousin Ethan, Envy in their family dynamic, and he agreed that the Dashiell's rich history made for excellent marketing.

At the landing, he let his eyes become accustomed to the dark. Then, picturing the engineer's computer screen, he moved forward in the maze to where he thought the void had resided. He used the light on his cell phone as a flashlight and dodged around columns and walls, making his way to the center.

It was true, Asher had no education in architecture or even history for that matter, but he was intrigued by what the monks had been thinking when they built the place. What reason would they have built over a giant, well, hole for the lack of a better word? Was it a cache of treasure? Maybe something from the old world they were hiding from the early American natives? Or even from the church? Perhaps it was only a crypt like those in the cathedrals of Rome and Paris and Spain. While that was less financially exciting than a cache of treasure, it could still be thrilling in its own right and seemed more realistic. And after all, crypts generally held some sort of religious artifacts of value.

There was already a cemetery filled with Monks and Dashiells on the property, but Asher couldn't get the thought of their very own catacombs out of his mind. The possibilities were wild. They could even give tours down here.

He turned a corner where he thought the middle should be and collided with a body as stout as a pillar. Too wrapped up in his gruesome fantasy, he let out a little shriek. Mercifully, the body was alive. Once he staggered backward and shown his light on it, he was relieved to discover it was only Esther.

"Shit! You scared me," he said and flashed his light about the room.

It wasn't as big as he'd expected. Really it was more the size of a large walk-in closet. Now that it was occupied by Asher, Esther, and Jeb, it seemed a bit claustrophobic. Especially once he noticed a bunch of rubble to the side. The pile of rocks and mortar looked newish. And come to think of it, the doorway wasn't square either.

"Did you guys do that?" he asked and pointed to the debris.

"Yeah," Esther admitted. "This room was sealed off."

"Really? Why?" he asked.

"That's what we're trying to find out," Jeb said.

The plot thickens, he thought, on the verge of glee. "What was in here when you opened it?" Asher asked the room at large.

"Nothing. Absolutely nothing," Esther told him. "Which seems like overkill, right?"

"I guess." He shrugged. "You know, if this was a horror movie, you guys would have set off the whole plot by letting some evil spirit out of its cage. Was there a loud whoosh or maybe a ghostly scream when you broke through?"

"Funny," Jeb said, but he didn't laugh at all. He did give Esther a suspiciously alarmed glance, though.

"No? Okay, consider this. Maybe it's the opening to a catacomb? Like something in Paris or Rome. That would be so cool, right? We could tie that all into the monastery and the vineyard. What a cool way to make this place stand out from all the rest."

For a split second, the air seemed to rush out of the small room like a vacuum and then burst back in fast enough to pop Asher's ears.

He worked his jaw a couple of times, trying to regulate his ear pressure. "Whoa, what the hell was that?" he asked.

"That would be the monks," Jeb noted.

"Seriously? This just keeps getting better and better. How many of them are in the room with us right now?" Holy shit! They were going to make a fortune off this haunted vineyard.

"I don't know, Asher." Esther was stern. "Maybe all of them. Listen, we have a problem. This room, right here, that this even exists, is a grave matter."

Asher snickered at the on-the-nose pun and she quelled him with a raised eyebrow.

"Right." He schooled his face and tried to tone down his enthusiasm. "Of course, we'll be very respectful of their crypt. We can get it designated as an historical place."

"We don't think it's a crypt." Jeb told him with a mirthless shake of his head.

"Well, ask them. I thought you guys could talk to these ghosts."

Esther sighed and rubbed her forehead with dirty fingers. She looked like a mess, which was very unlike her. "We can, but they're very agitated right now. Your presence here isn't helping."

He sent his light around the small room, taking in the construction. The walls were smoothed with plaster like the rest of the building, but the floor, at least in this room, was slightly uneven with huge stones laid down in a patchwork and cemented down. When he stomped his foot hard upon it, listening for an echo or the thump of a hollow, he heard nothing. The floor was solid, strong, and thick. In fact, the feeling he got from testing the floor was that it seemed excessively thick.

"Luke isn't going to let us fix the roof until he's sure the rest of the place is solid. This anomaly presents a huge problem. We need to know what it is. If these ghosts are not going to tell you, we'll just have to open it up."

The atmosphere did that weird pop thing again, but his time he thought he actually heard a voice say, '*Vetiti.*'

"I'm going to venture that will be out of the question." Esther was uncharacteristically grim, and this more than her words concerned Asher.

Some noise behind him signaled that at least Luke was on his way down and Mitchell was likely with him. Hadn't Esther said his presence in the room was causing the ghosts more upheaval? Luke's arrival as Wrath was sure to make it even worse. As if to punctuate his thought, what amounted to a dust devil of mortar debris began to swirl around their feet. Asher watched it with rapt fascination before it occurred to him to do something about it.

He spun back out the doorway in time to stop Luke and Mitchell. "Hey." He stood squarely in the way. "There's really nothing to see here."

Luke blinked at him. "That's the spot where the void shows up."

"Uh huh." Asher shook his head but didn't move. "But there's nothing to see."

Luke started to say something else, but Jeb stuck his head around Asher's shoulder. "Hey, boss." His inflection was super chipper—not at all suspicious. "Asher's right. Nothing to see in here. I was thinking though, maybe we should take another look at the building plans we got from the county."

A veritable eternity later of Luke glowering at his gargoyle and then Asher, he finally grunted out, "Fine."

Maybe in an attempt to get away from the tension in the basement, Mitchell volunteered to head back up to look for the plans. Jeb gave him ridiculously vague directions. All the while, Luke scowled.

Now that they were alone, Luke barked out, "What the hell is going on down here?"

Luke and Jeb stepped aside and Esther emerged from the room covered in dust and sneezing violently. The dust had finally settled around the room behind her.

"We've got a little problem," she said, her dry humor back in full force.

Luke appeared to finally take the situation seriously, realizing that they weren't being a pain in the ass just for shits and giggles. "What kind of problem?"

Asher filled him in. "There really is nothing to see in that room, but apparently the 'hole' for lack of a better description is under the floor in there. Maybe it's a crypt or a treasure horde of some kind. Either way, the ghosts are in some kind of tizzy about us knowing about it." He shrugged at the end, conveying how little they actually knew.

Esther shook her head, and a poof of dust blew from her hair. "It's not a crypt or a treasure horde. Sorry, Ashe, but your fantasies aren't coming true about that."

Luke pushed past everyone and stepped into the room. When they all crowded in behind him, the place was seriously tight. Ashe shined his light on the floor and they all stared.

"Let's get some pickaxes down here and bust this up." Luke said matter-of-factly.

Again, with the sonic pop, but this time, it was strong enough to rattle the walls a bit. Asher was concerned that some permanent damage was going to be done to his ears if the monks didn't cut it out.

"What the—" Luke grabbed his head.

"They keep doing that every time we mention digging it up," Jeb explained, pained expression mirroring everyone else's. "They're most adamant about it, and that's all they'll say."

Luke tilted his head back and looked at the dark ceiling. "Listen here, monks. We're not the bad guys here. We're trying to restore the place, not tear it down. You're going to have to help us out. What's down there?"

The four of them stood there, ears primed to hear any communication the monks were willing or able to give.

Nothing.

Luke tried again. "You've talked to us before. Or at least to these two." Luke pointed at the gargoyles in the dark.

"Help us to help you." Asher snorted in amusement until Esther and Jeb turned pointed looks at him. "What?"

"For fuck's sake, Asher." Esther raised her voice, and when she swatted at his shoulder with her granite hand it left not only a burgeoning bruise but a dusty white handprint as well. It looked like one of the ghosts had whopped him. "This is serious. Like, really serious. This isn't some stupid lark like you think it is." She turned her attention to Jeb who was shaking his head at Asher with disapproval. "I think we need to go right to Notre Dame with this. She'll know what to do."

What? WHAT?

Asher snapped to attention. "Wait a damn minute. Why would we need to go to the head of your order about some stupid ghost problem?"

The Sins had only just learned about Maison de Gargouille, the religious order their gargoyle protectors belonged to. Notre Dame was essentially their holy mother. The one and only time they had met her, she had literally morphed from a fearsome stone gargoyle into a lovely, tiny woman right before their eyes. She was much revered and a little scary, and the Sins were still leery of this entire bit of their family legacy they'd never heard of before. It seems the gargoyles had been the volunteer custodians of the Sins since the very beginning of the curse, and not the diabolical spies the Sins had thought they were.

Asher looked to his cousin for illumination. "What am I missing here?"

Luke eyed the gargoyles and risked their ire with a shrug. "I don't know."

Huffing out a beleaguered breath, Jeb held up his fingers to enumerate each point as he made them. "First, why do you think you were drawn here? To this particular vineyard? Two. It's in a monastery." Asher paid attention to the two fingers as Jeb continued. "Three. Don't you find it strange that Aaron has been showing up here so often? How often do we regularly see the Devil? Four. There's a giant mystery hole and the monk ghosts who live here don't want it dug up. I mean they *really* don't want it dug up."

"I'm starting to feel really stupid here," Asher confessed. "I was drawn to this place because I was looking for a new project and Esther found the apple wine here for your party." He poked Luke's chests for emphasis. "The place is named after Heaven. All of my investments have that in common, more or less. It's my 'fuck you' to the curse. And then I met Evangeline. Not hard to figure out from there."

Jeb shook his head. "I don't think any of this is a coincidence."

"Okay, I give up," Luke interjected with a wave of his hand. "What's in the hole."

"We're not positive." Jeb paused. "And don't freak out. You'll make it so much worse with the monks if you do."

Esther announced it as if she herself was quite positive what it was. "We're pretty sure it's one of the portals to Hell."

Chapter Twenty-Five

"A hole to where, now?" Asher asked. His brain flatly refused to believe what Esther had said.

"We think, we're pretty sure actually, that it might be one of the portals. You know they're all over the planet." Jeb was speaking carefully. He was used to dealing with irrational people, since he dealt with Wrath all the time.

Asher was feeling distinctly irrational at the moment.

Standing in his girlfriend's basement.

In the dark.

Over a hole to Hell.

"Why would there be a hole to Hell in Evangeline's basement?" Asher demanded. "Really? Why would we think this is a thing? The Dashiells don't have anything to do with our curse. I don't think the monks had anything to do with our curse."

Esther lifted her hand palm up to interrupt him. "Actually, I don't think that's true. It's possible the monks are curse adjacent."

Asher let his jaw flop open. He looked to Luke who had been mute about this scenario, and he still wasn't getting help there. Back at Esther and Jeb, he said, "Do you hear the words that you are saying? You sound insane."

Luke made a thoughtful humming sound. "In the scheme of things, our whole existence is kind of insane. Why is this particular development any more so than—" he pointed to himself and Asher, then to their gargoyles "—any of us? You're arguing with a living, breathing supernatural gargoyle. My father is the Devil. And you are the walking embodiment of Lust. Seriously, Asher, why is it any crazier that there'd be a portal to Hell in this basement?"

"I don't know," Asher bellowed. "Because I don't want it to be here. I don't want any of that vileness to infect her. She is good and precious and I..." He didn't say the last bit. He hadn't said it out loud yet. It wasn't a sentiment that should be bellowed in frustration.

Wrathful, gruff Luke gave him a sad smile and nodded his head. "I understand, man. I really do. But if there's one thing I know for sure, it's that we're not in control of this ride, we're just passengers."

Asher closed his eyes and slumped his shoulders, weary of his life. "I wanted to insulate her from all of this."

Esther linked her arm in his and bumped his shoulder with her own. "Except that you really didn't. You were only insulating her from the unsavory parts."

"No, I wasn't," Asher insisted, but he suspected there was a nugget of truth in her comment.

"You might have been against the idea at first, but when I brought the demons to work during Hell Week, you allowed it," she reminded him.

Damn it. Esther was right, as usual. If he'd really wanted to protect her from the worst of it, he would never have allowed demons on her farm. Maybe not even have introduced her to Luke and Mia. Probably not even Esther, but that would have been impossible.

Lust was weak, just like he was, and he'd permitted the demons because he hoped to best her in their little spat. God help him, he'd hoped to impress her. Finally, he'd welcomed Esther's intervention because it made Eva's life easier, and when she was relaxed, she was so beautiful.

Now he was horrified to realize that he was in love with her.

And he'd been so foolish as to introduce the nightmare of his reality into her existence.

Even if he was to leave her in a fit of honorable insanity, one of those I-must-leave-you-to-protect-you scenarios, it wouldn't do any good. There was a hole to Hell in her basement—a hole Asher was certain Eva and her sister were completely unaware of. Even if he pulled up stakes and took his malignant family with him, there'd still be a hole to Hell under her kitchen.

This was an unmitigated disaster.

Obviously, the hole was the reason the Devil was poking around over here. It really had nothing to do with Asher's own interest in Eva, other than the bastard's mean-spirited joy in upsetting him and Luke. That was somehow a relief. He certainly didn't want Maggie to get her feelings hurt, but he sure as fuck didn't want the Devil actively pursuing his girlfriend's twin sister in a romantic-feelings sort of way.

Holy shit, this was getting really complicated. They were going to have to fix this, but he didn't have the slightest idea how to go about it.

Well, except for one thing.

"We cannot tell Eva and Maggie about this." Asher gestured towards the floor and the godforsaken hole. "Let's just say it's not a problem, and get to the repairs. We'll leave it sealed under the floor and the monks can just continue keeping an eye on it."

Both gargoyles looked dismayed at this suggestion. Jeb crossed his arms, and Esther shook her head. Luke remained annoyingly silent.

"That only pushes the problem down the road. This will have to be dealt with at some point," Esther pointed out.

Asher deflated. "I know. I know. But I'm not ready yet."

He still had to make Eva love him. Somehow, he had to wriggle himself into her life so far that she thought of him as essential. The same way he felt about her. That way, when it all inevitably came out, she wouldn't throw him aside without a second thought.

A cesspool of doubt churned in the back of his mind. There was nothing he possessed, nothing that he brought to the table that was worthy of a second glance.

Lust brought him nothing but trouble. He was pretty. He knew how to fuck. Underneath that was just Asher Mephisto. A man with a business degree and dubious family connections. At least he had money, and that's what she needed most right now.

Pull yourself together, he told himself.

"Surely you're not suggesting that we open this thing up, are you?" he asked the occupants of the room as a whole.

"No!" all three answered at once.

Jeb continued, "Certainly not. The monks have kept it sealed for hundreds of years. We need to maintain that."

A little whirlwind of dust fluttered around their feet, seemingly bringing the agreement of the dead monks.

"Then we're not telling them." Asher sliced his hand through the air with finality. When he glanced at Luke, the big man nodded his head.

"You know, it's funny," Esther said, but her expression suggested it wasn't funny at all. "When I was bringing the demons here to work, one of them mentioned the back door in passing. I didn't know what he was talking about and I blew him off, but this must have been what he meant."

Luke and Asher gave her matching grimaces.

She mused on, "Think I should poke around, find out what there is to know about all this?"

Luke pulled a face that implied he didn't think much of that idea.

Asher shook his head in the negative. "Ummm..."

Jeb's calm voice overrode them both. "It would be a good idea to know exactly what we're dealing with here. Just make sure to keep it on the down low. We can't afford any undue attention here."

"Yeah," Asher agreed and poked his finger in the air to emphasize his point. "I don't want a bunch of unescorted demons trolling around the grounds. It's bad enough we have the few that are already here. Let's get them home ASAP, understand?"

Esther shrugged and Asher didn't know how to interpret that.

Jeb continued, "I'm going straight to see Notre Dame."

"What am I going to tell Mitchell?" Luke asked. "I have to give him some reason why we're blowing off the LiDAR."

Ashe snorted. "I don't know. Break out some architect stuff. You'll think of something. All I know for sure is that I want to get the repairs on this roof started right away."

Luke came up with something for Mitchell and the engineer was shuttled away from the vineyard. Jeb promptly disappeared to points unknown, and Esther rounded up the imported labor and she escorted them home, presumably asking subtle questions along the way. Asher brushed over the whole anomaly situation with the sisters, calling it no big deal and promised the repairs would start right away. If Eva tilted her head at him and squinted a bit at his breathy and unusually loquacious explanation, he pretended like he didn't notice and plowed on through.

To his immense relief, Eva and Maggie both accepted this story and picked up right where they left off.

As the week continued, Asher worked with Luke and Maggie to schedule the contractors as soon as possible. The next time Ashe saw Jeb, he pretended like he didn't know about any supernatural events in the basement. He pointedly did not ask any questions or ask for an explanation of the hole. In fact, when Jeb started a conversation with the words *Notre Dame said*, Asher turned and purposefully walked in the other direction.

It was a juvenile response, but Ashe didn't care. The less he knew, the less he was lying by omission. As if the court of broken hearts cared about semantics.

Of course, there was a stumbling block almost right out of the gate. It seemed none of the local contractors had a crew they could spare on immediate notice. Ashe tried to throw money at the problem, but that didn't actually get them anywhere.

"It's summer," Jeb stated as if that explained everything. "We've got bids from several of the top companies, but none of them can start for at least two months. This is a huge job and we're asking in the middle of the prime construction season."

"Can't you pull some strings or something?" Ashe asked Luke. "Surely you hold some sway in this town."

Luke snorted. "You'd think so, but not really. I do the plans, not the construction. That's a whole different ballgame."

"What about the crew Esther's had working here before?" Eva chimed in. "They were fast. They don't need to be brilliant, right? Just a grunt crew."

Jeb snorted. "Well, they do grunt."

Asher grimaced. Damn it, he really didn't want any more of Hell's influence around here than there already had been.

Esther shrugged and layered it with a sympathetic lift of her eyebrows. "I can get them here in a snap." Ashe wasn't even sure if that was just an expression or if she really could snap to summon demons. "They behaved before. I don't know why they wouldn't this time."

Eva nodded her head in agreement. "Yeah, give them a call. Let's get this show on the road." She laced her fingers in with Asher's and gave them a squeeze.

"Well?" Esther asked.

In the scales in his mind, he weighed the alternatives. Get the demon work gang back and finish faster or steer clear of any infernal influence and wait the couple of months. He knew what he should do. But he also needed to make sure he was keeping the project on track. It was integral to making himself necessary.

Luke nodded. "They've already been here. Nothing happened before."

That was true, but that didn't mean nothing still couldn't.

"I'll keep a really good eye on them," Esther assured him.

And with a resigned nod of his head, his good intentions went by the wayside.

Esther was true to her word. The crew arrived first thing in the morning and the new roof was done in record time. They used the same crew to load the furnishings and belongings back into the monastery. It was less than two weeks before Maggie's office and the vineyard gift shop were back in residency on the bottom floor.

Asher himself bricked up the opening to the tiny room that housed the hole. The monks seemed much relieved as there were no dust tornados to pester him while he worked.

When the last cases of wine had been lugged back into the gift shop and this part of the construction job had been officially completed, Asher wandered down to the Gewürztraminer vines to find Eva and share the good news.

And because he was desperate to touch her.

They'd worked separately during the roofing job. Even though the monastery was a disaster, the grapes waited for no one. So while Asher and Esther had supervised the work crew, Maggie had been at the picnic table handling the regular business of the vineyard while Eva and Ernie had been monitoring the grapes as usual. But every evening, Asher had taken Eva home with him.

He had never been so happy. At first, he didn't recognize the feeling. He'd thought he'd been happy all along. There was no reason to believe he wasn't happy. He had plenty of money which gave him the luxury of working at something he enjoyed and the added benefit of good looks that made life easier. And the supernatural advantage of what most people would consider an obscene amount of sex. He was essentially the superhero of all horny young men. Or women. Or anyone who has ever wanted sex.

Why wouldn't he be happy?

The truly astounding thing about being with Eva was that sex wasn't actually the end result of every encounter. When she went home with Asher, they spent as much time cuddling and talking and laughing as they did having sex. He wanted to know everything about her. What had her childhood been like growing up on the vineyard. Who had her first crush been? Where did she dream of going one day? When had she known that she could speak to the vines? There were so many questions to uncovering the fascinating truth of Evangeline Dashiell.

And it was a challenge to learn all he could about his favorite subject without giving much of himself away. It burned at his insides that he would never be able to give himself to her like she had to him. He tried to make up for that in a zillion other ways.

He watched her from the top of the row. When she removed her hat to swipe at her brow the sun shone bright on her mahogany hair, turning the thick braid into a rope of a hundred colors of brown and burgundy and gold. When she turned to smile at him, she had a swipe of zinc oxide on her nose and dark sunglasses to cut the glare. Her tee-shirt was faded and her jean shorts were dirty. Strong, shapely legs stretched into muddy Wellington boots.

Her beauty made him giddy.

"Hello, gorgeous," he said in greeting.

She strode forward, towing her work wagon behind her. "Hello, yourself."

Dropping the handle, she tossed her work gloves in the wagon, then slipped her hands around his neck. Asher wrapped his arms around her and pulled her tight against him. Her lips were warm, and her skin smelled of sunshine and earth. He tasted tart grapes on her tongue. She hummed deep in her throat when he grabbed her ass and hauled her in tighter still.

Finally, she broke the kiss with a giggle. "I do love these little visits of yours."

"We're all unpacked at the Monastery. Everything there is wrapped up." He turned her loose and plucked the wagon handle out of the dirt. "Are you done down here for the day?"

"Yup." She tucked her hand inside his free one, and they started back up the row. "You have perfect timing, as ususal."

"The gazebo lumber is supposed to be delivered tomorrow," he told her.

"Wow. This is all so exciting." She squeezed his fingers. "My grandfather would be ecstatic with all these changes. Wouldn't you, Pop?" She directed the last words out to the vines as if she was chatting with her grandfather now.

"Has he told you this personally?" he teased.

"Yup. Why not? If we all believe the monks are still poking around, then my grandfather would have hung around his favorite place, too."

He'd have to ask Esther about that.

With a kiss to her temple, he asked, "Are you still up for dinner tonight?" When she looked confused, he reminded her. "Remember, you, Maggie, and I are meeting with some of my cousins tonight."

"Oh, right!" She sounded like she was actually excited about it. Asher wished he could be. He'd set up the dinner to include Seth because as Gluttony, he knew all the greatest caterers and the best ideas for menus. Benji was bringing his art skills to the table. He'd expressed a desire to paint a mural in the new dining area being created in the cellar and the sisters had been super excited about the idea. Ethan was working up all kinds of ideas for marketing since Envy always knew the best ways to get to the core of what the masses wanted. Of course, Luke and Mia would be there. Luke had already done so much, and Eva and Mia had connected instantly.

"I can't wait," Eva said as she skipped up to the cab of his enormous red truck.

Asher forced a smile. He wanted to do everything to make the vineyard succeed, and the best way to do that was to bring on the experts.

If only it didn't worry him having so much devilish representation present at the place hiding a secret hole to Hell.

Chapter Twenty-Six

Eva was excited about meeting yet another of Ashe's cousins. Of course, she'd already come to know Benji because he seemed to tag around with Asher quite a bit. She'd already met Ethan as well, just that once, but Maggie had been out on her date, so she hadn't had the good luck. Eva had confirmed that Ethan was as handsome as Ashe, Luke, and Benji, and they both knew that Aaron Mephisto was remarkably good looking, too. The sisters couldn't wait to see if the next Mephisto fit in the pantheon as well.

Maggie rode into town with Asher and Eva and wandered around Asher's amazing apartment while Eva took a shower and changed into a pair of tight brown leather pants and an off the shoulder cream-colored blouse. A pair of kicky-heeled sandals completed the look, and she felt like maybe the farmer would fit in at a trendy restaurant. While she was finishing her makeup and putting product in her hair, Asher came up behind her, slipped his arms around her waist, and kissed the back of her head.

"You're gorgeous," he whispered, his eyes meeting hers in the mirror and holding her spellbound. "We can cancel dinner and I can just eat you instead."

"After all this effort to get dressed?" she teased. She arched her back the slightest bit to rub her ass against his crotch. As usual, Asher was ready to go. "Maggie would be so disappointed."

He didn't answer. Instead, he lifted the hair from the back of her neck and used his tongue against her nape to bring goosebumps to her arms. She let her head drop forward and hummed in appreciation, then sharply inhaled when his teeth nipped at a tendon.

It only took a light tug on the front of her blouse for the neckline to drop below her strapless bra and for his hands to cup her breasts over the flesh-colored lace.

"My favorite color," he said and retook her gaze in the mirror.

She gave her head a tiny shake. "It's nude-colored, you silly man."

"I know." Her gave a gentle squeeze through the lace. "My favorite color is naked."

She chuckled low in her throat. "We don't have time, Asher. Your cousins will be waiting for us, and Maggie is right downstairs." But. she didn't really want him to stop. She watched in fascination as he slid his thumbs under the cups of her strapless bra and tipped her breasts out. When he rolled her nipples, one in each hand, her breath caught.

He pressed one hand on the middle of her back and, still maintaining eye contact, he pushed her torso down towards the vanity counter. By now she was panting. The hand from her back slid down to her butt and massaged through the leather.

"I'll be quick," he promised.

She grasped the edge of the marble and swallowed hard. Her voice came out in a whisper. "I don't want you to be quick."

Both hands gripped her hips and jerked her back against him, his dick hard and straining against his pants. Oh, good lord, she wanted him. Right now. So much so, that she purposefully forgot about their dinner reservations and put her sister out of her mind. She arched her back further and gave her ass an inviting wiggle.

Asher growled. He actually growled, which thrilled her. The way he commanded her body, and the way her body responded to him, it was difficult to reconcile that he was the same man who seemed so inexperienced their first time together. If he was learning as they went, he was like a goddamned Einstein.

He sunk to his knees behind Eva and slipped a hand between her legs and cupped her.

"Hey, guys." Maggie's voice traveled up the stairs. "Are you about ready?"

With a heavy sigh, he answered, "We'll be right down. Two more minutes."

Two minutes? There were quickies and then there was ridiculous. She was worried until his teeth sunk into the flesh of her ass. He rose back to his feet behind her, crowding her against the counter with his body. Her mouth was dry, but her panties were soaking.

He thrust his hips against her butt while one hand filled its palm with one breast and the other delved down the front of her pants. The heel of his hand pressed against her clit and two fingers filled her hot, needy warmth. Now she was gasping for breath and pushing back against his crotch. Two pumps of his curved fingers and the perfect pressure from his hand and she was right at the edge.

"Beautiful," he whispered in her ear, his hazel eyes trapping her gaze in the mirror. "Come for me."

That was enough. His simple command and she was tumbling over the edge in less than two minutes. The man was a freaking wizard.

He held her up while her orgasm took over her body. When she felt like a languid version of herself, she opened her eyes to see him still watching her in the mirror.

"I'll go slower tonight," he promised and kissed her neck. As he turned away, he swatted her butt. "Come on, babe. We're going to be late."

He'll go slower tonight? she repeated in her head. That would likely kill her, but she couldn't wait nevertheless. If that was how she was going to go, well then, who was she to mess with fate?

While he walked away, she appreciated his butt in the mirror. The man could wear the hell out of a pair of pants. He shrugged his arms into a dark gray blazer and flashed her a rogue's smile, one that said he knew she'd be standing at the counter for a few more minutes before her knees were strong enough to move.

"I'll keep Maggie busy while you finish up." He blew her a kiss and strode from the room.

She grinned back even when she insisted, "Jerk."

Maggie couldn't believe they would get a table based on the parking lot alone, but Eva knew that if Asher said something was happening, it was a done deal. The lobby was packed and some of the city's chicest people stood around looking frustrated and hungry.

When Asher approached the hostess, the LA-pretty blonde perused him head to toe before saying, "Mr. Mephisto, right this way. Your party is in the blue room."

Eva tucked her hand inside the crook of Asher's arm, and they followed the model-thin girl to a glassed-in private room.

One long wall was filled with cross-hatched wine racks housing hundreds of bottles of wine. Eva gave Maggie a wide-eyed glance, and Maggie nodded.

"Someday," Maggie agreed, in an awed whisper, "Dashiell Vineyards will be everywhere."

"Sooner than you think," Asher promised with a cheeky grin. "It's all going to happen."

The wall opposite was glass and looked out into the restaurant, which itself was terraced and tastefully decorated in shades of green and brown. Enormous, tufted banquets and mid-century modern chairs and tables filled the floor while amazing pendant lights with tesla-style bulbs inside vintage bottles hung around the room. The place was so cool, Eva felt like she'd gained style points just being there.

The people in their private dining room only bumped up the cool factor.

Besides her sister and Asher, of course, Eva recognized Luke and Mia, Benji, and Ethan from their brief meeting before. There was also another man she didn't know. This one was enormous like Luke, tall and broad, but where Luke was clean cut and professional-looking even though he also did MMA fighting, this other one had long, black hair and a trim beard. He looked dangerous, piratical. A black linen button down, sleeves uncuffed and rolled halfway up his forearms, hung loose and untucked from dark jeans. Bracelets of woven string, beads, and leather wreathed his wrists, and she could see snatches of ink on his chest and arms as the material shifted when he gestured. Thick motorcycle boots finished his ensemble. With dark hair and dark eyes, he was intimidating as hell. Until he threw back his head and roared with laughter. He exuded merriment, not violence.

Good lord, the gene pool of the Mephisto men was unmatched.

Once the man noticed their entrance, he strode towards them. As he got closer, he took in the fact that Eva and Maggie were twins. She could tell that's what was running through his head after years of living through all the inane questions. She recognized the expression of wonder and amazement—as if twins were a completely alien life form or something only heard about in the freak shows of Barnum & Bailey.

The man clapped Asher on the shoulder with a meaty palm. "Well, look at this. Benji had said twins, but of course he left out the most interesting part." Before she knew it was happening, the huge man had separated her from Asher and had engulfed her in a massive bear hug. "So excited to meet you."

"Ack!" It was all Eva could get out before her lungs were squished.

"All right, dude," Asher said on the tail end of a laugh. "Let her go."

Eva wobbled on her feet, suddenly released from the embrace. "Hi." She didn't know what else to say. Everything seemed inadequate in the face of his avid greeting.

"Babe, this is my absurdly enthusiastic cousin, Seth."

Seth's grin widened, if that was possible. "And you must be Evangeline. I've heard very compelling things about you." Okay, that was a weird word choice. "I also knew you were a twin, but I didn't realize you were identical."

"Um, yeah. Nice to meet you, too." Eva stuck out a hand that was immediately swallowed up and kissed like a courtier. She couldn't help but giggle. For all that he was huge and effusive, he was also ridiculously charming.

"And you—" Seth turned to Maggie "—are clearly the sister, Magdalena."

"That's right," Maggie got out before she got the grizzly bear hug, too. "How did you know our full names? No one ever calls us by those."

Benji appeared from behind Seth's right shoulder. "Apparently I do share some of the good stuff."

Greetings and hugs were dispensed around the room. It appeared as though they were the last to arrive. Eva and Mia immediately caught each other up on their latest farming experiments and achievements. If left to their own devices, they would have easily retired to a corner and chatted about it for hours. Asher and Luke didn't allow it, however, and soon they were all seated at a large table in the middle of the room. Maggie was squished between Benji and Luke with Asher, Eva, and Mia on the opposite side of the table, and Seth and Ethan at either end.

"Is this one of your finds?" Asher asked Seth.

Ethan answered instead from the far end. "Nah, one of mine. I've done some charity work with the owner here."

"But I introduced them," Seth pointed out with a flourish. "I've known the chef for years. I staked him on his first venture when he was fresh out of culinary school. Dude's a genius with flavors."

"You didn't pee on him, Seth," Ethan countered. "He's not *yours*. You have to share your discoveries. You forget, I can do as much for his career now as you can."

"Oh really," Eva asked Ethan. "What do you do?" She expected to hear the smartly dressed man was a lawyer, or a hedge fund manager, or something of that ilk.

"I own a PR firm."

Ashe nodded. "He's the best. That's why he's here. We need to get the Dashiell Vineyards name out far and wide. Everyone has come here tonight to help."

To help? All of these people who didn't know her or Maggie. People who had no connection to the Dashiell family at all. They all wanted them to succeed. Eva felt a bit verklempt and, when she glanced at Maggie, her expression said she felt so, too.

"Wow," she said with an awed blink to those around the table. "That is... really generous. Thank you."

Asher squeezed her hand and gave her a rascally grin. "We each have a specialty that, when weaponized, can be very profitable. You know all about Luke. He's already done the retrofit designs for the new event space in the wine cellar. The work is coming right along on the monastery housing the new offices, tasting bar, and gift shop."

"Yeah," Maggie added with excitement. "My office is no longer in a tent with a picnic table."

"You do have a remarkable view," Mia pointed out.

Maggie lifted her wine glass high, "To the prettiest vineyard in the valley." The rest of the table joined in with "Here, heres" and cheers.

"And here's to Dashiell Vineyards and world domination." Ethan continued the toasting.

"That seems like a lot," Eva raised her glass to the toast even though she thought that idea was a bit over the top.

Asher clinked his glass to hers. "But it doesn't have to be. You and Maggie have all these amazing ideas to make the farm profitable. Together—" he swept his open palm across the expanse of the table "—we can make it real. We want to build on your ideas. Flesh them out. Show the world your talents."

Ethan chimed in. "Make you zillions of dollars."

"Zillions!" Seth repeated with a booming voice.

Eva blinked at the thought. Zillions? She'd never hoped for zillions. Neither had Gramps, honestly. Her deepest wish was far more tangible. A Platinum award at the Decanter World Wine Awards or an ever more seemingly untenable award for a tiny unknown vineyard in the States, Best in Show. If one of the wines from her hard work and experiments ever came home with a Best in Show from Decanter, well, she could simply lie down and die. Nothing would ever surpass it.

Asher's voice took on a softer tone. "Or the accolades you're dreaming of." He delivered another hand squeeze under the table.

"Yes. All the things!" Seth's voice rang out after he tossed back the contents of his glass. Did this guy do anything subtly? He was like a dark version of Thor. She fully expected him to hurl his goblet into a fireplace or something.

"Settle down there, big guy. You're scaring people." Asher rolled his eyes at his cousin. "As you can see, Seth's a great cheerleader for the cause."

"Right," Ethan cut in. "You'd think he was the PR guy or something. In all reality, we do want the vineyard to succeed in all the ways you're dreaming of."

Maggie leaned forward and put both elbows on the table across from Eva. "All we really need is for the place to keep itself afloat while Eva works her magic and tinkers with her recipes and stuff. We figured if we could also turn a profit as a party venue, then we could afford to take all the time she needs. We had some modest plans to do that. Well, they were modest before Asher arrived with his buckets of money, and Luke made some suggestions about the space in the wine cellar and before Benji asked to do a mural down there. Now they're much grander than we'd ever considered before."

"Go big or go home!" Seth bellowed good naturedly. "Wait until you hear what I bring to the table. You'll be internationally known before you know what hit you."

Like a mirror of each other, Eva and Maggie both sat back in their seats. Was this whole thing going to spiral out of control? It wasn't that she wasn't grateful for Asher and the power and influence his family could assist them with, but she also didn't want to lose control of their family legacy. She'd been afraid when Asher got involved because she had feared he would get bored and all his support would fall away just when she'd begun to depend on him. He'd eased her mind somewhat about that, but now she had to worry about all the rest of these guys falling out. Or worse yet, completely taking over.

Her distress must have been obvious from her expression because Ethan gave Seth a look to shush him. "How about if we just toss some ideas out there and you pluck out the ones you guys like and we can go from there, huh? This is just a discussion. Consider us a pro bono angel investor group with time at your disposal."

"Yeah, Seth. Jeez. Maybe you need to evaluate your meds." Benji was seated at his right elbow. Seated was an incorrect description. In actuality, he was more slumped in the chair, one leg literally slung over the arm in a posture that made her think of a bored and apathetic medieval king.

Seth deflated. "I don't take meds," he grumbled, his expression darkened.

Benji nodded. "Maybe you should check into that."

Mia chided him from across the length of the table. "Benji, be nice." She turned to Eva and said, "You'll get used to Seth. He just goes at everything a hundred miles an hour." Then directing her smile back at Seth, she said, "I think you're very charming, honey."

Seth shot Mia an air kiss.

Dinner got underway, a chef's tasting menu the waiter described as having been hand chosen by Seth and the chef to pair with Dashiell Vineyards wine. Seth beamed back at them.

"How?" Maggie asked, voicing Eva's question as well.

Asher answered, "A surprise."

Over the charcuterie and Pinot Grigio, Benji was convinced to describe the mural he was planning inside the newly realized banquet space inside the wine cellar. With some reorganization of the casks and copper drums, the addition of elaborate chandeliers, and a little magic, they would now have a fashionably rustic venue. Having spent much of the previous year in Europe and falling in love with the art and scenery, Benji seemed excited about the project. Well, as excited might have been a stretch, but his eyes did seem to brighten when he discussed his thoughts. He said he'd done some research on the part of France the Dashiell patriarch had emigrated from with the original root stock the entire vineyard was founded on. The mural would harken back to that time and space. Eva thought it sounded perfect.

A micro greens salad with apple and pear followed by sweet onion soup was the backdrop for a discussion of a landscaping design for the lawn surrounding the pond, which included a picturesque gazebo and a garden folly.

During the fish course of Monterey Bay abalone and Riesling, Ethan outlined a comprehensive plan for promotion and publicity that didn't seem nearly as terrifying as Eva thought it would be when she and Maggie had to come up with the plan by themselves.

During the meat course of braised rabbit, au gratin potatoes and Pinot Noir, Seth dropped the biggest news that he wanted to host a charity poker tournament to kick off their grand reopening to the world.

"A poker tournament?" Eva asked Asher. "Why poker?"

"Seth's a top ranked player," Asher told her in a low voice, as if that wasn't the most unlikely thing she'd heard tonight. Somehow, she'd always considered professional gamblers to be subtle people. Seth was as subtle as napalm.

"Professionally?" she asked.

"Yup. He donates everything he wins to charity."

She raised her eyebrows and felt like Alice. Curiouser and Curiouser.

In the most exciting way possible, Eva was beginning to feel like her life was morphing into someone else's. She barely recognized it anymore. When did she, the surly twin, the college dropout, the quiet farmer become the woman in trendy clothes with the zillionaire boyfriend who hung out with professional gamblers and fighters?

She hardly knew what to expect out of life next.

Hell XXI

The bar was completely quiet. It had gone from a raucous working-class bar to dead silent in the blink of an eye. One minute the dude on the stage was grooving some blues and the next all chatter had ceased along with the music and all eyes were on him and Juliet. It was a lot of eyes because a lot of the crowd had more than the standard two.

At least the flock of devilish beasties were no longer pawing at his angel. The path to the old men's table was clear ahead.

Neil leaned his head back and whispered to Juliet, "Just hang tight and don't panic."

Her arms around his neck tightened. "Uh huh. Don't let them get me."

He hated that he couldn't see her expression. She was braver than he could ever have predicted, but he still didn't like the idea that she was afraid. Of course, she was afraid. It would be easier if he could gage how badly. All he could do at this point was protect her—which he would do with every ounce of his being.

He hitched her higher on his back and strode purposefully towards the table of old men in the back. They were watching the two of them, their faces alight with interest. Empty booze bottles surrounded their feet. The tabletop was littered with used glasses and piles of what looked like kibbles of dog food. Gross.

"Well, what have we got here?" The speaker was an older guy with a big black, bushy beard and mustache and a white cowboy hat. His words came out in a smooth, lyrical drawl that made Neil think of the South.

"Looks to me like a hooligan." This guy was clean-shaven, but his drawl was maybe even more pronounced. He took a handful of kibble and tossed it into the center of the table to join a growing pile there as if he was betting on a card game.

A chuckle came from the guy at the furthest side of the table. Another one with facial hair, but it was salt and pepper and neatly trimmed. When he spoke he had a thick accent like that old guy who played James Bond. "I dinnae think he means the lad. He means the fair lass hanging on his back."

"That's right, Johnnie." Bushy Beard nodded, then asked, "What're you doin' with a girl hanging on yer back?"

"A fine question." The fourth man had closely shorn hair and long muttonchops but was otherwise free of whiskers. His accent sounded like that of the fine, rich Mexican ladies who would sometimes come to his orphanage to make donations. "Speak up young man."

Before Neil could come up with an acceptable answer, Juliet stuck her head over his shoulder and said, "I'm Juliet."

Neil suppressed a groan. "Didn't I ask you to shhh?" he hissed at her.

He could feel her shrug. "They're just old men. They seem pretty harmless."

He let his head drop and sighed. "If they're down here, babe, then they're not harmless."

"I say," the second man drawled again. He sounded like that giant chicken in the old Looney Tunes cartoon. "Harmless indeed. It's a pleasure to meet you, young lady." He touched the brim of an imaginary hat. "Johannes Beam, at your service, but you can call me Jim."

"Nice to meet you, Jim,"

Neil just knew she was flashing that endearing smile at these geezers.

"Come on down here and sit a spell," Bushy Beard suggested. He reached to the side and grabbed the back of a chair occupied by some imp with two heads. Yanking hard he dumped the imp onto the floor and dragged the chair to his side, then patted the ripped vinyl in invitation.

"Thank you, sir." Her sweet voice slipped over them like honey. "But I cannot get down."

"You mean he won't let you?" Bushy Beard demanded with a totally unexpected roar of anger. Juliet flinched and Neil instinctively backed up a step.

"Hush now, you brute." The Scottish guy pushed hard at Bushy's shoulder. "Dammit, Jasper, you're going to scare her away." Instead of Juliet, he spoke to Neil. "You're welcome to set her down and rest a spell."

The smile back in her voice, Juliet told them, "That's very nice, but I am unable to touch much of anything, I'm afraid. Magic, you understand." Well, at least she had the sense not to tell them she's an angel.

Jim slapped his own meaty thigh. "A tiny little thing like you. I'll bet you weigh next to nothin'. Why don't you sit down right here and keep me company for a while." His accent gave the word a soft "a" that elongated the word ending in a smile Neil didn't like the sheen of.

Neil narrowed his eyes at Jim but spoke to the table at large. "Yeah, she doesn't weigh anything and she's just fine where she is, thanks anyway. We're here looking for Johnnie, Jose, Jim, and Jack. Are you them?"

"Maybe," Muttonchops said. "Why?" He was dressed up all old fashioned and fancy, like he was from a long, long time ago. Even though his accent was Mexican, he seemed more like one of those stuffy old English dukes in a black and white movie.

"Housekeeper from the mansion sent me," Neil told them. "They're out of booze again."

It was that exact moment that it occurred to him who he was talking to. He squinted at Bushy Beard and realized Jasper was actually Jack Daniels. Which obviously made Jim Beam *the* Jim Beam. They had called the Scot Johnnie, making it painfully clear that he was Johnnie Walker. Neil stared at the old rich dude and tried to use context clues to sort him out.

"Dude." Neil pointed at the fourth man. "Jose Cuervo!"

"Don Jose Antonio de Cuervo," he said with a dignified nod. Not what Neil had thought Jose Cuervo of the world's most famous tequila would look like.

He threw up a hand to high-five each of them, but they left him hanging. Whatever. Jose fucking Cuervo. Whoa, shit! "Huh." Neil straightened a bit. "It never really occurred to me that you were all real people."

"Aye," Johnnie Walker said with a solemn frown. "Normally we'd have a few more of our esteemed lot, but Smirnov, Gordon, and Jameson aren't here just the now."

"Who are they?" Juliet whispered in Neil's ear.

"Famous alcohol guys. Which explains why they're in Hell, eh?"

"Oh, yeah. I don't really know much about that kinda stuff," she admitted.

"Aren't you just as pretty as a peach," Jim Beam drawled up at her with a look that was anything but grandfatherly. He was so smooth. If he wasn't directly trying to mack on his angle, Neil would have watched him for tips.

"Anyway," Neil growled at the geezer. "I need to pick up supplies for the mansion."

"We just supplied the mansion," Jack Daniels chucked at couple pieces of kibble into the central pile and then, almost as an afterthought, he popped a couple more in his mouth. He chewed a couple of times and then swore violently before spitting the mouthful onto the floor. "Damn it! I am so sick of this tired ass food. What I wouldn't give for some nice fried chicken."

Oh, fried chicken. Neil salivated even thinking about it.

"There's no use griping about it. It's never going to happen. Not that I don't agree. I'd even eat a haggis if given the opportunity." Johnnie Walker dusted his hands free of dog food crumbs.

"A cigar." Don Jose said the word with reverence.

All four men at the table looked off in the middle distance and moaned the word 'cigar.' Juliet giggled.

"Can't help you there," Neil told them. "Although I hear that the airline food is better than the other menu items."

"Bah!" Jack Daniels scowled. "I don't trust food from the sky."

"You'd eat a chicken," Jim Beam pointed out.

"Chickens don't fly, you idiot." Apparently, Jack Daniels was surly to begin with. Neil always assumed drinking the whiskey brought out the surly attitude of a drunk, but maybe that was already built in.

"They *can* fly," Jim insisted.

"Not with any damn finesse," Jack countered.

"Anyway," Neil interrupted. "The mansion needs more booze."

At the same time, Johnnie Walker held up an index finger. "I'd like a cigar, too. What say you get us four cigars, and we'll get you what you need."

Jose grinned wide. "What about the other boys?"

"Those dobbers," Johnnie said with a dismissive wave of his hand. "They're not here. Too bad for them."

"Cigars?" Neil had no fucking idea where he was going to get four cigars. "How in the Hell am I supposed to do that?"

Jack Daniels hooted. "A cigar! That's the ticket." He swept a hand across the table and brushed most of the dog food on the ground.

"Where the Hell am I supposed to get cigars?" Neil demanded of no one in particular. "Wouldn't you rather have chips? A candy bar maybe?"

Jim Beam perked up. "You have those?"

Neil squeezed Juliet's knee in a preemptive move to shush her. "I might have access to some."

"Nah," Jack said. "Cigars. Cigars. Cigars," he started to chant and pretty quickly Jose and Jim joined in.

Johnnie Walker leaned back in his chair and turned to face Neil and Juliet with a smug smile. "Four cigars and we'll get you the potables."

"I heard a Duke on Four had some cigars." Jose gave them a wink. "Go see him."

"If you like—" Jim patted his knee again. "—you can leave the little bird right here and I'll keep an eye on her."

Neil burst out in laughter. "Oh, hell to the fucking no, dude."

Neil hightailed it out of there and headed straight to the elevator. Juliet asked Charon as sweetly as anyone had ever spoken to that gnarly old bastard and he agreed to take them to Four at no charge and no questions asked. That little skill may turn out to be incredibly helpful. Eventually Juliet's backpack would run out of snacks.

Speaking of which...

"Hey, have you seen Cerberus?" he asked Charon over the sound of penny whistles playing that Lone Ranger song.

"Nope. Can't say that makes me sad," Charon said. It looked like he'd lost a tooth since the last time he smiled at them.

As if the dog already knew, he was waiting for them on the platform when the elevator opened on Four, tongues hanging out. All three heads woofed in excitement at seeing them.

It wasn't difficult to find Duke Gremory's home, a single-wide trailer on blocks. It was filthy from soot, and Neil regretted even having to knock on the door.

"I'm begging you, Juliet. Please be quiet while we're in there. Just don't say anything."

"Fine," was her curt reply. It didn't sound fine.

When the door opened, a cloud of acrid smoke billowed out the door. Oh, sweet lord, he couldn't bring her in there. Neil cast his eyes around the foundation and dirt yard for an answer on where she could wait. They were completely alone except for the dog.

"Hey, I have an idea. Cerberus, come here." The enormous dog lumbered towards them. He was so tall his wide back was over Neil's hip. "Climb on," he told Juliet, and he turned around and lowered her until she was sitting astride the three-headed dog.

"Hey," she said with a grin, "Pretty cool." She stroked two heads at once.

"I don't know why I didn't think of it before." Now that there was another solution, Neil felt a little sad there wasn't really any reason to carry her around anymore. On the other hand... He tilted her chin up and pressed his lips to hers in a brief kiss that managed to make him feel better.

"I'll be right back," he told her. "I'm just gonna run in there real quick and get four cigars. Won't take me more than a minute. I promise."

"We'll be fine," she promised. "Don't worry."

Chapter Twenty-Seven

Asher lay in bed. Alone. It had been weeks since the monastery had been put back to rights, all the furniture moved back in, and Eva had returned to her own home.

Damn, he missed her.

She'd slept over several times, but it wasn't enough.

The enormous expanse of his bed felt like an ocean of lonely high thread count sheets. To make it worse, he'd crawled in bed the first night after those sheets had been laundered, and her pillow no longer smelled like her. It would be really creepy for him to sneak up to her bedroom and steal her pillowcase, right? Right.

He couldn't go on like this. It was a truly pathetic epiphany, but he didn't want to sleep another night without her. Those days when she'd slept here with him had been the best nights of his life. In his entire existence, he'd never had a repeat bed partner, and then came Eva.

Brilliant, beautiful Eva.

Lazy, he turned his head to gaze out the window. The curtains were still drawn against the morning, but the color bleeding through seemed overcast. That would make Eva happy. The grapes would relish a nice soaking after all these long summer days.

That's the way everything presented itself to him now. After a lifetime of selfishness, everything he encountered ran through the Eva filter these days.

What would Eva think of the sky?

Hear a joke and want to tell her right away, knowing she'd think it was funny.

Pass a gas station and remember that the tank on her old pickup was low and remind himself to take it and get it filled for her.

His day dreaming was interrupted when his bedroom door swung open and Esther breezed in. "You know, I'm really missing ousting naked bodies out of your bed every morning."

Asher snorted. "I'll bet." He swung back the bedding in a wide arc and rolled out of bed.

"No, really," she said as she disappeared into his closet. "I haven't had to crawl under the bed to fish out tacky underwear or anything. I'm afraid if I tried to do it now, I'd pull a muscle or something."

"Funny," he told her with no mirth in his tone. Actually, he didn't miss it at all. His old life seemed like it belonged to someone else.

"I wonder what all the sexually frustrated people are doing these days?" She sounded muffled from the depths of his closet. "I haven't noticed an uptick on vice crimes reported on the news. They must be getting laid somewhere." She laughed at her own joke. "On the other hand, I do enjoy thinking of all the repressed Congressmen and religious folk who must be stewing these days."

Asher refused to think about any responsibilities he had to those frustrated people. As far as he was concerned, the world was about to experience a long, dark night of the sexual soul. He walked out of his underwear, leaving them on the bathroom floor, and into the shower where the rejuvenating pulsing water pounded his shoulders and back.

He didn't know what the day held for him, but he was going to be ready for it, whatever it was. Esther asked him if he ever got bored at the vineyard. He'd laughed at the thought. Bored? Tedium? Hardly. Every day with Eva, watching her work her magic, taming the stubborn earth, witnessing her brilliance transform into her bewitching wine. Every day was a gift, and he still couldn't believe she welcomed him every day.

Every day spent, bedazzled by her beauty.

Wearing a towel around his waist, he was shaving in the mirror when Esther stuck her head around the corner.

"You love her," Esther stated.

He'd already come to that conclusion, but he hadn't said it out loud to anyone yet. He met her eyes in the mirror. "Yes."

"What are you going to do about it?" she asked.

His hand paused midway to his chin. He screwed up his eyebrows in the reflection. "What do you mean?"

The rest of her body slid into view, and she rested her shoulder on the doorjamb. "You're sleeping alone again. She's by herself, too. Neither of you like it."

He nodded his head. Bringing the razor to his cheekbone, he rasped downward and pondered her question. "I hate it. I'm trying to work out how I can make that change."

"You're hopeless." She gave her eyes a dramatic roll. "Move in with her. Or move her here."

"I don't want to ask her to move away from her home." He splashed water on his face. "That would be horribly unfair. She would hate it." He paused and dried his face with a clean, fluffy towel. "I was thinking about building a house over by Ernie's." He envisioned a house built in the same style as the monastery on the large section of the property where Ernie's family lived. "Do you think she'd like that?"

He was nervous about introducing even more change into Eva's life. Anytime new challenges wormed their way into Eva's life, he could feel her retract in on herself. So long as he was patient, she would eventually uncurl and loosen her death grip on her comfort zone. That's what he'd have to do. Be patient. It was a long-term strategy.

But he was weary of being apart—even though he spent every day with her. He wanted every night with her, too. Forever.

"I think she would." Esther was earnest. "When are you going to talk to her?"

"About the house idea? Maybe this weekend."

"No, not about the house. About the rest of it. Before she can decide if she wants to continue with you into a lifetime commitment, she needs to know everything."

He flinched. Thank God he was done shaving.

Asher had been pretending his real life wasn't a thing now for months. He'd somehow managed to compartmentalize the fact that Esther was a gargoyle, his cousin who helped with all the architecture was Wrath, there were demons doing construction at his girlfriend's home. He wanted to have that conversation with Eva about as much as he wanted to be the next Devil.

Which was an actual possibility.

All evidence of Esther's usually stern personality was gone. "I know it's scary, but you have to do it. It's not fair, Ash. She's in love with you, and she could get really hurt."

He turned to look at his closest comrade. "How do you know she's in love with me?"

Esther's smile was mixed with pity. "Man, Lust really fucked you up. Yeah, honey, she loves you. Everyone knows it except you."

"And maybe her."

She gave her head a gentle shake. "All humans are a mess. It's a fact. Everyone can see she loves you. Just like they can see you love her. It's true. Hard for you to believe, I know. All of your experiences with intimacy are skewed. You can't even recognize when someone is showing you genuine affection."

Not especially thrilled with this conversation occurring in his bathroom while he wore a towel, he brushed by her and strode through his bedroom into the closet. Probably, he wouldn't like this conversation happening anywhere. The odd thing was, there wasn't a person in the world more comfortable in his own skin—usually. He was naked all the damn time. But just now, he was feeling more exposed than he'd ever felt before, and he didn't like it.

Esther trailed behind him. "You have to do it."

He snapped the band of his boxer brief around his waist. "How about if you do it?"

She snorted. "Me?" she sort of shrieked the word in disbelief. "Oh, Hell no."

"Yeah." Asher shoved his legs into a pair of jeans, really warming to the idea. "You can take her aside and gently explain to her as one woman to another."

She was silent for a long moment and when he looked up to see why, she was standing in the closet doorway with her mouth handing open. "You cannot be serious."

"No, listen," he said, "it would be perfect. She won't get mad at you, like she will at me. You can tell her all the stuff about Notre Dame and everything and she'll understand it better—"

"Dude, I'm not even a woman. I'm a gargoyle."

"See!" He threw his hands up. "I didn't even really understand that. You totally need to do this for me. You understand all the parts of this thing."

"Asher David Mephisto." She was very stern with his middle name. "Absolutely not. Do not ask me."

He put his fists on his hips. "I cannot believe you wouldn't help me out with this."

Esther narrowed her eyes and glared at him in a standoff in his walk-in closet. He held his ground and returned her stare. He was holding his own until he saw her jaw clench and he knew he'd never win. She could literally turn to stone and keep up that glare for a thousand years.

He let his shoulders deflate. "I'm sorry."

"You can talk to her. You simply must because you're not a villain."

He yanked a t-shirt off a hanger and jammed it over his head and shoved his arms through the holes. He brushed past her, out to the hall, and down the stairs. "That's very funny," he called over his shoulder, "because I very well could be the ultimate villain."

Esther didn't mention their argument again that weekend. Nor did she inquire as to any discussions he might have had with Eva about, well, anything. Surely she assumed he hadn't brung up the giant demonic elephant in the room. However, he did notice that she made herself scarce around the farm.

It was apparent the gargoyle cabal had discussed Asher's failings because Luke's guy, Jeb, had come out to bring permits or plans or something, and had given him a look of sheer pity that got Asher's hackles up.

He certainly didn't need help from anyone else to feel gutless. While he was an unrepentant coward, in his defense he could have never imagined he'd ever be in this position. What were the odds he would ever meet someone who mattered to him the way Eva did? The way he imagined his life playing out had been alone, fucking everything that moved, and finding some little joy and satisfaction in his business ventures.

He didn't want anything to interfere with the happiness he'd found with Eva. It was miraculous. Astounding. Extraordinary. He held on to it with a fierce, protective avarice.

The gargoyle cabal was right, of course. He needed to tell her, sooner rather than later, but there was no way that was going to go well. How could it possibly? So far, his working plan of ignoring it was succeeding. Not a great plan, but a viable one.

Until it wasn't.

To compensate for the glaring omission he was perpetrating, Asher worked his ass off. He personally supervised the demon reload into the monastery. He'd been mowing the grass between rows, a hot and tedious chore that Ernie was thrilled to pass off to him when he volunteered, when the equipment malfunctioned. Black smoke came out of the garden tractor. He took two days in the shade of the tool shed tearing the motor apart and rebuilding the tractor.

"What are you doing?" Esther asked after three solid days of ghosting him. She stood in the doorway blocking the noon sun.

He had his hands full of greasy piston rods. "Repairing an engine. What does it look like."

Her answer was several heartbeats too long to be believable. "I see. Do you want help?"

He grimaced. He wanted help, needed it actually. A positive outcome was looking iffy. But he was still feeling churlish from their row earlier that week. He grunted in response but, when she plucked the carburetor from a stack of newspapers and a can of cleaner from the work bench, he didn't stop her.

They worked in silence for the rest of the day. With her help, he got the ancient machine back together, and they both cheered when he turned over the engine and it fired to life.

"Look at you!" she crowed. "Fixing stuff. Well, with my help." She struck a pose with her greasy fingers forming a frame around her face.

"We're a great team." His first instinct was to hug her, but he pulled back at the last minute and slugged her arm.

"You'd have gotten it eventually," she told him while she tossed socket wrenches in the toolbox.

"Well, I appreciate it nonetheless."

Wiping her hands on an old shop rag, she said, "You know I've always got your back, even when you're an idiot. That's what we gargoyles do."

"Oh." He sighed in relief. "Then you've reconsidered talking to Eva. That's great."

Esther chortled and slugged him back, hard in the shoulder as she passed out the door. "Not a chance, boyo. This is all on you."

He spent hours upon hours in the rows, pruning the vines and working them up the training trellises like Eva had shown him. He pulled out the waterspouts and suckers, filling the wagon with the parasite fronds as he made his way along the rows. He'd been out alone for most of the day as he was feeling out of sorts and made bad company of himself.

"She's right, you know. You have to talk to her," he muttered to himself, referring to Esther. She was always right. He used his forearm to swipe at his forehead. "So stupid."

"Who's stupid?" The question came from behind him and was wholly unexpected.

He screamed and whirled around, a handful of sucker vines whiping around to smack him in the face.

Eva giggled, her face lighting up under the brim of her grandfather's straw hat. "I'm sorry," she said, but her grin said she wasn't really.

He threw the suckers in the wagon with emphasis. "You took years off my life."

She sidled up to him and pulled his cap off. When she tilted her head back to kiss him, her own straw hat fell back and hung from her neck by the chinstrap. She pressed a quick kiss to his lips and gave his earlobe an affectionate tug.

"Who were you talking to?" she asked.

"No one," he confessed. He tossed his gloves in the wagon on top of the refuse, then slipped them around the seat of her jeans and pulled her close. "I was talking to me."

"Oh, yeah?" She nipped his chin with gentle teeth. "What are you stupid about?"

"Nothing." The lie stuck in his throat.

"Hmmm." Eva's speculative gaze warred with the teasing turn of her lips for dominance. "Nothing, huh? I'm stupid about at least fifty things a day. You're not stupid about anything?"

"Really?" he asked. He found that hard to believe. He'd never known anyone so sure about things in his whole life. She seemed to know exactly what was happening with her farm. Every decision seemed to further a plan she had written down somewhere. "What are you stupid about?"

"Well." She hummed deep in her throat and ran an index finger from his chin, along his jaw line, to circle his ear. She gave the lobe a tug. "You make me stupid all the time. Every time I see you out here in my fields, I forget all about my chores." Her fingers tickled up his neck and tangled in the hair at his nape. "I'm like, 'what vines,' and I just want to do dirty things to you in my dirt."

"I'm completely on board with that kind of stupid." He encouraged her by lifting her by the buttocks into the thrust of his hips. Subtlety was never really his forte when Lust was involved.

"Then what did you want to talk to me about?"

And there was that feeling again, a creeping dread somewhere between terror of losing her and shame for what he was. Esther wouldn't help him. He was lost.

She tugged his hair. "Hmm?" Then she nipped his bottom lip. "Come on." She sang the words like a kid wheedling a parent for some toy. "I'm sure it's no big deal."

He kissed her as a distraction. He leaned into Lust and stroked the inside of her mouth while he molded her body to his. He tried to fill every one of her senses so that when he let her up for air, she would be dazed and uninterested in following that line of questioning. If he was lucky, he and Lust could lure her down into her fertile soil and fuck the curiosity out of her.

Unexpectedly, it was Eva who broke the kiss.

"Why are you nervous?" She was still teasing. "You've been like that a lot this week." She tugged on her bottom lip, deep red and swollen from their kiss. "The suspense is killing me."

The lure was there, just tell her and it would be all over. Except that was exactly what it would be if he opened his mouth and told her all she deserved to know.

Over.

A flash of a not-too-distant future showed him with a lifetime of strangers, yet always alone. Not a soul in the world who knew him or cared about him. Honesty was certainly how a brave man would move forward. The path a man who deserved Evangeline would go down.

He opened his mouth. Swallowed hard. Looked into her eyes to unveil the shitshow of his life.

"I love you."

Another distraction, but at least it was true.

Chapter Twenty-Eight

A sher blurted it out. "I love you."

Eva's heart stopped. She wondered if she'd heard him correctly, or if it was her mind playing tricks on her, making her hear what she wanted him to say.

Poor sweet Ashe. His expression was morphing a million miles a second. He went from hunted to lovesick then terrified. She was simply dumbstruck at his revelation. She needed to say something, because the terror in his eyes hadn't evolved into another emotion. When he started to pull away from her, she finally found the ability to respond.

She probably should have said the words back to him. Instead, she clutched his face on both sides and dragged his mouth to hers. Laying a kiss on him that she hoped would soothe his masculine ego, she allowed her body to sink into his. It worked because it was only a heartbeat before his surprise turned to passion and he wrapped his arms around her.

It was one hell of a kiss.

Her body was humming with need. She could sense the desperation leeching off of Asher, a need to be loved, to be seen, to be adored. She angled her face to kiss him even more deeply. She wanted to infuse all that she felt for him in the kiss. She hoped she could translate the thrumming desire he inspired in her into something that proved her devotion as well. Even more, she wanted him to know that he was the best thing that had ever happened to her. He made her stronger, braver, and more confident. Since he'd come into her life, the doubts had started to slip away. He made her feel like she could fulfill her dreams.

She really should have repeated the sentiment back to him, and she would have, but the kiss had set her girls parts buzzing. She was thrumming with the electricity of desire. They had always had amazing chemistry, but this was something else. How dazzling that simply tossing in the word "love" could get her amped up so quickly.

Maybe when a girl had heard it so rarely—.

Asher's hands grasped onto her ass and pulled her core flush with his, doubling the dazzling vibration of lust and it shook her to her core.

He pulled away long enough to tell her, "Your phone is buzzing."

She didn't care. No one could need her as badly as they needed each other right now. She pulled his mouth back to hers. When she ground her hips against his groin, it amplified the sensation and the realization sunk inside her sex-crazed brain that the feeling really was her phone.

She tried to ignore it, but its insistence was impossible to deny. Whoever was calling was persistent. They weren't leaving a message, just calling back over and over again. Now it was distracting, and annoyance was undermining her bliss.

Reluctantly, Eva broke the kiss. "Let me get rid of this." She jammed her hand in her front pocked and withdrew her cell phone. Maggie's face showed up on the screen. Her smile only brought Eva annoyance.

"What," she barked into the phone.

"Delilah's here." Maggie's voice held almost as many emotions as Asher's had when he made his confession.

Two words and all of Eva's euphoria withered.

Their mother.

What could she possibly want?

She planted a hard kiss on Asher's lips. "I'm sorry about this. I have to go up to the house."

Concern etched his face. "I'll come with you if you want."

She wanted, but she felt badly about throwing him in the deep end of her family drama. She shrugged, not able to ask for what she wanted. It was happening already. Every time their mother drifted back into their lives, Eva felt like all her maturity regressed to that of a needy little kid again.

"Never mind, I'm coming with you." He grabbed her hand when she turned to go back to the truck and walked with her.

The ride through the back rows was silent and fraught. Eva could feel Asher's gaze on her, but she kept her face straight ahead. If she looked at him, if she saw the concern she knew was carved into the lines of his forehead or the compassion in his eyes, she would fall apart. It was really important that she hold herself together in front of her mother. She was weary of the woman having any power over her.

Asher slid his palm over her thigh and rested it on her knee. "Are you okay?"

She gave a curt nod. "Sure. I'm fine."

"How can I help you?"

"I wish you could." Lord, she wished she could just send him, or better yet, Esther up there and have them demand to know what her mother was doing here. Esther would get to the bottom of it in a heartbeat. In truth, it could be any number of a million reasons. Certainly, she needed money. That was always the common denominator. But why this time? Legal trouble? Man trouble? Eva snorted at the thought that her mother might be pregnant again. Technically the woman was still young enough. That idea made her more nauseous than angry, and she didn't want to delve too far into that.

Eva downshifted the truck, turned the corner onto the long drive that ran the perimeter of the vineyard, and went through a catalogue of all the reasons her mother had turned up over the years to wheedle money out of her grandparents. There had been weddings. Not that any of the marriages had stuck—one had only lasted three and a half months. She'd brought one of those husbands home with her to con her grandparents out of thousands of dollars to invest in a treasure hunting business in St Thomas. Pop was a tough old bird, so Eva and Maggie could never figure out why he fell for Delilah's nonsense.

As the truck came over the rise, Eva searched the grounds for a hippie van, or a fancy Romany wagon, or who knows with Delilah, maybe a helicopter. The was only one vehicle in the parking lot that she didn't recognize, a white late model Honda Civic, so she parked next to it. She turned off the engine but didn't get out of the cab.

Asher reached for her hand. "Whatever happens, everything will be all right."

Eva gave a rueful chuckle. "Historically that is not true."

He squeezed her fingers. "Well, I'll be with you the whole time. If you want me to be."

She squeezed back. Oh, she definitely wanted him to be, but could she really drag him into the muck that trailed in Delilah's wake? Her family was such a mess. His smile seemed genuine, real enough to sway her, and she felt his support.

They walked past the rental car, Asher's steady concern bolstering her as they grew closer to the monastery office. She pushed open the door against the vacuum of the air conditioning to find her mother's dubious presence taking up the middle of the room.

Maggie wore a grim expression, and her hands were shoved deep in her jean's pockets. Delilah, however, greeted them with a beaming smile. Her mother was gorgeous, as usual. She was where her daughters got their height. She'd dressed to make an impression. However, Eva wasn't sure what impression she was trying to make. Or who the performance was supposed to be for.

"Hello, Evangeline."

It appeared her mom had outgrown her hippy phase. The same dark hair her twins shared was sleek and straight and shining instead of wild with natural waves. She was wearing tasteful makeup instead of the sun-kissed natural look she'd had during that ridiculous pirate hunting period. She wore a knee-length yellow sundress with pink flowers and cute little spaghetti straps, but her boobs were securely tucked inside. She looked like an adult.

Eva wasn't falling for this genial façade. "Let's just cut to the chase. What do you want?"

Her mother's expression showed a glimmer of emotion a more naïve person might have translated as regret. Eva was not naïve. "Nothing. I'm just here to see my family."

Maggie snorted, then turned her back and looked out the window.

Eva felt her nostrils flare before she steeled her expression again. "Truncated family, though, right? You weren't here for Pop's funeral, so I wasn't sure if you even knew he wasn't with us anymore. Just me and Maggie now. And Ernie. You remember little Ernie, right? He and his wife and baby are just like family. He's been here is whole life. Can you imagine such a thing? Being raised on a farm and feeling such a love of the land and the people connected to it that you become a part of a whole unit who go though life as part of each other's lives?"

Eva paused and let her bitchy speech wash over the room. She allowed a smile that could have been appropriate on Regina George. Her mother turned her into a Mean Girl.

Delilah swallowed. "I came to Gram's funeral."

"That's right. You came to your own mother's funeral. I'm sure your attendance was duly noted in the Giant Book of Karma Points in the sky." Her gaze darted to Asher who had come in behind her but moved to the gift shop side of the room. He was obviously trying to be unobtrusive. She really wished he wasn't here now, to witness her awful behavior, and yet she couldn't stop herself. "As I recall, you arrived an hour late, wearing a bikini under a beach muumuu, and left early with a ten-thousand-dollar check from Pop."

The woman was staring at the floor. "That was five years ago."

Eva screwed up her face in skepticism. "Now that I think about it, that last bit probably washes the Karma from attending in the first place, huh?" She tsked. "That's a shame."

"You don't have to be mean, Eva." Delilah sounded pitiful and small.

Eva's heart gave a little squeeze, but she remonstrated herself not to be a sucker. Her mother deserved any and all vitriol she could throw in her direction.

Maggie turned from the window. "Alright. Enough, Eva. What do you want, Delilah? Pop's not here to sweet talk. You've already taken the vineyard for well more than your inheritance. We don't have any cash to give you. Vineyards cost a shitload of money to keep up. Coffers are empty."

And there was no way in hell Eva was allowing Asher to give her any money. None. She didn't even want the woman to get wind of who he was.

"Girls," Delilah began.

"No." "None of that." Eva and Maggie spoke at the same time.

Delilah paused and started again. "I don't want anything. I promise. All I'm hoping for is... What I'd like is..." She paused and looked down at her hands clasped at her waist. "A relationship. Of some sort."

Maggie and Eva exchanged a glance. Maggie rolled her eyes, and Eva returned the look with a minute shake of her head.

Their mother blew a deep exhale as if to steady herself. "Look, I know I messed up. My life has been a series of fuckups, one following after another in a parade of horrible decisions. I've been working on myself a lot. I couldn't make it to Dad's funeral because I was in rehab. I'm not looking for sympathy—"

Eva snorted. "Good 'cause you're not going to get any."

"I understand I'll have to prove myself and I'm good with that." She gave them both a weak smile. "If you'll let me, I'm prepared to do the hard work."

Eva grunted in disbelief. She looked to her sister to share another eyeroll at the absurdity, but unbelievably Maggie looked like she might be buying in to some of this bullshit. Eva slapped her thigh to get her attention. Maggie's eyes whipped over to meet Eva's and she glared at her with stern eyebrows and mouthed the word, NO.

Maggie pulled her hands from her pockets and crossed them over her chest. "Just exactly how do you propose that will work?"

Eva felt Asher step up behind her, felt his concern wrap around her as if he used his actual arms. When he placed his hand on the small of her back she leaned back against it.

Delilah shrugged. "I don't know. I guess I hoped we could figure it out together. My therapist said you might be resistant."

Eva tensed with the desire to scream at her mother, but Asher rubbed her back in a small circle and she resisted the urge.

Maggie scoffed. "Very astute, Mother."

"I've rented an apartment in town. I'm not even going to ask to stay here." She took a step forward, as if she wanted to touch them, but stopped. "I really want to try. Can we try? We'll go slow."

A smooth, warm circle in her lower back.

"Whatever," Eva snapped. "We're not giving you any money. Do not ask. And don't steal anything." She turned to Maggie. "Lock everything up in here if she's going to be around."

Maggie nodded. Her sister might be soft enough to allow her mother a crack in her defenses, but she also wasn't stupid.

Delilah shook her head. "I would never—"

Eva waved off her mother's denial. "Just because we never caught you stealing in the past doesn't mean you won't do it now." She turned to leave, taking Asher's hand in the process. "You can't hold up this charade forever, and I don't want you clearing us out when you're done."

She wanted her exit to be dramatic and powerful, but instead the old monastery door stuck and she marched face first into it.

"God damn it," she yelled in frustration.

Asher reached in front of her and twisted the knob, giving the door a firm push. He kissed the back of her head and steered her out the door.

She stumbled out into the grass. Her nose and her psyche hurt in equal measure, and she wasn't sure which hurt the tears that brimmed her eyes was coming from.

"Come on, honey." Asher pulled off his linen shirt and held it to her nose to catch the blood.

She looked out over the expanse of her beloved vineyard through a watery haze and missed her grandfather. Actually, thank God he wasn't here. He would have just given her what she wanted and she'd be gone, out of their lives again, that much faster. She took an unsteady breath except that it caught in her chest and she hiccupped.

"Keep that on your nose," Asher said and pulled her away from the monastery. She could barely see anything with the shirt balled up in front of her face and the tears making everything blurry. Then he was swooping her up in his arms and they were going downward, and she recognized the cool of the cellars.

He carried her to the back by the casks of chardonnay where he slid down against the wall and nestled her in his lap. He kissed her temple and gently pulled the shirt from her face. "Let's see how this is looking." He swiped tenderly at her nose and mouth with a cleanish part of fabric. "Bleeding stopped. It's not so bad. You might have a little bruise there." His lips brushed the bridge of her nose.

She gave a tentative sniff to try it out.

"Are you okay?" he asked.

"I hardly know." Then she burst into tears.

Which made her furious.

Chapter Twenty-Nine

E va didn't speak with her mother for the rest of that day. Asher kept her in the cellar for well over an hour, holding her until she stopped crying. Angry tears suck so bad, and she resented her mother even more for making her feel weak.

Asher nuzzled her cheek with his own. "Are you hungry?"

She had to think about it. She was a lot of things at that moment, but she wasn't sure if hungry was on the list. "Maybe."

"Let's get out of here. Go get some dinner." He lifted her off his lap and patted her butt. "Distance might provide some clarity."

Eva shrugged. "It couldn't hurt. But I can't leave Maggie here alone to deal with this." It was bad enough that she'd been hiding in the cellar all afternoon.

"Three for dinner, then."

They emerged from the cellar and Eva noticed the rental car was gone. She was both angry and relieved. On one hand, thank God Delilah was gone because Eva didn't want to deal with her anymore today, but on the other hand, who knew when they'd see her again. She claimed to want to make amends, but that was likely just lip service. Why did Eva even care? If her mother was gone again, then they'd all be better off.

She listened deep into her heart for that little girl who hoped her mother was here to stay this time, but to her relief, that little girl was silent. Maybe Eva had cried her out back in the cellar.

They found Maggie in the office slamming drawers closed and dropping stacks of brochures and catalogues with loud thuds.

Eva called her name, but Maggie didn't turn around until Eva touched her shoulder.

Maggie plucked the earbuds out and said, "Oh, there you are." She sounded peeved, but she had a right. Eva should never have left her alone with their mother.

"I'm sorry. Can we buy you dinner?" Eva gave an apologetic shrug. "To repent."

Her sister narrowed her eyes at her for a split second and Eva thought she was going to get a dose of her sister's wrath. She would take it if Maggie dealt it, but instead Maggie blinked and calmly set the brochures in her hand onto the long tasting counter. That was so much worse.

Eva pulled her into a hug. "I'm sorry. I really am. I would be so angry at me if I was you. How long did she stay?"

Maggie's stiff shoulders curved into Eva's embrace. "Actually, not long. Maybe fifteen more minutes. She didn't even try to wheedle her way into the house, you know how she does. That staring thing where she waits you out until you offer the thing she wants." Maggie pulled away and Eva could see the danger of fireworks was passed. "I didn't, just so you know. She really does have a place in town."

Grabbing her purse and handing it to Maggie, Eva asked, "Did she give any more clue for why she's here? Like what she wants?"

"Maybe we should just give it to her," Maggie said. "You know, the more I think about it, the more I'm sure that's why Pops would just give her money. The sooner he caved the faster she left. Why prolong the misery, right?"

Asher pulled the monastery door shut behind them. "If that's what you want, I'll give her whatever amount you think will do the trick."

Maggie smiled at him, but Eva bristled. "No! I told her she wasn't getting anything, and I meant it. I'm sick of her swooping into our lives, fucking everything up, and then leaving with a wad of cash in her pocket. We get nothing out of the deal. We're just left with a devastating hole to fill back in."

He kissed her temple. "I'm just saying it's an option."

"Thank you." Maggie squeezed his arm. "Sorry. You shouldn't have to deal with this mess."

He barked out a laugh that held no joy. "I know all about dysfunctional families, ladies. You two certainly don't have a lock on relatives who routinely fuck things up. I'll participate in any way you guys want. I can make her leave, if you'd rather."

Maggie turned to him with a skeptical look. "That sounded final."

He squeezed Eva's hand, cementing the sentiment, but now his tone was teasing. "I'll have Esther drive her to the town border and see that she never returns."

"How very old west of you, honey." Eva squeezed back. "We'll keep that offer in our back pocket. Just in case."

Dinner was a nice escape. While their mother's presence was certainly in the front of all of their minds, the sisters made a concerted effort to discuss anything but her. The obsession was right there, waiting to be resumed and infiltrate Eva's entire being, but she resisted. There was so much good in her life now that Asher was in it. Just this morning, she was counting her blessings and feeling indomitable. Her vines were excelling, the vineyard was finally coming into its own, and she had a man who loved her.

He'd said so. She still hadn't said it back. Not because she didn't feel it. Oh man, all of her feelings were mutual. It's just that the time wasn't right now. His admission had been so heartfelt and honest. She felt like he deserved at least as much from her. She wanted him to feel as special as she had. She didn't want the sentiment to get lost in all the drama of her mother.

And there she was thinking about her mother again. God damn it.

The next morning when she woke up that was her very first thought as well. Usually, she would brush her teeth and run through a mental list of everything she wanted to accomplish with her day. She'd make lists.

Tour the vines. Check the irrigation in the west section. They'd replaced some of the hoses, and she needed to make sure everything was still grooving right along.

Turn some casks.

Vehicle maintenance.

Another trip to the hardware store—make a list for that: bailing wire, WD40, another roll of screening.

The lumberyard to make more vine cages and trellises.

On and on and on. There was always so much to do.

But she couldn't concentrate on any of it. The trip to the lumberyard was highjacked by concerns that maybe she'd see her mother there. Why the hell would her mother be hanging around in a lumberyard? Eva didn't know, but she could come up with all kinds of crazy scenarios. Now that Delilah was in the area, Eva expected to see her around every corner. She watched for her everywhere they went that day. She wasn't at the coffee shop when Eva stopped in there for coffee and a sweet roll. She didn't see her at the lumberyard when she picked up four by fours. Not even at the grocery store when she picked up some staples.

By the time she popped in the hardware store, she was feeling much more relaxed. Perhaps even complacent. She was reviewing her list, not paying attention as she breezed through the glass door and headed down aisle seven past the plumbing fittings and pipe tape, towards the key maker in the back. She dug the key ring from the bottom of her hobo bag and was twisting the new shed key off the ring when she heard her voice.

"Hello, Evangeline." Delilah wore a cautious smile and an employee smock on the other side of the counter.

Eva dropped the loose key, the key ring, and the shopping list in surprise. Her bag slipped from her shoulder and dropped with a thud at her feet. She stared at her mother for a heartbeat and then threw herself into retrieving her scattered items. Down on her knees, she found the paper and full key ring, but the loose key's location wasn't immediately obvious. Then a pair of pink flats appeared in her sight line and Eva knew the hand that plucked the key from underneath the key counter was attached to her mother.

Damn it. Damn it. Damn it.

"Do you need a duplicate of this one?" Delilah asked, holding the key between two fingers.

Feeling flustered and unsure of herself, she nodded, then cleared her throat. "Yeah."

"Okay. I can do that."

While Delilah was searching for the right key blank, Eva collected herself. Her mother was just a woman, she reminded herself.

"How long have you been working here?" Eva adjusted her purse strap on her shoulder.

Delilah looked up and smiled. "Four days."

Eva nodded and soaked up that information. Great, now she was going to have to switch hardware stores. She watched as Delilah fumbled through the process.

"I just learned how to make keys yesterday," she said by way of an explanation why it was all going so slowly.

Eva pursed her lips, raised her eyebrows, and nodded. If it made her mother more nervous, then Eva was happy with that.

A couple more minutes of stumbles later, and Henry, the store manager, appeared at Delilah's elbow. "Need some help there, honey?"

Her mother gushed. "Oh, Henry, thank you. I don't know what I'm doing wrong."

Henry patiently showed Delilah the procedure, and once he did, Eva had her duplicate key in short order.

"There you go, Miss Dashiell," he said, handing over a tiny paper sleeve.

Eva retrieved her wallet and pulled out a five-dollar bill. "Thanks, Henry."

Delilah pushed her hand and the money away. "I've got this one. No charge for your trouble."

Did she think this was going to score points? A whole dollar and a half for a key in exchange for a lifetime of deserting her children? Oh, hell no.

"A free key?" Eva said with boisterous false excitement. "You're totally forgiven."

Henry stood stock still, a frozen smile on his face.

Delilah cast an anxious glance at Henry, and said, "It's only a key. It doesn't mean anything."

"Damn right." Eva dropped the fiver on the counter and tucked the tiny key bag in her pocket. She turned on her heel and left, not waiting for any change and forgetting all the other items on her list. When she got in the truck, she was shocked to find her hands shaking.

Two days later, Eva couldn't find the utility wagon in the shed. When she asked Ernie about it, he took several long seconds before he replied.

"Your mom took it," he said. Her face must have turned scary, because he backed up a step before he continued. "She's down in the Zinfandels."

What in the ever-loving hell?

Eva stormed down the hill to the rows of black-skinned grapes only to find her mother wearing jeans, a work shirt, and a wide-brimmed hat. The wagon was laden with weeds. Even from the top of the row, Eva could hear her singing a fairly decent rendition of The Chain by Fleetwood Mac.

That woman was only down there to suck up. Weeding one damn row sure as hell didn't absolve her from shit.

But she was getting free labor. The row did need to be weeded. It wasn't like she could steal all the Zinfandel.

Eva turned on her heel and left.

Delilah came to the vineyard every day she wasn't working in the hardware store and did menial tasks. She never complained and she worked hard. Eva cut her no slack. They never worked together, and Delilah never pushed her daughters for more.

The sisters were unsettled.

Several weeks later, they'd planned a party in the evening. It was a tradition at Dashiell Vineyards. Their grandfather had refused the expense of a bottle labeler. Instead, they'd make a party out of putting hundreds of labels on bottles over the course of an evening. They'd have music, and their grandmother would make a feast. The night would end with everyone's shoulders aching and their fingers sticky. But also, having had a fun time. It was a night of laughter and raucous jokes and loud singing.

Asher had noticed they didn't have a labeler and had asked Maggie how many he should order, but Maggie had refused. When she told him about the tradition, Asher was one hundred percent in for the party.

He'd put his cousin Seth in charge of the food and bought a sound system for the cellar. Of course, Esther was there. Luke the architect came with Mia and Jeb. Ernie and Yesenia came and Asher's cousin Ethan brought Benji.

And out of nowhere, Delilah.

Incensed, Eva went to throw her out, but Asher intervened.

"Just let her stay," he suggested. "Ignore her. If you get all wound up and have a nasty fight..." He pulled her into an embrace. "Don't let her being here ruin our fun."

Maggie shrugged. "Whatever. She's been behaving herself."

Eva let her stay. She never engaged with her during the course of the evening, but she watched how their mother was with everyone. She was still a social butterfly, but something was different. While she laughed and teased with everyone, she wasn't flirting. When the night was over, she went home alone.

Eva hated to admit it, and she certainly didn't do so out loud, but it seemed like Delilah was actually trying.

Eva didn't know what to do with that information. She didn't know where to stow all her anger. She wasn't ready for peace, but maybe a truce was in order.

Heaven & Hell XXII

J uliet sat on Cerberus's back and watched the door Neil had disappeared behind. They were there for cigars in exchange for alcohol which was then to be traded for information on Rachel's whereabouts.

Neil had been inside the trailer for a really long time. Juliet would have checked her watch, but she didn't have one. Time didn't really mean anything once you were dead. But still, it seemed like she'd been waiting forever, perched on Cerberus's back and fussing with her backpack strapped to the dog.

All three of his tongues were hanging out as he panted in the heat.

"Poor puppy," she said and scratched the two outside heads between their ears. A stream of sweat ran down her own back. Ick. "Should we look around for some water for you? I worry about you overheating."

She placed her hands on either side of his middle head and aimed him towards the side of the trailer. "Let's see what's on the other side. We've seen everything over here. I mean, how long can you stare at burning tumbleweeds."

Cerberus swayed a bit when he walked like a slow pony. She held on to his wide leather collar with one hand and patted his side with the other.

"Yee haw. I never got to ride a horse when I was alive. No big deal really. They're really tall and a little scary. But you're not scary, are you? No, you're not. No, you're not." Her tone devolved into absurd baby talk while she roughly tousled his ears. The massive dog gave playful woofs and a little hop.

As they came around to the other side of the structure, the dog slowed down and the far-right head cautiously peered around the corner. It must have been clear because the rest of his body followed. This side of the trailer was no more attractive than the front. Tattered window screens dangled from the grime-smeared windows. A wooden stoop out the back door sagged heavily, and the metal skirting on the bottom was rusty and crumpled in places. Rustling noises came from underneath. Juliet recoiled, imagining what creature would choose to make a home beneath the wretched trailer.

And yet... While leaning away from the structure, she also found herself peering into the darkness with morbid curiosity, hoping for a glimpse of something. Cerberus paused and a low growl rumbled from two heads while the third raised its nose to the air and sniffed. The rustling from the darkness ceased, and then Juliet saw dozens of yellow eyes gawking back at her.

She patted the dog's shoulder with urgency. "This was a bad idea. Go back around to the front."

The growling continued, but the dog did pick up the pace and trotted back around the corner. Whatever was under there, Juliet never saw more than their eyes. Cerberus's growl was pretty horrific and, from what she'd seen already, he had a fearsome reputation in Hell.

Having made a full circle and back to the front, Juliet hadn't seen much more than filth. Certainly, no water to give the dog.

How much longer was Neil going to be in there?

Oh wait. Did he need help? Holy cow! God only knew what tortures he was going through. She needed to get in there. What could she do?

She patted the pockets of her sundress and considered what kinds of weapons she had. Candy bars wouldn't do much good except as bribes. Chips were even more useless. The sandals on her feet could be thrown or used to slap. And her ponytail holder would make a nice welt if she snapped it against someone's skin.

Oh, for heaven's sake, she was woefully unprepared. If there was any kind of physical altercation, she was done for. She couldn't contribute in any meaningful way. There wasn't even anything in the damn backpack that could be thrust or hurled.

If there was nothing on her person, what else was available? She couldn't—wouldn't—let anything happen to Neil. He'd watched out for her so diligently, with such concern for her wellbeing. She never felt so worthless.

She glanced around the immediate area. The trees were mostly occupied with fire, but maybe she could find a smaller one and break off one of the branches and use it like a flaming club. And there were some rocks on the ground, none of especially big size, but she had a fairly accurate arm and felt confident she could throw hard enough to hurt someone.

Cerberus! How could she have forgotten she had the dog? Surely with three viscous heads, he could take any out any danger they encountered in Hell.

She leaned down and plucked a couple of palm-sized rocks from the ground and tucked one in each pocket. Pointing towards the nearest tree, she said, "That one has some low branches. Go over there."

One of the lowest branches snapped right off when she pulled on it. A byproduct of burning for an eternity, she assumed. It was about two feet long and about as thick as a baby's arm. With the leafless end burning like a torch, she thought it was pretty threatening. Well, it certainly would be in Heaven. Who knew how it would do in Hell. These creatures seemed to take all of this horror in stride.

She urged Cerberus to trot back to the trailer. Neil still wasn't outside, and now she was certain he was in trouble in there.

Steering the dog to take the rickety stairs up the derelict porch, Juliet tried to peer in the windows, but the filth was caked on inches thick. She pressed her ear to the door and was relieved not to hear any screams of torment.

"Here's the plan, doggy." She held the burning limb with one hand and checked that the rocks were still in her pockets with the other. "I'm going to bang on the door like they do in the cop shows. I'll try to sound scary. You feel free to bark your heads off, alright?"

One head gurgled with a slobbery growl.

"That's perfect. Keep doing that," she said. She balled her hand into a fist and banged on the door three times. "Open up!" she yelled in as deep a voice as she could muster.

She'd barely had time to inhale a deep breath in preparation for another demand before the door opened with a skin-crawling squeal of metal against metal.

"Wait!" Neil threw his hands up in front of his face. "Don't hit me with that."

"Sorry. Sorry. Sorry." Juliet threw her makeshift club out into the dirt.

He bustled them all off the porch. "What were you going to do? Clobber someone with that?"

"You were taking so long, and I don't know what else to do. I thought you were in trouble in there." She dusted the soot from her hands.

Neil laughed, and it seemed like he was laughing at her. "It wasn't easy, but I'm fine. You bursting in would have made everything worse. Don't do anything crazy."

She narrowed her eyes at him. "I was trying to help."

"Well, don't, angel." He ran a hand down the back of her hair.

Now he was petting her? She still had those rocks in her pockets and considered popping him with one just to show him. "Why are you being a jerk?"

He steered them back towards the elevator. "I don't want you to get hurt. There's not a creature down here that wouldn't maim you, or eat you, or something worse. I want you safe, not charging into—" he flung his arm back in the general direction of the trailer "—that cesspit."

"Eat me?" Of all the things she'd thought of, eating her had never even registered.

"Maybe. And I don't want you gobbled up."

Her anger ebbed. They trudged along in silence for a few seconds toward the elevator platform in the near distance.

She took an inventory of Neil. She tried to be sly about it, but he glanced over at her and winked. "I can't help but notice you're not carrying any cigars," she said.

Neil groaned. "No. I'm not. He won't give me the cigars until I get him something in return."

For Pete's sake. "What now?" she asked.

Neil chuckled mirthlessly. "It's totally ridiculous. There's some guy on Seven who has a naked lady pen he wants."

Juliet gasped. "A what?"

He rolled his eyes. "You've seen them. Those pens with the lady in a swimming suit but when you turn it upside down the suit comes off and you can see her tits and stuff."

Oh. My. She should be scandalized but, heaven help her, she was intrigued. "So we're going to Seven to get this pen to give to this guy who will give us the cigars to take to the old dudes who will give us the alcohol to give to the maid who will tell us where Rachel is. Do I have that right?"

Now Neil's laugh was real. "Yep. That's where we are."

"Okay," she pointed forward. "Onward. I sorta feel like we're knights on a quest or something."

He nodded enthusiastically. "Yeah. Or maybe a video game. I hope there aren't any hard side quests."

The trip to Seven went smoothly. Juliet convinced Charon one of the rocks in her pocket was magical and he took them plus Cerberus to Level Seven with no complaint.

Once they were back outside and the elevator door closed behind them, Neil said to her, "I don't think you fooled him with that rock."

"What do you mean? He took it as payment."

"Yeah, I think that has a lot more to do with how cute you are rather than the mystical qualities of your rocks." He chucked her under the chin and gave her a quick peck on the lips.

He thought she was cute.

The most gorgeous guy she had ever known thought she, the nerdy book girl, was cute. She ducked her head so he wouldn't see her stupid grin.

"Well, this is horrible." Neil slipped his hand into hers. "I know you have the dog to protect you, but stay close anyway. This could get really bad."

Juliet's grin sagged and then fell away completely as she took in the landscape of Seven. There weren't fires in all the trees like on the last level. Instead, there were people hanging from them—by their necks or their hands and feet. Not a one of them was dead, either. They writhed in pain and misery, moaning or choking. Everywhere she looked there was some version of mayhem happening.

Bodies nailed to crosses. Whippings. People's arms and legs being perpetually pulled from their bodies. The whole place was filled with screaming.

Juliet was thankful she didn't have to walk because the tears filling her eyes made everything wavery. Even Cerberus didn't like it. All three massive heads whined in unison.

"Just close your eyes, babe." Neil squeezed her hand.

"I feel like I should bear witness or something." She swiped at the tears streaming down her face. "This is just so, so..." She couldn't finish. They passed a man who was collecting the blood from his many open wounds in a jar and then drank it down in heaving gulps. His movements were jerky with desperation, as if he could keep himself together by putting the blood back inside himself somehow.

Neil grimaced, too. Even though he was from here, he was not unaffected. That had to be good, right? She knew he was a good soul even if he didn't believe it. She had hope for him even if he didn't.

"That's stupid," he told her. "You don't need to witness anything. You don't belong down here. These are not your sins."

He tucked her tear-streaked face into his chest to keep her from seeing any more, but that made it very difficult to walk. She and Neil and Cerberus all jammed together were a slow-moving, jerky, awkward mess, and she wanted to get in and out of this Level as quickly as possible. She pulled away and buried her face in the scruff between the dog's heads one and two. Neil kept his hand on her back, rubbing in slow circles. It would have been really nice if she couldn't still hear the screams and moans and keening from the tortured.

She lost track of time, but it wasn't very long before Neil was saying, "We're here."

When she lifted her head, they were in front of a low concrete building that looked like an old bunker. There wasn't a door barring the entrance, so the three of them took a deep breath and walked inside. A long hallway lead past dozens of doorless rooms so that as they walked past, they could glance in to see what was happening in each space. After the first room showed a demon with a human body and the head of a vulture tearing the innards out of a shrieking man strapped down to a table, Juliet kept her eyes trained steadfastly forward.

Several times Neil gasped or groaned, and Juliet was grateful she hadn't seen whatever horrors were happening in there. She still couldn't ignore the sounds of whipping or tearing or ominous dripping. She kept her curiosity firmly in check.

As they got closer, Juliet realized the room at the end of the hallway was a throne room of sorts. A hairy ogre stood guard at the entrance; his telephone pole-sized arms crossed over his chest.

"What do you want?" he demanded in a deep rumble.

"We're here to see Count Råum," Neil answered. Juliet was impressed with how level his voice was, not a note of trepidation or anxiety.

"No." That was it. No explanation, just no.

Juliet swallowed hard and then said, "Please."

The ogre's black, bulgy eyes slowly shifted from Neil to her, and her stomach dropped. He stared at her and slowly a crease formed on his forehead as if his brain was very slow in sorting out what she was.

"Please," she repeated. Neil tucked her body into his side again and wrapped his arm around her shoulders.

The ogre let his arms drop to his sides, his eyes still trained on her, and then his mouth slowly gaped open. After another second, a hand rose slowly in her direction, fingers reaching out as if to touch her. Neil pulled her further behind him and Cerberus's heads let out a snarly growl. The creature blinked and pulled his hand back.

"Okay," he said and moved aside to let them pass. Neil exhaled a long breath.

The room was mostly empty except for a huge throne made up of twisting rose vines complete with thorns jutting out from every angle. A yellow-skinned demon perched on it, thorns and all, while a goblin and a woman sat on the floor in front of it. The woman was sobbing as the goblin slowly pulled out her fingernails with its teeth. Her feet were scabbed over and oozing puss as if they had already had this same treatment sometime before.

Juliet jerked her eyes away from the scene to look at the demon in charge. Count Råum's skin was the color of old egg yolks with a rat's nest of hair coming off its head in tangles and knots. The count took in their arrival with gleeful interest.

It squeaked in high excitement. "The dog!" Råum's voice was much higher pitched than Juliet expected. It pushed a knot of hair out of its eyes. "Want a treat?" Cerberus kept up the low growl, which did not deter the Count. It nudged the goblin with a booted foot. "Give the dog a finger."

The goblin promptly snapped the index finger off the woman's right hand. She screamed as one would expect. Juliet watched with mounting horror as the goblin extended the finger towards the dog with a shaking hand.

"No," Juliet said to the dog, but she didn't need to worry. Cerberus wasn't interested in eating a woman's finger.

Count Råum snorted in disappointment. Its attention moved to Juliet instead, which was infinitely worse. To her and Neil's dismay, Råum's beady eyes laser focused on Juliet. It slowly rose to its feet and kicked the goblin and his victim out of the way.

"Who are you?" it asked.

Neil spoke up, "Her name is Juliet."

The Count whipped its head to Neil and hissed, "I'm not talking to you." Back to Juliet, it's voice tempered back to the high pitch it had used before. "Who are you?"

Juliet cast a quick glance at Neil who subtly shook his head. She ignored him. "I'm Juliet."

"Why?"

"Why?" Juliet repeated. "Because that's what my parent's named me. Everything has to have a name."

Råum approached in a weird slither motion that didn't seem to work on a creature with two legs. Juliet pursed her lips and struggled to remain still. She held her breath as its face got impossibly close and smelled her hair. "Why is your hair?"

When bony fingers extended towards her, she shied away, but it still managed to loop a finger under the hair tie and break it. When Juliet's hair streamed loose over her shoulders, Råum yawped in glee.

"How your hair?"

Why did this thing ask such unanswerable questions? She took in Råum's hair. Filthy and snarled, it was so tangled owls could nest in it. Impossibly, Juliet thought she might understand what it was getting at.

"I take care of it," she told it. Råum clearly didn't understand something so simple. "I wash it and brush it."

"Do me!" Råum whirled around and gave its back to them. It fluffed out a clump of the knotted mass like one of Charlie's Angels. "Do me!"

It was hopeless. There was no way in God's green earth Juliet could fix that mess.

"Do you have a brush?" she asked. This was madness.

"No." Count Råum sounded crushed. Suddenly, it clapped in excitement. "Stable. Stable has brushes."

Neil spoke up then, although Juliet didn't know if that was wise considering Råum's response the last time he said anything. "We want the naked lady pen. If you give us that, we'll go get a brush from the horse stable."

The Count narrowed its eyes and clenched its fists. "Get brush. Then pen."

Juliet pulled the focus back to herself. She genuinely feared for Neil's safety. Obviously, violence was not an issue when dealing with any problem on this Level. She spoke calmly and clearly. "If we go get a brush, you'll give us the pen we need, right?"

Råum spread its lips in a horrific grin full of lots of pointy teeth. "Yesss."

"Promise?"

"Do me, then pen."

Neil and Juliet shared a look. "Okay, then. Off to the stables," he said with a weary eyeroll.

"There's stables in Hell?" she wondered aloud as they passed back by the ogre doorman. "What do they keep in there?"

Neil shrugged. "The Four Horsemen of the Apocalypse."

Juliet nodded. "Of course."

Chapter Thirty

"I love it," Asher told his cousin, Luke. They were alone, standing over the open tailgate of Betty, his giant red pickup. He'd had Benji paint the vineyard name on the side. Asher loved driving it around town, feeling like a farmer.

"And she still doesn't know about it?" Luke's raised eyebrow told him everything he thought about Asher keeping Eva in the dark.

Ashe rolled the blueprints of the new house, the one he was planning to build for him and Eva right here on the vineyard, and tucked them safely in a tube. "I want it to be a surprise."

"Because historically that always works out."

Ashe laughed. "I'm going to show her after the grand opening party. I just want to get past this event and all the stress that comes with it, and then I'll show her what you created. She's going to love it."

Luke had known exactly what Asher was going for when Ashe mentioned how he wanted a house on the property. He'd picked up a pen, and while Ashe was talking, Luke had been drawing. Two stories, like if a Spanish hacienda had a baby with a Catholic cathedral, this house would be their love child. It would blend right in with the feel of the old monastery.

Ashe was so excited and was dying to tell Eva about it, but with the grand opening party, the construction, and the wholly unexpected arrival of her mother, Asher didn't want to add any more things for Eva to think about. He hadn't even told Maggie. The sisters were in no mood.

Asher didn't know how to help them. He certainly understood about difficult family members. Still, he couldn't explain to her how he knew what she was feeling. Anything he said was just lip service when he couldn't give her any backstory. He sounded like a dick when he tried to give her any advice. Mostly, all he did was make eye contact, nod in the appropriate places, and agree with her.

He was surprised, though, that things seemed to be going so well with them. He had a pretty good idea how Eva and Maggie thought this whole visit was going to play out, and reconciliation wasn't even on the map. Yet Delilah kept showing up at the farm and working. She'd asked her girls for nothing. She'd taken nothing. She'd even kept her apartment in town instead of moving into a room at the monastery.

During one of Eva's bitch sessions, Asher had floated the idea that he'd be willing to pay for a private detective. He'd mentioned it before, but they'd roundly declined, saying it was pointless to waste the money and she would most certainly leave within a matter of days.

Four weeks later and Delilah was still hanging in there. Asher honestly had to give her props. Able to observe from a distance, though not necessarily detached, he saw what he characterized as an honest working attempt to make amends.

There was no opportunity for the Mephisto family to come back together. That wasn't in the cards. The curse made sure of that. But he'd sure like to see Eva's family heal. And if Delilah was genuine about her desires, then he wanted to support that. It would be good for Eva in the long run—he just didn't want to do it behind her back.

So he continued to listen to Eva's complaints and theories and fears and tried to steer her towards, if not forgiveness, then amnesty.

That's why he casually mentioned that Delilah should come to the meeting to plan the open house.

The whole crew was gathering on the lawn outside the monastery. They'd pulled up a bunch of chairs in the shade and Maggie was filling goblets with cabernet. Asher had invited several of his cousins along with Luke to participate. With Eva, Maggie, and Ernie with Yesenia, the crowd was loud and excited about inviting the world to come and fall in love with their vineyard.

He noticed Delilah in the tool shed. She was diligently putting away the big wagon and sheers but surreptitiously eavesdropping on the excited chatter.

Her look of longing squeezed his little black heart, and he found himself waving her over, despite the laser eyes of fury he got from Eva.

"Come have a glass of wine," he said as she drew closer. Eva's head turned toward him on a slow swivel. He squeezed her fingers to let her know she still had his support.

"We're planning a big event to open the vineyard up to the public," he told her.

"Oh, that sounds exciting," she said. "Your grandfather would be so excited if he knew what an amazing job you girls are doing here."

Maggie handed her a glass of wine, then turned her back on her mother. Eva didn't say a word.

Asher turned a soft smile to Delilah. "Eva and Maggie really are awesome." He dropped Eva's hand and wrapped an arm around her waist. Pulling her tight against his side, he gave her a loud smacking kiss on the cheek. She shoved at his shoulder, but he held on tight.

Jeb, the gargoyle hidden under the guise of a pretty gay man, took control of the group. "What kind of a party are we thinking about?"

"Casino night would be fun." Seth's voice boomed over the chitchat as if he'd been anxiously waiting to tell everyone the idea.

Benji's voice was softer. "Sure, professional-gambler-man. You just want a casino night so you can win everyone's money."

"No," Seth protested. He stood from the bench and walked through the crowd until he was at the edge. When he turned around, he was ready to present to the group, like he was in a boardroom or something. "There are several different companies we can hire. They bring all the tables and the dealers and everything. People love it. They won't play with money; they'll have chips. At the end of the night, they can use their chips to buy Dashiell wine and stuff. It'll be a huge success."

Eva nodded, picking up where he left off. "That would be a lot of fun. We could make up the cellar to look like Monte Carlo. String lights and—ooh, it could be so beautiful."

The group murmured and nodded thoughtfully. Seth beamed and looked proud of himself. Asher couldn't help but laugh at the big goof as the idea picked up steam and the crowd talked louder.

A small voice on the fringe spoke up. "What about a circus?"

No one heard or even noticed when Delilah spoke up. They were all too busy tossing out decorating ideas and dress codes and prize ideas to pay attention to the little suggestion. Asher heard though and looked at her with interest.

"Say that again, but louder," he told her.

She cleared her throat and spoke again more assertively. "A circus would be really memorable."

The talking slowed and eyes turned her direction. She shrugged. "I've been to several casino parties and they're fun, but they're not especially memorable. They've sorta been done already. But a really cool stylized circus with a big top on the lawn over there—" she pointed at the vast expanse of grass by the pond designed for outdoor parties. "*That* would be memorable."

No one spoke, but en masse they turned and took in the expanse of green.

"That could be really cool," Benji murmured, staring into the near distance with an artist's eye. "Really colorful, but still dark. Very stylized."

"With fire eaters and jugglers walking around with the crowd," Ethan added.

"And tightrope walkers," Ernie chimed in.

"No clowns, though," Luke punctuated himself with a slashing gesture.

Ernie's wife, Yesenia, shuddered. "Agree."

A disgruntled hum came from Maggie. "I was thinking of a much more elegant party, something inspired by like Breakfast at Tiffany's or something. You know, black tie and pearls, really fancy with cocktails."

Speculative silence settled over the group. Asher watched as everyone mentally picked the party idea they liked the most. Seth pouted, likely at the possibility that his idea might not be getting traction.

It was Eva who started the debate. "Whatever we do we must include the cellar, because that's a brand-new venue spot for us. We need people to see it and imagine their own party. And well, I guess the monastery, too, since it has that beautiful stained-glass window to showcase a gorgeous party."

Maggie pursed her lips in thought. "But the lawn and gazebo, too. Whatever we do has to be big."

Jeb spoke up, commanding attention in that magical way the little man could. "Why choose? Why can't you have all three parties at once? We put flashy Monte Carlo in the cellar. Roulette and craps tables. It can be very fancy. Out on the lawn we have the mysterious striped tent for a cirque. I know we can hire some carnival workers for fire breathing and acrobats and what have you. Make it very exaggerated and theatrical. Then do the monastery like a swanky New York society party with wine and fancy canapes."

Eva gasped at the realization of what he was suggesting. "A showcase."

"Yeah," Asher agreed. He pulled away so he could face her and Maggie full on. "We want people to see Dashiell family vineyards in as many lights as possible."

"This is going to be really exciting," Ethan told them. He'd taken out his phone and was taking furious notes. "I'm going to bring in every influencer, party planner, and mover and shaker in this part of the state. The buzz is going to be epic."

The rest of the evening was spent planning. The weather was so nice they simply turned on the newly strung café lights and stayed outside. Jeb ordered a stack of pizzas and Ernie brought out bottles of pinot noir.

When Delilah edged away from the group, Eva noticed and exhaled an exhausted breath. She left Asher's side and went to her mother. Ashe couldn't hear their exchange, but Eva's body language wasn't as hostile as usual. After Eva spoke, Delilah gave a timid smile. Eva's answering nod was brusk, but not mean, and then she came back to Asher's side.

"I told her to stay for dinner." Eva said it like it was a punishment, but Asher could sense the child inside who was afraid to make overtures fearing she would be rebuffed. She lifted her shoulders in a classic I-didn't-care-either-way gesture. "I mean, she did come up with the best idea. She should get dinner out of it."

"Yeah," Asher said, pulling her into his embrace. "It's just crappy pizza."

"Right. It's not like there's any effort into it." Her eyebrows grew tangled. "It doesn't mean anything, right?"

Asher kissed that spot just above her nose that was crinkling up with worry. "I'm not sure, babe. It might actually mean something. These days, with your mom, it seems like everything means something."

"Oh, no," she whispered into his chest.

He wrapped his arms around her tighter, turning their space in the crowd into a snuggly cocoon that seemed to isolate them from all the noise around them. "It's going to be alright. I know it's scary to feel like you're setting yourself up to be hurt again, but what if the risk pays off?" He rubbed her back, and she fitted herself flush against him. "And if she leaves again..." He shrugged. "We'll deal with that if it happens. I don't know how it's been before, but it seemed like in the past it was always a wham, bam, thank you, ma'am sort of situation. I feel like this time, she's working in good faith."

"I hope so." She turned her face up and kissed him.

She still hadn't told him she loved him, but these moments, kisses like these, told him so not in words, but in actions. He was keeping a very firm rein on his anxiety. He was feeling real emotions for the first time in his life and, although they were scary, he had never been happier. This was what a relationship was like, right?

He would be patient. After this huge party, after everything had settled down, that's when he'd press his case.

In the back of his mind, he heard Esther's disappointed reminder that what Eva still didn't know about him and his family could fill the Library of Congress. Earth-shattering information that would most certainly change Eva's fundamental feelings about Asher, his family, and everything she thought she knew about Heaven and Hell.

Asher had faith that all that stuff would work itself out.

It had to.

Chapter Thirty-One

The vineyard was a flurry of activity. The little details of the remodeling work were finishing up. The wine cellar was painted, and the old stone floor was polished to a high shine. All the casks had been outfitted with the new logo for Fiery Monk Cellars. They'd been arguing about a new name for days and finally landed on that one because it harkened back to the monastery and the fire that made the place so distinct. They were still Dashiell Vineyards, but now they had something catchy and specific to market.

When the gambling tables were loaded in, they'd fill the center of the great room with the racks of casks circling the outside. Eva didn't know how they'd done it, but Esther and Jeb had moved the massive stainless-steel fermenters out of the way to the back of the building, and all the buckets and other flotsam and jetsam of vintner life had been stored away in an out shed. She wasn't sure where Diablo had relocated to, but he and the rest of the cats had made themselves scarce, at least while the party was coming together.

A bar had been installed on the far end and they'd all be working on fun but fancy wine cocktails to serve in the Monte Carlo style casino the place would become in less than a week.

It was beautiful. The old building had always had style, but now it was classy and just on the right side of glamorous.

Her grandfather must be pissed he was missing this party, as he watched from wherever he was these days.

Eva climbed the steps and closed the big oak door behind her and headed off across the grass toward the pond and soon-to-be site of a magical circus.

This had been Delilah's brainchild and as much as Eva and Maggie hated to admit it, their mother brought value. Maggie was ostensibly in charge, but everyone knew that burden actually landed on Esther and Jeb. They had connections that just made everything come together in a way that was almost eerie.

Esther had located a circus complete with a troupe of performers, including a ringmaster, firebreathers, trapeze artists, tightrope walkers, and acrobats. The tent had started going up this morning, and it was everything they had imagined. Wide red and white stripes with two peaks, the tent looked like something from a circus fantasy. It took up nearly the entire yard. Inside the tent, two rings would be able to show two acts simultaneously.

She waved at Esther who was supervising the assembly of the tent while on her cell phone. She returned the gesture with a thumbs up. Eva grinned at her. She was such a character. Today she'd obviously taken the circus into account when she got dressed, because to top off the outfit of a black lace body suit lined with some scarlet red stretchy material was a top hat. It stayed on her head at a jaunty angle as if the hat itself was afraid to fall off for fear of angering her. No one else in the world would risk stiletto heels in the grass, but there she was, storming around on the lawn, barking into her phone, and waving her arms at carnies. God love her.

Inside the monastery, she skirted past the tasting room and store to avoid Maggie and Jeb talking with all the caterers and ducked into the office. She did not want to get roped into that meeting. With three entire parties happening in one night, there were three catering teams as well as the venders with the popcorn and cotton candy trucks. An army of waiters would be coming in with bartender counterparts. It was going to be an amazing party, that was for sure, but Eva was trying to stay out of it as much as possible. She'd get all dressed up and press the flesh at the party, but she didn't want anything to do with the minutia. She conceded any decisions to people with an opinion. When arguments happened and the inevitable pair of them would approach her with two colors of napkins or different fonts on invitations, Eva would literally close her eyes and point at one. Finally, everyone stopped asking her. It was the perfect plan.

So, while everything was coming together, Eva worked herself to exhaustion among the vines. Except she wasn't alone. Ernie was always around, like usual, unless he was roped into some task at the monastery. Of course, Asher was never far. There was always some point while she was working that he would find her.

Even if it was the furthest corner, down the furthest valley, or the most out of the way hill, he and his ridiculous truck would roll up.

She anticipated it every day. She'd hear the rumble of the big diesel engine while he was still rows and rows away, and her heart would skip faster. One of her favorite parts of the day was to observe his exit from the vehicle. She wouldn't be able to see in the driver's door because the tint was so dark, but then the door to the cab would swing open and he'd hop down. She'd see his long legs under the door first. Invariably he'd have on worn denim and a pair of soft suede lace-up boots. Her breath would catch waiting for the rest of him to come into view.

It would be his smile she'd see next after he stepped away from the truck. Even if he was on his phone, his gray eyes would meet hers, then the stark planes of his face would relax and curve into a smile. Tall, slim, and graceful, he'd saunter down the row, eyes on hers, ready to scoop her up and devour her with a kiss.

Toe curling, leg jellying, womb tightening kisses.

Her life had never been so good. She couldn't be happier about how the grapes were coming along. Even her experimental projects made her giddy with how well they were ripening. The business plans for the monastery were surpassing her wildest dreams. Asher made her all squishy inside with his compliments and attention and general gorgeousness. After all her protestations, he'd slid into her world, nice and snug like the world's most complicated jigsaw puzzle.

Her life was turning out so unexpected and wonderous.

But then there was the problem of her mother. If Asher showing up every day was new and novel, then her mother's continued appearances were even more so. What did she want?

After the first week, Eva and Maggie couldn't just pretend that everything was normal and her visit was going to go the way they usually did. She wasn't acting normal, for one thing. Where was their frivolous yet sneaky mother? Eva studied her and couldn't figure out what her new angle was. There was no sob story. No new business scheme. No long tale about a mysterious illness. There wasn't even a new despicable man in tow.

Delilah just kept showing up and finding work to do. She didn't complain. She wasn't snotty or whiney or difficult. She just...worked. Something she'd never done willingly in the entire history of Eva and Maggie's collective memory.

If it was suddenly revealed soap-opera-style that Delilah had had a lobotomy, the sisters would totally believe it.

If she didn't look exactly right, they would have considered that she was an imposter, but they'd tried tricking her up on family lore and she knew all the things she was supposed to. They were puzzled.

Over coffee one morning two weeks ago, Maggie suggested again that they cut to the chase and just offer Delilah something to see if she'd go away. The idea had grated on Eva, but she was also tired of playing this game. Asher said he was willing to bankroll Operation Evict Delilah without a second thought.

That very afternoon, they'd offered her two handfuls of nicely stacked wads of cash bound with a paper band from the bank that read one thousand on each one. Delilah had smiled sadly and refused.

"I don't want anything from you," she'd said. "I've taken much more than my share in my life. This time I'm only here to give back." She'd given each of her girls a peck on the cheek and left to do her afternoon shift at the hardware store.

Maggie had frowned. Eva had stewed. Asher took the money back with a shrug and put it in the office safe.

"Maybe she's legit," Maggie had murmured as they watched their mother get in a beat-up old Mercury Sable she'd bought from an ad posted on the hardware store bulletin board.

"How is that possible," Eva protested.

Her sister shrugged. "I don't know, but we can't seem to get any evidence to the contrary."

"This is a long con. I'm sure of it."

Maggie and Eva would just have to be patient. Their mother's true colors would show eventually.

Today though, Eva wasn't out in the rows. She'd done her best to avoid getting roped in to any party decisions, but now the whole event was only days away and she was going to have to pitch in. So she hid in the office while the showroom was bedecked in super-fancy, marvelously chic decorations for the hoity toity New York style party.

Once she heard the meeting with the caterers break up, she emerged.

"Everything good?" she asked Maggie.

Her sister feathered the papers in her notebook. "I think so. Sheesh, there's so much to do. At least five times this week, I decided we were crazy to try and do all this at once."

Jeb snapped his laptop closed. "Don't worry. We've got everything under control. We've organized this event within an inch of its life. Nothing would dare to go wrong."

Eva spread her arms wide. "Well, it was suggested that I needed to kick in some manpower, so here I am. What do you need?"

"Excellent." Maggie tore a page free from her notebook and started listing off things they needed from town. "Pick up the boxes at the printers. Here's a list of stuff we need from the hardware store. And it would be super helpful if you would stop by the tailor's. I need to do a final fitting, and you can do it as easily as I can." Having the exact same measurements had its conveniences.

Eva took the list happily. The prospect of leaving the site of the bustling activity improved her spirits exponentially, having assumed she was going to be forced to deal with all the strange people running around the vineyard. Other people were fine, so long as she didn't have to deal with them.

She hopped in her faded old truck before anyone could think of something else she needed to do. Asher was always trying to get her to drive the new truck, but she loved good old Miriam. She was steady and trustworthy, and Eva didn't feel like she was pretending she was fancier than she was when she was driving it. Asher was fancy, however, and his over-the-top truck accurately reflected him.

Eva stopped at the hardware store first. She was in such a good mood, she hadn't even considered Delilah would be putting in her shift while she was there. She was working, because of course she was, but this time Eva wasn't blindsided. In fact, when she saw her mother standing there, that usual heavy ball of anxiety wasn't weighing down her gut.

Delilah was organizing paint sample chips when she walked in. She gave Eva an official hardware store smile. "Hello. What brings you in this afternoon?"

Eva waved the sheet of notebook paper. "A whole ton of crap."

She placed the cards with the myriad of colors on the counter and approached with her hand out for the list. "It's going to be a hell of a party."

"Parties," Eva corrected, but then added a smile to soften the tone. "I really hope it turns out. There's so many moving parts. It could go so wrong, you know."

"But it won't." Delilah assured her while glancing at the list. "Grab a basket and follow me."

Eva followed behind her while her mother competently led her around the store with confidence, selecting things off the list and popping them in the cart. It was a dramatic turn from the first time Eva had seen her in the store.

Delilah handed Eva a package of finishing nails, which she added to the cart. "You any better at making keys?" she asked.

Her mother laughed. It didn't sound nervous or forced. It sounded nice.

"Yeah, thank goodness. I just had to get my footing around here, know what I mean?"

"Sure." They turned down the adhesives aisle where Delilah pointed out the wood glue. "That's the way Maggie and I felt after Pop died and we had to figure out how to run the vineyard."

Delilah paused and nodded contemplatively. "That must have been really hard on you two. I know how close you were to him. I'll always regret that I wasn't there. Not that I could have helped any. But I should have been there." She sighed a breath that seemed like it came from the bottom of her soul. "You and your sister are truly amazing. Mom and Dad would be so proud."

Eva didn't say anything. She found she couldn't. That stupid lump from her gut had moved up to her throat. She was dangerously close to allowing feelings for this woman, and that could be a huge mistake. Except that she'd been pushing and pushing for weeks now, and holding up her defenses was making her weary.

She stayed quiet while Delilah gathered the rest of the list. Eva followed along mutely behind as they went back up to the counter and she rang up the purchases.

"Should I put it all on the Dashiell account?"

"Yeah." Eva nodded. "When do you get off work today?"

Delilah blinked and then looked at her watch. "Actually, five minutes ago."

"What do you have planned for the rest of the day?" This was undoubtably a mistake.

"I was going to grab some lunch and then head over to the vineyard and find some chores to do." Her mother stuck her hand in her smock pocket and nervously fiddled around with whatever was in there.

Eva nodded. "I have a few more errands to do for the party in town." She paused, but then, *what the hell*, and went for it. "You could come with me and then we could grab some lunch. I can take you out to the farm later."

Her mother grinned and suddenly she looked so young. And so much like her sister. Eva could no longer deny that she wanted her mother. It was never going to be a Hallmark kind of relationship, but maybe, *maybe*, they could be friends?

"I'm game," Delilah said with obvious delight. "Let me put away my smock and grab my purse. Two minutes."

"I'll wait in the truck," Eva called after her as she dashed away.

While she was dropping the hardware store bags in the big wooden box she kept in the bed of the truck for just these times, Delilah appeared at her elbow.

"Where next?"

"Printers."

Her mother was nearly bouncing on the bench seat. "I remember when Dad got this old truck. He was so excited when he came home with it. He hadn't told Mom he was going to do it, either. He'd just shown up at the farm with it. On the way home from the dealer, he'd stopped off at the truckstop , you know the one just outside of the city, and bought her some cheap ass earrings to soften the blow." Delilah cackled at the memory. "He didn't want to come home without some present for her. Boy, was she pissed."

Eva chuckled at the memory. She could actually see it in her mind's eye. Her grandfather, so handsome and rugged, sweet-talking Gran into not being mad. He'd grab her and kiss her neck until she'd squeal. Eva was pretty sure she knew the earrings in question. They were still in the box of jewelry that had belonged to Gran. Mostly costume pieces, only her wedding ring set and one pair of ruby studs that were of any value. She leaned towards subtle, understated jewelry. There was one pair of large blue chandelier earrings that didn't fit with the rest. They were ostentatious and flashy. They had to be the ones.

Gran never wore them, but she wouldn't let the girls play with them either.

"I guess it explains why she always called this truck Pop's mistress," Delilah said. She patted Miriam on the dash. "She's a good old gal."

"Your boyfriend's truck is a doozy," Delilah noted.

Eva stiffened. Aha, this was when Delilah was going to show her true colors. She waited for a sly feeler about money to slide out of her mouth. "Yeah. He's a bit of a doozy himself."

Delilah fiddled with the radio button, trying to find something on the FM dial. "He seems very nice, though, from what I've seen. He loves you, that's obvious."

Yes, he did love her. She was really going to have to say that back to him soon. "Well," Eva said noncommittally.

The radio landed on an old Moody Blues song. "But he's good to you, right? He treats you nice?" Her mom's hazel eyes studied her from across the cab. "You have to be careful with the pretty ones. Sometimes they can be so underhanded and cruel."

Eva concentrated on the road, stopping at a crosswalk for some school kids to dart across. "What do you mean?"

Delilah waved her hand. "Oh, nothing." She took a deep breath and patted her knee while she reflected. "Some people aren't good, that's all. They act one way, but they really want something else."

Eva shot her some side-eye. Her mother did not seem to appreciate the irony, and Eva didn't want to pick at a scab that was just starting to form.

Delilah continued, back in the present, "Asher seems like the real deal, though."

"I believe that he is."

"Then at least I don't have to worry about you. I can concentrate on Maggie."

What the hell did that mean? "When have you ever worried about us?" There she was, picking at the scab. "You didn't even know enough about our lives to be worried about anything. And when there was obvious stuff, like people actually dying, and you weren't here to do anything about it."

Delilah shifted on the bench, her knee catching a corner of duct tape and rolling it up a bit. "I was an awful mother and a bad person," she admitted.

Eva really wished she'd stop doing that. It made it harder and harder to hate her when she wouldn't fight back. She closed her mouth tight.

"But I always loved you girls." Delilah looked at Eva straight on. "I'll be atoning for my sins for the rest of my life."

Pulling the truck into the parking lot at the printers, Eva didn't reply. "We're here."

After they loaded boxes of napkins, pricing sheets, menus, and business cards into the bed of the truck, Eva took them to the tailors. She shucked her work clothes and slid into the little black dress Maggie was wearing for her cocktail party.

"Put these on, honey." The tiny seamstress handed her a pair of black stilettos.

"Are these what Maggie's wearing with this?" Eva asked, agog. "These are crazy high." Her already long legs looked even longer in the mirror with the extra three inches. She was now so tall and the skirt so short, the little old lady barely had to bend to adjust the hem. "And she wants the skirt that short?"

Delilah laughed from a club chair in the corner. "You're young. Live a little."

"Okay," Eva said and didn't even try to keep the skepticism out of her voice.

"What are you going to wear?" Delilah asked.

The old lady brought over a step stool and climbed up to adjust the neckline.

"I don't know, and don't think for a minute that doesn't terrify me to my very soul." Eva mentally sucked in her chest to avoid stabby pins.

Her mother was leafing through fashion magazines. "What does that mean?"

"We're going to be hosting the circus, Asher and me." Oops, that was a real pin into the collarbone. "His assistant, Esther, told me she had my whole outfit covered and not to worry about it."

Delilah looked up from *Vogue*. The cover looked to be from somewhere around 1972. "Esther's style is...interesting."

Eva laughed, and the seamstress scowled at her. "Hold still," she said.

"Esther is extraordinary. She runs Asher's life like a machine, and I guess now that includes me. She has an almost supernatural ability to anticipate what you need at any moment. She's a little scary and very stern, but you feel very well taken care of, you know what I mean."

"Turn." The old woman made a circle in the air with her finger. Eva gave her access to her back and she futzed around with the zipper.

"So, what are you wearing, then?" Delilah asked.

"I don't know," Eva admitted with a touch of alarm. "You saw what she was wearing today, right? I'm filled with dread."

"I can see why you'd think that." Delilah rose and went to stand next to Eva in the mirror. They looked so alike; it was eerie. There were three of them, the Dashiell ladies, and Eva had to confess to herself the idea was beginning to grow on her.

"Whatever it is," Delilah said, "I'm certain you'll be able to pull it off. Your handsome boyfriend will be gob smacked."

He already couldn't keep his hands off her when she was in grubby jeans and old t-shirts. The idea of his reaction to her being all tarted up was thrilling.

Eva met her mother's eyes in the mirror. "You're coming, right, to the party?"

"Am I invited? I wasn't sure and I didn't want to push my way in."

Who was this woman? "Yeah, you're invited. A third of this party was your idea."

"I'd love to," Delilah said with obvious glee.

"I'll have Esther find you something to wear."

Delilah held up her hands and chuckled. "No, that's alright. I got this covered."

Eva blew out a slow breath.

Your life is coming together, she told the woman in the mirror.

She even allowed herself a ridiculous thought.

It's going to be everything you ever dreamed of, baby girl.

Chapter Thirty-Two

It was early and Asher didn't want to get up yet. Eva's warm body was snuggled up against his back with one arm slung across his waist. They'd slept at the monastery that night since today was the day of the big party. There was so much to do, it just seemed smarter to start off from there rather than in the city.

Unsure what had woken him, he kept his eyes closed and enjoyed the comfort of Eva's bed. But then rumbling started up above his head and something very sharp sunk into his scalp.

"What the—" He leapt out of bed. He didn't know what to expect, but a giant gray tabby cat wasn't in the top five. Diablo, the cat from the wine cellar, was stretched out across the pillows. His front feet were making air biscuits right where Ashe's head had been.

Eva shot up in bed, the sheets falling from her chest, leaving her half naked. Eyes wide in confusion, she turned around to follow Asher's gaze.

"Oh, holy crap!" she exclaimed and squinched down further in the bed, farther away from the cat.

Diablo's eyelids were at a sleepy half-mast. His mouth opened wide, showed all his teeth, and yawned. While Asher and Eva watched, he rolled slightly over on to his back to expose his fuzzy, striped tummy. His front feet continued flexing while he purred loud enough to be mistaken for a diesel engine.

"Where the hell did he come from?" Eva asked, eyeing the feline warily and clutching the blankets.

Now that Asher's heartbeat had slowed down, he chuckled. "The cellar, I guess. He sorta got kicked out of his home, so I guess he's moving in here."

She shot him a dismayed look. "On our pillow? I'm not comfortable with that. He'll kill us in our sleep."

Asher gave the cat a moment to smell his hand while he asked if he could pet him. The cat nosed his fingers, so Ashe started with a scratch on his striped head. "Nah, he won't."

"Don't touch him," she whispered, as if afraid she'd frighten the cat and he'd lash out.

Ashe scratched his way down the cat's side until he got to his belly. Diablo fully opened his eyes and observed Asher carefully while he scratched the warm belly fur. Asher was gentle, and the cat's eyes slipped closed again and the purring ratcheted up a notch.

"He's really friendly," he tried to assure her. "Look at him, just a big ole pussycat.."

"He's not, though," she protested. "You're tempting a fuzzy demon while you're totally nude. Just offering up your junk for his destruction." Asher realized he'd been standing there one hundred percent naked. Eva retreated via the end of the bed, taking the covers with her.

The cat stretched and yawned and meowed. He looked very comfortable on the bed, nestled into the pillows.

Asher put his fists on his naked hips, fully aware of the pose he struck. "Well, it looks like he's made himself at home."

Eva scowled at the cat and him in intervals. Finally, she shook her head. "So basically, my home is being overrun by pompous, vain scoundrels, and there's nothing I can do about it."

He fisted his burgeoning cock and smirked at her. "Nope."

She snorted and chucked a throw pillow at him. "You're ridiculous."

He rounded the end of the bed and stalked towards her. He could tell she was fighting the urge to flee. "Scoundrel, huh?" He chuckled deep in his chest.

She clenched the wad of sheets tighter to her breastbone and took a step backwards. "Uh huh." She was breathy. Tousled dark hair against tanned skin contrasted the cream of bedsheets. Her blue gaze was captured by his, and sweet rosy lips opened in a lusty pant. The swell of her breasts drew his eyes to their rise and fall.

He was only about five feet from her now. He pumped his hand up and down the length of himself then squeezed the head. He dragged her attention to his fist and the bead of precum that glistened on top. When he rolled his thumb across the top and smeared the liquid, she made a delightful little noise of anticipation. He moved the last few feet to her until the head of his cock actually brushed the front of her sheet.

"Open," he commanded and slipped his thumb into her mouth.

And the minx bit him. Fuck, he loved this woman.

They took advantage of her dresser and closet door. As some point, Asher got his feet tangled up with the hamper and nearly killed them both. Instead, Eva tumbled to the floor in a paroxysm of laughter.

Legs tangled in sheet and dirty laundry and using a work boot as a pillow, Asher nuzzled Eva's neck.

"You're going to leave whisker burns," she said but turned her face so he had better access. "Is the cat still up there?"

Asher lifted on his forearms. "Yup. He's holding up both paws. I think he's given us ten out of ten."

Eva pinched his rib. "Nice. I've thought we'd lose points for that dismount."

"Any points lost were made up when you screamed my name." He lifted over her and raised his voice to a girly pitch. "Oh Asher. Oh Asher."

Her mouth dropped open, comically insulted. "I hate you."

He climbed back over her, resting his weight on her lower half. He shook his head. "No, you don't."

"Yeah, I do."

"No, you don't." He kissed her, hard, deeply, while keeping her prisoner on the floor.

When he finally lifted his head, she whispered, "Yes, I do."

Asher booped her nose with his own, and whispered back, "No, you don't."

"No, I don't." She took his face in both hands. "I don't hate you. I love you."

"I knew it." He sounded cavalier to his own ears, but his heart soared. He had known it. At least he'd been pretty confident about her feelings, but now that she'd said it, the knowledge wrapped around him, embracing him with tenderness. The sense of security in knowing that she loved him, too, inflated his skipping heart.

He wrapped his arms around her and rolled her on top of him. "I have something I want to talk to you about after the party."

Eva raised her eyebrows. "What?"

"Just stuff, but I want to wait until all this chaos is over." He feathered her eyelids with kisses. "I love you, too."

Sometime later, Asher was standing outside the monastery drinking coffee and watching the first of the work crews arriving. In the next hours, the place would be bustling with activity.

They had left Diablo to his beauty sleep in their bed. Asher delighted in the arrival of the cat. He seemed like a good omen somehow. Like he was really and truly accepted by the vineyard. Even the ghosts no longer seemed to regard him as a harbinger of evil.

This was his home now, and he never wanted to leave. He'd show her the architectural plans he'd commissioned and get her input on them. Eventually, when he thought she was ready, he'd ask her to marry him. They'd make little Evas and Ashers, and they'd grow up to love the vineyard like their mother and aunt had. He was picturing their children playing with cousins on the very lawn now covered with a circus tent. He was glad there was so much room here because there would be so many kids.

Maybe they could get some horses, too. His mind was wandering into far distant futures with a petting zoo and nannies and jumping castles.

"What are you doing?" Esther asked him.

He sipped his coffee and landed back in the here and now. He did a double take over the rim of the cup. "What are you wearing?"

Esther had on plain jeans, a pair of -swear-to-God Keds on her feet, and a white t-shirt. Her hair was gathered into two pigtails. She wasn't wearing makeup or jewelry. Was she ill?

She waved a hand in dismissal. "I have other clothes to change into later." She had her iPad open and was scrolling through an impressive list.

That wasn't enough of an answer. "But why are you wearing that now? Is there a costume party I'm unaware of?"

"Don't be a dick. What are you doing staring off into the distance like a weirdo anyway?" When he didn't answer because she'd make fun of him, she swiveled her head and raised an eyebrow. "Daydreaming?"

"Yeah," he confessed with a goofy grin. "Eva told me she loved me today."

She nodded, understanding coloring her gaze. "And you're dreaming of your future. Let me guess. Your sweet little house. Lots of children running around."

His grin grew wider. Some people might not appreciate someone knowing them so thoroughly, but with Esther there was a level of comfort.

"You haven't talked to her yet, have you?"

On the other hand, it could also be annoying. "Why you gotta rain on my parade?"

Esther sighed and looked up at the heavens. "Dude. For your own well-being, I'm begging you to have this conversation with her. You're going to be annihilated when she finds out if you don't do this soon."

"I will." He repeated it when she rolled her eyes. "I will. After tonight. I'm going to sit her down and show her the house plans and everything."

"And *everything*?" She emphasized. "The house is the least of your worries."

"Yes," he agreed. "Everything."

She looked at him for a long moment. "Finish that up—" she indicated the coffee "—you've got a lot of work to do. And I'd suggest you wear something that can get sweaty."

Asher took in his own clothes. He was wearing linen trousers and a favorite silk t-shirt. He went back inside and changed into something that could get grubby. His mood was effectively squashed.

Upon his return, there were a stack of rakes and clippers and lawn bags on the step.

He grimaced.

Esther called from her meeting with Jeb and others he didn't know. "Just give that lawn a once over so it's nice and neat."

"Don't we have landscapers?" he mumbled churlishly. He didn't say it loud because he didn't want to talk to Esther anymore.

Over the course of the day, a million different workmen came and went. The caterers set up in the monastery kitchen and the bartenders were putting together their workstations in all three venues.

As Asher left the circus tent hours later, he met up with Eva on her way back from the makeshift casino.

"Oh my gosh," she exclaimed. "Why are you so dirty? What have you been doing?"

He wiped his brow on the shoulder of his t-shirt before he kissed her hello. "Esther has me working on every single nasty job she can find."

"Poor baby." Eva patted his butt. "Go get a shower. People will be arriving soon."

There were two giant white boxes on Eva's bed waiting for them. Along with the cat.

"I'm almost afraid to see what Esther has in store for us." Eva gnawed on her thumb while she looked down on the closed boxes anxiously.

"She's usually pretty good at this sort of thing. I'm sure it'll be perfect, but if you don't like it, we'll figure something else out." He kissed Eva on the temple then tickled the cat under his chin. "I'm going to hop in the shower. Wanna come?"

Eva rolled her eyes at the double entendre and shooed him along.

When he emerged, squeaky clean and cooled off from all the labor, Eva was almost completely dressed.

She was stunning. Esther was a goddamned genius.

Eva had wrapped her mile-long legs in fishnet stockings. She had on black, skin-tight hot pants and a sleeveless, white tuxedo shirt with a white bow tie. She was slipping a bright red jacket over her arms with long tails that came to about midcalf. It crossed over her waist and buttoned in a wrap style with a vee of six brass buttons. Gold braid looped over one broad shoulder. Shiny black boots with gold leather bands sat near her on the floor, and a black, silk top hat rested on the bed.

"Holy shit!" he said, as his hair dripped onto his shoulder. "You're the hottest master of ceremonies I've ever seen."

Eve snorted. "How many hot masters of ceremonies have you seen?"

Actually, she'd likely be surprised. The number was shockingly high. "Enough to know you leave them in the dust."

"Let's reserve judgement until we see what she's got in that box for you." She padded in stocking feet to the bathroom.

He didn't know why Esther was irritated at him, so he kind of expected a fat man's suit or something in the box. But it wasn't.

He shook out a shiny burgundy silk shirt with pearl buttons. Next, a pair of sleek black pants. In an interesting twist, a black leather corset with velvet boning and leather lacings. Two leather arm garters with buckles. In a separate bag, he found a duplicate silk top hat and buttery, black leather boots.

He was admiring his look in the mirror when Eva emerged with deep red lipstick and her light blue eyes lined in kohl. She'd ironed her hair to hang straight down her back in a stream of mahogany brown.

"Oh wow." She breathed. "A corset. I wouldn't have thought that would be so sexy, but then here you are."

Asher pulled her into his arms and turned them to their sides so they could look in the full-length mirror together. "Damn."

"Agreed."

"Hotsy totsy," Maggie said when they came down the stairs.

She was wearing the little black dress Eva had tried on at the tailor's. Her hair was pulled up in a *Breakfast at Tiffany* coif, showing off her long neck. There was a sparkly comb in her hair and pearl and diamond earrings on her lobes.

"You look amazing," Eva squealed.

"I know!" Maggie squealed back. "Where did she get this, do you suppose?" She indicated an almost perfect replica of the necklace from the movie.

Asher kissed her on the cheek. "These were not questions you ask of Esther or she'll likely tell you. It's usually best not to know. Plausible deniability and all that."

"I love it," Maggie confessed. "It would be worth a fortune if it was real."

Asher whispered in Eva's ear. "It's probably real."

Eva shot him an astonished look, and he winked at her. She grinned, thinking he was kidding. He wasn't.

Out on the grass, Ernie and his wife were strolling up. He had on a bespoke tuxedo and Yesenia was wearing a full-length beaded silver gown. They were hosting the Monte Carlo casino night, and they looked every bit the part.

"Esther is remarkably good at this," Maggie noted.

"Agreed," Yesenia said. "She didn't even ask us our sizes. Boxes showed up, and perfect clothes were inside."

"One of my many talents," Esther said as she rounded the corner. Dressed head to toe in hot pink—except for a black whip—she made a fearsome lion tamer. "Is everyone happy?"

"You're a wizard."

"So happy."

"Oh, yeah."

"Alright then," Asher clapped his hands. "Let's rock the hell out of this party."

He couldn't help thinking with excitement that this was the start of a new beginning. After tonight, everything would change.

Heaven & Hell XXIII

N eil had hoisted Juliet into her previous position on his back. It wasn't because Cerberus protested carrying her anymore, and certainly not because the dog couldn't. Neil felt like he could better protect her when she was physically attached to him. Also, he just missed her steady weight around his shoulders and her breath in his ear.

"Where are the stables?" Juliet asked. "Have you been there before?"

They were following Cerberus back to the elevator platform. The dog stopped periodically to investigate things. At one point, he wandered off the road to snuffle at some bodies suspended from trees by their feet. Neil hoped Juliet wasn't watching, but she must have been because when the dog came, back two of the heads were carrying human bones and she made him drop them in the dirt

Neil kicked the bones to the ditch on the side of the road. "I think it's on One, but I haven't been up there before. Charon will know for sure."

"And you think he'll tell us?"

"I think he'll do anything you ask him." Neil tossed a grin over his shoulder. "That old man has a crush on you."

He could feel Juliet straighten her spine a bit. "That's an old man? Wow. I honestly didn't see that. I thought he was a demon or something. I mean, with the teeth and, and the color of his skin, and, well, ew."

Neil chuckled. "I'm pretty sure he was a man once. Hell is, well, hell on people. Maybe when I've been here as long as him, I'll look like that, too."

"Oh, no way," she protested. "You're way too handsome, no matter how long you were down here."

She thought he was handsome. Neil knew he was. He'd used his good looks plenty when he was alive. A person would have to be an idiot not to take advantage of an asset like that. It didn't help with jack shit down here though, so it had been a long while since someone had said so, and it was nice to hear.

She went silent for a moment, and then she said in a soft voice. "I don't want to think of you down here."

He shrugged which made her rise and fall a fraction. "Well, it's where I am and where I'll be so..."

"I'm going to talk to Hashmal when I get back upstairs. There has to be something." She'd said this before, but Neil put no stock in it at all. What kind of pull could this sweet kid possibly have.

"You're sweet for trying," he said and patted her knee, "but don't get upset when there isn't." Hell isn't really a place people come and go from, know what I mean?"

"Maybe," she said with that tone he was beginning to recognize didn't appreciate being told no. "I'm just saying when we manage to do all this crazy stuff and get Rachel reunited with Lucifer, I have no doubt I'll figure out a way to get you out of here, too."

"You won't mind if I don't wrap all my hopes and dreams into it, though, okay?"

Juliet kissed his cheek again. It was getting to the point where he'd do stuff just to get a cheek kiss.

Cerberus trotted up to the elevator platform. There was still no one at the entry desk, which really didn't matter. He was sure they were off torturing some pathetic soul. Either way, one less grisly gatekeeper for Juliet to have to deal with.

The elevator doors were open, and they could see Charon sitting on the floor criss-cross-applesauce. Neil wasn't sure, but it looked like he was playing solitaire.

"There you are," the ancient old man croaked. He rolled forward on his knees and then climbed to his feet. The process was slow and agonizing to watch. Finally, when upright on his spindly legs, he spread his lips and bared his ghastly teeth in proximity to a smile. "What took you so long?"

"I'm telling you, honey, the old man loves you. Just ask him to take us to the level with the stables," Neil whispered

Juliet groaned in his ear. If he didn't know that it was directly related to the gross old man, the sound would have been arousing.

"Hi," she said brightly. "Are you playing cards?"

The old man appeared to blush. It was hard to tell; his skin was already so mottled.

"I was killing time waiting for you guys," Charon said by way of explanation. He shuffled the cards around in his hands. They looked to be from several different decks.

"It doesn't look like you have enough cards for a complete deck, there." She might find the old man gross, but she was awfully sweet to him, and it didn't feel fake.

He shrugged his skeletal shoulders. "Nah, there's not." He showed his cards. It looked like there was about thirty, and they were of different sizes and several different decks. The assortment included some little white kittens, a number of different Vegas casinos, a brand of cigarettes, a soda pop, and a couple of red Bicycles.

"How can you play solitaire without all fifty-two cards?" Neil asked. "You can never win."

Charon barked out a laugh. "I was never going to win."

Still, that seemed absurdly depressing to Neil, even considering where they were. Why would anyone do anything "for fun" that you lost every time? Had absolutely no chance of winning? Maybe he really did have some hope left because he couldn't imagine ever being able to give in that completely.

"Ah, poor Charon," Juliet cooed. "That's very sad."

"Why?" the old man asked. He tucked the cards in his breast pocket. "It doesn't matter."

"It's just... Well, I mean..." Juliet floundered. "Never mind, I guess."

Charon swept his hand in a wide arc, welcoming them into the elevator car. He scowled a bit at the dog, but he allowed him in, too, without complaint. "Where to now?"

The doors slid shut and the sound of cats yowling in unison to the tune of Small World filled the car. Well, that was wretched.

Neil didn't complain. He didn't want to distract Charon from the spell Juliet had spun around him. Truly, the old bastard was entranced.

"Do you know where the stables are?" she asked him, her angelic voice sounding extra sweet.

The ferryman cum elevator operator paused for a moment. "Yes." He said it tentatively, as if he wasn't sure he wanted to tell them.

"Will you take us there, please."

Charon wrinkled up his nose. "I'm not sure."

Oh, crap. Perhaps Neil had miscalculated. Maybe the old man's infatuation wasn't going to be enough. Was there anything left in that backpack Julie had slung around Cerberus for them to bribe him with.

"You're not sure where it is?" she asked.

"I know, I just don't know if I should take you there."

"Why not?" Juliet straightened up against Neil's back.

Charon looked to Neil for support. Neil didn't know why not either. The old man had already taken them to the mansion, for crying out loud. Neil would have thought that would have been far more dangerous and forbidden.

"What's the big deal?" Neil asked. He pushed the dog's shoulder with his thigh. The elevator was really too small with all three of them and this massive dog.

"There's scary stuff there." Charon might have shivered. One couldn't really tell since his uniform was so big on his skinny frame, his old bones could shake a hell of a lot in there without even ruffling the material.

Juliet gasped. "Scarier than this level?" she asked, horror rounding out the timber of her voice.

"Dangerous stuff," Charon clarified.

"We're on a very important mission, you know," Juliet explained. "And we've got the puppies with us. We'll be all right."

Charon gave the dog a disapproving glare, then squinted at Neil. "Don't let anything happen to her."

"On my honor," Neil said and crossed his heart with this index finger.

"Honor?" Charon croaked. "Do I have to remind you that you're in hell?"

Sweet Juliet reached her arm around to Neil's front and patted his chest. "Neil is very honorable. Maybe the most honorable person I've ever met. It makes no difference that he currently resides in Hell."

Neil's stupid heart doubled in size. Talk about lovesick.

"If anything happens to her, I'll tell the big man," Charon threatened.

Neil cocked his head and gave the old fool a *Really?* look. "You talk to the big man. Sure."

Narrowing his eyes, Caron said, "Everyone rides the elevator."

Neil snorted. "Don't worry, pops. I've taken care of her this far." His conscience reminded him that when the shit hit the fan before, it was the dog who actually rescued her.

With a huff, Charon started up the elevator and they listened to another round of "It's a Small World." "Sweet Caroline" was starting up when the car came to a halt and the door slid open. Cerberus exited and hopped off the platform, trotting away, seemingly not at all worried what danger they could get into.

Neil toting Juliet followed. She patted the top of the old man's hat as they passed by. "Thank you," she said and Neil just knew she was dazzling the old fucker with a bright smile.

"Take care," he called after them. "Be honorable, you little pissant."

Neil tossed a peace sign over his shoulder, but he didn't really mean it.

"So, where are we?"

"One, I think."

There was nothing on fire. No screaming. No active torturing.

"It's not so bad," Juliet noted. "It's not even as hot here."

True. It's not like there was a breeze or anything, but still it felt markedly cooler. Then it dawned on him. "Oh, this is Limbo."

"Limbo," she repeated. "Can I be honest? It's freaking me out a bit. Why would Charon be so worried about it?"

Neil shook his head. He didn't know the answer to her question. He was busy trying to figure out how he could get transferred out of Gluttony on Three and move up here.

"Oh, over there." Her arm appeared over his shoulder again, this time pointing to a large barn-like building. "That has to be it."

Wooden and at least two stories tall, there was no apparent entrance inside. They circled the entire perimeter and never found a doorway.

"That's weird, don't you think?" she asked him.

"Well, yeah." Neil admitted.

He lifted his leg and planted a motorcycle boot against a wide wall slat and pushed, hard. Not even a smidgeon of movement. As they walked around a second lap, they pushed against the walls, hoping to trigger a hidden doorway. No windows, either. Neil backed away and peered up at the roof, looking for a way in from up there. Nothing.

"Hey," Juliet called. "Hey, you."

"Shhh," he hissed, whirling around, looking for whom she was talking to.

Too late. A hobgoblin loped forward, bouncing to a stop in front of them on webbed feet. Hair hung in front of its face to the point where its nose stuck out, but no other facial features were visible. It didn't speak. Instead, it smelled the air around them as if trying to figure out what Juliet was by aroma alone.

"How do we get in there?" Juliet asked pointing to the barn. "Where's the door?"

The shaggy head shook back and forth. "It's a secret." His voice was high-pitched, as if it was being played back at high speed.

"Can you tell me?" she whispered as if she should be in on the secret, too. Neil would bet that smile was back.

"No."

Juliet laughed at the bluntness. "Pretty please?"

"If you can't get in," the hobgobblin explained, "then they can't get out."

"Well, that's pretty fucking ominous," Neil pointed out.

"Shhh." She covered Neil's mouth with her hand. "We don't want to let anything out. We just need one little thing from inside and then we'll leave. I promise."

Neil kissed the inside of her hand because he could. When she didn't immediately take it away, he smiled.

"It's a secret," the hobgobblin squeaked at them. "You need a special key to get in."

"Do you have the key?" Juliet asked.

"No one does." Actually, the pitch of its voice was rather nasally. "That's how we know they'll never get out."

"Ah, that makes sense." Juliet nodded. Neil nodded along with her. "We've been hunting for all kinds of crazy things. Will you tell me what the key is in case we might have seen it."

The hobgoblin straightened and preened a bit as if proud he knew something that they didn't. It smoothed down its hair with a hand webbed all the way to the fingertips. "Impossible. You'd have to find an angel feather."

Juliet and Neil both grew impossibly still.

"You have got to be fucking kidding me," Neil mumbled, her hand still over his mouth.

They were finally going to catch a break. Un-freaking-believable.

Juliet giggled and then Neil felt a great whoosh of air as her pure white wings unfurled and spread wide behind them. The hobgoblin gasped in awe. Neil wished with everything he held dear that he could see her like that again. She gave a little grunt of effort and then her free hand appeared before him, holding a pure and virtuous primary feather.

Neil pulled the hand from his mouth. "So pretty." He took the feather between his thumb and forefinger and brushed it across his lips. Soft and dainty, it smelled like spring and warm bread. He turned them back to the barn, and the hobgoblin followed. They couldn't see his expression, but Neil just knew its mouth was agape. As they grew closer to the barn, the feather began to vibrate as if it was actually pulling his hand towards the wall. The instant it touched the wood, the building creaked and popped and before their eyes a massive set of double doors made themselves known.

"Cool," Juliet and Neil said in unison.

A hellacious racket sounded on the opposite side. Something clattered closer with a terrifying cacophony until with a thunderous boom the doors crashed open, sending the hobgoblin tumbling out of the way. Neil was barely able to twist his body clear of a collision with the wildly swinging door. Juliet screamed but not from pain.

Backed against the side of the building, they watched as four of the biggest horses Neil had ever seen burst clear of the barn. Bigger than those Budweiser horses: a black one, a red one, another so white as to rival Juliet's feather, and a pale grayish green horse. Upon each one sat a cloaked rider, whooping battle cries as they galloped free.

"What the hell?" Neil and Juliet watched as they bolted away, dread filling Neil's gut.

"Who was that?" she asked. Neil was afraid to guess.

"The Four Horsemen." The hobgoblin breathed.

"Of the Apocalypse?" Juliet shrieked.

"Oh, you guys are in such trouble," the hobgoblin gasped.

Chapter Thirty-Three

With the exception of a little row among the valets at the beginning of the evening, the parties were going off without a hitch. The guys they hired to park the cars were messing around with the portable chargers Asher had arranged for the electric cars that would be coming out for the event. By the time Eva heard about it they'd already had to replace two of the valets. Apparently, the chargers packed a hell of a wallop when attached to someone's tongue or, God have mercy, put down their pants.

"What kind of idiot does that?" Eva asked Maggie and Esther when the three of them met up in the monastery office by accident.

Esther looked furious, and that was pretty impressive when one was dressed entirely in hot pink. Esther managed to make it look fierce instead of cutesy. In fact, Eva was pretty sure she'd kick anyone's ass who suggested she looked anything so offensive as cutesy.

"They're complete fucking idiots," Esther exclaimed. "I'd kill them all if it would make any difference."

Maggie raised her eyebrows. "Everybody's all okay, though? Our insurance is never going to cover electrocution."

Eva hadn't even considered what that would mean to the insurance. That's why Maggie was in charge of the business part of Dashiell vineyards and not Eva.

"Don't worry," Esther told her. "Those assholes would never file insurance claims. Trust me."

Eva didn't ask for an explanation. She assumed the workers were as terrified of Esther as everyone else was. "Except for that, obviously, and the fact that my fishnets combined with these tiny shorts are giving me a wedgie of epic proportions, everything is going great though, right?" Eva asked. She did a little, wiggle hoping things would adjust themselves.

"My party is going off without a hitch," Maggie said with glee. She held two packages of branded napkins. "The wine tastings are going really well. The hors d'oeurvres are a hit." She beamed at them. "There've been so many compliments about the remodel."

"Really?" Eva asked. "I didn't realize so many people had been here before."

"Well, not *so* many compliments, but the mayor likes it and there was a lady who'd been here once when Gramma was still alive, and she recognized the changes."

"Squee!" Eva emphasized with jazz hands.

"I know," her sister chirped. "How about the casino, Esther?"

Esther's gaze rose from the hand mirror she was using to reapply her hot pink lipstick. "I haven't been down there for a while, you know, keeping my eye on the valets and all, but I'm sure it's going well. Jeb is down there, and I'm certain he has it all under control." Just then, her cell phone started up with "Crazy Train" by Ozzy Ozbourne. "Speaking of the Devil." She capped the lipstick and touched the Bluetooth in her ear. "What's up?... Uh huh... I already told them no." Eva and Maggie exchanged a look. "That wasn't the arrangement... Let this be a lesson to us on using them too often... No, I'll be right there." She tapped her ear with an angry finger. "I'm going to strangle those demons."

She shoved her lipstick between her breasts, presumably next to her cell phone as there weren't any pockets visible in her hot pink tutu skirt, and waved goodbye.

"Yikes. That woman scares the hell out of me. Thank God she's on our side, huh?" Maggie jostled the napkins and added another to the pile.

"Agreed." Eva made an "eek" grimace while rifling through a desk drawer. "Where are our business cards? Never mind. I found 'em. Between Asher and his cousins, they know *everyone*. Have you met anyone good?"

"Yeah, I met another cousin, Jacob. Wait till you get a load of this one." Maggie comically fanned herself. "Not as tall as Ashe, but holy moly. Dark beard. So pretty."

Eva chuckled. "What is with that family? Seriously."

"Good genes, I guess. Maybe something in the water? I don't know."

"I gotta get back. Keep holding down your fort."

Maggie waggled her fingers as Eva left the office. She could hear the live music through the French doors, an interesting quartet of piano, violin, cello, and clarinet. It had sounded odd when Benji had suggested it, but when they looked them up on YouTube, they had been duly impressed.

Once outside, she was impressed again by the magnificence of the circus tent. Now that it was evening, the darkness added an otherworldly quality. There were flaming torches around the perimeter of the pond and highlighting the paths from the casino to the circus and then to the fancy party. Popcorn, salted nuts, and cotton candy vendors had booths lit up with carnival lights, and of course the glow from inside the tent flowed out to the lawn. Roaming around the grounds and talking to the guests were a collection of "freaks": a guy on crazy-tall stilts, a bearded lady, and a man and woman wearing tiny swimsuits completely covered, head to toe, in tattoos. There were some old-fashioned carnival games near the pond, and a small crowd had assembled around a man guessing people's weights. Mia was cheering on Luke as he bashed a comically giant hammer down on the strong man plunger and then shrieked with delight when the bell rang.

This party was simply the most magical thing Eva had ever seen, and she was inordinately proud that her vineyard was at the heart of it. Before returning to the tent, she followed the path that led to the cellars and the casino. She hadn't seen the place once it was in full party mode, and she was not disappointed.

The dark, cold cellar had been transformed into a James Bond movie. Ashe's cousin, Seth, held court at a poker table while Ernie and Yesenia mingled around the roulette wheel, craps, and blackjack tables. All the guests had been given poker chips to play with and all the proceeds were going to the community food banks. Exotic cocktail waitresses paraded around the room with trays full of specialty cocktails made from the wine at Dashiell vineyard.

They had all had a blast coming up with the recipes for those. Seth had brought in a friend who was a mixologist at some trendy bar in the city. He showed them things with foam and whipped cream and smoke, of all things, that were so freaking cool, and the fact that they were all made with the house wine was such a great advertisement.

There was a good crowd in the room, and she saw some recognizable faces. There was a senator, a state representative, and a few local celebrities. A closer inspection of the crowd revealed a couple of Asher's cousins, Benji with Seth at the poker table and Ethan laughing with a handsome gentleman she didn't recognize, maybe Jacob based on Maggie's description, by the bar.

She didn't fit in with the glamorous crowd in her ringmaster outfit, so she waved to Ernie and shot him an encouraging thumbs up. On the path to the circus, she passed a group of laughing partygoers, no one she recognized, but they toasted her as they passed. This whole event was such a success, she felt like she could fly. Why had she been so afraid of this, of sticking their necks out and taking a risk? Thank God Asher had come along. Otherwise, Eva might have spent her entire life among the row of vines, growing grapes and tinkering with wine until she died a lonely death and never got any recognition.

Boy, was Asher getting laid tonight.

She passed through the gaping flaps of the tent and glanced around for her man. Being inside the tent was bewitching. She wasn't sure how the circus guys managed to get that old-fashioned glow with the lights, but everything seemed to be coated in honeyed nostalgia. There were two big rings in the center of the tents. A woman in a pale pink leotard and a skirt made with sparkly fringe was using a matching umbrella to balance herself across a tightrope. The second ring had a troupe of contortionists, knife throwers, and flame eaters amazing the crowd.

She found Asher keeping company with a tall, thin man with perfectly styled hair. He looked like a Ken doll if Ken dolls were actually stunning.

"Babe," Asher called to her. "This is my cousin, Ian."

The aesthetically perfect specimen of a man raised an eyebrow at their introduction. He extended a hand and a dental advertisement smile. "Evangeline. I'm delighted to meet you. Nicodemus has told me a lot about you and your sister."

Eva looked to Ashe who rolled his eyes and shrugged. "Nico is his Esther."

"I've never met Nicodemus." She loved the sound of that name. "How would they know anything about me?" she asked Ian while shaking his hand. It was warm and, she didn't know how exactly, but friendly.

Ian smirked. When Asher smirked, it was randy and almost always sexual, but not so with Ian. The man oozed congeniality. "That group talks about everything. It's weird. Like a hive mind. You'll meet them all eventually and then you'll see what I mean."

"I can hardly wait," she said.

"I'm going to find the boys," Ian told Asher, then turned to her. "This is an amazing party. It was great to meet you finally."

"You too," she told him with a grin. "I'm sure I'll see you again soon." Then she added, thinking she'd dissected the cousin code, "You'll find several of your cousins in the casino."

"Thank you." He winked as he turned. It was the first time she didn't find a wink offensive and icky.

"I like him," she told Asher. "Of all your cousins—"

Asher closed his eyes on a long blink and nodded. "You'll like him the best," he finished her sentence. "Everyone does. He works very hard at it."

Eva slipped her arms around his waist and pinched his butt. "But I love you," she whispered and kissed him.

"I know."

"This has been an amazing party," she gushed. "Thank you so much for everything."

"It's your wine, babe. You're the genius."

She pinched his other butt cheek. "Thank you for noticing."

"I notice everything about you, babe." He nuzzled her neck and then whispered in her ear, "You're my favorite thing."

She groaned and then stepped back. As much as she'd like to peel off that sexy corset and molest him immediately, she wouldn't, not while she was hosting a party.

"Hey," Esther's voice coming from behind her startled Eva. She dropped her arms and spun around to find Esther approaching. The woman looked rattled. That in and of itself was enough to put Eva on alert. "I just heard from Judith."

"Who's Judith?" Eva asked.

"Benji's," Esther tossed out as an aside and then added with gravity, "Aaron is here."

Oh! "Maggie's Aaron?" Eva asked. "Does Maggie know?"

Esther and Asher ignored her. "Where is he? What does he want? Does everyone else know he's here? Who invited him? What are we going to do?"

"First, we're not going to panic," Esther told him. "Judith is watching him, and she'll let us know if he seems up to shenanigans. Right now, I just wanted to let you know about it."

"Judith?" Asher cried. "Judith? She's way too nice to be expected to have him under control. Oh, holy crap."

"Second, Judith is every bit as capable as I am. Don't forget she is a—" Esther paused and looked to Eva "—she's one of us."

Eva narrowed her eyes at them both. What in the hell was the deal here? She didn't appreciate being left out of important details, and yet it often felt like

Esther and Jeb didn't give her and Maggie all the information they needed. She'd had enough of that bullshit.

"What's the big deal here? You're pissing me off with this high drama. What difference does it make if he's here? If you don't like him, just stay away from him. You don't need to interact with him if it's going to cause you all this distress."

Asher and Esther just stared at her. She could see their minds whirling. Were they debating letting her in on whatever the big secret was? Esther raised an eyebrow and looked to Asher, but he shook his head and waved her off.

He reached for Eva's hand, but she clasped her hands behind her back so they weren't available. "It's just that he's notorious for causing trouble, and I don't want anything to jeopardize your successful party."

She gave him a dazzling smile. "Nothing is going to ruin this party. It's going so well. I say we just ignore him." Besides, she assumed Maggie would keep him busy.

Two and a half hours later, the party was still booming. The valets were too busy parking cars to electrocute each other. The crowd had only grown and so few people had left that the parking area extended down the dirt track around the vineyard. Guests flowed from one party venue to the next. The guest list was extensive, and Eva assumed it was due to the Mephisto cousins knowing absolutely everyone who was anyone. Eva met area politicians, Fortune 500, and sports figures. Mia had introduced her to her best friend, Cassandra, who worked for one of the area's biggest party planners. All the movers and shakers were there.

Eva was reeling from the amount of people she'd met.

It turned out every one of Ashe's cousins had an assistant, and they were all present. She had a lot of questions about these people. They were all insanely competent, very interested in Eva, and inordinately stern to the hired help. The valets, waiters, bartenders, and circus folk kowtowed to them at every encounter. Except for Esther and Jeb, none of those assistants had been involved in planning the function. It was odd. Not that Eva minded the free help in keeping this monstrous party rolling smoothly.

Asher and Eva had wandered out onto the lawn where they found Luke and Mia, Benji, Ethan, and the man she'd seen before whom she assumed to be another cousin. Held in the thrall of a juggling team, they watched from a safe distance as two men tossed three running chainsaws back and forth. All these performers were so amazing. A round of applause and cheers went up as the jugglers bowed.

Benji noticed Eva and Asher's approach and lifted his arm in a wave.

"Hey, honey," Benji said and kissed her cheek. "Great party."

"Thank you. I think it's going to be a crazy success."

"You look gorgeous," Ethan told her and kissed the other cheek. "Of course, it's going to be a success. Look at this crowd. We invited everyone who is anyone."

"And thank you for that." She turned to the man she didn't know and extended a hand. "Hi, I'm Eva. This is my party."

"Oh shit." Asher jumped in. "I'm sorry, babe. This is our cousin, Jacob. Jake, this is the love of my life, Evangeline."

Deep brown eyes twinkled good naturedly, and a white-toothed grin contrasted against the warm tan of skin the color of harvest acorns. He wore a very close beard and short, curly black hair. It was obvious what Maggie had found so attractive about him.

"There's seven of you, right? I think I've finally met you all now."

"I feel like I should apologize then." Jacob's voice was smooth as warm caramel. Wow, this dude.

"Alright," Asher scowled and pulled her to his other side, opposite of Jacob's. "That's enough of that."

"I heard Aaron is here. Has anyone seen him?" Benji asked.

Luke's cheeks bloomed red. "What? Who said he's here?"

"I haven't seen him," Benji explained. "I heard from Esther."

Asher spoke up. "Stay calm, Luke. Let's not make this worse than it needs to be. This could be an epic disaster if you start letting go in this crowd."

"I'm not getting mad," Luke insisted, but he definitely sounded mad to Eva.

"Take some deep breaths, honey." Mia was petting Luke's biceps.

Eva did not understand. She knew as well as anyone what having a difficult family was like. She wanted to be as supportive of Asher as he had been of her when her mother showed up. If only he would tell her what the issue was. "I'm sure he's here to see Maggie." Then she swept her hand to show the crazy party happening around them. "And to come to an amazing party. It's only going to be a big deal if you all make it one. Just ignore him. I'm sure it will be fine."

Six pairs of eyes blinked at her for several long heartbeats with no one saying a word. Finally, Jacob turned to Asher. "She doesn't have any idea, does she?"

Asher clenched his jaw shut and exhaled through his nose but didn't say anything.

"We'll just take turns keeping an eye on him. I'm sure the cabal has every-thing under control." Ethan looked at Luke with his eyebrows gathered together. "Except maybe Luke. Maybe you should steer clear."

Cabal?

Benji raised a hand like a kid asking permission to speak in class. "Umm, I just want to point out the work crew around here." He cast a furtive glance at Eva, but continued. "If he wants to cause trouble, it won't take any effort at all to make this party an historical fact."

"Oh shit," Asher breathed. "I hadn't thought of that. Fuuuck."

"Well-—" Eva pointed towards the path coming up from the monastery and the fancy party. "—here he comes with Maggie and my mother. You'll have all kinds of opportunities to keep an eye on him now."

All of them turned where she was pointing to see Aaron Mephisto coming up the walk with Maggie and Delilah, one on each arm. She didn't know who invited him, or why he caused such melodrama with the cousins, but Maggie seemed to like him and he seemed to treat her nicely.

"Boys," Aaron said as they grew closer to the group. "Beautiful night for a party."

And like fifteen-year-old boys caught doing something they shouldn't, they all stood there with their focus on their shoes and said nothing.

Except for Mia.

All five foot nothing of her in a yellow dress with a bow on the back stood next to her giant of a man and said, "What are you doing here, Aaron? It's hard to believe that you've got no agenda showing up here just now."

Aaron Mephisto turned his attention to Mia. It was unsettling how his focus was so intense, but Mia didn't blink. "You expect me to have no entertainment until your wedding? I can't very well sit at home the whole time twiddling my thumbs now, can I?"

Mia didn't back down, but Eva did detect a blanching of her usually rosy cheeks. "No, we understand that you have an empire to run, but I hope you keep in mind that this vineyard is very important to these people, my friends."

Eva could feel Asher gasp next to her and then whisper, "Oh, shit."

Aaron chuckled. It was deep, mischievous, and bawdy. "Oh, Luke. I do adore my daughter-in-law-to-be. She might actually be too good for you."

"I know she is," Luke admitted, and pulled Mia tight into a one-armed embrace.

"Don't worry, Mia." Aaron's focus was still on her. "I enjoy a good party, and this is an amazing party." His gaze traveled to Eva, and she felt his regard like a physical caress. She recoiled from it, taking a half step back before she caught herself. "There is no cause for concern. I have no intention of bringing you any trouble. You're much more likely to have brought the trouble on yourself. Was it the gargoyles' idea to hire the staff?"

"We've had no trouble," Asher insisted.

"Have you not?" Aaron raised a knowing eyebrow. "Regardless, I'm here for the party and the company of the lovely Magdalena. I didn't imagine I'd also make the acquaintance of your charming mother, too."

Delilah smiled. Eva saw just a hint of the old Delilah in her eyes. For a moment she wondered if their mother would revert totally and make a play for Aaron, but she relinquished her hold on his arm.

"I haven't had cotton candy for years. I'll be right back," Delilah said and made her way across the lawn.

"Shall we go inside the circus then, my dear?" Aaron asked Maggie.

"It'd be cool, right?" Maggie asked Eva. "I haven't had a chance to check it out yet. Esther is in the monastery, so it'll be okay for a few minutes."

"Yeah," Eva told her. "Make sure to watch the contortionists. It's kinda nauseating."

Their little crowd watched Aaron and Maggie walk away and then pause to catch the juggling act at the other side of the lawn. This time the jugglers were tossing hatchets and a bowling ball back and forth.

"I think he's just here for the party," Ethan ventured. "Maybe to get laid. Sorry, Eva."

Eva shook her head. "I don't think so. The getting laid part. The party, yes."

"I know what you're all thinking, but maybe they're right." Jacob watched Aaron with a speculative look. "I mean this is an amazing party. Maybe he's not always up to something."

"Usually..." Luke's arms were crossed over his chest, and if he wasn't careful, he'd grind his teeth into nothingness.

"I say we still keep an eye on him," Asher cut in.

Benji scratched the back of his neck in a contemplative way. "What choice do we have?"

"None," Ethan agreed. He punched Asher lightly on the shoulder. "Let's not panic. He doesn't seem like he's up to anything, and we really shouldn't antagonize him or he could change his mind."

Once again, Eva felt like an entire conversation was happening around her that she didn't understand. She was going to demand some explanation, but a huge cheer rang up from the monastery.

As if they were all on a swivel, Eva and the cousins all turned towards the fancy party. The French doors to the lawn exploded outward in an eruption of glass and shards of wood. The cheering got louder as four massive horses with riders burst clear of the building and thundered out onto the grass.

Eva's jaw dropped open as the horses paused for an instant, their enormous hooves ripping up the lawn. She wasn't sure if it was her imagination or what, but she'd have sworn great puffs of smoke came from their flared nostrils and that their eyes glowed red. The riders all wore cloaks with hoods so Eva couldn't make out their faces, although it was likely too far to see any details anyway. Still, she knew the lead rider's eyes were on her when his arm raised to point a level finger in her direction. His war cry was thrilling and terrible at the same time.

An involuntary squeak came from her as the four horsemen wheeled the animals in their direction, taking off around the perimeter of the pond.

The partygoers from the fancy party were streaming out of the monastery, clapping and cheering.

As the horses pounded closer and time seemed to slow in that crazy way, Eva catalogued what she saw. No regular thoroughbreds like you'd see at the guest ranches in the valley, these might have been draft horses or Gypsy Vanners. Absolute giants, each was a different color with the rider wearing a matching cloak. A pale grayish green horse led the pack followed by black, roan red, and white. The identity of the riders was mysterious. You'd never be able to pick them out in a lineup, as the hoods of their cloaks came down over their faces. You'd only be able to say that they wore colors to match their horses.

A tickle in the back of her brain suggested something familiar about this group, but spiking adrenaline clouded her thinking.

As the string of horses passed the midway point, Eva saw that revelers were also exiting the cellar, abandoning the casino party to see what all the commotion was outside. They joined in on the cheering as well. Eva imagined that the spectacle was amazing—from the outside. They hadn't booked any riders and they sure as hell hadn't planned for anyone to crash through the freshly remodeled monastery and make rubble out of the showroom.

The horses pounded around the wide turn at the end of the pond and bore down on the field in front of the circus tent. The crowd was applauding and spreading apart to create a wide path for the horses to pass through. Eva was separated from Asher when she stumbled over a bowling ball forgotten by those damn jugglers, so her eyes were off the horses for a moment while she gained her feet.

When she lifted her eyes, the riders were only yards away from her, bearing down faster now that they were on a straightaway.

Eva wanted to scream. She even opened her mouth to let it out. Asher was steps away from her, shoving through the crowd to get to her in time when she lost her feet again. This time from a massive shove to her back. She careened into the crowd and Asher's arms as the first of the horses churned up the ground where she'd been standing.

A shriek sounded behind her and, when Eva followed the noise, she saw the rider at the back of the pack, the one in black, had snatched up Delilah from the crowd and slung her across his horse as they all disappeared into the night.

Chapter Thirty-Four

Asher caught Eva as she was flung clear of the approaching riders. He'd known only panic when he'd realized she was directly in the path of the pack of horses, thundering through the crowd. It was her mother of all people who'd saved her. Delilah had seen the danger and in two giant steps had shoved her daughter as hard as she could, sending Eva and her freshly purchased cotton candy clear of the massive hooves.

The Pale Rider.

Some instinct recognized the horse and rider at the front of the pack, and the name dropped in the forefront of his brain. And on the pale horse sat Death.

And the three other horses matched up to the story.

There wasn't any chance the Four Horsemen of the Apocalypse appearing at their party the same night the Devil showed up was a coincidence. No fucking way.

"That guy just stole Delilah." Eva was regaining her balance, using his arm and shoulder to steady herself. She hadn't noticed yet that her long hair was hopelessly tangled with cotton candy. "Who the hell was that?"

The Four Horsemen churned up the grass then gravel as they charged furiously down the long driveway out of sight.

"Asher," Eva shrieked. "Who was that?"

Ashe didn't want to ignore her, but he also didn't know what to say. *I'm pretty sure that was Death, but don't worry about it. We'll talk to the Devil and get her back. It'll be fine.*

He grabbed her by the hand. "Hang on."

Where were his cousins? Where the hell was Esther?

Benji, Ethan, Jacob, with Luke and Mia had gathered together in a tight clump on the grass. En mass, their mouths hung open in shock. On the other hand, the general crowd of partygoers believed the whole thing to be a fantastic show to go along with all the rest of the party. After a significant round of applause, the people began to disperse and filter back into one of the three parties. Not even having the party crashed by a herd of cloaked riders on demon horses stopped the fancy party in the monastery.

"What the ever-loving fuck was that?" Luke's eyes were wide.

"Did you know that was happening?" Ethan asked. "I don't remember hearing anything like that in your plans."

"No, that wasn't planned! I don't have any idea where they even came from," Asher snapped. He wanted his cousins to have answers, or at least theories, not ask stupid questions.

Esther came trudging up the walk from the party. "They came from the hole in the basement."

"What hole in the basement?" Benji asked. "There's a hole in the basement? Like how big? What's in there?"

Luke answered his cousin curtly. "Jeez, did you just wake up or something. I don't think that's the main issue we need to be worried about here."

Benji blinked. "Why not? There's obviously a hole that needs to be dealt with if things are coming up from Hell. How is that not the issue?"

Maggie, having just arrived from the other side of the yard, joined Eva in asking in unison, "What do you mean 'coming up from Hell'?"

The Sins and Esther ignored them. Instead, Luke pointed a finger at his father trailing behind Maggie, and his voice thundered. "What have you done?"

The Devil laughed. The motherfucker actually laughed. "This wasn't me, kiddo. I had nothing to do with it. This is all on you, boys."

It was Luke who continued the argument. "You're really going to try and tell us that you, the Devil, having come directly from Hell, had nothing whatsoever to do with the Four Horsemen of the Apocalypse coming up from a hole that leads from Hell?"

Aaron, the Devil, tucked his hands in his pockets and rocked back on his heels. "Not that it's any of your concern, but I did not come directly from

Hell. And I don't care if you believe me or not, but I did not turn the Four Horsemen loose."

Eva had clearly had enough. "What are all you people talking about? None of this is making sense. Who were those men? Why are they coming out of the monastery? My mother is in danger and you are all just standing around and arguing?" She dug around in the waistband of her tiny black shorts and pulled out her cell phone. "I'm calling the police."

Asher pulled her phone from her grasp before she'd completed dialing nine-one-one. "Honey, we can't."

"What the—"

"Fine, I'll call." Maggie carried a tiny black purse which she whipped open and pulled out her own phone.

Esther relieved Maggie of her cell as well. "I'm sorry, Maggie. You'll have to wait a bit." She turned to Asher and said very sternly, "This is it. No more putting it off."

"Somebody had better tell me what the hell is going on right fucking now!" Eva was shaking with fury. "I've had enough of these weird conversations that seem to be about something else entirely that I don't understand."

Asher reached for Eva's hand, but she yanked it away. Maggie was next to her in a flash, and they shot him matching glares of death.

"Talk," Eva ordered.

He looked to his cousins for help. Ian and Seth were jogging up the pathway from the casino to join up with everyone else. Aaron stood a few feet removed from the rest of them, but clearly still part of this pack. Along the fringe, most of the gargoyles had shown up, too. Only Judith, Benji's gargoyle, looked to be missing, and when he glanced around he saw her supervising the cleanup of the destroyed French doors on the monastery lawn.

One raised eyebrow from Jeb, then he was directing the guests into the circus tent for more of the show. Within moments their group was the only one on the lawn. All the time for bullshitting was over.

He looked to Luke for help, but Wrath was studiously avoiding his gaze. *Thanks, man. The only one of us who's done this already. You'd think he'd have some advice.* Mia met his eyes, though, and she gave a little nod.

"Asher." Eva uttered his name like a threat.

He reached for her hand again, but she kept it out of his reach. He searched her face for some sign she still loved him, but all he saw was anger and frustration.

With a deep sigh, he removed his top hat, desperate for something to look at that wasn't Eva. "There's a story I need to tell you. It sounds really crazy and impossible, but it's true."

"Um hum."

A snort of humorless laughter escaped him. "I don't even know where to start."

"How about with who they were," Eva suggested with a point of her finger in the direction of the Horsemen.

"I'm not certain, but—" he looked to Esther for confirmation and she nodded with conviction "—yeah, they are the Four Horsemen of the Apocalypse."

When she didn't say anything, he glanced up from his hat. She merely blinked at him and then turned to her sister. They shrugged at each other and communicated in their silent way.

They are," he repeated and shrugged. "The Four Horsemen. It seems that they came up through that hole in the basement. Esther thought she closed it, but apparently not."

"I did what I could. I mean, it's not like any of us have a lot of experience sealing portals." Esther said, sheepishly. It must have been hard on her to admit there was something she wasn't a star at.

"Is that all? That's your story?" Eva asked, nodding her head in a furious motion, suggesting she was preparing to blast them with sarcasm.

"No, there's more. Lots more." He took a deep breath. Here's where he was going to lose her. "You know the saying, the Seven Deadly Sins? And you know how there are seven of us?" He pointed out his cousins, each of whom nodded in acknowledgment. "Each one of us represents one of the Sins."

"Really! This is the most fascinating bullshit I've ever heard."

"I told you it was crazy, but it's also true." He met her gaze and tried to send as much honesty through it as possible.

"Why would you make up this ridiculous story? Give me back my phone. I'm calling the police."

"It's real, Eva."

"You—" she waggled her finger at all of them "—are the Seven Deadly Sins."

Every one of his cousins nodded solemnly.

Eva closed her eyes on a long blink. "All right, Asher, then who are you?"

He swallowed again. "I'm Lust."

She laughed, sort of a giggle. It wasn't a happy sound and it felt hopeless to Asher. "You're Lust," she said in giggling disbelief. "Okay."

Asher was taken aback. "Wow, that's hurtful."

"No!" she raised a finger indicating to give her a moment to get control of herself. "I'm not saying you're bad in bed. Not at all. But you're supposed to represent Lust? Okay, I'm just... I don't know."

He put his hands on his hips, completely offended at this point. "My powers don't work on you."

"Of course, they don't." Eva nodded with complete irony.

Mia, God bless her, piped up. "That part really is true. Luke is Wrath and it doesn't work on me. And I'd bet it doesn't work on you, either."

Eva turned to Maggie as if to say, *can you believe this shit?*

Maggie snapped her fingers at Esther. "Give me my phone. I'm calling the police."

"Hang on everyone. I've got this." Benji stepped forward and raised his eyes to meet Maggie's. They all watched as he gave her a slow blink and a complete change came over her. Her angry expression sort of melted from her face, replaced with a languid sort of bliss. She looked around her, lazily searching for something, and then sunk to a seat on the ground.

Eva stared at her sister. "What are you doing?"

Maggie lifted one shoulder then let it drop. "This whole thing is an awful lot of work."

Her jaw hanging, Eva demanded, "Magdalena, get up. We need to get the police out here looking for Delilah."

A yawn stretched Maggie's face. "I'll call in a little bit."

Eva's face was pink. "What the—"

"It's the Sin." Asher explained. "Benji is Sloth. He sent her a little zap. She'll be fine."

Now, Eva's eyebrows were mashed together on her wrinkled forehead. "I don't get it."

"You see," Esther cut in. "The Sins don't affect you because you and Asher belong together. It never works on their 'person.' But Maggie's not you, even though you're almost exactly alike."

"That's completely insane."

Ethan raised his hand and then looked at Maggie on the ground. With a little blip of Envy, Maggie rose to her feet and glared at Eva.

"I don't understand why you got the cool, sexy outfit and I get this stupid, old black dress. It's boring. You always get all the cute stuff. I want yours. Let's switch."

Eva took her in with an astonished expression.

Ethan took a bow and said, "Envy."

Jacob was next. He gave Eva a wave and then sent Maggie a shot of Greed.

Maggie clutched the necklace Esther had given her. "I'm keeping this necklace. I don't care if it's a loan. In fact, is it a set? I want it all."

With two fingers to his temple, Jacob gave her a salute. "Greed."

Eva turned to Mia. "This cannot be true."

"I know. It's totally crazy." Mia let go of Luke's hand and came to stand in front of Eva. "Let him finish the whole story. It gets weirder."

Eva didn't look convinced, but she seemed less angry and more curious at this point. "So you're Lust and you're Sloth." She pointed to each of them. "Envy and Greed. That's four. Who are you other three supposed to be?"

Luke signaled. "As mentioned before, I'm Wrath."

Seth and Ian from the back piped up with, "Gluttony." "Pride."

"Well, that's all Seven of you," Eva noted.

"And don't forget me." Aaron stepped forward from the periphery of the group. As he passed Maggie, she wobbled a bit and he caught her by the elbow.

Ever the gentleman, Asher thought bitterly.

"Watch out there, sweetheart. You're a bit out of sorts there with all the blipping and whatnot." Aaron tucked her under his arm as he turned to Eva. "You've met me as Aaron Mephisto. Luke's erstwhile father. But many know me as the Devil."

Before Asher could intervene, the Devil showed his true nature. It was just for an instant, just long enough for the facts to register in Eva's mind before his charming mask was replaced. A wave of heat rushed past them, ruffling their hair and singeing the inside of their noses. Maggie moaned and sagged, but Aaron kept her on her feet.

Eva however, had a reaction Asher hadn't seen coming. He'd been watching her keenly, trying to read her face for signs he could interpret, so he saw her expression go from terror to rage.

"Let go of her," Eva growled at the Devil and grabbed her sister by the forearm and yanked her free of his hold. She wrapped her arms around Maggie and backed the two of them away from the Devil.

Or rather, Aaron let Maggie go. Either way, a flush of pride filled Asher that the woman he loved was so fierce.

Esther approached like she would a wounded animal. "Let me take her for a few minutes. I can fix her and she won't remember."

"What are you?" Eva asked Esther.

Esther looked to Asher, and he gave tacit approval. "Me and Jeb and the rest of the 'assistants' are Gargoyles. Each one of the Sins has one."

Eva didn't reply. She stood there and took everyone in as if she was weighing how much of this bullshit she believed. As much as Asher hated the Devil, his showing her his true face was what brought the whole absurd story into the realm of reality. The Devil was impossible to dismiss once his handsome face cracked open like a lava flow and black eyes radiated bottomless depths of misery.

"I cannot believe I'm buying into this insanity." Eva finally turned to Asher. "I don't understand what any of this has to do with me or my family."

"Because I love you," he said.

"Okay. Well, thank you for telling me your story." Eva backed her and Maggie up another couple of steps. "You're a really nice guy…"

Here it was. She was never going to go for this. He was losing her. He fucking knew this would happen. He'd known it all along.

"Honey, we can get Delilah back," he said.

Eva's eyes filled with tears and his heart ached for her, but he was desperate. If he had to use the snatching of her mother, he would. The Devil who put him in this position could also help him keep her.

"We can get her back," he promised. 'But there's a lot more to this story."

Chapter Thirty-Five

*B*reathe, Eva, breathe.

The story being unfolded before her was something out of the most outlandish fantasy novel ever written.

She wanted it to be some elaborate ruse. Like the practical joke of the century.

Except that she'd seen the face hidden underneath Aaron Mephisto's mask, and it was horrifying. She could still see it when she shut her eyes and she was certain she'd see it in her nightmares. It had been as if someone had peeled the skin from a skeleton. She couldn't help envisioning a boiled and peeled tomato with solid back eyes, except that wouldn't have been scary. What she'd seen had been more than scary.

Her brain wouldn't have been able to make that up, so she knew it was true.

Aaron Mephisto was a real honest to God devil. Maybe *the* Devil. She'd panicked when she'd realized that he was holding Maggie in his arms, and before she'd had an opportunity to second guess herself, she'd yanked her sister free from the demon's clutches. His expression had been surprise not anger, thank goodness. She was ill-equipped to wrestle him if it was required.

Who he was remained very clear in her mind.

The gargoyle thing, however, that she didn't understand. What the heck did that mean, a gargoyle? The only ones she'd ever heard of were made of stone and hung on the sides of buildings, and that didn't make any sense. Did they all belong to a professional organization, maybe? Like the Moose Lodge or the Elks. Or was there an agency called Gargoyle? She was going to have to Google that later.

Even though she and Maggie had spent their entire lives living in an old monastery, apparently even with ghost monks in residence, they'd never been an especially religious family. Eva could probably even count the number of times she'd been in a church, since every time had been someone's wedding. Thus, her understanding of scripture was severely limited. Nevertheless, she had to assume the arrival of the Four Horsemen of the Apocalypse was a horrifically bad scenario.

And what could they possibly want with Delilah? Why would they snatch her up out of all the people available? She'd pushed her out of the way. Was it her they'd actually wanted?

Maggie collected herself and stood on her own, though she remained dazed and a bit shell-shocked after the Sins had been messing with her head. Eva could hardly fault her for that. She was feeling distinctly addlepated herself.

Eva's hands started to shake at the realization that perhaps it had been her they'd wanted. Was it her they had even come here for? She couldn't understand why. She'd never done anything she could imagine would bring on the attention of a group so vaulted as the Four Horsemen.

But then again, the actual goddamned Devil was at her vineyard, so who knew what was going on in the conversations of the underworld movers and shakers.

Her trembling hand rose to smooth her hair from her eyes. Instead, she encountered a wad of sticky hair. When she pulled it away, her fingers were covered in blue cotton candy. She stared at her tremulous fingers, not really understanding what she was looking at. What was she supposed to do with this mess now?

"Oh, baby," Asher crooned and took her messy hand into his palm. Out of nowhere, Esther appeared with a packet of wipes and he used one to clean off the crud. Even with the sticky stuff gone, her fingers still had a blueish tinge, and she continued to stare at them stupidly.

Asher wrapped his arms around her and said, "It's going to be alright. I promise."

Eva remained ramrod straight. As confused as she was, she still had enough sense to remain furious and untrusting of anything he tried to say to smooth over this absolute shit show. It only took a second before Asher let her go. Maybe he was getting frostbite.

"Enough of this," the Devil said, the smirky expression gone from his incongruously handsome face. "I don't know what they're doing loose up here, but I'm going to go find out. Probably get your mom back while I'm at it."

Jacob, Ian, Ethan, and Seth came to stand next to him. "We're going, too," Seth informed him. He turned to Maggie and Eva next, "We'll get her back. I promise."

"Yeah," Asher added. "Don't panic. I'll make sure she's fine."

"No, you won't." Mia pulled Luke by the hand, towing him towards his father and cousins. "Asher, you're going to stay here with us. You have a lot of explaining to do. Luke and the boys will see to Delilah's safety."

Luke glared at the Devil before saying to his fiancée, "Are you going to be alright?"

"Definitely." Mia nodded. "Eva and Maggie need me here. You go." She seemed to notice that Benji was hanging back. "You, too, Benji. Get going."

Benji trudged his way to the group, a sour expression on his face. Now that he'd introduced himself as Sloth, a whole lot of his behavior made sense. "Why doesn't Ashe have to go?"

"Believe me, it won't be more fun for him here." Mia shooed Benji towards his cousins.

Ethan wrapped his arm around Benji's neck and rubbed his head with his knuckles. "Come on, little buddy." Ethan spoke to him like he was a child, until Benji slugged him in the ribs.

The Devil's smirk was back when he told the cousins, "Come on if you're coming. I don't need your help, but—" he shrugged "—the horsemen are unpredictable. I'd rather not have to track them using those idiot demons."

Seth was the big guy with the toothy smile. Eva liked him despite what she now knew. Gluttony, she thought and tried to pick out memories that would confirm his proclivities.

"Regardless, we need to get them wrangled up. They obviously can't be running around loose up here." Seth shook his head with disgust. "Not running a very tight ship down there, eh?"

The Devil's grin went from smirky to scary in seconds flat and, without even thinking about it, Eva stepped slightly behind Asher.

"When you get down there you can run Hell any way you wish. I can assure you when I get home, there'll be hell to pay." The Devil winked at Eva with the pun. "Miss Magdalena. Miss Evangeline. I will return with your mother no worse for wear."

"One would say if you hadn't let them out in the first place we wouldn't be going after Delilah at all." Luke crossed his arms over his chest and showed no fear.

Luke was taller than the Devil, but Eva could see a familial relationship. They looked approximately the same age. Brothers, perhaps?

The Devil raised an eyebrow. "Nice try, son. The Horsemen are not mine to command. They may have been in residence, but only because of the remodel. You're an architect. You know how unreliable workmen can be. It's not like they can use my demon workforce up there. Although..." He chuckled and there was a second when Eva could clearly see his horns again.

Her stomach roiled and for a passing moment she thought she might vomit.

"Come on," Ian called. "Let's get rolling before they get too far."

The cousins and the Devil started for the parking area. They argued about whose fault it all was, who was driving, and where they should start. Ethan didn't let Benji lollygag behind as he towed him along with his cousin's head in the crook of his arm.

That left Maggie and Eva bunched together to stare at Asher, Esther, Jeb, and Mia.

"You have a ton of questions," Mia stated.

Eva snorted. Now that the audience of people staring at them had shrunk, she was feeling slightly more in control. It also helped considerably that the Devil was no longer regarding her or Maggie with creepy interest.

"That's an understatement," Eva said.

Maggie cleared her throat. "First, I need to know if you think it's safe to send the Devil out to find Delilah."

With an expressive sigh, Mia answered. "Truth? I don't know. I've only known about him for less than a year. Esther? What do you think?"

Even in her hot pink getup, Esther carried herself with an air of authority. "I believe he will bring her back safe. He's the Devil but he's also Luke's father, so—"

"What?" Maggie and Eva shrieked in unison.

Eva looked to Mia with wide, shocked eyes. "What is she saying?"

Mia nodded. "It's true. Like Asher said, there's a lot more to this story than the Sin part."

Eva hesitated to ask. She let her mouth hang open while she digested this latest nugget. Finally, she turned to Asher. "How can the Devil be Luke's dad? Although, I guess that explains his open hostility to the man. What does this have to do with you? I don't understand how your Sins fit in here."

Asher cast his eyes down and shame seemed to flit across his face before he took a deep breath to shore himself up. He reached for her hands, and she debated allowing him to hold them. In the end, she only let him have one.

"What I'm going to tell you is crazy, but I promise you, it's all true. Please just let me get through it and tell you everything, okay?"

Eva didn't reply with words. Instead, she closed her eyes, raised her eyebrows, and allowed a shrug that gave tacit permission to continue.

"So, it all started with Adam and Eve."

"Oh, come on." Eva tried to pull her hand back, but he held strong.

"Please let me tell this story."

"Fine," Eva said, but she didn't even try to disguise her annoyance. This was ludicrous.

Asher went on to spin an over-the-top tale involving Adam and Eve and Lucifer and some girl named Rachel. As fantastical as the part about being a Sin was, it was believable because she'd actually seen it with her own eyes. What they'd done to Maggie was barbaric, but it brought the whole thing home. Her sister would never have behaved that way without prompting. This outlandish tale... Well, no.

But Asher told it with conviction. Eva had to give him that. He told her this wacky story and maintained eye contact with her the entire time. She didn't believe any of it, but she also found that she wanted to. She wanted there to be a reasonable explanation for the chaos Asher had brought to her life.

"So, every generation is saddled with a Sin and then the year we turn forty, one of that generation's Sins becomes the Devil and the whole cycle starts over," he finished up. "That's how the Devil can be Luke's father."

Eva looked at the watch on her free wrist. They'd been gone forty-five minutes. "How long do you think this rescue will take? Will they be back tonight, do you think? I'm just wondering how long to give them before I call the police."

"Ummm," Maggie hummed. Her forehead was furrowed with anxiety as she peered at Asher. "Are you saying that you might be the Devil someday?"

Asher closed his eyes and swallowed hard. His skin took on a pallor, and his nod was almost imperceptible.

"Oh, Maggie." Eva rolled her eyes. "Tell me you're not falling for this nonsense."

"Well..."

Mia settled her hand on Eva's shoulder. "I know this sounds—"

"Crazy? Insane? Ridiculous?" Eva suggested.

"Yeah," Mia agreed. "All those things. But it's also true."

Eva was so disappointed in Maggie and Mia both. Maggie she'd forgive because she had a bit of fancy in her since childhood. She was the sister who had held on to Santa and the Tooth Fairy for so long. Mia, though, she'd seemed like such a reasonable person. She should know better.

What Eva needed was to get Delilah back and then have a really good sleep. She'd been overworked, that was all. In the clear light of day, after about twelve hours of good shuteye , all of this would make sense. Some reasonable explanation would be put forth that Eva could wrap her head around. Until then, it was clearly time to get the authorities involved.

Esther spoke up then. "Enough of this. Come with me, all of you."

When Esther spoke like that, she didn't leave much room for argument. With a brusk gesture, she led them towards the circus tent: Eva, Maggie, Asher, and Mia with Jeb trailing along in the rear. Eva didn't know how much explaining was going to take place in there. It was crowded and loud with partygoers and circus folk. Esther lifted aside the flap and entered with the others following inside like ducklings.

Except when Eva entered, the smell of people and popcorn fell away, replaced with the chill of hewed stone and the smell of history. The tent was gone. Where she expected sawdust and canvas, she found marble floors and ancient wooden pews that seemed to stretch forever. Echoes of their heels on the floor spread thoughout the massive hollowed out space. Eva looked around in awe, unable to reconcile what she was seeing.

Mia stepped next to her. "Even crazier, right? Prepare to have your mind blown."

"Are you alright?" Asher asked and squeezed her hand.

"I have no idea," she answered truthfully. Although she knew it shouldn't, Asher's steady, warm hand brought her comfort.

"Notre Dame will explain it all to you so you can believe the truth," Esther assured them as she led the pack up the wide aisle.

Eva tossed Mia a quizzical look.

Mia answer with a broad smile. "Wait 'till you see this." She made a little explosion with her fingers near her temple. "Mind. Blown."

Was everyone on drugs? Had some sort of hallucinogenic drug been piped into the party?

At the top of the aisle, Esther paused at the altar. The church, because that was clearly where they were, was magnificent. Enormous marble statues were built into the walls with ornate classical designs carved into the rock.

Breathtaking. She allowed her eyes to feast on the architecture and design of the place and thought how much it reminded her of the ancient churches she'd seen in Europe.

"Notre Dame," Esther called. "We have brought her."

Her? Was she 'her', Eva thought. Now beginning to consider that she was being indoctrinated into some weird cult, Eva looked to Asher of all people for assurance. He, however, was staring intently over her shoulder. When she turned her head to see what captivated him, she stopped breathing.

The air around an especially majestic carving of a formidable gargoyle was shimmering. Eva squinted at it. Then the statue moved.

What the ever-loving fuck was happening?

The gargoyle stood on its haunches, then seemed to stretch and shrink at the same time, morphing itself from a stone carving into a petite woman. The air settled down, and the lady stood before them. Truly lovely, she wore soft, white robes and a pleasant expression of welcome.

"Evangeline," she said in a lilting, accented voice. "I am delighted to meet you at last. Esther has told me so much about you."

"Oh. My. God." Eva was pretty sure she was going to pass out. "Gargoyles."

Chapter Thirty-Six

E va looked a little woozy so Asher took the opportunity to slide in next to her and wrap an arm around her shoulders to pull her in tight to him. He couldn't blame her reaction, honestly. He'd known who and what Esther was his whole life, but he could only imagine seeing a gargoyle change for the first time was a shock to the system. He and his cousins had only ever met Notre Dame and seen the cathedral where she lived for the first time a couple of months ago and, full disclosure, that had blown them all away even as jaded as they were.

With the freakout Eva was experiencing, he was grateful for Notre Dame's presence. The supernatural qualities the lady brought with her were undeniable. Eva could pretend that what she was being presented with was untrue, but she couldn't deny what she saw with her own eyes.

Notre Dame observed Eva's reaction to her transformation with interest. With a beatific smile, she stepped down from her pedestal and seemed to glide toward them. As she neared, Eva shrank backwards against Ashe's body. He wrapped his arms tighter around her, thrilled that she was still able to find solace in him. She must not hate him too much. Thank the lord for small favors.

"Perhaps you should sit down, dear," Notre Dame suggested. "This can be an awfully big realization to come to terms with in the beginning."

The Lady extended her hand to Eva. Settling her hand in the lady's, she accepted her assistance to one of the ancient pews. They settled down together with Mia and Maggie taking seats on the next pew where they twisted around to sit sideways and look over the back to converse. Asher found himself lingering on the outside of their little tableau, an extra, unnecessary person.

"I'm certain you have many questions," the lady said. "But first you look like you could use a cup of tea." She gestured to Esther. "Will you please get our guests —" she stopped speaking and turned back to Eva with a question on her face "—or I guess maybe you'd prefer wine?"

Eva shook her head. "No. I think a calming tea would be just the thing."

"I thought so." Then back to Esther. "Tea then, if you would."

Esther nodded, and she and Jeb walked away from them and disappeared behind a pillar. Asher shifted his weight from one foot to the other and wished he had an assignment.

"So how did you know my name?" Eva asked.

Notre Dame took Eva's hand in hers again and patted it. "We are the watchers. The protectors. We have seen you coming."

Asher's eyebrows rose. They'd seen her coming? Had Esther seen her coming? Why didn't she say anything? What else did they know?

"Something very important is possible," Notre Dame continued. "We see how the forces are aligning for the first time in millennia."

"Like astrology?" Eva said with skepticism coloring her question.

"Oh, nothing so mundane as astrology," Notre Dame assured her. "The silly stars are not involved."

Maggie found her voice then, timid and full of awe. "Can you predict the future? You saw her coming. What does that mean?"

"It's not that we can see the future, but we've been watching for so long that we can—" the lady paused as if looking for a word, and then finally settled on one even though it didn't really fit. "—predict what will happen."

"And you saw me? Why me?" Eva asked.

"Ah, the tea has arrived." Notre Dame gestured for Esther to come forward. "Thank you, *chère*." She doled out teacups to Eva, Maggie, and Mia and kept one for herself.

Asher turned to Esther. "None for me?"

Esther scoffed at him. "You don't like tea."

He tried not to look like he was pouting when he pointed out, "I am thirsty."

It wasn't that Jeb materialized necessarily, but one minute he wasn't there and the next he was. It was off-putting whatever mechanism it was.

"Here." Jeb thrust a glass of tepid water at him. No ice cubes. No nice sprig of mint or wedge of lemon. He'd have even taken a cucumber slice. Was he being punished or something?

"Spring water?" he asked hopefully.

"Tap," Jeb replied.

Asher took a sip so as not to appear ungrateful, but it really was just water.

"This—" Esther gestured at the expansive interior of the cathedral and said to him "—isn't really for you. You understand, right?"

Asher pursed his lips and nodded, refocusing on the conversation with the ladies.

"... found Mia and then you were there on the horizon. I knew it was you who would bring completion to Lust. It is remarkably rare for a Sin to find the one, and now there have been two."

"The *one*?" Eva asked.

"Yes." Notre Dame nodded. "The person who negates his Sin. The one who makes him a mortal man, without the supernatural curse of Lucifer's kin ruling his life. Only then can the Sin experience whole love. A love not diminished by provocation or incitement born of the nature of the sin." The lady turned her smile to Asher and nodded for him to come closer. "For the first time in his life, Asher can know that the reason you love him is because of the man his is, and it's not the lust driving you."

Asher felt a rush of emotion course through him, lighting up his limbs and setting a glowing fire alight in his belly. He raised his eyes to look at Eva, to see if she was enjoying that same sensation, and when their eyes met, he hoped she was. The warmth of embers bloomed into a bonfire, making his heart ache and his breath hitch. He wanted to hold her and whisper in her ear how much he loved her. Tell her how beautiful she was and how smart and generous.

But maybe she didn't feel that way anymore. Not after the revelations of the evening. Maybe she never really felt that way. What if her depth of feeling wasn't as acute as his?

He couldn't imagine how his life was going to continue without her. The thought of going back to the way he'd been before her, back when Lust ruled, filled him with despair. He couldn't do it. He couldn't go back to the way life had been before. All the meaningless encounters that had colored all his interactions. The faceless, baseless sex.

Eva had ruined him.

"And I believe Asher fills some reservoir in you, Evangeline, just as Mia does for Luke." Notre Dame tipped her teacup in Mia's direction.

Mia returned the lady's smile with her own. "I know this whole thing feels like too much," she told Eva. "It's surreal and feels impossible, but it's so important."

Maggie nodded at her sister. "This is really big." Her gaze took in Notre Dame and the cathedral. It even lit on Asher for a moment, and the look she gave him was charitable and not full of the pity he'd expected. If only he could read Eva as easily.

Eva shook her head and stared into the teacup. Asher did the same with his water, realizing that he was subconsciously mirroring her as a way to keep that connection with her.

"I can't believe any of this is real," she said. "Like I stepped into a magic circus and drank one of those crazy cocktails we made up and now I'm in some sort of Alice in Wonderland scenario."

"I get it," Mia said. "I was in your shoes not too long ago. It's going to take some time to sink in, but it *is* real."

"What if I don't want anything to do with this?" Eva studiously avoided Asher's gaze as if the liquid swirling in her cup was less confusing than everything else. "What if this is too much? What if I'm not ready for this? Maybe I'm not really *the one*? Or I don't want to be. What then?"

Asher nearly dropped his water.

After a long second, Notre Dame answered. "That is your choice. You are always free to choose. No one can make you love someone just as no one can make you unlove someone. Not Asher, not me. Not even God." The lady mused for a moment, taking a sip of her tea before completing the thought. "I believe that is an important part of lifting this curse."

"How do you mean?" Asher asked, making himself a part of the conversation for the first time instead of a timid eavesdropper.

"The curse happened because God couldn't make Rachel stop loving Lucifer. Love is the basis of everything. As all of these seemingly random pieces started to align, we pondered how the Sins played a part, and we have been unsure. However, we believe love is the answer. We think—" she paused and gave Eva and Asher a look in turn "—each of the Sins must find the one who cancels out his Sin. That alone won't break the curse, but combined with everything that is going on in Heaven and Hell at this time..." She shrugged. "We have hope."

"So, it's all ruined if I leave?" Eva asked.

The lady's expression grew contemplative. "In order for the curse to be broken, all the pieces must fit. If you aren't the right one for Asher, it won't matter if you stay or not."

She was his one. Asher was certain. What did he have to do to convince her?

"Let me make sure I understand." Eva set the cup and saucer on the pew and stood. She turned to walk out into the aisle, but Asher was standing there. He didn't know if it was his puppy dog eyes that repelled her or the stench of rejection that did it, but she took one look at him and turned the other direction.

Eva paced up and down the row as she spoke. "In a few years, some ceremony will happen and either Asher or one of his cousins will become the Devil." Mia and the lady nodded. "And their sons will take over as the Sins in that same ceremony."

Esther nodded both yes and no at the same time. "More or less."

"What if they don't have sons," Eva asked.

This time, Jeb answered. "It's part of the curse. It just happens that way. They always have a son, since the first generation."

"So, if Asher and I are together, we will have a son and not only do I risk losing my husband to the job of the Devil, but I could also lose my son?" She waited for confirmation before she went on. "And either way, even if it doesn't happen, if Ashe is not the Devil, we'll lose one of our friends slash cousins, and for years we'll have this thing hanging over our heads?"

Eva turned to look at Asher for the first time. He nodded, clutching his half-full glass of water like a life preserver. She stared at him for an excruciatingly long time before turning on her heel and pacing back the opposite direction.

"And you're saying you think I'm *the one* for Asher?" When there was no answer, she paused and looked to Notre Dame for an answer.

"There is much evidence to suggest you are."

"But you're saying the choice is mine, right?" She took her time and looked at each of the gargoyles in the room. "Esther? Jeb? You agree with...?" She indicated the lady with a toss of her head.

Jeb and Esther nodded in unison.

"You're the one," Esther said with confidence. "I knew from the moment he met you."

Asher pursed his lips and glared at her in annoyance. "'The moment,' really?"

Esther's expression went blank with challenge. "The moment," she repeated.

"But," Eva said forcefully to interrupt any argument they were about to launch into. "I don't have to stay. I don't have to participate in this. Is that right?"

Esther's eyebrows knit together in concern. "No. If you want to leave, Jeb and I won't force you. No one can force you. You decide."

"But if I leave," Eva started slowly, clearly ordering the thoughts in her head. "The curse won't be broken."

Notre Dame stood then and took Eva's hands in hers again. "If you leave and the curse is not broken, that only means it wasn't time yet."

Eva nodded, her gaze concentrating on the floor.

Mia inhaled sharply. "Don't you love Asher?"

"No, that's no—" Eva said.

"The boys are back with Delilah," Jeb interjected and then realized what she said. "Oh."

Asher did drop the glass then and it's shattering seemed to fill the room, echoing the sound of his heart smashing with it. "You said you loved me," he whispered the words, embarrassed, ashamed, humiliated in his pitifulness.

Mia and Maggie looked as astonished as he felt crushed.

Eva blinked at the sudden change in topic. "Wait. Delilah's back? Already?"

It was Esther who answered. "It's actually been about five hours since they left. Time is a little iffy over here."

"Oh," Maggie said in surprise. "She's alright?"

"Yes. Apparently, the Horsemen didn't actually want a hostage. Death just grabbed her as a spur-of-the-moment, she-was-in-the-way sort of thing."

Eva swallowed hard. Asher knew this because he couldn't stop looking at her, begging her without words to see how much he loved her. "So, there is nothing standing in the way of me leaving? My mom is back, and the danger is gone?"

Esther looked as stricken as Asher felt. "I guess so."

Eva took a step and Maggie grabbed her by the arm before she could get away from her. "Eva! Are you sure?"

The sisters stared at each other with that twin telepathy zipping silently back and forth. Asher wished with all his might that he could participate. He closed his eyes and begged through his thoughts for her to hear him, to think about how good they were together, to feel his love for her.

"I'm sure," Eva said.

Maggie dropped her hand and let her sister go.

Eva didn't look at anyone as she made her way past Notre Dame and into the aisle from where they'd come. She paused in front of Asher, her heels crunching in the glass at his feet. She didn't say anything until he raised his eyes to meet hers.

"Asher," she began. "This story, the curse, is really scary. You understand that, right? You've had a whole lifetime to get used to it. To the Devil and gargoyles and magical powers. I've only had like five hours, I guess, but it felt like twenty minutes. I'm not angry that you didn't tell me before this. How could you have possibly told me? I mean when, right? It would have even been more ridiculous than hearing about it the way I did. You're not holding anything over my head anymore because Delilah is home."

"It's all right," Asher whispered. "You don't love me. Or not enough. I understand."

She stepped closer. "No, you don't." She kissed him then. She wrapped her arms around his neck and pressed her lips to his with tenderness. She angled her mouth to take him more completely and when he opened his mouth in surprise, she kissed him with furious possession. He couldn't think. His synapses were firing a zillion times a second. His hands gripped at her hips, handfuls of the little back shorts she wore as he held her to him.

When she finally broke the kiss, he realized they were alone and no longer in the cathedral. A quick glance told him they were back in the vineyard. In the distance, the glow from the party suggested maybe down in the south quarter with the cabernet.

"I love you," she told him. "I told you I love you and I meant it."

"But that story?"

"Is fucking terrifying. But I'm the one. I'll admit there was a moment..." She paused and shrugged. "But the stone lady said it was my decision. If they tried to force me..." She shrugged. "But I choose. I choose you."

"You're not afraid?" he asked, his inquiry full of wonder.

"Sure. But, we're going to break that curse," she said with confidence. "Because I love you and you love me. You're my one."

Epilogue

The vineyard was decked out in fairy lights and apricot roses. The bride was gorgeous in a silver and cream vintage flapper-style wedding dress. The bead work was exquisite. The artist in Benji could appreciate the time and skill it took to craft. The vows took place at the crest of the hill where an arbor had been erected using the natural backdrop of the rolling hills of vines.

The ceremony was perfect as far as Benji was concerned. It was short. All kidding aside, it was really nice. The bride giggled nervously during her vows, and the Benji was pretty fucking certain the groom had tears. Nice probably wasn't the word to describe it. Maybe epic was more appropriate.

Jeb, Luke's gargoyle, didn't even try to disguise his tears. He blubbered shamelessly into a handkerchief, but he was always an emotional sort. As the first of the cousins to get married to his *one*, it was a big damn deal. Benji might have felt a bit verklempt himself, but he at least held it together. Next to him in the row of white slatted folding chairs, Asher sniffled a couple of times, but he was also overly demonstrative these days since he and Eva...

Benji was happy for all four of them. He really was. Perhaps Notre Dame was right, and something was brewing. Maybe the four of them had started a trend that could end their curse. Anything was possible. That's what he said out loud, but his internal monologue was more cynical. It seemed awfully early in the game to start thinking so big as curse removal. On the other hand, he had no intention of throwing away the opportunity should it make itself known.

He was crossing the grassy expanse to where the reception was taking place and pondering what his perfect girl would be like—so he didn't blow her off should she wander along his path someday.

Her favorite movies would likely be rom-coms, but he was okay with that. He could Netflix and chill with rom-coms as easily as thrillers. Maybe she was a knitter. He kinda liked the idea that maybe she'd be cuddling on the couch with him and making a fuzzy blanket at the same time. She'd love takeout. Maybe she was a reader. He imagined someone a little plumb and soft with rounded edges. He saw light brown hair and chocolate eyes. Maybe she'd wear her hair gathered up in a clip, all messy like with wispy curls falling loose. That was really sexy—a woman who didn't have to try hard.

Well, if it happened, it happened.

He chose a table near the buffet for proximity. There was a woman already sitting there, but Benji wasn't averse to chatting people up.

"Hi," he said. "Do you mind?" He indicated a chair at three o'clock from her position, leaving several between them for her presumed date. She was sitting slightly sideways, so he sat in her eyeline.

"No, please." She gestured for him to sit anywhere.

Once seated, he allowed his gaze to linger on her. Very pretty in that California way: blond hair, perfect teeth. Her eye color was strikingly ice blue. In his mind's eye, he used his colored pencils to sketch her profile, shading in the hollows of her cheekbones and behind her ear.

"I'm Benjamin," he said. "Everyone calls me Benji. Groom's cousin."

"I'm Cordelia. Cory," she said. "I'm here with my cousin, too. She was in college with Mia. Same sorority, I think." She pointed at bridesmaid number two.

Benji hadn't met the cousin, but he assumed she was very nice if she was friends with Mia. Mean old nasty Wrath had found the sweetest girl on the planet to marry.

"Ah," he nodded. The table was festooned with wedding flowers and short candles that would look pretty once the sun set. He considered how the shadows would fall on Cory's face by candlelight. How he'd pull out the drama of her eyes with the glimmer of the flame.

The crowd had almost entirely migrated to the reception, but the tables were slow to fill up. A band had launched into their first set across the lawn, playing your standard low-key wedding fare. The buffet was spread out, but Benji knew from previous experience at these kinds of functions, it was frowned upon to dig in until the bride and groom had made their first pass.

"Food looks good," he noted aloud.

"Yeah," she agreed. "I'm starving." After another moment of silence, she asked, "So what do you do?"

Benji grinned wide. "Not much." Cory laughed, showing off those perfect, straight teeth. Benji's fingers itched for his pencils. "How about you?"

"I work in customer service. It's not a great gig, and the pay is shit, but they give me lots of time off for when I have tournaments."

Benji raised his eyebrows, showing interest in her continuing her story.

"I'm a competitive fencer."

"Really? That's pretty cool. How competitive?"

"At the moment, not very." She leaned down and pulled up a pair of crutches laying at the grass by her feet. He realized she was sitting sideways because a foot was propped up on the chair next to her.

"Bummer. What happened?"

"ACL injury."

"Man," he said with a teasing grin. "That's what you get from all that moving around."

She laughed again. "Agreed."

"So now I'm going to show my ignorance. You don't really hear a lot about fencing except for the Olympics."

She gave a one-shoulder shrug that mocked modesty. "It's a good thing I was in the Olympics, then, huh?"

Benji didn't try to hide his surprise. "No shit? Wow. You should lead with that. 'Hi, I'm Cory, Olympic fencer.'"

"That seems awfully prideful, doesn't it?"

A waitress came around and Benji took two glasses of white wine from her. Dashiell cellars, of course. "Prideful is not my concern. My other cousin Ian deals with Pride. Did you medal?"

"Silver."

Holy shit! "Wow, Cory. I'm impressed."

"Thanks." She jiggled the crutches again. "But now I'm lame."

"I assume not for long, though, right?" Benji asked. "ACL tears get fixed all the time."

Before she could answer, Mia and Luke appeared at his elbow. He pulled himself to his feet in order to hug Mia.

"You are gorgeous," he told her and then extended his hand to Luke. "Smile looks good on you, dude. Congratulations."

"Thanks," Luke said, his smile not dimming one bit.

"You both know Cory the silver medal-winning fencer?" He asked, indicating Cory.

Mia bent down and hugged Cory. "Of course. We met at the bachelorette party." Luke's smile faltered ever so slightly at the mention of the bachelorette, which amused Benji.

"Can you believe she doesn't introduce herself that way to everyone?" he asked them.

Mia giggled as she asked Cory, "Did he tell you that portrait of us is his? I'll bet he didn't brag about that, did he?"

Cory's smile dropped and she indicated the large canvas propped up on an easel . "Wait, you painted that portrait?"

It had been his wedding gift. He'd done it in oils in the style of the old masters, since Mia seemed to really love those and he loved playing with shadows.

"He did," Mia confirmed. "It's embarrassing having a giant picture up of myself, but it's too gorgeous to hide away. I wanted everyone to see it."

Benji slumped back into the chair and leaned way back. He stretched his legs out in front of him and laced his fingers over his belly. It was a good piece. He'd worked hard at it, and he was happy with the end result. He simply couldn't bother to put the energy into bragging about it.

"You didn't say you were an artist," Cory scolded him.

Luke asked, "Out of curiosity, what did he say he does?"

Cory scoffed. "He said, and I quote, 'not much.'"

Luke barked out a laugh. "Well, he didn't lie." He and Mia excused themselves to go get the buffet started.

When Benji turned back to Cory, she was staring at him with a tilted head. Like the RCA dog trying to figure him out. "What?"

"You're very interesting," she told him. "I thought I was being modest, but really you have like a gold medal in humble."

"No." Benji emphasized that word, drawing out the syllable. "It's just too much work to toot one's horn. Humility has nothing to do with it. Again, that's not my gig."

She blinked at him and shook her head. Then her stomach growled loud enough for him to hear. Her eyes grew in surprise and embarrassment. "I did say I was starving."

"I could eat," Benji said, but didn't move from his comfortable position.

Cory scowled at her crutches. "I hate these things. I hate not being able to move around. I'm not a sedentary person and this sucks."

Benji, the most sedentary person in creation—at least of this generation—gave her his biggest grin. "I won't stop you. You can get my plate, too."

Her jaw dropped for a second, then she side-eyed him through narrowed slits. "You don't think I can do it, do you?"

He looked at the crutches and then at the buffet. "I think you can do anything you put your mind to." He said it with diabolical flirtatiousness.

"I can, though. I'm going to prove it." She popped up to her feet and put the crutches under her arms. "Just watch me."

Benji crossed his ankles. "All right then." She was cute, but that competitive streak must be exhausting. Still, he was curious to see how she was going to juggle this.

"If I pull off dinner, then you have to do cake," she said as she hobbled away.

"We'll see," he said with a contented sigh.

The Devil was wearing one of his bespoke suits. In a nod to the occasion, he'd pinned a sprig of apple blossoms to his lapel. In the shade of an old oak tree some distance from the party, no one at the reception had noticed him or his companion yet.

"And the woman was fine, you say?" In his motorcycle leathers, Michael had not dressed for the occasion. Aaron assumed he didn't plan to hang around for cake.

"They claimed she was in the way, so they just scooped her up."

"And you don't know how they got loose?" The archangel was tall and blond and looked to be plucked out of a casting call for heavenly beings. Or he would if he didn't march around looking so surly all the time, trying to pass as a Hell's Angel. The irony did not amuse the Devil.

"I do not. I'm not taking the blame for it though. I'm not in charge of the Horsemen. In fact, I was doing you guys a favor putting them up all this time. You all said a remodel. How long is that going to take?"

Michael ignored the question. "Did they say what they were planning to do while they were up here?"

"Nope." Aaron turned to face him. "We got her back, but we weren't prepared to subdue them. They gave her up willingly. Don't start thinking about punishments for my people. This is not our fault," he reiterated.

"No one's blaming you, but it is a problem," Michael grumbled.

Aaron adjusted his cuffs. "Then you best get on your bike and ride."

***

JOIN IN THE FUN!
Don't miss a thing! Sign up for the newsletter at:

Amylynn Bright

https://amylynnbright.com/

About the Author

Amylynn read her first romance novel in 2008 after being a lifelong literary snob. By the time she was done, she was hooked. Now she pens Regency, contemporary, and paranormal romances that will make you laugh.

She in an Arizona native and lives in the same house her husband owned before they were married. Amylynn fears she will never call another state home unless someone tells her husband there are forty-nine others to chose from. In reality, she'd settle for a walk-in closet.

Her family consists of the aforementioned husband, two very loud children, two dogs, four cats, and a hankering for a panda. She'd like it mentioned she's never been in prison, but we'll see how that panda thing works out.

Also By AmyLynn Bright

The Devil's Descendants - Book 1

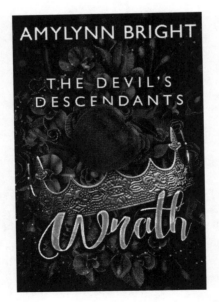

Luke Mephisto has carried the burden of Wrath since he was ten years old when his father was chosen as his generation's Devil. Luke is certain it's only a matter of time before that heavy crown falls on his own head. He is already a celebrated architect and currently designing the building of his dreams, one that will put him on the map for long after he's gone. But there's a new liaison with the client's company and she's ruining everything—coming to their meetings in her cute outfits and making kooky demands. And suddenly Luke doesn't feel so wrathful anymore.

Mia avoids conflict in her life. She got plenty of that from her parents. But when she's put in charge of her family's new corporate headquarters, she takes a stand. She knows what she wants, and the surly architect will just have to deal with it. Underneath his grumpy exterior lurks a guy who makes her feel special, like her intelligence and talents are valuable. Except her nightmares have been especially hellish lately, and the Devil in her dreams looks an awful lot like her new boyfriend.

THE BENNET FAMILY SERIES

COOKING UP LOVE

Is there anything more pathetic than a food critic who can't cook? That's Holly Darcy—secret socialite, wannabe author, lousy chef and "The Covert Connoisseur." Feeling like a fraud for critiquing restaurants when she can't boil a pot of water, Holly joins a cooking class for beginners...and quickly cooks up serious chemistry with the sexy instructor. Mark Bennett was born to be a chef, but his foray into restaurant ownership fell far short of his dreams thanks to a scathing review from The Covert Connoisseur. Now teaching is the closest he will venture into a kitchen. Luckily the job comes with an unexpected perk: the attraction simmering between him and a curvy, clever writer with pinup-girl looks. Flirting over pasta soon leads to passionate kisses and a sizzling relationship. But how can Holly be honest about her job when Mark blames his restaurant's failure on her review? And when Holly's secret is exposed, how will Mark be able to forgive her for ruining his life?

BUILDING UP LOVE

Five years ago, Lee Bennett's whirlwind romance with Candace Claesson ended as abruptly as it had begun, and just when he needed her the most. Since then, Lee's built a successful construction company and a satisfying, if solitary, life. When he's hired to build Candace's new veterinary clinic, Lee finds her as irresistible as ever—but he's never forgiven her and he's sure as hell not letting her break his heart again. For years, Candace has wrestled with regret and guilt over leaving Lee. At the time, nothing was going to stop her from achieving her dreams of studying in Scotland and becoming a vet—not even young love. They'd been inseparable for six months, but anything that intense couldn't last. Or so she thought. Reunited in their hometown, neither Lee nor Candace can resist picking up where they left off. But with so much from the past standing between them, how they can rebuild what they started so long ago?

HEALING UP LOVE – COMING SOON

Sarah Grant is holding it all together after the accidental death of her husband, the same accident that left her with a disabled child. She's doing a pretty good job of it, too, until her son gets a new therapist. While Mr. Miller is full of unrealistic—and possibly dangerous—ideas, he's also incredibly attractive. Driven by guilt, she'll never let anything bad happen to Sidney again. Unfortunately, the more she's forced to deal with Mr. Miller, the more she remembers she's more than just someone's mom. It's hard to focus on getting the man fired when she's set aflame whenever he's around.

Zachary Miller didn't expect his forced retirement from the military to be easy but dealing with Sidney's mom was more than he'd bargained for. He'd faced down the enemy in combat and survived, but this woman could oppose anyone and win with her cool, no-nonsense gaze. She's a force to be reckoned with even while she makes him want to forget the scars that define him. He'd bet good money that under her ice queen façade burns a fire ready to illuminate the dark future that terrifies him and keep his demons at bay. Maybe Sarah Grant and her son are exactly what he needs to pull himself into the light.

Can Sarah and Zach leave their broken pasts behind and find healing in each other?

THE SECRET SERIES

LADY BELLING'S SECRET

Francesca Belling is torn between two worlds—her past infatuation with her brother's best friend and her future obligations. She never intended to end up in the bed of her longtime crush, Thomas Wallingham, but that's exactly where she finds herself. Unfortunately, mail is slow during a war. She thought he knew everything. He had never suspected. Thomas has always wanted to be a part of the Belling's family but he was too foolish to grab the chance when she threw herself at him before. Instead, he ran off to war. Emboldened by his new-found appreciation for a grown-up Francesca, he finds that dream is within his reach. If she thinks he's running away this time, she has no idea what she's in for.

MISS GOLDSLEIGH'S SECRET

When Henry Cavendish, Marquess of Dalton, leapt to catch the fainting woman before she hit the cobblestone, he never thought that one chivalrous act would set his well ordered life on end. His ingrained need to protect her has every bit as much to do with her enchanting beauty as it does his desire to wipe the hunted look from her startling blue eyes. He thinks he has everything in hand, but the lady has secrets that put everything he loves at risk. Olivia Goldsleigh just wants to live without terror, but a gunshot in the night proves things can always get worse. The beautiful and god-like Lord Dalton swears to protect her, to make the danger go away. She wants the man, the life, the family, the bliss he promises, but her secrets are certain to destroy them all.

THE DUKE OF MOREWETHER'S SECRET

Thea Ashbrook comes to London on a mission to do right by her half-brothers — not to find a husband. Homesick for Greece, she causes an incident at a Salon lecture on Greek architecture where she is introduced to the annoyingly handsome Duke of Morewether. The gossips have told her of every deviant escapade for which he's so famous, and she is not impressed. When she discovers that his love of family mirrors her own, she gives herself permission to open her heart to him. Christian, Duke of Morewether, is infamous for his scandalous ways. He thinks his life lacks nothing, until he meets Miss Althea Ashbrook and, for the first time in his life, he finds himself tongue tied. When his past comes back to haunt him, it will take all his powers of persuasion to convince Thea he is worthy of her love. The duke has a secret – one that Thea thinks she could never forgive and sends her racing for home. To find redemption and win her back, Christian must realize mistakes can't be ignored forever. The secrets you keep can change your life forever.

MISS SINCLAIR'S SECRET

Anna Sinclair is an English lady who refuses to settle—not if all her friends have love matches. When she receives notification that her father, General Sinclair, is missing and presumed dead in America shortly after the War of 1812, she knows she has nothing to lose by going to find him. In an untamed country, she'll need to navigate the Mississippi River, miles of wilderness, earthquakes, Indians, and one absurdly attractive American sea captain.

Nathaniel Johnson is an American patriot whose only goal is to return to the country he loves with his recently located brother, a sailor impressed by the British. The money offered to escort a young English woman to the United States is too much to pass up when he's desperately trying to save his family's shipping empire. The beautiful lady spins a ridiculous tale about looking for her father, but Nate has powerful reasons to believe she's a spy for the Crown. He'll help her on her quest, at least until he can prove her villainous intent. Will Anna's secret destroy his country and be his undoing?

Made in the USA
Columbia, SC
09 September 2024

41437157R00204